© James Sherwin

Hiroko Sherwin was born in Nagoya, Japan, and was evacuated to the countryside when the city was bombed during World War II. She later moved to Princeton, New Jersey, where her three daughters were born. She served as a special correspondent for the Japanese newspaper *Yomuiri USA*, and wrote four books in Japanese about American women and society. She now lives in Bath, England, with her husband, three cats, eleven sheep, and four alpacas. This is her first novel.

EIGHT MILLION GODS AND DEMONS

HIROKO SHERWIN

A PLUME BOOK

PLUME
Published by the Penguin Group
Penguin Group (USA) Inc., 375 Hudson Street, New York, New York 10014, U.S.A.
Penguin Books Ltd, 80 Strand, London WC2R 0RL, England
Penguin Books Australia Ltd, 250 Camberwell Road, Camberwell, Victoria 3124, Australia
Penguin Books Canada Ltd, 10 Alcorn Avenue, Toronto, Ontario, Canada M4V 3B2
Penguin Books India (P) Ltd, 11 Community Centre, Panchsheel Park, New Delhi – 110 017, India
Penguin Books (N.Z.) Ltd, Cnr Rosedale and Airborne Roads,
Albany, Auckland 1310, New Zealand
Penguin Books (South Africa) (Pty) Ltd, 24 Sturdee Avenue,
Rosebank, Johannesburg 2196, South Africa

Penguin Books Ltd, Registered Offices: 80 Strand, London WC2R 0RL, England

Published by Plume, a member of Penguin Group (USA) Inc.
First published in Great Britain in slightly different form by Robert Hale Limited.

First Plume Printing, December 2003
10 9 8 7 6 5 4 3 2 1

REGISTERED TRADEMARK—MARCA REGISTRADA

LIBRARY OF CONGRESS CATALOGING-IN-PUBLICATION DATA
Sherwin, Hiroko, 1936–
Eight million gods and demons / Hiroko Sherwin.
p. cm.
Includes bibliographical references (p.).
ISBN 0-452-28451-1 (pbk.)
1. Japan—Fiction. I. Title.

PR9515.9.S47E54 2003
823'.914—dc21

2003048269

Printed in the United States of America

Set in Sabon
Designed by Leonard Telesca

PUBLISHER'S NOTE
This is a work of fiction. Names, characters, places, and incidents either are the product of the author's imagination or are used fictitiously, and any resemblance to actual persons, living or dead, business establishments, events, or locales is entirely coincidental.

To Jimmy: with love

ACKNOWLEDGMENTS

Without my husband Jimmy's unflagging support and enthusiasm, this book would not have been possible.

I am grateful to my editor Kelly Notaras, who helped focus the story on Emi and Taku and kept me from amusing distractions. John Hale had faith in my book and is its United Kingdom publisher.

My friends Ralph Sonnenberg and Michael Lynton were enormously helpful in connection with the publication of the book in the United States. Professor Martin Collcutt, East Asian Studies, Princeton University, has been of invaluable help to me.

Many thanks to my six daughters and stepdaughters: Mako Yoshikawa, herself a novelist, for her invaluable advice, Professor Miranda Sherwin for her insightful suggestions, Yoko and Aiko Yoshikawa for their perceptive comments, and Ali and Galen Sherwin for their moral support.

My brother Takuro Inoue, my late uncle Shinroku Inoue, my mother Masako Inoue, and the late Professor Hyong-tai Oh provided historical material and told me about family life in the old days.

I am greatly indebted to and relied for my background material on:

Cook, Haruko Taya & Cook, Theodore F., *Japan at War, an Oral History,* The New Press, New York, 1993.

Duus, Peter, *The Abacus and the Sword: The Japanese Penetration of Korea 1895–1910,* University of California Press, California, 1995.

Itabashi, Morikuni, *Troubled Industrial Development in Hokkaido,* Hokkaido Shimbun, Hokkaido, 1992.

Listen to the Voices of the Sea Gods: The Letters of Students Who Died in the War, Kobunsha, Tokyo, 1959.

Modern History Group, Sofukan, *Document, the Great Earthquake,* Tokyo, 1993.

Sensho, Asahi, *Our Fathers' Memoirs of War,* Tokyo, 1982.

Sone, Kazuo, *Private Notes on the Rape of Nanking,* Sairyusha, Tokyo, 1984.

—Hiroko Sherwin

CHAPTER 1

Emi remembered the day she discovered that her husband was betraying her. She was on the way home from visiting a new doctor. The sky in Tokyo was dark that autumn afternoon. The capricious wind whirled leaves in the air and rolled up the hems of women's kimonos.

Going to a doctor was a ritual for Emi, like visiting a Shinto shrine. She knew he would not cure her, just as the eight million gods of Japan could not, but she would at least feel better for having done something.

The doctor was a gentle old man. He gave her Chinese herbs, acupuncture and a massage, and tried to impress on her the importance of spiritual tranquility. Nothing was new, but she was cheerful for a change as she sat on the rickshaw with her mother, Chiyo.

"I'll be tranquil and won't have any more attacks, Mother," Emi said, half-jokingly.

"You've always been tranquil. The doctor didn't have to lecture to you about that," Chiyo replied, her cheeks furrowed by a sad smile.

The rickshaw was running slowly, threading through the busy streets of Tokyo. "Downtown is always like a masquerade party, isn't it, Mother? Look at the fat sumo wrestler in the black kimono, walking with three geishas," Emi said looking out of the little window.

Emi had grown up in a little village near Hiroshima and was still a country girl. She had moved to Tokyo two years before with her husband, Taku, who had been elected a member of the first Diet in Japan in 1890. These days she rarely saw him since he had accepted a second job as head of a coal mine on the northern island of Hokkaido. So Emi spent a lot of time with Chiyo who had moved to the city to help her daughter.

The rickshaw moved on from the center of town to an elegant street flanked with red-brick buildings. Open horse-drawn coaches passed by, carrying men in Western suits. Emi's eyes lighted on one pulled by two black horses.

"Look, Mother," she cried out. "Taku-san is sitting on that coach. But the Diet isn't in session; he's supposed to be in Hokkaido today."

"Some business must have brought him back. Let's prepare dinner for him tonight," Chiyo said.

The dinner got cold. Taku didn't come home and Emi could not sleep. Every time she heard the slightest noise, she stood up and ran to the door. There was nothing there except the wind. She looked at the clock on the wall every fifteen minutes. In the end, she tried not to look, but the ticking clock woke her every time she dozed off.

She dreamed of the three geishas she had seen walking with the sumo wrestler that afternoon. The wind kept opening the layers of their colorful kimonos. A strong gust stripped off a few layers and blew them into the air. They ran after the kimonos that were flying away like butterflies. When they finally caught one, in it was a man who looked like Taku. The image kept Emi awake all night.

Emi was worried about Taku. They had lost Ume, their second baby, just four months before when she was only five weeks old. They had had six months with their first child. Taku was sad but had been kind to her both times.

But now she felt something else had died between herself and her husband. Taku came home less often, saying that his coal mine kept him away. When he was home, he stayed up late working. He came to bed late and seldom made love to her. Emi was secretly relieved because she was fearful of having another baby who might die, but it also made her sad to think that the carefree, passionate lovers they once had been were now a pair of wounded birds afraid of touching each other.

Taku had been crazy about Ume. Born premature during the season that the *ume,* a plum tree, was in full bloom in the garden, Ume was as pretty as its flower, but as pale and ephemeral as its petal. Every evening, Taku came home and called, "How was Ume today?" He held the sleepy baby in his arms, danced around and sang off-tune lullabies he made up, half asleep himself. "Ume, Ume. My little blossom. You'll grow as big as an *ume* tree. Birds will come and sing for you. Bees and butterflies will come, cats and people will come. After the flowers, it will bear fruits as sweet as Ume baby."

Ume was attended every minute of the day and night by Taku, Emi and her mother. She was wrapped in a silk floss and kept in a warm basket. Emi and Chiyo went to shrines, temples and roadside deities to pray for the baby's survival. The only thing the household talked about was whether Ume had suckled that day, and how much she drank—whether it was more than morning dew on a *ume* leaf, or as much as a robin's tears. The cat, Momo, had lost Emi's favor. Shut out of the baby's room, he often went unfed. When he meowed during the baby's nap-time, he was unceremoniously put outside.

Then Ume developed a fever and stopped drinking milk. One evening, Taku picked her up and held her gently in his arms. Her eyes were closed, dark shadows etching their rims. Her fingers were tightly clenched and her soft pink cheeks were gray and cold.

"Ume, Ume, don't die," Taku cried desperately. She opened her lips slightly as if trying to smile or cry. She opened her eyes, too, and gazed at her father one more time as if to say *sayonara*. Then her face contorted with a faint cough. She gasped for a last breath and trembled. Ume died in her father's arms.

Taku burst into tears and cried louder than Emi had ever heard a man cry. Emi cried, too, for the life that lasted only a little longer than that of a plum blossom, for the life that had no chance to bloom, no chance to grow fruit.

Emi felt not only sad but guilty. It was her fault Ume had died. She had played her *koto* when she was seven-and-a-half months pregnant. If only she had not played music that day and had not bent down so much, she might not have had a premature baby. Or were all her babies doomed to die because of her frail health? A wife who did not bear an heir was herself to blame, and Emi accepted the guilt without question.

A gulf formed between Taku and Emi. One day Emi overheard her mother saying to their maid Yoshi, "Taku-san is devastated. After losing two babies, he may find another woman. What do you think, Yoshi-san?"

"I know it's easy for a man to find other women whether he has a child or not," Yoshi said. "But Taku-sama is a special man: he's a Buddhist and he adores Emi-sama. We can only hope he'll be faithful to her."

Somewhere down deep, Emi believed he would be. She knew he still loved her though in an inhibited way. Taku's mentor, Professor Fukuzawa, a happy family man with nine children, had told him never to go to a geisha house. Taku worshiped him and blindly believed whatever he said. Fukuzawa said that geishas were poor women exploited by men—pimps and rich clients.

Besides, Taku was much too busy to be distracted by other women. His mind was full of ideas about freedom of speech, Korean independence, universal suffrage, tax cuts for the poor, his coal mine, and his plan to build Japan's first steel mill. At night in bed, the abacus in his brain was counting the multi-million yen he had to shuffle to run his operations. Where would he find time for women?

So Emi rejected the idea that Taku was being unfaithful, even when he did not come home that night.

Taku's face, disfigured by the smallpox he had suffered when he was eight, had pockmarks as deep as the moon's craters. Swollen lids drooped over eyes that shone shrewdly like a fox's, and made him look drowsy. But he had command of 10,000 Chinese words and could compute eight-digit numbers in an instant. When he stood up on the podium, his arguments were so logical, his grasp of facts and numbers so accurate, his language so eloquent, and his voice so clear and loud, that people forgot how ugly and sleepy he looked. There was always a hushed silence at the end of his speeches. Once, when he spoke in a public meeting, a paper wrote: "Taku Imura makes tsunami waves out of a flat sea."

But he was so fearless and outspoken that he made many enemies. Emi remembered a night Taku came home with a black eye and a bruise on his forehead. She chilled the wounds with ice, while Taku bragged, "As I came out of the office, two men ran from a corner and attacked me. I grappled with them, twisted one man's arm and kicked the other in the stomach. These barbaric attackers show how uncivilized Japan still is. It's deplorable." And yet he had not only been a victim, but also an aggressor himself. He once hit the nose of a political enemy with his walking stick and had to apologize, though reluctantly.

One day Taku came home with sword slashes on his forehead. When Emi asked who had hurt him, Taku snarled like a bulldog and said, "Probably the hired attackers of Foreign Minister Uno. He didn't like the article I wrote, criticizing the government for enforcing the Act curtailing freedom of speech and assembly. An outrageous law for a modern country."

"I know how you feel about freedom," Emi said, "but please don't provoke Minister Uno again, Taku-san. You'll be put in prison again, or lose your life, let alone freedom of speech."

"All right. All right, Emi," Taku said. The next day he gave a major speech in the Diet attacking the government about the Act, his head wrapped in a bandage.

Taku had been imprisoned for having insulted Minister Uno in earlier days, but as soon as he was free, he became an outspoken opponent of the government. Vengeful Uno might be after him again.

Therefore, Emi imagined the most terrible scenarios: Taku stabbed and left in a dark lane to die, or taken to jail again; or in the dark, he might fall into a ditch or be hit by a running horse. Since he was a baby, Taku had "a bird's eye" and was "night blind as a bird."

The morning after Taku didn't come home, Emi contacted the police, but they had no record of any accident involving Taku Imura.

At a loss, Emi went to see her best friend, Mariko. Mariko's husband, Hora, was an old friend of Taku and had recently joined Taku's coal company in Hokkaido. Mariko might know of Taku's whereabouts.

Emi found Mariko looking pale, her normally twinkling eyes swollen and red. Emi asked if Hora had come home the night before.

"Yes. But after midnight and dead drunk," Mariko said in an angry voice. "After I nagged and nagged him, he confessed he'd been with a geisha."

"Was Taku-san with Hora-san? He didn't come home last night."

Mariko turned paler and looked outside the window.

"Please tell me anything you know," Emi said.

Mariko hesitated for a while and then said, with a heavy sigh, "If you insist, I'll tell you, but this won't make you happy, Emi-san. Taku-san was with Hora. There was a dinner party entertaining bankers at a geisha house. It was nothing; they do it all the time. But after dinner, Hora spent some time with a geisha in a separate room and when he came out, Taku-san wasn't there any longer. Hora left, thinking Taku-san had gone home already. He said, 'Taku is a chicken about geishas, you know.'"

Mariko saw Emi's face quiver like rice paper in a wind. "I feel sorrier for you than for myself," Mariko said. "Because probably you have had no experience like this before. Hora said he had been encouraging Taku-san to have fun with geishas because he had been so sad about having lost two babies. So I said, 'What about Emi-san? What kind of consolation would she have for her husband going to other women after losing two babies?' He said, 'Going to a geisha house doesn't always mean sleeping with them.' But I know it often does."

Emi had the sensation of being hit by an avalanche of rocks. Her heart had been bleeding for her lost babies; now it ruptured, crumbling like a fragile shrine in an earthquake. Emi had thought her married life was solid, but her two babies had left her and now her husband had, too. Before, whenever she felt sad, Taku consoled her in his arms. With whom could she share her sorrows now?

Mariko patted Emi, looking into her eyes. "Cheer up, Emi-san. Do you know what we should do? These men are hopeless. If they forget us and do whatever pleases them, we should also forget them and do whatever pleases us. Luckily, both of us have something we love to do. You are a talented musician and I'm a good dancer. You know how much I love your music, don't you, Emi-san? Why don't you compose and play more? I choreographed a dance to your piece, *Murasaki*. I'm pleased with it. I can't wait to dance it for you." She twirled around twice with her arms up, starting to dance.

Emi opened her eyes wide and gazed at Mariko. Mariko always surprised Emi with her strength. She was angry at her husband's infidelity, but she would rather think about her dance. Emi loved music, but she was too upset now even to think of the *koto*.

Emi went home and tried to be strong. She took the dusty felt sack off her *koto* and sat in front of the long rectangular body of the instrument. Her mother was a *koto* teacher and Emi had been playing since she was five.

Emi had always been a sickly child, though the attacks had not started until she was seventeen. As a girl the sun gave her headaches and the rain colds, so she had to stay home like an indoor plant. But the gods had given her a special ear for music. Her mind was full of happy tunes and she made songs of trees, the wind, birds and animals.

But recently only sad melodies had filled her ears when she played the *koto*. Nevertheless, Emi tried to practice. She put three ivory plectra on her right fingers and strummed randomly. To her delight, the music glided into the happy tunes of her two babies, Taro and Ume, bubbling and chirping. They even started to laugh and dance on the *koto*'s silk strings. Her cat, Momo, romped around Emi, wiggling his stubby tail, as he always did when she played the *koto*.

But gradually, low vibrating notes crept in, growing ominously loud. The happy images of her children disappeared. "Oh, I can't go on," Emi said to Momo, and put her palms over her face. Momo watched her with a melancholy gaze.

As Emi tried to stand up, she felt a familiar thinness of the air. The eerie sounds of the jammed strings vibrated in her ears and faded into silence.

There was a long blackness. Emi felt a warm drop of water on her cheek and opened her eyes. Blinking, her vision still blurred, she saw her mother gazing at her with tears in her eyes, which the strong-willed Chiyo seldom let anybody see.

Emi felt sorry, watching her mother wipe her eyes with her kimono sleeve. Having lost her husband when she was relatively young, Chiyo lived for her daughter. She had been proud of having married Emi off to an important man. But ever since Emi had developed epilepsy, she was afraid she had given her mother more heartache than joy.

"Are you feeling better, Emi-chan?" Chiyo said.

"Why are you here, Mother? How did you know I fell?" Emi asked. Chiyo lived in the teahouse across the garden, but she was almost always there when Emi awoke from an attack.

"Did I shake like a tree in a winter storm and kick you as usual?" Emi asked.

"This was an easy one. It was only a few minutes," Chiyo said, combing Emi's disheveled hair with her fingers.

"I didn't have tranquility of spirit. That's why this happened. Right, Mother?" Emi said.

"How can you be tranquil when your husband didn't come home last night?" Chiyo's frown etched three lines on her forehead. "But don't worry, Emi," she said, forcing herself to be cheerful. "Important men often have long nights of parties. It doesn't mean anything. Why don't you rest this afternoon since you didn't sleep much last night? Read a book. I have to go back to the teahouse. My *koto* students are waiting."

Emi obediently picked up a book, but her thoughts wandered again to her husband. She felt like a dog trampled not only by her husband, but also by Hora. It had been he who suggested Emi play *koto* the day Ume was born. He and Mariko had been over for tea, and he had seen the *koto* in the corner.

"Emi, don't you think it's too strenuous for you to play *koto*?" Taku asked.

"I'll only play gently, Taku-san," Emi said.

It was difficult for Emi to bend down over the instrument with her big belly. But as soon as she plucked the first string, her discomfort faded, and she almost forgot that anyone else was present. The joy of music, which had escaped from her during her months of morning sickness, welled up again. It was her fingers, not her mind, which had memorized the melody, the rhythm, the fortés and the pianissimos. The music started gently and progressed into a passionate finale.

When she finished, Emi felt dizzy and was suddenly worried that she might have been carried away and used too much of her strength. Was she about to have a fall? Was the baby all right? But she felt better when she heard the cheerful voices and clapping hands of Hora and Mariko.

"It was beautiful," Hora said, his eyes gazing at Emi in a way he had never done before. It was as if he was seeing in her a different woman than Taku's sickly wife.

"Lovely, Emi-san," Mariko said. "I wonder if you'd mind my dancing to that music wearing a violet kimono just like yours?" Mariko stood up on tiptoe and swirled, letting her kimono sleeves swing like the wings of a bird.

That evening her waters broke prematurely, and Emi gave birth to a girl Taku named Ume.

After the sleepless night waiting for her husband and the stressful day learning about his geisha house visit, Emi did not know what to expect in the evening. If Taku returned, Emi wasn't sure how she would welcome him. Would she confront him and ask him where he had been the night before? Wasn't it she herself who had pushed her husband into the present predicament?

Emi had not decided how to face him when she heard her husband striding into the house, his steps as vigorous as a *samurai.* She felt faint, but managed to say, "Taku-san, you are so early today."

Opening his thin crescent eyes to a half-moon size, Taku said, "Early? I'm one day late. You'll laugh at me when you hear what I did last night instead of coming back to you, Emi." Smiling, Taku squeezed Emi so tightly that her bones creaked.

So, was the long night of anxieties and suspicions just a bad dream after all? He did not look like a man who had something to hide. Emi burst out crying and laughing at the same time and said, "Taku-san, oh, I'm so happy to see you."

"Guess what I did last night, Emi. What a waste of a night. I came back from Hokkaido in the afternoon because I had a meeting with engineers about a steel mill. Steel is absolutely necessary for modern industry. I had to see bankers, too, to negotiate about loans. It was a difficult negotiation and Hora insisted we entertain them at a geisha house. You know I don't like geisha houses but we went there anyway. It's boring enough to talk to the bankers and even more boring to have geishas around. They insist on playing stupid games with toothpicks, bean bags and flower cards. Games for children. I was so impatient and in such a foul mood that they said they'd cheer me up and drowned me with saké. This morning I found myself on a pink futon in the geisha house. A young geisha brought me a tray of breakfast and smiled mischievously, saying, 'Did you enjoy yourself last night? You are quite a man.' So I asked her, 'What did I do?' She said, 'You fell asleep as soon as we started to flirt with you.' Emi, can you forgive me for this stupidity?"

So the mountain of agonizing amounted to a molehill. Taku looked embarrassed enough and Emi did not want to make him feel worse. She laughed and said, "It's typical Taku-san." He had often fallen asleep in the middle of a boring party, particularly when he drank too much. Emi could tell Taku was telling the truth; he was incapable of telling lies anyway.

Emi told him she had seen him riding in a horse-drawn coach in the afternoon and was waiting for him all night. "I was worried you might have been attacked by someone's hired killers," she said. "I'm so glad you are alive and well, Taku-san." They laughed and hugged, and were happy again.

Before too long, Emi was pregnant again. She was determined to have a healthy baby this time. She wrapped her belly with many layers of warm cloth and confined herself to rooms with no furniture, no fire, no knives, scissors or needles—nothing with sharp edges she might fall on. She did not play the *koto,* even when she wanted to, and read books in order to calm herself.

But one day she had an attack on the stone bridge over the pond in her garden. She was holding the railing with both hands and walking sideways like a crab to cross it, but still she fell. Although the water was only knee deep, she slipped to the bottom and was drenched to the skin. Chiyo and Yoshi ran to her, waded in and pulled her out. But the shock of the fall and the cold water killed the five-month-old child in her womb.

Taku did not blame Emi for the miscarriage. "I'm sorry about the baby," he said. "But we're grateful you're alive." Still, this incident must have made him face the fact that Emi was not made to have a child. Another pregnancy would further ruin her precarious health.

He began coming home even less frequently. "The steel mill is finally coming together. It involves enormous time and effort, as you can probably guess. I'll be staying in Hokkaido more often."

The strange thing was, that even during the Diet session, when he was staying in Tokyo, he did not come home to Emi. On the rare evenings he did come home, he looked preoccupied. He confined himself to his study and did not talk much during dinner.

Chiyo and Emi agreed that he was overworked. Chiyo invited him to her teahouse. "Taku-san, we'd like you to relax with a tea ceremony and music," she said. "I'll make tea and Emi will play *koto*." Taku grumbled a little, and came reluctantly.

While Emi played, he sipped his tea with a frown and glanced at a clock on the wall every two minutes. As soon as the music ended, he said, "I'm sorry, Emi and Chiyo mother. I must write a big speech for tomorrow's Diet," and stood up. On his way out, he bumped into Momo, who had been listening happily to his mistress's music, and shooed him away. Momo jumped up and ran off.

Emi remembered the days when Taku's eyes shone as she played *koto*. Now he did not have the patience to listen. She knew that he didn't love her any longer.

As she watched her husband leave the teahouse, her head reeled and her body quivered. "Emi," her mother was calling from a distance.

Still in a faraway place, Emi heard Chiyo saying to Yoshi, "I'm glad Taku-san didn't see her fall."

At least music consoled Emi. Every time she played *koto,* Momo sat and gazed at Emi with mournful eyes.

"Momo," Emi said to her cat, holding back tears, "Beethoven composed his most beautiful music after he became deaf. Dostoevsky wrote great books after he had spent ten years in prison, where he became an epileptic. So even though I have lost three babies, I'll still make my little music."

She listened to the recordings of Bach, Beethoven, Mozart and Schubert Hora had given her, on the gramophone Taku had bought. She worked out the differences between Western and Japanese musical scales. By playing some half notes, she was able to make music with the Western scale. Momo walked around her, beating time to *Minuet Momo* in G major and *Tokyo Waltz* in F minor.

Occasionally when Taku was home, he made passionate love to Emi. She did not know from where his passion came and who inspired it. Maybe he was rejuvenated by his secret escapades. He smiled a sheepish smile, as if he had been teased by words whispered into his ears, or by spidery fingers that stroked him. He lived far away in a different world from Emi; she lay rigid and cold as if she were a corpse.

Then Emi became pregnant for the fourth time. Her doctor told her to have an abortion and Taku agreed. Even Chiyo did not oppose it. But Emi stubbornly insisted, "This will be my very last chance. I'll do my best to protect the baby and myself. The rest is up to the gods and to Buddha." She thought that the baby might bring Taku back to her. It was a matter of life and death for Emi.

She went with her mother to a Fox God shrine in a faraway village. It was early spring and among the green rice fields stood a shrine painted in bright vermilion, the color of foxes. Foxes were messengers of the gods. It was said they came down from the mountains and listened to your wishes. Emi and Chiyo did not see the animals, but they prayed and left pieces of fried tofu, the favorite food of foxes, at the altar.

Emi and Yoshi often visited a miniature guardian deity standing at a street corner. He was the patron of pregnant women and had a benign, baby face. Emi left a bowl of rice in front of him. Yoshi covered his shoulder with a red mantle and his head with the padded hood she had sewn for him.

The gods and Buddhas took pity on Emi. They gave her a baby boy, Jun, and a chance to win back her husband's love. The whole house was besotted with the baby.

"Look how dark blue his eyes are. They look really intelligent," Chiyo said, her cheeks pink. "And he's always smiling. He has a good disposition as you do, Emi."

"I'm glad he doesn't have my bad temper," Taku said with a big smile, his eyes in crescents. "He gazes at me with serious curiosity. I bet he's wondering why my face has pocks."

"Look, how big his feet are. He's going to be a big boy," Yoshi declared, her eyes shining. "See how they are kicking, Emi-sama. It's a sign of health."

Jun was not all that healthy and caught every possible illness a child could have. Once he was even on the verge of death, so that the whole household did not dare to breathe and Momo was not allowed to meow, but the boy managed to survive.

At first, Taku was cautious not to be too involved with Jun. He was guarding himself from grief. But his fatherly love grew as Jun surprised him with early signs of intelligence. At the age of two, he matched the picture of a horse and a dog with their Chinese characters and divided numbers with an abacus.

Taku would dash home in the evening, asking, "Where's Jun?" If he was asleep, he woke the child. "I'm here. Papa's here, Jun. I've brought you a present," he said, showing him miniature trains, or his factory's machine models. Emi was glad that Jun, if not she, had captured Taku's heart.

Jun stuttered a little as he started to talk, but Taku reassured Emi, saying, "It's common for a bright boy to have a little stutter. He'll grow out of it soon."

Jun was fascinated by all kinds of machines and loved to go out on the streets to see them. Every morning he would say to Emi, "L-let's go and see the di-ding-ding." Emi and Yoshi took him to the main street and they watched the chocolate-colored tram cars rattling on the tracks, singing "ding-ding." Round the sharp curves, they seemed to struggle to keep themselves from derailing and toppling over. They made squeaky noises and gave off blue sparks as the metal pole touched the electric line above.

Jun had a watchful eye for all the other vehicles—rickshaws, horse-drawn coaches and bicycles. "L-look. That's D-Daddy, in a horse carriage," Jun shouted, pointing at the black shining carriage in which Taku was sitting, a tall silk hat on his head, together with a distinguished-looking man in a similar hat.

Emi's thoughts flashed back to the bad dream that had long been buried. Her husband was supposed to have been in Hokkaido today. It was exactly the same scene as the one she had witnessed on the way back from the doctor several years before. She realized how naïve she had been to think that Jun had brought her husband back to her.

There had been clues. She had overheard Taku's personal assistant Honda telling Yoshi, "I'm going to the second house for an errand."

"The second house? Which house? To whose second house is Honda-san going?" Emi asked Yoshi.

Yoshi quickly turned her back and said, "I don't know what he's talking about."

Emi also noticed that three of Taku's suits and some of his favorite ties had been missing for a long time. When she asked about them, Taku said, "It's strange. I have no idea," and immediately changed the subject.

One day he came back wearing a fancy English suit Emi had

not seen before. "You look so elegant, Taku-san. Where did you buy that nice suit?" she asked innocently. He looked embarrassed and said, "This suit? I didn't realize I was wearing this today. I bought it in Hokkaido."

"You told me your coal-mine office in Hokkaido is in an absolute wilderness," Emi said. "It must be getting quite civilized if there's a store selling English suits."

Taku found her comment either too sarcastic or censorious. "It's none of your business where I buy my clothes," he snapped, in a voice that gave her goose bumps.

On the day Jun saw his father in a horse carriage, Emi asked Yoshi later when they were alone, "You must know where Taku-san goes at night. Where's the 'second house' Honda-san talks about? Who lives there? Please don't hide anything from me; tell me as much as you know, Yoshi-san."

Seeing Emi's thin body stiffen like a prisoner waiting for a sentence, Yoshi realized that the time had come. It was a moment she had been dreading for a long time. Up to now, Yoshi had told Honda to keep the secret from Emi and Chiyo, although even many outsiders seemed to know about it already.

"Taku-san's business acquaintances often flatter him by saying what a beautiful mistress he has," Honda had said to Yoshi. "They are openly invited to the second house to discuss business. As if in the eye of a typhoon, Emi-san is the only one who doesn't know about the storm around her."

"The time will come when she finds out. But isn't it better later than sooner, because there's nothing she can do about it anyway?" Yoshi said.

"It's time for her to realize that it's only natural for a man of Taku-san's stature to have a mistress," Honda said coolly.

"After all you are a man," Yoshi shouted at him, enraged by Honda's comment. "You don't care how a woman feels."

But now Yoshi knew that she had to tell Emi the truth.

"You don't deserve this, Emi-sama. You really don't," Yoshi said, her eyes gleaming with tears.

Emi took Yoshi's hands and caressed the rough skin. "Please go on," she said in a quiet but determined voice.

"I heard that he bought a geisha woman named Hana," Yoshi said. "Paid a big sum and freed her from the geisha contract. He bought a house for her in Mita. She already has a baby boy, a little younger than Jun-san, and she is expecting a second child. So he has a whole household set up there with three maids, an assistant, and a gardener. I don't know how he has time to do everything. An executive managing a coal mine, an important member of the Diet, husband, lover and father running back and forth between the two houses and Hokkaido."

Emi trembled, her face ashen. Yoshi circled her arms around her mistress, afraid of an attack. But Emi did not fall. Tears welling up in her eyes, she stayed in Yoshi's arms like a wounded child before collecting herself.

"Thank you for telling me this, Yoshi-san," Emi said. "I know why you didn't tell me before, because there's nothing I can do about it, is there? If I reproach Taku-san for what he's done to me, he won't get rid of this woman and her child, will he?"

"I was really disappointed by him," Yoshi said. "After all, he is no different from all the other men. I thought he was religious; he must be a rainy-day Buddhist. He's on top of a mountain, blinded by the sunshine of his own success. When one conquers the world, one conquers women. When I first met him, he was so modest and ideal."

"You mean 'idealistic.' He still is," Emi said, trying to distract herself from the thought of Taku's mistress.

After a pause, Emi continued, "What kind of woman is this Hana-san?"

"You don't have to worry about her; she's only a geisha after all," Yoshi said, her round brown eyes gazing at Emi, eager to cheer her up. Yoshi's eyes reminded Emi of acorns. Yoshi was as small and bouncy as an acorn. She was in her early twenties and her excessive energy often caused problems. She broke good dishes and tore paper screen doors with her broom, but Emi loved Yoshi because she had a kind heart. She was eager to please everyone, particularly Emi to whom she was fiercely loyal.

"A geisha can be a nice person. Some very nice women are forced to become geishas. They are just as human as we are. Anyway, I wonder what kind of woman this Hana-san is who has made Taku-san go crazy enough to buy her."

"Honda-san knows Hana-san well because he often goes to the second house. He told me Hana-san is beautiful. I said it's only natural for a geisha to be beautiful. What else? He said she's got a brain. I said how do you know that. He said she has a sharp tongue. I said that doesn't mean she has a brain, it means she has a wicked mind," Yoshi said, casting a glance at Emi to see whether she was holding up.

"As you've noticed, Taku-sama's clothes disappear. He goes to the second house and leaves his underwear and socks. At first, I refused to go there and I asked Honda-san to bring them back. But he's sloppy and forgets. So, finally, I went there. Hana-san is indeed a beautiful woman, but she has nothing to compare with your purity of mind, Emi-sama. Hana-san is all wicked, like a witch," Yoshi said, trying hard to find words to comfort Emi.

"It's nice of you to say that, Yoshi-san, but you don't have to compare me with her. I'm just curious what kind of woman she is."

"You know, she's tall and slim. Her face is a bit like a Western woman's. It's the kind of face you'll never forget once you see it. Like a picture an artist would paint, nose as straight and thin as a chopstick, eyes as wild as a cat's. She and Taku-sama write *haiku* for each other."

Yoshi saw Emi's face turn pale. She stopped, and added hastily in a chirpy voice, "But you are so much more intelligent and beautiful, Emi-sama. Do you know why? Because once

Hana-san opens her mouth, she talks like a lower-class woman, like me. She curses and speaks dirty words. She talks to me as if I were a slug, 'Get out of here if you came to spy on me. Tell your mistress never to send you here again. I'll never leave here if that's what she wants to know. Ha, ha.'

"If a woman talks like that, she's ugly, no matter how beautiful her face is, and no matter what expensive kimonos she wears. Besides, she dresses too much like a geisha. Her kimono's pulled way down her back to show her painted nape. She walks, shaking her hips and pulling up her hems to show off her pink slip. She paints herself ghastly white. You have naturally pale skin, Emi-sama, but I suspect her skin is purple. I saw her naked hands—purple, like wisteria. Strange color for skin, isn't it? She's a doll when she keeps her mouth shut; she's a vampire when she opens it." Yoshi caught her breath after talking nonstop and looked into her mistress's eyes eagerly to see if she had succeeded in raising her spirits a little.

"But it's understandable that Hana-san's not nice to you because you belong to us," Emi said calmly. "She must be jealous of me just as I am of her. She probably talks like that because she had a hard time in the geisha house."

"My father wanted to sell me to a pimp, Emi-sama," Yoshi spoke in a proud voice. "My father's a hopeless drunk and spends all his money on drink, the cheap muddy kind. It's made him a sleazy, good-for-nothing man. He thought if he sold me to a pimp, he could make his fortune. But I refused, Emi-sama. I told my father I'd work hard in any other job and send money to him. That's why I'm here, Emi-sama. But, come to think of it, it may not have been such a bad idea to be a geisha and become a rich man's mistress. Unfortunately I'm not so pretty, but I know how to play my cards well. I'd flatter a man to death and pretend to love him no matter how ugly he was. I'd tell him I've never met such a handsome man in my life even if his skin is as rough as an elephant's and his nose's as round as a dumpling. Then he'd buy me out."

Emi laughed and said, "You are too honest. If you try to flatter and tell a lie, it'll show clearly on your face. Yoshi-san, you are a lovely woman; you'll have no problem finding a nice man."

"Do you think so?" Yoshi's round eyes became rounder.

"Have you met Hana-san's son? What's he like?" Emi asked.

"He's a cute boy. Ken. A little younger than Jun-san. Unlike his mother, he smiled at me and said, 'What's your name?'"

Finding out about Taku's mistress did not make Emi happy. It was particularly difficult at night when she was alone, wondering if her husband was at Hana's place, having dinner with her and Ken, chatting and laughing. She was jealous not only for herself but for Jun. Why must Jun be deprived of his father on the precious few nights he was in Tokyo? The image of little Ken sitting on Taku's lap, talking and reading, brought tears to her eyes. Taku was probably more relaxed with Ken because he would not stutter. Emi lay next to the sleeping Jun and hugged him. Her tears wet his cheeks and made it seem as if he had been crying with her.

Taku must be passionately in love with Hana. It was one thing to go with a random geisha overnight. It was understandable for him to leave a grief-stricken home and look for some solace in a pleasure house, but this was a serious affair which had lasted for several years. How romantic it must be to correspond with each other in poems.

The vacant futon next to Emi looked emptier and colder than before. She tried to erase from her eyes the colorful images of Taku and Hana together on their futon. But as soon as she tore them to pieces in her mind, the torn flakes danced and flashed in front of her like summer moths around a lamp.

The joy of music died. It stopped singing in her ears. When she sat in front of the *koto,* her fingers froze. Emi was a canary who had forgotten how to sing.

Chiyo said to Emi, "What's happened to you, Emi? You look so wan these days." Emi had not told her mother anything because she did not want to give her more reason for grief. But, as her mother kept asking, Emi broke down in tears and told her about Hana. Chiyo's face lost color. She staggered and sat down as if her legs had failed her. Gradually she regained a calm look and said, "I've been suspicious that something like that is going on. He's managed to keep it a secret from us for a long time, hasn't he? But I knew this would happen sooner or later, Emi. Successful men have big egos. They want to fill the world with their descendants. Taku-san wanted a lot of children."

Seeing that Emi was unimpressed by her deliberate calm, Chiyo continued, "You think those men who decide the fate of the country are only busy with politics, but they seem to have plenty of time to wander."

Sometimes Emi played with the idea of becoming a nun. She would shave her head, don a black kimono and pray to Buddha, rubbing her prayer beads. She would rise above the world of jealousy and competition. There would be no more long, anxious nights, staring at a clock and tortured by dreams filled with images she tried to erase and could not. She would listen to birds, play the *koto* and walk among the trees, feeling calm and serene about Taku's love for Hana.

But what would she do with Jun? She could not leave him and run away to a temple. Jun meant everything to her now that she could not count on her husband.

Emi visited Mariko, whom she had not seen for some time. When Emi told her about Taku's second family, she said, "Hora told me about it some time ago, Emi-san. Forget about Taku-san for now, if he's forgotten about you. It's a waste of time to cry over an errant husband. Hora still frequents a geisha house, but I don't think about him anymore. I don't even have a child as you do."

"What's your secret? How do you look so cheerful, Mariko-san?" Emi wondered aloud, looking at Mariko, whose cheeks were pink and eyes shining.

"Rather than moping, find a lover yourself," she said, smiling mischievously at Emi. "It might wake Taku-san up. If not, at least you'll feel better about yourself. Between you and me, I've had an affair with a young man. Nothing serious. He's just a university student who came to work for Hora. I sort of flirted with him. He fell in love with me. You know, Emi-san, he freed me. It cleared my grudges against Hora. I'm able to be nicer to him than before. I feel like my own person rather than a neglected pet of a man."

Emi gazed at Mariko, amazed at what a modern woman she was. "I don't think I could ever do such a thing. I'm timid, Mariko-san," Emi said in a resigned voice.

"Look at Taku-san, he used to be timid, too," Mariko said.

"I don't want to play games with him," Emi said in a feeble voice.

"Well, then, at least forget about him and the Hana woman," she said. "Do you know what I would do if I were you? I would enjoy being a good mother to Jun and making music."

"I'll try," Emi said, trying to believe it herself.

One afternoon Mariko came over to visit Emi. "Guess what?" she said. "That Hana woman is in my dance class. She said she had another baby. A girl. But she was bored watching the babies every day and wanted to dance. You see, she danced before as part of her job as a geisha. She is not a bad dancer. Being tall and beautiful, she has presence. Would you like to come and watch her dance? I need a musician at the studio. If you don't want to meet her, I won't tell her who you are."

Emi was not sure whether she wanted to meet Hana. But her curiosity won out. She went to Mariko's studio. In the dimly lit room, several women were learning how to walk on tiptoe. "One, two, one, two. No faltering," Mariko exhorted in an imperious tone.

"Stop. Now this time stand on one leg. Without swaying or tottering."

It was funny to watch the women in colorful kimonos stand

on one leg. They stood like flamingos for a few seconds, but one by one they swayed, wobbled, and dropped the other leg. As Emi became used to the dim light, her eyes were drawn to a tall woman in a pink kimono stretching her arms like wings and struggling to balance on one leg. She was the queen flamingo. Emi's heart stopped beating. This must be Hana. Yoshi was right: one would never forget this face. Her body had the subtle curves of a mermaid, of the eternal woman men had adored since Venus.

It was only natural that Taku had fallen in love with Hana. Emi would have, too, if she had been a man. She felt strangely ecstatic, imagining what her naked body looked like. Then a feeling of despair attacked Emi like cold rain. This woman has cast a spell on Taku-san. He'll never leave her, she said to herself.

"What did you think of her?" Mariko whispered to Emi after the class was over. "She's striking, isn't she? But she's a mean-spirited woman. Taku-san won't be able to stand her for long. He'll come back to you soon, Emi-san."

"I'm not sure," Emi said, her face drawn.

"Emi-san, you must be strong," Mariko said. "You must be a fighter like me." Mariko patted Emi on her shoulder.

Emi walked out of Mariko's studio, trying to shake off Hana's image. But it was burnt into her eyes. The trees and people outside blurred like gray mist, while the pink flamingo stood in front of her triumphantly, flapping her wings.

At night the flamingo kept her sleepless. Momo came up to Emi's futon and sat by her. Momo was getting very old and recently he slept day and night, often snoring. But tonight his eyes were wide open and anxious. Emi cuddled him and he purred. They fell asleep together.

Momo slept by her every night, curled up, his fur touching her cheek. Emi thought he did so to keep her company. But she noticed there was something Momo wanted to tell her and did not. When the morning came, he looked morose, his eyes gray, and he did not move. Emi asked Yoshi to take him to a cat doctor. According to Yoshi, the doctor only said, "There's nothing wrong with Momo. He's just very, very old. He won't last too long." Emi did not tell this to Jun because he loved Momo, too, and would be upset.

One night when Emi was asleep, Momo crept up on her bed, and rubbed her cheeks with his nose. "*Sayonara,* Emi-san. It's time for me to go," he said.

"Don't go, Momo," Emi begged him, cuddling his thin body.

"Emi-san," he said, "you haven't been happy. I'm worried about you. Take care, Emi-san. This is the very last night. I'll see you again in heaven."

"Don't go. I love you, Momo." Emi cried and held him close to her chest. "You've been more faithful to me than my husband."

Momo's faint snoring awoke Emi. He was curled up, his fur touching her cheek. She was so terribly happy he was there. She talked to him for a while and fell asleep, holding him and feeling his warmth. But before morning he was gone.

"Mama, w-where's Momo?" Jun said the next day with a worried look. "I can't f-find him anywhere."

"I've been looking for him, too," Emi said.

Jun and Yoshi went out in the street and looked all over. Momo was nowhere to be found.

Four days later, gardener Lee found his lifeless body deep under the camellia bush. Emi felt she had lost another child. Lee and Jun dug a grave near the spot where he had been found. They planted a small peach tree by the grave, for *momo* means "peach."

CHAPTER 2

Taku was on the deck of a steamship crossing from mainland Japan to Hokkaido. Dark-blue waves knocked against the side of the ship, splashing cold water on him as he stood clutching the rail. He watched two seagulls following the ship, flapping their wings and screeching their rough cries. They somehow reminded him of Emi and Hana, the two women in his life.

Men of means openly had mistresses and society took that for granted. Still, Taku felt guilty about having established a second family with Hana. He often left Emi alone, though she had suffered much for him since their marriage. She had endured misfortune with good grace and had always been a sweet and loving wife. So, what right did he have to be disloyal to her and give her more grief? Had success, power and money gone to his head so that he had lost his heart?

Taku had been bewitched by Hana's charm. He had met her at a dinner party given by Prime Minister Ito at his favorite geisha house. Ito had been kind to Taku, although it was his Foreign Minister, Uno, who had put Taku in jail. The prime minister was a fair-minded man who did not allow personal enmity to interfere with his political decisions. He was sympathetic to Taku and always found a kind word for him.

"Taku," he said, "I hear Standard & Chartered Bank of England has granted a loan of ten million pounds to your coal mine. With your horrible English, how did you manage to convince them to give such a generous amount? I couldn't get a loan from them for my government."

"Perhaps because my company has a better record than your government, sir," Taku said smiling.

Ito was a famous womanizer. Each time Taku visited him, Ito was surrounded by beautiful geishas. He was a revered politician, the founder of the modern government and the author of the new Constitution, but he enjoyed talking to geishas for hours on end and making them laugh. That night, Ito was talking about the first journey he had made to England with Uno forty years before in 1863, on the *Pegasus,* a three-masted British ship. They had sailed for 130 days without ever putting into port.

Taku was listening attentively to Ito's story, when the door slid open and a tall woman in a golden kimono appeared with plates of sushi. Suddenly the whole room brightened as if a yellow flower had opened in a dark forest. There were beautiful women in the room, but they all paled in her shadow. She sat, bowed, and put a dish in front of Ito in the composed and slightly haughty manner of a woman who had supreme confidence in herself.

"Hana, where have you been? Now sit down and listen to my story," Ito said.

"I will, Prime Minister Ito," she said, but went on serving dishes to the other guests. She brought one to Taku and stared at his pocked face. His heart started to pound when he saw her luminous black eyes gaze at him. When she poured saké into his cup and her lithe fingers almost touched his, he turned red like a boiled crab and she smiled. She smiled again when his hands trembled and he almost dropped the cup.

"Your eyes are like black stars in the night sky," Taku whispered to her. It was cheap flattery he would normally have disdained, if anyone else had said it.

"How can you see black stars in the night sky?" Hana said, with an air of scorn. "How about black pearls or diamonds? They sound just as tacky, but at least you can see them in the night sky."

"You are right. I was foolish," Taku said, ashamed of himself.

Hana left him, but Taku could not take his eyes off her for the rest of the evening as she went around the room serving the guests.

As they left, Prime Minister Ito patted Taku's shoulder and said, "I've never seen you flirt with a geisha as you did tonight with Hana. You have good taste, Taku, but watch out: she's very proud. She's refused so many men that she's been punished and has to serve and wash the dishes."

That night after Taku returned home, Hana's image kept him awake for hours. It was as if a force like a typhoon had swept him up into the sky. With Emi, it had been more gradual. She was only fourteen and a half when his mother had arranged for them to meet. His mother's single-minded eagerness about the match made him a little resentful and cautious. He had only fallen in love with Emi when he realized how sweet, intelligent and talented she was.

Taku pursued Hana with the same impetuousness that had helped him achieve everything he wanted to do in life. He had forgotten all the sympathy he had felt for Emi, for her illness and loss of the babies; he was a wild animal.

He invited Hana to a quiet teahouse in a moss garden far away from her geisha house. She came in wearing a blue kimono embroidered with a magnificent green peacock in full feather, and she looked like one herself. As she walked, her hips swayed gently left and right. Her face was thinly powdered, rather than covered with heavy white paint, and her hair was done in a simple oval chignon, on top of which was a blue hairpin like a peacock's crest, in place of the convoluted geisha hairdo she had worn the other night.

"You look like a real woman, Hana-san. I like you that way," Taku said.

"I feel like a real woman, breathing free air. I'm glad you invited me here, Mr. Imura, so far away from the prison I live in," Hana said with a sigh. "Don't you think I deserve a better life than being a dog to men, Mr. Imura? Of course, I only sleep with the very few men I like. Dirty old men have no chance to touch me. The other day I slapped the face of a man I didn't like. I received a reprimand and I've been cleaning lavatories for two weeks."

"So, am I a dirty old man who is not allowed to touch you?" Taku asked.

"That depends on how you treat me," Hana said, with a bemused smile.

"Tell me why you became a geisha if you don't want to sleep with dirty old men. Most rich men who come to your place are dirty old men, aren't they?"

"Do you think any woman would choose to be a geisha?" Hana said angrily. "My father was an antique dealer—a connoisseur. He loved to collect beautiful things. He was a compulsive buyer and was deeply in debt, because he could not let go of what he had acquired. He polished and rubbed his antiques as if they were his lovers.

"He was cold-blooded about people, even about his family. He didn't care if my mother and I didn't have much to eat. He had no money to send me to school. As a child I buried myself in tales of queens and princesses, imagining myself as the heroine. My father ended up sending my mother to an asylum and me to a geisha house. He paid off his debt by selling me, but all his possessions burnt to ashes in the fire—you know, the big one—which swept Tokyo five years ago. He drank himself to death, unable to accept the loss. My mother died in the asylum last year. So I'm stuck in my prison, hating every minute of it," she said, her black eyes showing a trace of a tear.

Taku had a hard time suppressing a desire to take her in his arms, or at least to hold her hands in his and console her. Hana certainly did not deserve to be stuck in the geisha house for the rest of her life. She seemed to be an intelligent woman with a strong mind of her own. Taku felt justified in spending money to free her from prison. After all, he would be saving a woman's life. It would be as worthwhile a cause as the flood victims and the orphanage he had supported recently. Emi always encouraged Taku to be generous about charities.

Of course, there was nothing generous about this charity. Taku was not about to set Hana completely free. He had a wild desire to possess Hana and make her his own woman. Emi had just miscarried her third baby. The thought of another doomed pregnancy was too painful for him. With Hana he might have healthy babies.

Hana was a shrewd negotiator. "There's a man who adores me and he's been saving money to buy me out. He almost has enough. He's a very handsome and sweet man," Hana said, pronouncing the word "handsome" slowly as if to rub it in, glancing at Taku's face which looked like a bumpy potato.

"Do you love him?" Taku asked, seething with jealousy.

"I'm fond of him. He's very intelligent, too. His wife died last year. So he wants to marry me. But I don't know how successful his business is. . . ."

Although her story might not be true, Taku's blood boiled wildly. He had to act quickly. Since he knew he wasn't handsome, he had to prove to himself that women could love him for other reasons. His mother had said that Taku used to be a good-looking boy, with skin as soft as a freshly pounded *mochi* rice cake. Everybody had loved him for his looks and his sweet nature.

Taku had caught smallpox when the epidemic blew through his village like an ill wind. The evil god of smallpox came at night in a red kimono and looked into the window of each house to find prey. It was said that the evil god loved to catch beautiful children.

In order to please and intoxicate the god so that he would not take Taku, his mother placed in front of her house saké and the pimply smallpox dumplings she had made out of crushed and steamed soy beans. She also organized a god-chasing party. Radiant in her scarlet kimono, her normally tidy hair flying loose and her arms in motion, she danced passionately with her neighbors all clad in red. The neighbors followed her and circled around each room of her house like a red snake, waving their kitchen fans to chase the intoxicated god out of the house.

But the god caught Taku two days later. Taku's stomach ached violently, his skin oozed pus, and his eyelids stuck together. The doctor shook his head when he saw Taku's violet-colored spots and his black lips. Taku was in a delirium for two weeks.

The first day he was allowed to go outside, all the villagers came to see him. They said they came to congratulate him on his recovery, but he soon realized that they had come to see how ugly he had turned. Children stared at his face, laughed or shouted in horror, "He looks like an iguana," "He's a monster," "A polka-dotted bulldog." They ran away and came back with more children. The grown-ups hid their shock and said with a smile, "How wonderful to see you well again." Then they turned their backs and whispered, "Poor thing. He used to be the prettiest boy in the village. In two weeks he has become the ugliest."

Taku ran back into the house and looked at the mirror that hung in the hall. When his mother had washed his body a few days before, he had caught a glimpse of his reflection and had been so horrified that he had avoided mirrors since. He figured that the scars would eventually disappear if he did not see them. Now he saw himself again. His skin was filled with holes like the miniature craters of a volcano he had once seen in a picture. His face was so swollen with the mounds the volcanoes had created that the nose seemed indented, and the eyes thinner than the thinnest moon.

He had a violent urge to scrape and peel off the ugly skin from his entire body and face. If only he had been a snake and could slip out of the worn-out skin. He shook, jumped, kicked, stamped on the floor and scratched himself all over. Blood oozed, but no skin peeled off.

His mother used to say that not only his looks but also his personality had changed since the illness. People didn't love him readily any longer. In order to be accepted by the world, Taku had become a fighter.

Taku paid off Hana's debt right away and freed her from the geisha house in the same bold and decisive manner that he carried out his business decisions. He bought her a big house with a fancy rock garden. He bought her handsome furniture, beautiful kimonos, jewelry and everything she wanted. He did this gladly, because she said she loved him. He was blissfully happy and felt rejuvenated. He had more energy than ever and was never tired despite the work he had to do for the Diet, the coal mine and the proposed steel mill which was making progress.

Occasionally, he felt sorry or guilty and went back to Emi with a heavy heart, but, like an addict reaching for opium, he returned to Hana again. Hana bore him healthy children one after another. There was no turning back.

But wasn't Hana getting too willful and manipulative lately? She kissed him with crimson lips, caressed him with her spidery fingers and used all sorts of wiles when she wanted him to buy something. If Taku did not buy it, she called him names and exercised her sharp tongue. Did she really love him?

Recently, she bought what she wanted even without asking him. Every time Taku returned from Hokkaido, he found new furniture or ornaments in the house. On his recent return Hana said happily, "Did you see the Korean chest in my dressing-room with gorgeous iron handles, Taku-san? I bought two more chests, one Japanese and the other Chinese. They are coming tomorrow. The dealer says I have an excellent eye for antiques."

"Hana, why do you need three chests?"

"Because I've bought quite a few kimonos this week and my wardrobe's overflowing."

"Did you buy even more kimonos? I received a huge bill from your kimono tailor last week."

"Do you love me, Taku-san? It costs money to keep a beautiful woman."

"By the way, who's the new maid who greeted me at the door? Almost every time I'm back, there's a new maid. What happened to the last one . . . what's-her-name?"

"She's gone. I saw her put her filthy fingers into my bathtub to see how hot the water was. I'd told her to wash her hands before she did it. And she folded my kimono with dirty hands. So I was cross with her and she left."

"Don't you think you are a little too strict with the maids, Hana? Besides, you have too many of them. I saw a new gardener outside, too. Emi has only one maid and one gardener. She and Yoshi adore each other. Her gardener Lee is the one whom I invited from Korea because he protected me there. Emi treats him like a part of our family."

"Always Emi, Emi. If she is so great and if you love her so much, why did you bring me here?"

A seagull came and perched on the railing. She had sad eyes like Emi, tilted her neck sideways as Emi often did, and looked at Taku. A sharp pain stung his heart. Had he become so arrogant that he thought he could have two families and make two women happy at the same time? How could he apologize to Emi for what he had done? Of course, apologies would not mean anything unless he abandoned the second family, which he was not ready to do.

When Taku had graduated from university, his mother urged him to return to her village and marry a girl she had selected from the neighborhood. But Taku told her he was too young to marry and went to Korea as a member of a cultural mission organized by his mentor, Professor Fukuzawa. Japan was a little ahead of Korea in modernizing itself. The professor thought it important to help turn Korea into a strong, independent country like Japan, so that it would not easily be gobbled up by China, Russia or the West, which were watching it like eagles hovering over prey.

Hora had been typically cynical about Taku's enthusiasm for helping Korea. "I bet the Koreans will be suspicious of your intentions. They'll say you're a hypocrite because they consider Japan more of a threat than Europe. A wolf comes to a rabbit's hole and offers help; the rabbit will surely say, no thank you."

Hora was right and Taku had a difficult time in Korea. The government was pro-Chinese and an army of 3,000 Chinese was guarding Seoul. Taku and his colleagues were ostracized and stones were thrown into their home. Everyone, except Taku, went home in three months.

Taku stayed on alone and, at age twenty-three, became King Kojong's foreign adviser. He also started the country's first newspaper, written in Chinese, the language of the educated.

Everyone liked the paper except the commander-in-chief of Seoul's Chinese military, Yuan Shih-kai. He strode into Taku's office, rattling his saber and growling with rage. He pointed to an editorial Taku had written about Korean independence and shouted in a thunderous voice, "Korea is not independent. It belongs to China. A Japanese has no right to start a Korean paper here. It's supposed to be a Korean government paper and a greenhorn Japanese like you, Taku, is not allowed to express his personal opinion in an editorial."

"Korea is an independent country, or at least it's supposed to be," Taku said coolly.

"Be careful what you say, Taku," Yuan said proudly. "You'll regret it, because I'll be emperor of China one day. If Napoleon, at just five feet, conquered Europe, I can conquer Asia easily at five foot three. Remember, China is twenty-eight times larger than Japan. Ha, ha, ha." He laughed vociferously and left, stamping his boots.

Shortly thereafter, posters were pasted on lampposts all over Seoul, *Hang Taku Imura, a Japanese imperialist!* Leaflets captioned *Kill Taku Imura* were distributed with critical comments about his paper.

One day when Taku was walking down the street, he saw Chinese soldiers marching, their green sabers pointing forward. A large paper poster was impaled on the points of naked steel. Taku walked up close to read it. *Kill Taku Imura, a Japanese imperialist!,* the poster read in dripping red ink. Fortunately, the soldiers had no idea what Taku Imura looked like and ignored him like a stray dog, when he was under the tips of their noses. Taku passed by them nonchalantly and walked home safely. His housekeeper Lee managed to hide Taku in a closet when the soldiers broke into his house.

Half a year later, Taku again made Yuan boil with rage by an article with the caption, *The Savagery of a Chinese Soldier,* reporting on a Chinese soldier who had shot to death a Korean grocer for refusing to give him free ginseng. Yuan protested to the Korean Government and demanded that the paper be suspended and Taku fired. The Korean Government, which kowtowed to the Chinese, summoned Taku and told him to apologize for the article.

"I don't think it is necessary to apologize unless they prove that the article is wrong," Taku said. But he resigned from the paper and decided to go home to Japan, so that the king and the high officials who had been supportive of the paper would not get in trouble with China.

Taku had been away from Japan for almost two years when he returned to visit his aging mother in Nogami, the village near Hiroshima where he had grown up. On the second day he was back, his mother said to him, "Last time you didn't even meet the girl I'd chosen for you. Too bad, she has already married away, but I've found an even better one for you. She is a very special girl, Taku. Perfect for you. Finding the best possible wife for you is my last important duty as a mother. I can't die until then.

"Taku, did you know that your schoolteacher, Mr. Yamato, passed away last year? And did you realize that he had a lovely daughter named Emi? He asked me before he died if I would consider Emi-san as your wife. He said he would go to heaven in bliss if Emi would marry a man like you. I didn't promise him for sure, because first you must like her. But you know that she's from a family of well-respected scholars. She's only fourteen and a half. She's the brightest student in her class and well-liked by her friends. The neighbors say she's shy, but gentle and kind. Her mother, Chiyo-san, is a *koto* teacher. Emi-san is very talented and has taught herself to compose music." His mother chattered away like water gushing from a gutter after rain.

"The only problem is she's an indoor plant pampered in a greenhouse. She catches cold easily. But I'm sure she'll grow healthier as she grows older. If you don't mind, Taku, will you pay a visit to Chiyo-san and tell her how sorry you are about your teacher? That way you can meet Emi-san in a casual manner, you see. I already told Chiyo-san about it and she is expecting you. I'm getting old and won't last forever. So, please give it some thought."

As his mother went on talking, her enthusiasm started to annoy Taku. He was intending to return to Korea to start a new paper, written this time in Hangul, the Korean alphabet. Korea was no place for a honeymoon; Japanese were not loved there. Why couldn't he think about marriage after he returned from Korea next time? Wasn't a fourteen-year-old girl too young to marry? Besides, why did he have to marry a girl from Nogami? When Taku went to university in Tokyo, he found women there so much more elegant and sophisticated. It had been his dream since to marry a beautiful Tokyo woman after a passionate love affair, the kind he had read about in Western novels.

But he found it difficult to turn down his old mother's ardent request. Taku's father had died when Taku was only six and his mother had raised him alone in absolute poverty, sending him to school by selling kimonos she had sewn and cultivating vegetables on the poor land. He felt forever indebted to her.

Taku missed his father even after he grew up. He remembered sitting on his father's lap, the warmth of which he still felt, listening to him read Chinese folk tales, his knotty fingers tracing ideograms, and watching him count by flicking amber abacus beads. His father talked about the squadron of American Black Ships that had arrived in Japan. "Giants of men with golden hair and green eyes were on board," he said. "The ships woke up our country from hundreds of years of sleep and ever since Japan has been in turmoil."

His father was a samurai who had been unhappy about the latter-day Shogun regime. Taku listened to him argue with his samurai friends who gathered in the house. "If we don't modernize ourselves, those giants will conquer us," he said. His normally stable and comfortable lap swayed and rocked as he grew animated and Taku could feel the thudding of his father's heart. The revolutionary fever of the times was spreading through Japan, infecting even the remote village of Nogami.

On a bright summer day in 1867, Taku followed his father to the port near Hiroshima where he and his several samurai friends were to embark on a journey by steamship to Kobe and thence by horseback to Kyoto, the site of the revolution.

The sea was blue and serene, and a wooden ship in the harbor was chugging, ready to leave. "Taku, this ship is small," his father said. "But someday you'll board a big one and go to faraway places like America." Then swooping down, he picked up Taku and held him high above his head. Taku felt dizzy, but he laughed. Lowering Taku down to his chest, his father squeezed him and his mother together and whispered with a radiant smile, "Don't worry. I'll be back in no time and tell you all about the victorious revolution. Taku, take good care of your mommy. I love you both."

His father never came back. He contracted typhoid fever and never reached Kyoto. He did not see the victorious revolution—a peaceful coup d'état to end the two-hundred-and-sixty-year-old Shogun dynasty and to restore young Emperor Meiji as the ruler of the country. The whole village celebrated the birth of a modern nation one night, but Taku and his mother stayed home. Taku cried in her arms as they watched the lantern parade from the kitchen window—an endless string of red beads floating away along the dark rice paddies to the village.

His father's last words never left Taku. He felt responsible whenever he saw his mother cry, hiding her face between the tomato plants and dropping tears on the kimono she was sewing. He was determined to take good care of her as soon as he grew up. He had sent her money from Tokyo and then from Korea, but he felt guilty for having been away from her for so long; now he found her suddenly aged, clutching a walking stick and her hair gray, though her eyes were still sparkling. He had turned down her previous request to meet a girl. Now he was twenty-five, still young, but not at an unreasonable age for a man to marry.

If he did not listen to his mother now, and if she happened to pass away before he returned from Korea next time, he would carry a lifetime of guilt. His mother would take along with her to his father in Heaven the tale of an unfilial son. Not only Confucius and Buddha, but also the eight million gods of Japan would punish him. None of the gods had done much so far for Taku and he always suspected that at least half of them were evil ones, like the god of smallpox. No god had saved his father from typhoid either. So Taku was not overly respectful of the Japanese pantheon but he was still too cautious to be outright rebellious. After all, they were the ones who had originally created the world.

Besides, meeting this girl would not necessarily mean marrying her. He could decline her. It was very likely that she would not like an ugly, pocked man like him. There was nothing wrong with paying a visit to Mrs Yamato to say how sorry he was about her husband. He had been a good teacher to Taku.

Taku agreed to his mother's request and she was all smiles. Regaining her youthful exuberance, she said, "I'll go to the village temple and tell your father the good news. I haven't visited him for ten days." She emphasized "the good news" as if it was news of marriage. She added, "And I'll go to the village shrine to ask Priest Kono to preside over the ceremony. Then I have to send that fast letter—what d'you call it, a telegram?—to all our relatives."

Taku was frightened that his mother had already taken it for granted that he was going to marry this girl he had not met, and was orchestrating the wedding.

"Taku, now go see Emi-san," she said, almost pushing Taku out of the door. "Be polite to Chiyo-san. She's a good lady and a hard worker. Without her husband, she's raising her daughter very well."

Taku was not watching where he was walking, still unsure if he wanted to meet Emi or not. He missed his step and found himself in a rice paddy. His white *tabi* socks and wooden *geta* clogs were all muddy, but he said to himself, It doesn't matter if I don't look elegant. She is only a fourteen-year-old.

This was the familiar path he had walked every day as a child, wearing straw sandals and carrying books, rice paper and a *sumi* ink brush wrapped in a straw sack his mother had made. He often ran there in those days, either because he was late or for the fun of it. Taku liked his school, as Mr. Yamato lent him good books to read.

It was numbingly silent all around. The boys must have gone to school elsewhere, after their teacher had passed away. This neighborhood used to be a lively place, not only because of the boys, but also with girls coming in and out of the back of the house where Mrs. Yamato gave lessons on *koto*. In those days, Emi must have been just a baby and it would have been premature even for his eager mother to have arranged a marriage with Taku.

As he approached the house, a faint sound of *koto* drifted in the hushed silence. When he went around to the back of the house, the air was flooded with resounding music. It was so beautiful that the wind had hushed itself to listen and the crows on the trees had stopped cawing, ashamed of their ugly voices. Who was the musician? Was it Chiyo, a student, or was it Emi herself?

Taku stood in front of the entrance for a while, unwilling to interrupt the music. He spent a deliberately long time cleaning the mud off his *tabi* socks and *geta* clogs. But the door slid open gently and a middle-aged lady in a maroon kimono with thin, gleaming eyes and a gentle, oval face smiled at Taku. "You must be Taku-san. I'm Emi's mother, Chiyo. My late husband talked so much about you. You were a very special student for him. Emi will be here right away. She was a little nervous about meeting you and was playing the *koto* to calm herself," she said.

Before she finished speaking, a little girl in a pink kimono was standing in front of Taku, her eyes thin but sparkling just like her mother's, and silky hair hanging down to her shoulders. She looked as fragile as a dainty Japanese doll in a glass case that one must handle with care.

Chiyo led Taku into a room, three walls of which were covered with shelved books. Taku recognized some of the titles Mr Yamato had lent him in the old days. The room was otherwise sparsely furnished with a calligraphy scroll and a flower arrangement in an alcove, a table and a few *zabuton* cushions to sit on. "Please sit down, Taku-san. I'll bring you tea," Chiyo said and left. Emi sat in front of Taku and cast her eyes down wistfully, as if to avoid looking at him. Did she not like his pocked face? Was she sad about facing marriage at such a tender age?

"I'm sorry you lost your father. He was a great teacher," Taku said.

"I miss him. He was a sweet father," Emi said in a sad voice. "He gave me a little kitten not too long before he died and I think of him every time I cuddle the cat. His name is Momo. He isn't a kitten any longer. He's big and fat." She smiled.

"I listened to your *koto* from outside. You play so beautifully, Emi-san."

"Oh, thank you very much," she said, and looked down again at her fingers on her lap, so as not to make eye contact.

Taku wanted to find something exciting to talk about, but he did not know what to say to a girl of fourteen. After all, wasn't she at an age when she would be happier playing house with her friends? At a loss, he asked, "What do you like at school, Emi-san?"

"Lots of things, but I particularly like music, arithmetic and English. I love to read, too." Emi spoke in a musical voice like a bird singing.

"What kind of books?"

"At the moment I'm reading *Brothers Karamazov* in a new translation. It's the last book my father bought for me before he died. It's a gripping story. So many people in the book are tormented, possessed by demons. I wonder if people are like that in real life," Emi said, deep in thought as if absorbed in the pages of the book. Then she continued, "But I love Alyosha. He gives everybody hope."

Taku was astonished that a Russian book had arrived in the cultural desert of Nogami and a fourteen-year-old girl was reading it. Emi had a dreamy look in her eyes when she carefully pronounced the exotic name, "Alyosha." Obviously, she was more interested in Alyosha than in the man who was sitting in front of her.

But suddenly she came back to reality.

"Oh, have you read the book, Taku-san?"

"No, I haven't yet," he said apologetically. "I've been too busy lately. But I'd like to read it someday soon."

"Your mother told me about the newspaper you've published

in Korea. What kind of articles do you write? I suppose I can't read your paper because it must be written in Korean," she said, tilting her head and looking with curiosity into Taku's eyes for the first time.

Taku told Emi the paper was written in Chinese and she was surprised. "Why do you write in Chinese, when your readers are Korean?"

"You're right. My next project is to write in Korean."

As Taku told Emi more about Korea—about his feud with Yuan Shih-kai and about the king and the queen—how the serious King Kojong was eager to modernize his country, while the beautiful and clever Queen Min appointed her relatives to all the important positions of government and turned the court into a pleasure house, while people were dying of hunger—the wistful look disappeared from her face. She kept asking questions, her eyes shining. She often smiled at Taku, as if she liked him more than in the beginning.

Encouraged, Taku asked about her music. "What kind of music do you compose, Emi-san? Did you write the music I heard outside?"

"Yes, I did. I'll play more for you, if you want. Would you like to come to my music room? I'll show you my cat, too," Emi said. Taku was happy to hear her say that; she would not offer to play music if she did not like him.

She took him to a small room in the back of the house, where in the center of the *tatami* mat lay a *koto* with its elongated wooden body, longer than Emi. Patting the cat, who was peach-colored with a bobtail, asleep on a cushion in front of the instrument, Emi said proudly, "Taku-san, this is Momo. He's very intelligent and understands everything I say. Momo, this is Taku-san, whom I told you about."

Momo yawned, totally unimpressed by Emi's guest. As if a yawn were not enough to show his contempt, the cat stood up, stretched his legs and arched his back like the Arc de Triomphe. Then he sat and went back to sleep again.

"So what kind of music would you like to hear, Taku-san?" Emi asked.

"Any music you want to play for me," Taku said.

"Let's see. I'll play the first music I made, when I was nine. It's called *The Song Contest of Tree Frogs and Meadow Frogs,*" Emi said, and sat in front of the instrument with her legs folded neatly inside her kimono. She put ivory plectra on three fingers. As she bent down and touched the instrument, each of her fingers started to dance up and down the strings as if they were little magicians, and the funny voices of frogs, *ga-ga, gue-gue, gakko-gakko, gekko-gekko,* cried out in chorus. Emi tilted her head to listen to her own song, her cheeks glowing and smiling, as if amused by the frogs' voices. Momo purred in his catnap and joined the chorus.

Taku smiled, too. He loved the light-heartedness of the music. He liked the innocent way Emi had played, forgetting her shyness.

Walking his way home in the dusk, Taku felt perplexed. He tried to tell himself that Emi was just a precocious young girl and no candidate for marriage. But he found himself smiling, reliving the entire scene, the way she talked about Alyosha with dreamy eyes, the way she was animated by his stories of Korea, and the way her fingers danced on the *koto* strings like little magicians. How could he be so easily attracted by a mere child? Taku shook his head, trying to banish her image, but her music kept flowing in his ears and her soft voice kept talking to him.

Emi was still only a timid bud of a flower. It would be cruel to pick the bud before it had given even a sign of softening. It would be a sin to domesticate such a young girl and turn her into a housewife. Shouldn't she enjoy being free and unfettered for a while, nourishing herself with books and music as much as she liked? In a way, it was lucky that Taku had to leave here soon. Emi could wait for a few years before she was ready to be his wife, if she so chose.

Two rice paddies away from home, Taku saw his mother pacing nervously outside her house. When she spotted her son, she rushed out so fast she stumbled. Picking up her cane, she called out, "What did you think of her, Taku? Isn't she lovely?"

Taku said cautiously, "Emi-san is sweet and very intelligent. I don't mind considering her as a future wife, but I still have things to do in Korea and she's very young. She can wait until I return here and then we'll marry if she likes to."

His mother's cheeks stretched into the ripples of a happy smile as she heard Taku's favourable impression of Emi, but she did not agree with him about postponing marriage until later. "Make haste to do a good deed, Taku. I'd like to see your happy face while my eyes are open. Let's have a wedding now and she'll wait for you here."

"Please let me sleep on it, Mother," he insisted.

"Only until tomorrow morning," she said.

The next day Taku received a telegram from the Foreign Ministry in Tokyo asking him to visit Minister Uno in his office at his earliest convenience. Taku said to his mother, "I have no idea why the foreign minister wants to see me. It's probably something to do with Korea. If someone important like him tells me to visit him, I suppose I have to. Now it's impossible to have a wedding before I leave, Mother." Taku was secretly relieved that he did not have to have a wedding right away.

Taku never imagined that meeting with Uno would lead to a lifetime of tragedies and grief. He was only excited to meet the famous minister. Uno was a powerful man, known to be tough and cunning. A close friend of Prime Minister Ito, he was a perpetual winner in the political upheavals.

Taku did not think it was possible even for his over-enthusiastic mother to arrange a wedding before he went to Tokyo to meet Minister Uno.

"Yes, it is possible." His mother's animated voice shocked Taku. "The foreign minister can wait a few days if you send him a telegram saying, 'I'll rush to your office right after my wedding.'

We'll have the wedding the day after tomorrow, because it's a Big Luck Day according to the lunar calendar."

She spoke of her plan as if it had been set up long before. "You can leave the following morning for Tokyo. You know, I've already asked Priest Kono at the village shrine. He said he's available on the Big Luck Day. I've talked to Chiyo-san, too, and she is beside herself with pride and joy at her daughter's having the good fortune to marry a man with a bright future. She's eager to rush the wedding before you change your mind. Obviously we can't have a big reception, but I've sent telegrams, and some of the relatives will be here."

"What about Emi-san? Did she like me? Did she say yes to marrying me?"

"Of course she liked you, Taku. Before she met you, she didn't like the idea of getting married so young, although it's not an unusual thing here, you know, but yesterday she said to her mother, 'I admire Taku-san because he's so idealistic and brave. There are many people who have idealism, but there are few who put their thoughts into action. I'm not really ready for marriage yet, but if he wants me to, I'll wait for him until he comes back from Korea.' Isn't she bright, Taku? At such a tender age she has a good appreciation of what you are like."

"So Emi-san has the same idea as I have. We'll marry after—"

"I have some reason to rush now," his mother interrupted, her eyes moist and gray. "I have a feeling I may not last too long. My heart feels strange. My bones are brittle, I fell twice last month and my knees hurt. This may be my last chance to see you, Taku. That's why I want you to marry now."

She whined like an old nagging woman, which she had never done before. This might have been a clever trick she used to persuade her son, but it was an ultimatum for Taku. He said to himself, if I say no to her now, she'll fall ill with disappointment and the gods only know what will happen to her. Besides, the more Taku thought about Emi, the more he liked her. He thought she was the kind of woman he wanted to have as his wife.

Taku sat straight and said in a resolute voice, "Mother. I will marry Emi-san." Then he added, laughing loudly, "People tell me I'm like a steam engine when I set my mind on something. I know from whom I get that, Mother." His mother wrinkled up her face in a triumphant smile.

The wedding took place at the village shrine, presided over by Priest Kono in a white silk kimono and a tall hat. He shook a scepter like a big rice spatula and exorcised evil spirits ftom the bride and groom. He unfolded the rice paper pleated in layers of rectangles and read the words to call for the eight million gods of Japan to bless the new couple. The words were dreadfully boring and incomprehensible.

Taku kept stealing glances at Emi, who was standing next to him in a snow-white brocade kimono with white cranes embroidered all over. She was looking like a crane herself—pure, delicate and noble. A traditional bride's headdress, a big box called a horn-hide, looked heavy and painful on her small head, but each time he looked at Emi, her cheeks blushed pink and she smiled shyly.

As the priest's mumbling went on and on, Taku noticed that Emi's face had turned paler. A minute later he was catching in his arms the bundle of kimono falling toward him. With her eyes shut, Emi looked frozen. Taku excused himself from the priest, carried her to the back room and laid her down on the *tatami* floor.

Chiyo ran after him and quickly took the horn-hide off her daughter's head. She was as pale as her daughter, and apologetic. "I'm sorry she interrupted the ceremony, Taku-san. This horn-hide is a nuisance; she has no horns anyway. The *obi* was stiff, too. It's just a little fainting. She'll be all right soon." As Chiyo undid the layers of *obi* sash that had been binding her daughter's thin body like a punishment, Emi opened her eyes and looked around quizzically. When she caught Taku's worried eyes, she smiled faintly, tried to sit up, and faltered like a fallen crane. Taku laid her down again and said, "Don't rush, Emi-san. Take it easy." By that time Taku's mother was also there, looking upset.

The ceremony resumed when Emi returned in a loosened *obi* and looking prettier without the heavy box of the horn-hide. After the ceremony, everybody toasted, ate, sang and talked at the village inn. Emi was quiet during the feasting, but toward the end, she stood up and surprised everybody, saying in a soft voice, "I'm sorry I fainted and disgraced myself at the ceremony. In order to apologize to all of you, I'll play a little music."

She walked to the corner of the room where a *koto* was placed. She sat in front of it and bowed a deep bow, placing her fingertips together on the floor. She put the ivory picks on her fingers and sat still for a minute, as if to calm herself.

With the decisive manner of a karate chopper cutting still air, she plucked a string. A deep voice came from far away, striking one's inner chord. Her fingers started to move all over the strings as Taku had seen three days before, but this time they danced to a melancholy tune, at times quiet and other times surprisingly loud coming from the delicate fingers of a young girl. The theme melody had been woven into many variations, ending in a resounding finale, echoing the chorus of sound from the walls and ceiling of the room.

The music enraptured everyone and the room was still for a long time after the last echoes had died down. Then cheers and clapping of hands erupted. Taku's mother was all smiles again.

Emi sat next to Taku again, her cheeks flushed pink from the hard work. He had a hard time resisting an urge to embrace her. He felt proud to have her as his wife. Until this morning, he had felt as unready as half-cooked rice about the wedding, but at the ceremony he was engrossed by Emi's painfully innocent beauty. Then her music had swept him away. It was not only the beauty of the music, but also her quiet grace and courage that had enchanted him.

Emi and Taku were taken to a room where two futons had been laid side by side on a *tatami*. Emi looked exhausted after the long, strenuous day. Taku thought he should let her sleep right away. But as soon as they were left alone, he could not help hugging her as hard as he could. Her body was so thin he thought he had cracked a bone or two.

Taku whispered to Emi, "I love you, Emi-san. I want to express my passion to you with my whole body. But you are so young and may not like it. I won't do anything you don't want me to do."

Emi looked frightened, but then she answered in a timid voice, "I've read in the novels what married people are supposed to do. Now we are married, so I don't mind trying."

Taku was still hesitant. But he could not contain his passion too long. Before he knew it, millions of fireballs spread like the most beautiful fireworks in the night sky. Taku whispered to Emi, "Did you see the fireworks, Emi-san? I'm night blind, but I saw fireworks for the first time." She did not answer. She was already asleep, or pretending to be.

The next morning Emi was well rested and looked like a fresh morning glory in a blue kimono. Taku's heart thumped with the pain of imminent parting. When he kissed her, her eyes shone with a teardrop. Taku told her to take care of her health, read books and make music. They promised to write to each other.

Emi rode on a rickshaw with Taku to the port where he was to embark on a steamship sailing to Tokyo. She sat on Taku's lap, curled up in the rickshaw box, normally claustrophobic but perfect for the lovers. As it shook and squashed them together, they kissed and caressed. Taku tried to memorize every square-centimeter of Emi's delicate features, her voice soft as a breeze, and each careful word she uttered.

As the ship left the port, Taku watched Emi, who stood on the shore waving her hands at him until she disappeared behind the horizon. The wind from the sea chilled Taku. He found himself clasping his arms together. Only the wind went through the ring of his arms where Emi had been wriggling and giggling a little while ago. He had hoped he would be a happy man for a long time, remembering the love he felt for her, but he was already feeling acute pain as if part of his body had been severed.

At the foreign minister's office in Tokyo, Taku found a tall man in a fancy pin-striped suit shouting loudly at a man who shook like a mouse in front of a lion and bowed obsequiously. Uno was red with anger and two old scars on his face, one above an eyebrow and the other on a cheek, were twitching. These sword gashes Uno had suffered during the revolutionary war, which he was known to be proud of, were enough to frighten anyone, but Uno also had blue veins on his forehead swelling up like bolts from the sky. The crude way he was shouting at his subordinate upset Taku and he took an instant dislike to the minister.

Seeing Taku enter, Uno dismissed the man with his chin and pasted a smile on his craggy cheeks. Then he made his point right away to Taku.

"I've heard about the furor you've caused in Korea with Yuan Shih-kai. You have guts, Mr. Imura. You should go back there and continue the paper before Yuan takes it over and uses it for his propaganda. As you've proven, the newspaper can be a powerful political tool." Uno was as shrewd as a fox. He wanted to use Taku's paper as a Japanese political weapon.

"Right Honorable Minister Uno," Taku said defiantly, "it was not my intention to publish a paper as a political tool. Fukuzawa *sensei* wanted the paper to help enlighten the Korean people."

Taken aback by the audacity of this young man, Uno pinched his eyebrows. "No matter what your intention, your paper sent an excellent message to China about Korea's independence," he said, feigning calm. "I'll provide some funds for you to continue the paper."

Taku knew that Uno's idea of Korea's independence was different from his own. Uno only wanted to push China out of Korea so that Japan could take it over. But Taku could not resist the offer of the funds. He could use them for buying a Hangul printing machine and hiring Korean assistants. He promised to promote Korean independence.

"By the way, you know that Kim Ok-kiun is organizing a *coup d'état* in Seoul to assassinate government ministers, don't you?" Uno said, lowering his voice.

"I know, sir," Taku said. "Kim talked about it."

Kim Ok-kiun was a young Korean aristocrat Taku had known since the days he had lived in Fukuzawa *sensei*'s house in Tokyo. Kim visited the professor, disguised as a priest, and asked for advice about the coup he had been planning with the members of his Independent Party. Kim discussed it with *Sensei* for many days. At night he walked back and forth along the corridor, tottering, his intense eyes glittering, his slim face pale and drawn. Taku, a Buddhist taught not to kill an ant, was disturbed by Kim's idea of murdering seven officers of the government and argued against it.

"If you save millions of countrymen by killing seven, it should be justified," Kim said. "Money is lavished on banquets every night while people are dying from hunger. The situation is so bad that there is no alternative but to kill them."

Even Fukuzawa *sensei* said, "Think about the French Revolution and the American Civil War. Sometimes bloodshed is inevitable in the name of justice."

Taku was still not sure about the idea of murder. But when he went to Korea and saw people in rags sitting listlessly on the road begging, and found the skeletons of people who had died from starvation or epidemic lying in the empty ruins of their houses, he began to agree with the idea of killing seven in order to save millions.

The Japanese Government had been secretly supporting Kim, because Japan would benefit if Kim established a pro-Japanese government after overthrowing the current pro-Chinese one. But Taku heard that the government had begun to have second thoughts about helping Kim.

So, when Uno asked, "What do you think of Kim? Suppose his coup is successful and he takes over the government, could he be a trusted political leader?" Taku defended Kim enthusiastically.

"Kim has big dreams. He is highly intelligent, ambitious and charismatic, and I'm sure he is capable of changing the country for the better. His party members are all bright young men, too. But without soldiers to fight against Yuan Shih-kai's army, his coup won't succeed, and without money he can't carry out his ideas in a new government. Kim told me that, when he was in Tokyo last time, you, Minister Uno, kindly offered him a generous loan and 3,000 soldiers to help him. Kim was worried he hadn't heard from you since. It would be very helpful if you—"

Before Taku finished talking, Uno stood up impatiently, the old scars on his face twitching again, and said, "That's enough. Thanks for coming," so that Taku had no choice but to leave.

When Taku returned to Seoul, Kim came to talk to him. He said, his voice quivering and his eyes bloodshot, "Minister Uno has shifty eyes like a cat. I wrote to him again asking about what he had promised. He wrote back, saying that he had decided against sending the troops, but that I could certainly count on the 200 Japanese soldiers stationed in Seoul in case of the coup. About the loan, he said he might send some money later, when the coup worked out successfully. It was terribly disappointing because we were counting on him so much. But we can't wait any longer. China is in a dispute with France over Vietnam, and half of Yuan Shih-kai's soldiers have been sent there. This is the best time to strike."

"Even half the Chinese soldiers will be seven times more than the Japanese stationed here," Taku said, trying to talk Kim out of rushing into action. "You don't even have money to pay for the Korean soldiers who might work for you." But Kim was not listening, his eyes staring faraway outside the window.

* * *

Taku's heart hurt even now, more than twenty years later, to think of those three cold nights of December 1884, in Seoul. Those brief hours crushed all the dreams of Kim's party. Many lives were lost, Taku's good friends murdered, the party members killed and punished. Six out of the seven high officials of the government were murdered, but that did not save millions of Koreans.

The original plan was to invite the would-be-victims to a celebration of the new post office. Dynamite laid at the back of the building would then explode. At the shock of the explosion, the ministers were expected to run out and be murdered by hired killers waiting outside the front door. The plan did not work because the dynamite did not explode on time. But, one of the plotters quickly started a fire on a bushy hill nearby. In the confusion, the ministers left by the back door instead of the front.

Losing no time, Kim managed to summon the escaped party guests to the palace under the pretense that it was the king's order. Taku and Lee, who had been hiding near the palace in case they could be useful, saw the guests ushered into the courtyard. There, masked killers grabbed them and stabbed them from behind, cupping their mouths and muffling their screams. Their bodies bent limply like straw dolls and fell on the ground, blood gushing over their gold and silver brocade.

Early the next morning, a change of government was declared, and a triumphant Kim announced the policy blueprint he had worked on for years: the independence of Korea to be declared; the class system abolished; schools to be opened; employment opportunities to be given not by birth but by merit; the tax system to be reformed.

But, by the next day, the Chinese Army led by Yuan Shih-kai, together with the Korean soldiers who had switched sides when they were not paid, had laid siege to the palace, chased the Japanese soldiers who had been protecting the king and took him to their camp.

Japanese civilians in Seoul were stoned and killed and the women raped, when it was reported that Japan was behind the coup. A mob banged on the door of Taku's house and demanded that he come out, shouting, "Death to Taku Imura, Japanese imperialist!" Lee whispered to Taku to sneak out by the back door, and told the mob Taku was not there. As the mob set fire to the house, Taku ran out. Stones hit him in the back, but he made it to the Japanese Legation building where hundreds of Japanese refugees were thronging. Eventually, the entire Japanese contingent walked all night in the snow to Inchon, the southwestern port, flanked by the 200 soldiers who fought off the pursuing Koreans and Chinese.

Six of the defeated coup organizers followed the Japanese, hoping to escape. They were dressed as monks, wearing yellow gowns, but it was hard to disguise their identity, particularly Kim who was moaning like a wounded lion. Taku walked among them, carrying on his back a five-year-old girl. The old pocks on his cheeks cracked with tears that had turned into ice. It seemed an endless funeral procession, mourning for Korea's lost cause, winding through dark, desolate forests indifferent to the sorrows of men.

In the end, Taku walked sleeping, dreaming of Emi weeping for him and almost dropping the girl on his back. Eventually, the trees loomed blue-white in the forest. A gust of wind brought a salty smell. Down the hill stretched the sea. Two big ships, one military and one civilian, stood at anchor flying the flag of the rising sun.

Everyone was happy to have escaped to safety, except the six Koreans. The Japanese Legation minister refused to take them on board. Taku boiled with rage and shouted at him, "Have you lost your head, sir? You know what will happen to them if they stay here. Are you going to leave them here to be murdered?" His screaming fell on deaf ears.

After the minister, the soldiers and the legation personnel embarked on the military ship, Taku secretly met the captain of the civilian boat and begged him to smuggle out the Koreans. The captain was a humane man and said, "Normally I wouldn't accept this request because I will lose my job if it is discovered, but I can tell you are asking this out of sympathy for your fellow men. I believe that heaven has assigned me the task of saving these men's lives." The last minute before the ship sailed, the captain guided the fugitives to the hold and whispered to them to get into the empty bags of rice and lie among the hundreds of other sacks piled there. The ship arrived at Nagasaki Harbor with the "monks" peacefully asleep in the rice bags.

Taku considered this the one good thing he had done in the failed coup attempt. However, the Chinese and Korean governments revenged themselves on Kim ten years later. They sent an assassin to Tokyo, enticed Kim to Shanghai and murdered him. In the main square of Seoul, Kim's body was hung under a large sign saying, "Kim Ok-kiun, a loathed criminal, guilty of the highest treason, rebellion, and immorality." Amidst frightened cries from the packed crowd, the body was chopped into segments that were taken around the country and displayed on the streets.

Back in Tokyo, Taku rushed to complain to Minister Uno about his indecisive and half-hearted support for the coup. Taku had already sent him a telegram as soon as he landed in Nagasaki, but he felt he had to confront Uno. He should not have laid all the blame at Uno's door, but he was sad and tired, and needed to complain to someone.

At the entrance of the imposing brick façade of the Foreign Office building, a guard stood like a tin soldier with a bayonet at his side. He asked Taku why he was there. Taku said bluntly, "Minister Uno would see me if you gave him my name."

Looking up and down at Taku's crumpled suit, his pocked face and disheveled hair, the guard must have taken him for a lunatic. "Excuse me, sir. Do you have something to prove your identity, or a letter of appointment?"

"Just go!" shouted Taku in such a loud voice that the guard jumped and went inside. Taku was asked to sit in the foyer and waited there seemingly for hours. He could not complain since he had no appointment, but he was irritated by the slow welcome of the minister who knew what Taku had gone through. By the time Taku was allowed to enter the inner sanctum, he was seething with rage.

Without any greeting, Uno blurted out, "Don't you think those Koreans were outrageously reckless to start a coup without enough soldiers, or the money to pay them?"

Taku burst out, "Minister Uno, you once promised Kim you would send soldiers and a loan. Since then, Kim was often confused by your conflicting messages, but he counted on you till the last minute. It is true Kim and his Independent Party members were reckless, but I'm afraid you played a role in their failure. After all you don't care about Korea, do you, sir? You just decided to sit and watch Yuan Shi-kai swallow Korea and kill the dream of the courageous young men trying to save their country."

Blue veins at Uno's temple swelled up and the sword scars on his face twitched. He was enraged by the impudence of this young man blaming an important man like himself. Uno could have had Taku thrown out of the office, but he could not afford to make an enemy out of a newspaper man who might write damaging articles about him and the coup.

"In the end, Prime Minister Ito didn't want to be involved with the coup," Uno said, his voice trembling with anger. "Political situations shift all the time. Recently, we've been too busy with domestic politics to deal with Korean affairs. I hope you'll understand." Uno stood up irritably, and said, "I'm busy today."

"I'm afraid that my cordial relationship with Your Honor has ended for good today," Taku said bluntly, turned his back on the minister and left without bowing.

Gazing at Taku's back, Uno must have decided that a cordial

relationship, if it had ever existed, had indeed ended, and that this unruly horse could not be left free to run wild. This man had to be punished for his insolence.

Taku went out of the gate. The streets of Tokyo, with their fancy brick buildings and women dressed in pretty kimonos, were coldly indifferent to his rage. No one here knew what had happened in Seoul and no one seemed to care. Korea was a lost cause here. Nothing would change if Taku shouted at the minister or not. Against the powerful Uno, Taku was only a small bee, who stings and dies. Not only would the small sting make no prick in the bastion of power, it was also a sure way to kill his future career. Why had Taku done something so stupid? Now he was *persona non grata* to the government.

Taku found himself at the Fukuzawa's door. *Sensei* dashed out and hugged him. "I received your telegram," he said, his face pale, his hair grayer and the furrows on his forehead carved deeper.

The professor's face turned even paler when Taku told him what he had said to Minister Uno. "I'm afraid you made a serious mistake," *Sensei* said. "Uno is not a man to play with; he's well known for his vindictiveness. Didn't you stop and think for a minute about what might result if a young man came in rudely and shouted at a foreign minister to his face? I know how much you care about Korea and how sad you feel about the coup, but I don't think Minister Uno was trying to be malicious to Kim. As he said to you, political circumstances often force one to compromise. Don't rush into such criticisms, Taku."

As he left Fukuzawa, Taku was despondent. *Sensei* was right. There was no excuse for such an outburst of temper. Was it the trauma and the sadness of the coup, or the fatigue of the long voyage from Korea that had caused him to act so rashly? He had only himself to blame for this colossal blunder. Anger turned to remorse and self-pity, and Taku found himself weeping.

CHAPTER 3

Taku sat in jail in Tokyo, wearing a prisoner's red kimono. The moonlight was seeping through the iron-barred window, casting pale square shadows on the dark floor. Taku felt his way to the window and pushed his face against the bars, but the window was too small for him to find the moon. It was as small as the pocket of his confiscated winter coat that he wished he had because he was freezing to the bone.

The little window was his only contact with the outside world. He was not allowed to read, write, or see anyone. He felt as if the only thing he could do to express himself was to scream. He did so a few times and the guard rushed in to grab him and cupped Taku's mouth with his hand. He looked sympathetic though, probably thinking that this stupid criminal had finally gone crazy.

Taku lay down on the futon as thin as a cardboard and hugged a worn-out pillow, the only thing that remotely resembled the soft warmth of Emi in this icy cold cube of a cell. He cried thinking about her as always, holding the pillow.

Although Taku had been insolent and regretted his ill behavior to Minister Uno, he had not dreamt the punishment would be as harsh as this. He thought over and over again about what else he had done to merit this incarceration.

After the tempestuous encounter with the minister, Taku returned to Nogami and had a brief and happy reunion with Emi. Then he went back to Seoul and toiled away to create a paper readable by the common people. In the end, he used Chinese characters along with the Hangul alphabet to accommodate the educated men who only read Chinese. On the day the first paper came out and was pasted on posts, townspeople stopped and read aloud, perhaps to show off that they could. The children found a picture of the world map in the paper and tried to pronounce the names of the foreign lands.

The paper was a success, but Taku missed Emi so much that he asked his Korean colleagues to continue it and went back to Japan. Emi had finished her high school in the village and they moved to Tokyo, excited that finally they would start a life together.

It was a big move for Emi. It was the first time she had left her mother, home and Nogami. Momo, the only companion Emi brought with her, missed his home as desperately as did his mistress. He scratched and banged his head on the door, trying to get out and go home.

Their Tokyo home was a cozy two-story wooden house with a garden and a pond with twelve gigantic *koi* carp and numerous frogs. The owner of the house said that the *koi* had lived here for a hundred years before he was born. Momo, attracted by the idea of fresh fish for dinner, forgot his homesickness and roamed about the pond like a charmed man. But the fish, twice as fat as Momo, acted as if Momo did not exist and swam along nonchalantly. The idea of jumping into the dirty pond did not occur to the fastidious cat. The frogs were amused by Momo's vain struggles and sang away, "*Gua. Gua. Gekk. Gekk.*"

In the evening when Taku returned from work, he found Emi

and Momo lying next to each other on the *tatami* mat, both looking unhappy.

"What's the matter?" Taku asked.

"We're just complaining about the cruelty of city life," Emi said. "This morning Momo ventured out into the street through the crack in the wooden fence. Soon he came back covered with mud and soot. He told me he was shouted at by a rickshaw man and splashed with mud by its wheels. He sat and licked himself for the rest of the day, but he never recovered the pristine color he was so proud of back home. He's permanently dyed gray, just like all the alley cats he disdains.

"I went to a market. When I said I wanted to buy a sack of potatoes, the storekeeper looked at my face and said, 'Eh? Say it again. I don't understand your accent.' I pointed at a potato and said, 'I'd like to have *imo*.' The woman stared at me, my coarsely woven cotton kimono and my country-style hairdo, a sumo wrestler's bun, with total contempt. 'You mean *o-imo*? Where do you come from? No nice ladies in Tokyo say *imo*. Only rickshaw drivers say that.' I ran out of the shop without buying *o-imo*. But don't worry, we'll get used to city life soon, Taku-san."

Taku took Emi to his mentor and friends, but otherwise she stayed home, shut all the windows and curtains and made music like a silkworm weaving thread inside a cocoon. Momo swirled around her like a faithful windmill, wiggling his bobtail back and forth.

Taku started to work at Professor Fukuzawa's newspaper company in Tokyo. One evening when he came out of his office, two men in black masks ran from a corner. Fukuzawa *sensei* who happened to be at the office heard a commotion and ran out. The men in masks ran off when they saw *Sensei*.

But after a second attack, *Sensei* invited Taku to his house and said, spreading a map of America in front of him, "Taku, what do you think of going to California? You have to stay out of Minister Uno's hair for a while. Going away is the only way to escape his desire for revenge. The government is punishing all of its opponents severely now."

"California? That's the other side of the earth," Taku said.

"It's a golden country," *Sensei* said. "Lots of Chinese went there, cultivated land and built railroads. When they became too successful, the white people made a law to exclude them. Now America is pressing the Japanese to emigrate as they need cheap labor. Obviously, it's only a matter of time before they'll make the same law against us. So I've been thinking how to prevent it from happening. Taku, you've made good friends in Korea and so you'll do the same in America. You'll escort a group of emigrant farmers to California and promote good relations with the Americans."

Taku went home, and discussed it with Emi.

"How long are we going there?" Emi said, not knowing how to react to such an astonishing proposal.

"At first, maybe we'll stay for six months. If you don't like it, we'll come back," Taku said, sensing Emi's hesitation.

Moving to Tokyo had been disconcerting enough for Emi; moving to America was like going to another planet. But Emi realized she could not say no if this was a device *Sensei* had come up with to protect Taku from Uno's pursuit of revenge.

"It'll be fun to see the New World," Emi said. "I read in a high-school book that the sky is vast and the fields flame golden in California. The mountains glow orange in the afternoon and turn purple in the twilight. People have yellow hair and blue eyes."

The next evening when Taku returned home, Emi was standing in front of a mirror posing like a mannequin in a Western shop window, her hands on her waist. She was wearing a blue velvet dress with puff sleeves, and on her head was a matching hat with a feather. "The lady at the shop said this is the latest fashion in America," she said, smiling.

"You look lovely," Taku said and added hesitantly, "But

velvet may be too hot in California. And we may have to live like farmers."

Emi ignored Taku's comments and pointed to her feet, saying, "Look, Taku-san. I can walk in high heels." But when she took two steps, her ankles wobbled and she stumbled. Emi pouted and said, "She sold me all these strange-looking things." Kicking off the shoes and stockings, she showed Taku the things piled up on the floor—a heavy, boned corset and a metal frame for hoop skirts.

Emi quickly adjusted to the idea of going to America, but somehow she often felt sick. She did not pay special attention because feeling sick was more of a normal condition for her than being well. Every time she had her period, it was a trial for her. So, she was more relieved than worried when she missed it two times. But when Emi, at Taku's suggestion, wrote a letter to her mother about it, Chiyo wrote back telling Emi to go to a doctor. The doctor said she was pregnant. He also said that traveling on a ship could be life-threatening for the mother as well as the baby. "Particularly because Emi-san isn't too strong."

"Unfortunately, I can't change my plans," Taku said reluctantly. "The eighteen emigrant families I'm accompanying are ready to leave. Why don't you go back to Nogami and stay with your mother until you have the baby, Emi? We'll survive this separation as we did before. The harder the parting, the happier we'll be when we reunite."

Taku left on a big boat from Yokohama Harbor. The melancholy gong of the ship howled like the call of the wild from the faraway continent. The hundreds of colorful tapes connecting the people leaving and the ones staying were cut and the pink one linking Taku and Emi was torn. Taku watched Emi until she became a dot on the horizon. When only the sheer line dividing the sky and the sea remained, he still kept gazing at the spot where Emi had been. Nothing else in the vast space of the sea and sky mattered.

On the first day in San Francisco, Taku went to see Mr. Miller at the Immigration Office. He was a brown-haired man as tall as an electric pole. Taku was impressed by the way this tall man bowed politely down to his waist to greet him, but then he realized he was bending down to study Taku's face. Probably he had never seen a face so badly pocked and was wondering whether this man from a barbaric land, with a terrible skin disease should be kicked out of his country.

"Don't worry, Mr. Miller. This isn't communicable," Taku said, not realizing it was his English that was incommunicable.

With the funds *Sensei* and his friends had raised, Taku bought, on Mr. Miller's advice, fifty acres of wasteland in Valley Springs at the foot of the Sierra Nevada. He worked with the emigrant farmers, cultivating the land, planting enough to be self-sufficient and building cottages to live in. They grew beets and beans on the reclaimed land, but the soil was so poor that it would be some time before the produce could be sold at a profit.

Women worked side by side with the men, their babies tied to their backs, and they also cooked, washed and helped their husbands build their houses. The woman who often asked Taku to come for supper would doze off with food falling off her chopsticks, oblivious to the laughter at the table. Taku was glad Emi had not come here. He could not imagine how the greenhouse plant of Nogami could survive a pioneer's life.

But Taku missed Emi so much that he was more than happy when, after three months, the emigrants asked him to raise more money in Japan so that they could buy better land. On the boat returning home, he hummed and hopped on the deck, thinking of the day he would arrive. By that time it would be New Year and he would celebrate the holiday with Emi with saké and *mochi* soup. Emi would have a baby before long and he would be with her when it arrived.

When the ship finally arrived in Yokohama, the minute he disembarked, his heart dancing with the expectation of seeing Emi and the joy of being on the soil of his motherland after the long, tiring trip at sea, Taku was surrounded by men in black police uniforms and found himself coiled with rope like a viper. He struggled to untie it, asking why he was being arrested. They shouted at Taku to shut up and threw him into a windowless, hearse-like black van. They slammed the door and whipped the horses so hard that they started to gallop.

Taku shouted all the way to Tokyo in vain. The van stopped at a gray building surrounded by a high wall topped with barbed wire. At the iron gate stood armed sentries with glistening bayonets. Inside, Taku was stripped naked and put in a prisoner's red kimono. He was screaming and kicking until then, but when he was thrown into a dark hole of a room, he fell on his knees, having no strength left to utter a word. As he heard the heavy padlock with an iron bolt click behind him, he burst into tears, calling, "Emi. Emi." All the happy dreams of going home to see her were crushed and he sat in the cell weeping with his head burning, chest aching and limbs frozen numb.

Life came to a halt; the world ceased to exist. Lying in the cell, a scroll of the blue Sierra Nevada Mountains stretched like a long forgotten dream before his eyes. The faces of the people who were waiting for him in California haunted him. Taku had promised to return after he raised money and buy a great piece of land in San Joaquin valley which he had found after traveling extensively on horseback with land experts. He had also talked with American businessmen and saw the possibility of making contracts to build streets and railways. It would be a terrible breach of trust if he did not return and did not even send a letter of apology. He begged the prosecutors to let him write, but they did not care as much as a frog's tears about his problems.

On some mornings, Taku was taken to the courthouse where important-looking investigators, prosecutors and detectives were lined up. They said that this was a pre-trial to determine Taku's guilt. No matter how many brilliant brains were put together, how could they present proof of a nonexistent crime? But their job was to prove him guilty. Once a man was detained, he was presumed "not" innocent. And the proceedings were held behind closed doors with no defense attorneys or jurors.

Months passed and they had not found enough evidence to accuse him. They came up with a report Taku had written on the Korean coup and pointed out mistakes on minor facts.

Exasperated by the stupidity of the whole exercise, Taku often exploded with anger, banged the desk and yelled at the prosecutors. He knew very well he was repeating the same mistake that had brought this ignominy on him in the first place: utter insolence toward authority. The prosecutors told him his sentence would be heavier because of his contemptuous manner. He did not care.

As time went by, Taku became more irked than angry. Every morning he assumed the lotus position and pretended to be a zen monk practicing asceticism. He repeated the words he had once read in Buddha's book, "When a man is born, an axe grows in his mouth; a fool abuses it and cuts himself down." Taku was a fool. He had been too arrogant, grown a big axe in his mouth and shouted at Minister Uno which had brought this misfortune on him. He said aloud, "I'm not angry. I don't hate the man who put me through this ordeal. Hate will not solve my problem."

When he was bored, he asked himself mathematical questions. He kept squaring a number as far as he could go. With his fingernails he picked up the dirt accumulated on the windowsills and used it to write down the numbers on the floor.

For physical exercise, aside from the calisthenics every inmate was taken out to do, he did push-ups and jumping jacks every day. The number of push-ups he could do had increased from 75 to 155 in six months.

These activities did not quench his craving for reading. He borrowed a brush and paper and wrote a petition asking to be allowed to read. Eventually the petition was granted. Only religious books or educational ones were allowed, but Taku was beside himself with joy. He asked for the book of Buddha's teachings and for the Bible that he had skimmed through in America and wanted to read more. He was also given French, German, and geometry textbooks. Though rebellious in the courthouse, Taku was polite to the guards and scrubbed the floor in his cell and in the dining hall. So a guard even brought a desk and a bright lamp for him.

Suddenly cell life became a blessing in disguise. He was lonely and missed Emi, but otherwise he had few complaints. "Do not fear those who kill the body but cannot kill the soul," the Bible said. Whoever put Taku in jail could never kill his soul.

Although the window of his cell was tiny, there was one three times as big on the corridor leading to the courtroom. Each time he passed it, he enjoyed a glimpse of the outside world, a ray of sunshine, floating clouds and the tip of a tree that suggested the changing of the seasons. There was even a trace of an old bird's nest in the tree.

On an early spring day, when the twigs were dyed with tinges of pink and yellow, Taku saw the old nest repaired with a few new twigs and a pigeon sitting on it. She was plain with brownish feathers and a beige neck, but for him she was sublime. She had a roundness and fluffiness alien to the prison environment. He was sure that God had sent her to him. Didn't the Bible say the dove is a holy spirit? Isn't it a sign of meekness? The bird reminded him of Emi. She tilted her neck as Emi did, looking as gentle and soft as she. He named her Emi. "Good morning, Emi. Blessed are the meek," Taku said on the way to the court. She was always there, patiently waiting, like Emi in Nogami.

One day he saw three fluffy balls under Emi's wings. They had ugly beaks, but they were life itself, clamoring for food and growing bigger every day. Taku wondered if his own baby had been born by then. Was it a boy or a girl? Were both Emi and the baby doing well?

After several months of interrogation, a small piece of paper with three lines of Chinese scribbled on it was presented to

Taku. Asked about it, he said, "Yes, this is my handwriting. I wrote it in Korea when I had no command of Korean yet and had to communicate in Chinese."

The investigator said that the note was found inside somebody's drawer in the Korean Government office. The note explained the makeup of the Japanese Government. It said, "Prime Minister Ito and Foreign Minister Uno are extremely clever. With a few others from their party, they've formed an oligarchy that decides all the important issues of the country. They are ambitious and are hoping eventually to control China." The prosecutors argued that Taku insulted the Japanese high officials in a foreign country. The officials were offended since they had never intended to control China.

Taku insisted that the note was no official statement. It was written as part of a casual conversation. Though a foreign adviser to the king, Taku was not representing the Japanese Government; he had a right to speak as a private individual.

The pre-trial finally ended. A magistrate quoted the three-line scribble and concluded that "the defendant delivered a speech on the above quote. He committed the crime of 'contempt of high officials.'"

As a prisoner on remand, Taku was sent to the Minor Offence Court to have an official trial. But it did not begin until three months later. It was again to be held behind closed doors with no attorney to assist Taku.

Soon, a change of the political climate outside the jail brought fresh air to Taku's life. Uno was no longer foreign minister. Taku was not released, but was allowed to communicate by mail. Letters came in piles. Friends had not forsaken him—at least some of them.

Sensei wrote him, saying that he had written to the people in California about the circumstances that had made it impossible for Taku to keep his commitment. "They were extremely sorry for you, but wrote me to tell you not to worry because they are doing well."

Hora wrote, "Taku, the world is too quiet without you. Come out soon. I've never known a man who gets punished so much for his good deeds. What a shame. You are a brave wild boar, but you can't win, charging head-on to a tiger like Uno. . . ."

Emi wrote to him frequently. He read and re-read her letters until his tears wet them and made them illegible.

Dear Taku-san,

After you left for America, I returned from Tokyo to Nogami. I was happy being back, like an uprooted tree replanted where it belonged. Momo was the same way; he catnapped beside my koto, *purring the loudest and the most musical of purrs. But I missed you and pictured your whereabouts on my mind's canvas like an artist painting random pictures. Sometimes I painted you riding a horse on a golden Californian hill, as tanned as an American Indian. Other times I drew you drinking tea at a local café, chatting with a blue-eyed waitress. In the long nights, wild imagination has a way of growing like toadstools after rain. I read somewhere that in America everybody kisses everybody and I wondered if you had gone crazy with kisses and kissed every woman you met. Did Taku-san fall in love with a golden-haired American woman? Did his love for me melt away with the California sun and wind?*

The silly toadstools would wilt away in the morning sun and I happily played duet on the koto *with my mother, cooked and sewed with her. I let her fuss over the baby growing inside me and tried to be a carefree seventeen-year-old, reading, dreaming and playing with Momo.*

But it was mind-boggling to think of the distance between you and me and I was weary of the long months I had to wait for you. So, how excited I was when I received your telegram, saying you would be home on New Year's Day and would be with me when I had the baby.

I hugged my tummy and patted the baby inside me. I talked and sang to him about his father's homecoming. The baby kicked back vigorously. Time passed quickly. As the New Year approached, my mother cleaned the house frantically and planned a feast. Momo noticed the sudden liveliness in the house and ran about, wiggling his stubby tail.

New Year's Day was always a special day when I was a child. The whole world was reborn that day. Before the old year ended, all the eight million gods worked hard, like millions of elves, to sweep the sky to make it crystal clear, polish the stars and the moon and shed old leaves from the trees. My mother worked even harder than they and the whole house looked new. Old tatami *mats were replaced with fresh rush ones that shone with a green sheen and smelled like sun-drenched hay. I helped my mother tear the faded rice papers off the screen doors and paste on snow-white ones. Then we would decorate the gate with freshly cut pine branches. On New Year's Eve, my mother trimmed my hair, clipped my nails and scrubbed my back in the bath.*

On New Year's morning, I would get up before the sunrise and listen to birds sing newly composed songs with freshly tuned voices. I put on a new kimono with long sleeves and a flowery pattern and went out to see the sunrise. Then I would sit in front of the family shrine and pray, asking the eight million gods of Japan to bring a good year for me and my parents. My father would ask me to drink ceremonial saké, but merely sniffing it befuddled me.

Then my father would take me to the village shrine, which he normally avoided. He was in a good mood and greeted all the villagers, saying, "Happy New Year. This is my daughter Emi," as if fishing for a compliment. He would smile broadly, showing his white teeth, when they said, "Oh, what a pretty daughter you have, Yamato sensei.*"*

This New Year would be even more special than usual because Taku-san would return and our baby would arrive soon. I helped my mother prepare for the feast and cooked. We made a square omelette, caramelized fish with saké, soy sauce and honey, and cooked chestnuts, black beans and lima beans. We put all the food in three-tiered lacquered boxes and kept it for the seven days of the New Year holidays.

In the morning of the New Year, as in the past, I got up at dawn to see the first sunrise of the year, with the happy expectation of seeing the big sun coming up from behind the mountains, heralding a peaceful beginning of the year, dyeing the sky violet, red and then gradually golden. As you know, the winter sky is always clear here in Nogami where the ancient gods lived, and the sun never failed to smile on this day, as far back as I could remember.

But on this New Year's morning, the sky was covered by clouds and the sun did not shine, keeping the whole world gray. The chilly air made me shiver and I came inside.

I wore my blue kimono so that I would look pretty for you. My middle was so round that I looked like the full moon embroidered on the kimono. "Taku-san will laugh when he sees me so big," I smiled. I kept looking out of the window, waiting to see you running with heavy luggage in both hands and smiles all over your face. Would he speak English to me? Did his English improve, or was it still broken? I wondered.

I waited and waited, but no sign of you was seen all day. The sun never came out either. The gray day turned into a grayer evening. The three-tiered lacquered boxes that kept all the delicacies we had cooked had not been opened. We wanted to show you how beautiful the food looked and eat together with you. I didn't feel like eating anyway, not even the square omelette and the sweetened beans I normally love.

"Maybe the ship from America hasn't arrived on time," I said to my mother.

"Even if it has arrived, Taku-san will first visit with Sensei *in Tokyo. Then he must take another boat to get here.*

Perhaps the boat didn't leave because of the bad weather, or because it's a holiday," my mother said. "Why don't you read a book. Worrying isn't good for the baby."

As I sat down to read, there was a loud knock on the front door. "Who can be banging on the door so rudely on New Year's Day?" my mother said, frowning.

A man was standing at the door, out of breath. He said, "Are you Chiyo Yamato-san?" As my mother nodded yes to him, he handed her a yellow telegram sheet. "A Happy New Year. We usually don't work on a holiday, but this is a special service, because it looked important," the man said. After gazing sympathetically at our alarmed faces, he left quickly.

As my mother read the telegram, her face turned white and her hands trembled. She pushed the yellow sheet deep under the layers of her obi *and ran inside her room. I followed her, but she would not let me in the room. After a few minutes she came out and said calmly, "My uncle died in Tokyo."*

"Which uncle?" I enquired. "You never told me you had an uncle in Tokyo. Can I read the telegram?"

"N-no," my mother stammered. "I didn't want to talk about him because we haven't been close. We had a fight once. Don't worry, Emi. I won't go to his funeral since you're about to have a baby."

I was disturbed by my mother's unusual secretiveness. During the whole evening she had a forced air of cheerfulness. She talked loudly and even hummed as she moved around the house. But her eyes were unfocused and her humming often came to a sudden halt. As if dazed, she carried the same flowerpot from one room to another and came back with it again. She stood in the kitchen, saying, "Let's have supper," but forgot even to sit down.

I said, "What's the matter with you, Mother? The telegram has made you crazy. It can't be the death of an uncle you've never bothered to talk about," but she didn't respond. In the night she sat and gazed into the darkest corner of the room. I knew something terrible had happened. "It must be something to do with Taku-san. He usually sends us a telegram when anything happens."

"I think he's late because the ship hasn't arrived yet," my mother said, looking away. I decided not to pry into it for now. If it was such horrible news that she was determined to keep it from me, I should not know it. For the baby's sake.

Seven days passed without any sign of you and the New Year holidays were over. The sun came out only a few times during the entire week. It had been a joyless holiday with clouds hanging even in the house. My mother was unusually quiet, often in deep thought, her cheeks frozen hard. The food in the lacquered boxes was hardly touched and went stale.

The eighth day was another gray day. The wind rattled the doors and windows, and the crows were circling over the house with ugly cawing. I didn't feel well and was resting on a futon. Momo, who had been looking outside the window, suddenly crouched in a ready-to-jump posture, his hips and tail swaying and his eyes glittering with hostility.

"You can't catch a crow. He'll catch you, Momo," I said to him and got up to look out of the window myself. Then I screamed and covered my mouth. I saw eight or ten men in policemen's black uniforms riding on black horses and heading in the direction of our house. They were not the friendly, kimono-clad village policemen carrying sticks, but Tokyo policemen in imposing square-shouldered Western uniforms, with brass buttons all over and leather sacks hanging at their waists.

Why did Tokyo policemen suddenly appear in this faraway village, trampling the ridges of the rice paddy? Did their horses fly like Pegasus over the sky from Tokyo? The horses in the Chinese poems my father used to recite also flew over the mountains and fields.

Hearing my scream, my mother rushed to the window, and turned as white as she had when she received the telegram.

"They're coming here." Her voice was shaking.

"Why are they coming here? What for?" I asked.

Mother looked resigned now. "Emi, I tried to keep you from the shock and told you a lie, but I must tell you the truth now. The telegram was from Fukuzawa sensei, *informing us that as soon as Taku-san had disembarked at Yokohama, he was arrested by the government police and put in jail.* Sensei *wrote to me in order not to shock you. They must have come here to interrogate us. Try to be calm, Emi."*

Before she finished talking, there was an enormous commotion outside, with the jangling of swords, stamping of boots and the banging of the door. Mother had a determined serenity on her face and opened the door gently. The police stormed into the house without bowing or greetings.

The most arrogant-looking one with affected whiskers like a cat's pushed a sheet of paper in front of my mother's face and said, "Are you Chiyo Yamato? And where's your daughter Emi Imura?" He glared at me and cast a rude glance at my belly.

"We are the investigators from the federal police. We came from Tokyo by the order of the government. We'll search your house for evidence concerning Taku Imura's activities. We'll ask you questions about him. You aren't allowed to tell us lies, hide documents or interfere with our search."

"Could you tell me why my husband was arrested?" I said in a firm voice. "It must be a mistake. He's not the kind of man who would do anything criminal."

"We aren't allowed to discuss the case," cat-whiskers said bluntly.

They clomped all over the house, opening every closet and drawer. One of the policemen stepped on Momo's paws. Momo yelped a gasping meow and bit him on his trousered thigh. It couldn't have hurt him much, but the man kicked the cat out of spite. Momo's yellow eyes flashed with rage. I picked him up and comforted him.

They went into your study and looked through every sheet of paper in and out of your desk. They threw boxes from the shelves all over the floor and opened them one by one. The room you kept neatly organized, now looked as if a typhoon had hit it.

They went to my room. They overturned the boxes filled with my music and ransacked my kimono drawers. A young policeman stumbled over my koto. *The discordant bang of the strings struck me like the last blow. The world blackened in front of my eyes and I fell backward. The eerie vibrations of the thirteen strings faded away.*

There was a long silence. When I opened my eyes, I had no idea where I'd been. Through still blurred vision, I saw my mother gazing at me. As my sight cleared, I saw Dr. Imai, behind Mother. The doctor asked me, "How do you feel?"

I didn't understand why he was there. "I'm fine, Doctor Imai, but why am I lying here? Is there anything wrong with me?"

The doctor looked at Mother first and, receiving her nod of approval, answered hesitantly, "I'm afraid you had a traumatic epilepsy attack. It's a falling illness."

"A falling illness. A traumatic epilepsy attack. . . ." I repeated his words, my head reeling. "I think Dostoevsky had the falling illness. An illegitimate Karamazov brother had it. Poor Smerdyakov. But I don't remember falling."

"In an epileptic attack, one doesn't usually remember falling," the doctor said. He told me to take care and left. I overheard Mother, who had gone to see the doctor off, ask him, "How often will the attacks occur? Do you think the baby was hurt by this?"

"It's completely unpredictable," the doctor replied. "It's important for Emi-san to live a peaceful life from now on, without trauma. Get rid of hazardous objects around her. As for the baby, let's pray that it's all right. I hope it survived her fall."

I saw the policemen tiptoe around the house, now subdued and chastened at the terrifying consequence of their delinquent behavior. Cat-whiskers, who had been insisting on interrogating me, had given up. They quickly finished their search and left furtively, one by one, as if they feared being accused of having triggered my illness.

For me the seriousness of the illness had not yet sunk in. I just tried to reconstruct the terrible string of events that had caused the blackout. I did not remember the fall, but the images slowly returned to me: Mother running away with a telegram; the policemen on the black horses; Momo stepped on and kicked; and the policeman tripping over my koto. . . . But somehow I could not find the key piece, the crucial centerpiece of the puzzle. Was my brain damaged because of the attack?

Suddenly I remembered. "Taku-san's in prison!" Now I understood why I'd had an attack. I fell in the abyss when I heard Taku-san cry out from the prison. The terrible dissonance of the koto strings tangled together was your desperate scream from the prison. It was your sad voice echoing in the dark cell.

Now I was back to a reality that was blacker than the darkness into which I had fallen. How dark and cold it must be in the cell. How long must this ordeal last? How cruel of them to catch you just before we were about to be reunited after a long separation. All of a sudden I burst out crying and my tears did not stop falling.

In my mind, there was no question that you had done anything unlawful. You are honest to a fault. Your crime was being a little too rash. You were so passionate about Korean independence you were carried away. But wasn't this too much of a punishment just for being a little headlong and impolite to the Foreign Minister? What a shame to put in prison a man who'd been working so hard and so selflessly for good causes.

Mother was normally a strong woman, tougher in spirit and in health than I. But the string of events—receiving the telegram, policemen trampling into the house, her daughter wriggling and bubbling like an upside-down crab, and the doctor telling her that it was the onset of a lifetime illness, that would occur as unpredictably as an earthquake—was so traumatic to her that she suddenly became religious.

She used to be an atheist, secretly thinking that the gods do not exist and that if they did, they wouldn't do much for her. I'm not so different from her as you know. Whether we prayed or not, people suffered, died and became ashes. My father died in spite of our fervent prayers. But in the face of the recent events, my mother felt she was being punished for her impiety. Now she is a polytheist. She has been going on pilgrimage to the shrines, temples and miniature roadside deities. She prayed that my illness, if not cured, would be light, Taku-san would be freed quickly and a healthy baby would be born.

Thanks to her prayers, a perfect baby was born, a boy who looked like a little bulldog. It took a whole night and I thought I was going to die of exhaustion. But I did pretty well for a weak woman like me, didn't I? His first cry was not a bark, but a whimper, but it was a miracle that a miniature human being came out of my body with ten fingers and ten toes intact. I wished you had been here, Taku-san. How overjoyed you would be to see the baby. Sensei named him Taro.

I have to write to you sad news about your mother. On the day Taro was born, she came to visit us. She laughed loudly when she saw Taro and said he looked exactly like you when you were born. She was in good spirits as always, although complaining about pains in her chest. Today her neighbor came and told us she had suddenly passed away. Dr. Imai said it was a heart attack.

Both my mother and I were saddened. We'll miss her very much since we became good friends and visited each other often. She was a bright and brave lady till the very end. I feel terribly sorry for you, Taku-san, for having been unable to be with her in her last days. The only consolation was that she had at least met Taro and that she still thought you were in America. We had not told her where you really were.

Taku was shocked by the news of Emi's illness, saddened by his mother's death and overjoyed by the good tiding of his son's arrival. The series of the events were so overwhelming to Taku that he asked a prison priest to pray with him every day.

Emi kept writing about Taro like a doting mother: "*He sits up on bed, but falls over in any direction like a top-heavy doll. I'm in bliss when he sucks my breast, smiling playful smiles which remind me of you. . . .*"

Occasionally, Emi wrote about herself. "*This morning when Taro was asleep and I went outside to wash diapers, the whole world became black again. When I opened my eyes, Momo was sniffing at me with anxious eyes. I was lying on dirt and water was dripping on my face. I found it strange because the sky was blue. It was the drops from the washing I had hung on the bamboo rack. I remained lying on the ground, looking at the sky. How I wished you had been there, looking at the crystal sky with me. I hope we'll do it soon, because no matter how nasty they are, they can't keep you forever for whatever petty crime they've concocted against you."*

Then Emi's letters stopped coming. Taku was afraid that no news was not good news. Had Emi had a fall and hurt herself badly, or had something happened to Taro? Two weeks later her letter arrived.

Dear Taku-san,
This is a sad letter to write. Ten days ago, Taro was listless and whimpered all day. We took him out and walked in a strawberry field, my mother carrying Taro on her back. The strawberries looked so lovely that I picked one for him. He did not show his usual curiosity and it slipped out of his fingers. The birds did not interest him either, when they screeched and flew over him. My mother said he felt hot. By the time we came home, he was as red as a boiled octopus. Mother grated a white radish and put it on his forehead to cool him. She made garlic juice and gave it to him. He brought up everything he had in his stomach. Dr. Imai gave him Chinese medicine for the fever and Taro calmed down. He looked serene as a pale moon.

But at night his temperature climbed up again and suddenly he fell into a fit of convulsions. Mother shivered and said, "Oh, gods. He's also epileptic."

After a few horrible spasms, he fell into a coma. Dr. Imai looked grave and said that Taro might have contracted the brain fever that is going around. My mother and I fervently prayed to the gods and Buddha.

The next morning Taro opened his eyes. He squinted his eyes as if light bothered him. He drank sugar water and dozed on and off. In the afternoon he gazed at me and smiled faintly. It was a Buddha's smile and I cried with relief.

But when we tried to change his kimono, somehow he did not move his limbs. My mother turned ashen and said, "I hope he wasn't paralyzed from the brain fever." I put my little finger on Taro's palm and he didn't wrap it in his fist as he used to do. I held up his arms. They fell on the futon like pieces of stick.

Dr. Imai saw Taro and shook his head. "It's possible one could get partially paralyzed from this brain fever, but it's too early to tell," he said.

Dr. Imai is a sweet man and was reluctant to tell the truth, but it was enough to confirm our fears and I burst into tears. Taro looked at me with innocent eyes, knowing nothing of his own fate or of my despair. Dr. Imai said, "Taro is still very ill. We should concentrate on taking good care of him and help him recover," and left quickly as if he could not stand facing the tragedy.

Indeed Taro was still very ill. He was breathing heavily. His nose jiggled and his throat throbbed. The dim lamp beside his bed was casting a dark shadow on his face. Deep lines had crept into the sunken hollows around his eyes.

Later in the evening, Dr. Imai came back again and opened Taro's kimono to listen to his heart. The frail blue ribs were throbbing as if painfully counting his time. Doctor frowned and said, "He now has pneumonia as well."

"Does he have to die?" I asked. The doctor nodded hesitantly.

"If he must die, I want him to die in my arms," I said and hugged him to my chest. He was soft and warm. I'll remember this warmth forever. This minute will stretch to eternity and Taro will live with me as long as I live. In my arms Taro breathed calmly. He even opened his eyes. They gazed at me in the dim light. The sad, dark eyes. He drank sugar water. "He may be all right tonight," Doctor said and left.

In the middle of the night, my breast became unbearably

hard and started to drip milk. When I nudged Taro with my nipple, he sucked it. You don't know what ecstasy it was to feel his mouth on my breast again, Taku-san. The breast got softer. Doctor was wrong. My baby will live. How can he die without even being held once by his father?

But soon he vomited everything he had drunk. In the morning he was cold to the touch, his face gray. The eyes that had been gazing at me closed halfway. I called, "Taro, Taro," but his eyelids did not move. His breath came out clogged like hiccups, pushed painfully through the throat. Then he sighed long sighs. Sighs of sayonara *to me and to his brief life.*

"Mother," I cried. She was already there. She put a drop of warm water into his mouth. It spilled over. She cupped Taro's hand with hers and cried. He was not breathing any longer. "Sayonara, *Taro," I said and closed his eyelids.*

Is this death? Taro died as he had gone to sleep every day after he finished drinking my milk. As if the tide had ebbed. Roosters crowed and crows cawed. The world went on as if nothing had happened. It took only a brief second for Taro to cross the border of death, but he would never in eternity cross back to life again.

I miss his warmth and softness. My arms are empty. My breast is hardened with no baby to feed. Milk has turned into tears and spouts uncontrollably, trickling down and wetting my kimono. It is chilling my whole body. As Mother and I cleaned Taro's body with warm water and put on the silk kimono and the little bonnet you had worn as a baby, he looked like a little Buddha. At least he went up to heaven.

Since Taro's death, Emi's letters to his prison had been so desperately sad. Taku was hoping the sentence would be light so that he could be with her soon. He had waited for seven months while they looked for a reason to condemn him and yet another three months to wait for the sentence. Wasn't that enough for whatever crime he had committed? He hoped that they would take his term on remand into account and lighten the sentence.

It did not work that way. When Taku heard the words, "Five months in prison," his head reeled and his heart bled for Emi. He fell to the chair, his whole body shaking violently.

But in a month, he was called to the prison governor's office and told that he was the beneficiary of a pardon under the new Constitution that was to be promulgated in three weeks, in February 1889. Taku tottered like an intoxicated man and cried out, "Hooray for the Constitution."

Outside the prison, the noise and frenzy of Tokyo was too much for someone who had lived like a monk inside silent walls for almost a year. Taku took the first boat home to Emi in Nogami. It was early spring and the emerald green of the rice paddy stung his eyes that for so long had been used only to the color gray. The village river he had grown up with was rushing down in torrents and stretching out its long body like a calligraphy stroke. The air was sweet and the sky infinitely big.

As he approached the path near Emi's house, he heard no *koto* music. Emi had not mentioned music in her letters for a long time. She must still be too sad about Taro to think of music. Or was she ill? Then Taku saw a shadow move—a silhouette of a flowery kimono behind the camellia bush. It came out and ran toward him, calling, "Taku-sa-an!" It was Emi running, her kimono sleeves fluttering like butterfly wings. She threw herself into Taku's arms, pale and breathless, but smiling. Taku burst out crying. They held each other until they felt choked, and walked home hand in hand.

"Are you all right, Taku-san? You are so quiet. But for a man who has had a terrible ordeal, you are looking very well. You seem as if you were back from another exotic land like Korea or

America," Emi said and laughed. Nothing made Taku happier than hearing Emi laugh.

The next morning after a happy reunion, Emi was up early playing with Momo. "Momo loves this little ball my mother knitted for Taro," she said, throwing the ball for the cat to chase. "Look. Isn't he funny, Taku-san?" Emi smiled watching Momo tangle with the yarn. But Taku saw a shadow pass over her face right after the brief smile. In order to hide her wet eyes, she looked outside and at the sky. She was still living with Taro and his death, although pretending to be cheerful.

"This is our second honeymoon, isn't it, Taku-san?" Emi said after a while. "The first one was when you returned from Korea after the failed coup and you were sad, although I was blissfully happy being reunited with you. This honeymoon is a long-postponed one since the last New Year's Day. This time both of us have known sadness; I'm no longer the innocent girl I used to be. You were put into prison for no good reason and I was sentenced to epilepsy for life. And we've lost our first baby. But we'll be happy again since now we have each other."

Emi lived not only with sorrow, but also with fear of collapse. She sat on a pillow and read in a room devoid of furniture except a table, the corners of which were wrapped with pads. She did not sew because Chiyo did not allow her to use needles and scissors. She did not cook because the kitchen was full of hazardous things like fire, knives and pots.

"It's so beautiful out, Darling Emi. Let's go for a walk and visit Taro in the cemetery," Taku said. "I'll visit my mother's tomb, too."

"It'll be lovely," Emi said, her face brightening up. "Taro will be so happy to have his father's visit. Oh, I have a good idea: let's have a picnic with Taro there." Emi made rice balls. She put plum pickle in the center of each ball and wrapped it with seaweed. She put water in a dried gourd.

Taku and Emi walked along the rice paddy and Emi picked

dandelions here and sweet peas there, saying, "Aren't they sweet, Taku-san? I'll give these to Taro."

She talked about Taro, her eyes shining and her cheeks as pink as the sweet peas. "Every day we took him out and walked along this footpath, my mother and I. He loved the outdoors. He kicked his legs and shook his hands with excitement. He loved flowers and put them in his mouth whenever I picked them for him."

Then Emi stopped talking. Suddenly her eyes were filled with tears.

"Look, Emi," Taku said, quickly pointing to a green frog sitting in the mud. "Doesn't he look funny? I wish I had big eyes like his." Seeing Emi still in tears, he kept talking, patting her shoulder, "Look, there are two mud eels, wriggling. I wonder if they wriggled all the way from the village river."

"No, they were born here in the rice paddy." Emi shook her tears away and smiled at the brown, slimy creatures. "They love mud. They're so ugly, aren't they?"

By the time they reached the temple, it was already past noon. The temple was unusually crowded with the villagers who had come to enjoy the cherry blossoms under the pagoda. People spread rush mats on the ground and sat on them, eating sushi or rice balls. Some were drinking saké and singing drunken songs. Taku and Emi walked past them to go behind the temple to the cemetery.

Emi ran to a small new granite tombstone, hugged it in her arms and said, "My little Taro, how are you today? Say hello to your daddy. Aren't these dandelions and sweet peas pretty, Taro?"

They had lunch with Taro, visited Taku's mother's tomb and took a rickshaw back home.

Taku said to Emi that evening, "Emi, *Sensei* suggested I should run for the new Diet, which will start next year. I said to him, 'Do people vote for an ex-convict?' He said, 'People can tell if you are a good man or not. You went to the end of the world, Korea and America, and further down to hell in the jail and somehow managed to come out a hero. It looks to me like you might make a good politician. Why don't you ask Emi-san what she thinks about the idea? Emi-san suffered a lot and she has that illness now. You can't do what she doesn't want you to do.'"

Taku paused and asked hesitantly, "So Emi, what do you think of my running for the Diet? I'm afraid I'd have to leave you alone again because I'd have to campaign."

Emi thought for a while and said, "It's a good idea, Taku-san. You've always worked for good causes. You have big ideas and you know how to carry them out. You are a passionate speaker. You'll make a good politician. Why don't you run, Taku-san?" Emi patted Taku on the shoulder.

Taku was elected and moved to Tokyo with the whole family—Emi, Chiyo and Momo. It looked as if life was finally settling down and happy days were in store for them.

CHAPTER 4

"Thank the gods, Buddha and the Christian God," Chiyo said to Emi with a happy smile. "It's like a dream that today is Jun's tenth birthday. It is a miracle he has survived measles, pneumonia, chicken pox and mumps, Emi. I must thank all the heavenly figures today for what they've done for him. I'll make a quick pilgrimage to Masago Shrine, Fuji Temple and Azabu Church. I'll stop by Inari Fox Shrine if I have time. Will you come with me, Emi?"

"Mother," Emi said, smiling, "if we pray to so many of them at once, don't you think they'll be jealous of one another? Actually, I'm not too different from you, but doesn't it mean we are hopelessly confused and can't make up our mind which god we believe in?"

"I just feel like praising the entire heaven, eight million gods, Buddha and the rest, for blessing you with such a nice son. I'm going anyway."

"Have nice visits, Mother. I pray a lot for many things these days, but I just prefer to do it inside here," Emi said, placing her fingers on her heart.

Chiyo hired a rickshaw and went on a whirlwind tour as she had planned. The reason she was so eager about this pilgrimage was not only to thank the gods for her grandson's tenth birthday, but also to ask them to cure his stuttering. It had persisted in spite of the speech lessons Emi had given him every day. Another item on her list of prayers was for Emi's illness to get better, if it was not cured.

The last item was a troublesome one: in the past Chiyo had prayed many times that something terrible would happen to Taku's mistress, Hana, but no matter how she prayed or cursed, Hana did not disappear from Taku's life or from the surface of the earth. Hana had already borne four healthy children for Taku. Chiyo feared that if she wished more ill luck for Hana, it might bring retribution on herself or Emi. They say curses come home to roost.

To lay a curse on Hana, Chiyo had once donated to the fox god shrine a pair of scissors, in the hope that the fox god would cut the tie between Taku and Hana. The scissors had gone, but the tie was not cut.

Another time Chiyo had read in a book that love would cool off if the lovers ate the powdered seed of Chinese hackberry. So after visiting twelve Chinese medicine men, she finally got hold of the yellow powder that was supposed to be the ground seed of this holy tree. But, as she was figuring out how to make Taku and Hana eat it, it disappeared. Somebody must have thrown it away by mistake.

When Chiyo had heard Hana was pregnant with a fourth child, she went to a temple famous for the power of aborting a baby and fervently prayed for her to miscarry. Chiyo came home feeling sick. A healthy girl was born to Hana in spite of Chiyo's wicked wish. They say cursing digs two hells to fall into: one for the cursed and one for the curser. It had made the curser sick, but did not seem to have dug any hell for the cursed. So Chiyo decided not to pray for a big misfortune to fall on Hana any more, only a small one like Hana falling off a step or catching a cold.

Chiyo had not told Emi about the curses she had laid on

Hana. She knew that Emi would not approve. "Emi doesn't have a single wicked bone in her," she said to Yoshi. "That's why she's taken advantage of by Taku-san. She's as stoic as a zen Buddhist about the whole thing."

"She's too nice for her own good, but that's why I admire her," Yoshi said.

Today, instead of cursing Hana, Chiyo went to a temple well known for the power of binding love relationships and left at the altar an *obi* for binding kimonos, so that Taku and Emi would be bound together with love again.

While Chiyo was on her pilgrimage, Jun ran in from the door with his schoolbag on his shoulder, shouting, "Mother, is there any p-present f-for me?" He was tall for his age, but had a pale complexion and a slight build. His eyes were indigo blue and had a gentle gleam like his mother's.

"Yes, Jun. From your father," Emi said, holding up a big package.

As Jun opened the present, his cheeks reddened. "Mama, l-look. It's a t-train set," he cried out. "D-do you know that th-this is the model of the train I took on the t-trip with Daddy in Ho-Hokkaido, the one going from the co-coal mine to the h-harbor? See. This coach has the s-same number as the one I took, 1246."

Jun studied each piece carefully, connected them with the hooks and let them roll on the rails. He set up traffic lights with an electrical device he had made. Miniature lamps turned on and off as the train approached. Checking against the map of Hokkaido, he drew a landscape on cardboard where the tracks were to be laid. He wrote down the names of the rivers, the mountains, the mine and the port.

"Mama, wh-why isn't Daddy home on my b-birthday?" Jun asked, watching the train run on the track winding through the landscape he had drawn. He usually took it for granted his father did not come home. Jun was always so absorbed in books, solitaire *shogi* or the electrical devices he made by using wires that he did not even notice his absence. He had his father's single-mindedness for anything he did. But today he said, "I wish I could sh-show this to Daddy. He's never h-home, is he? Aren't you lonely, Mama?" Then he came and whispered into Emi's ear, "But you are my b-best friend, Mama."

It was true Emi was his best friend. Jun did not like to play outside with other boys. Once they mocked his stutter and shouted in chorus, *"Do-do-domori no do-do-donguri,"* meaning, "S-s-stutterer a-a-acorn." Jun came home and said, "They said that I s-stutter because I've eaten too many acorns. I haven't eaten even one. They aren't edible and must be too h-hard to chew."

Emi looked outside the window so that her son did not see her tears. "Look, Jun. The sky is red with the setting sun. And look at the red dragonfly on that beanpole." Emi started to sing a song and Jun sang with her.

"*Yuuyake koyakeno akatombo. . . .*"

(A little dragonfly burned red in the sunset sky. . . .)

His singing made Emi happy because he never stuttered when he sang. He had a clear voice and perfect pitch.

Emi wondered where Taku was this evening. Was he really in Hokkaido as he had told her, or at his second house with the four children? Emi tried to believe what he had told her, because he loved Jun and would not go to his other children on his birthday. Or was it possible Taku could not bear listening to his persistent stutter? An impatient man, he did not understand why his son's speech could not be perfect.

A few weeks later, a delivery man brought Emi a package beautifully wrapped with layers of rice paper. Inside, there was a handwoven brocade *obi* with dozens of phoenixes embroidered with a gold thread. A note was attached, saying, *Happy birthday, Emi. Unfortunately I'll be in Hokkaido on your birthday, but I'll be thinking about you. Much love from Taku.*

Emi was happy that Taku remembered her birthday this year.

He had never forgotten Jun's birthday, but in recent years he had forgotten hers a few times. Last year, a silk scarf had arrived two days late with an apology. This year Emi had not remembered her birthday herself, until she was reminded of it by Taku's present.

Then, sitting at breakfast, she was blindfolded from the back by slim fingers and a high-spirited voice said, "H-happy birthday, Mama." As Jun removed his hands, she saw in front of her a big bouquet of flowers—Chinese bellflowers, cosmos, Japanese pink and chrysanthemum.

"These are the flowers we collected from the garden Jun-san and I tended," Lee, standing behind Jun, said with a shy smile. Yoshi was also there with the pink rice cake she had made for her mistress.

Yoshi helped Emi try on the *obi* Taku had sent her. "You look gorgeous, Emi-sama. It looks striking on the light blue kimono you are wearing today," she said, her acorn eyes shining.

Chiyo was about to leave for her whirlwind pilgrimage, but stopped to see the *obi* Emi had put on. "Isn't a phoenix a bird that never dies? Taku-san wishes you to live forever," Chiyo said, her cheeks regaining a youthful glow. She was tempted to tell Emi that the other day she had left an *obi* at the altar of a temple known for tying lovers' bonds, but she did not and just smiled happily.

The same afternoon, while Lee was working in the garden, whistling his favorite Korean tune as usual, he looked toward the front gate, drawn by a faint smell of tropical flowers and a rustling sound of silk, and saw the most stunning woman he had ever seen in his life standing there in a fluorescent emerald-colored kimono.

Looking as standoffish as a peacock, with a crest-like golden hairpin on top of her complicated coiffure, the woman said, "Can I see Madam Emi? I came to congratulate her on her birthday. My name is Hana."

Lee felt faint and mumbled something incomprehensible in Korean. He knew that Hana was the taboo name of the lady of the second house. She was the woman who had caused his lady Emi's anguish over the years. Indeed, this was an enchantress who could knock out any man at first sight. No wonder Taku-san had been trapped by her, Lee thought. But what was she doing here? She had a nerve to come and see Emi-san. Should he send her back, saying that Madam Emi was not home?

Inside the house, Yoshi saw Hana from a window and screamed, "Oh, my goodness. That Hana woman's here. She must've come for Emi-sama's birthday, 'cause she's carrying a wrapped-up box. What a nerve to come here uninvited. Shall we spatter salt on her, wish her ill luck and chase her back with this broom, Emi-sama?" Emi heard Yoshi shout this loudly and saw her run toward the door, carrying a tall broom in her hand.

"Oh no, Yoshi-san. Don't shout so loudly. Leave that broom and let her in."

"Are you sure, Emi-sama?" Yoshi said.

"Yes." Emi's face was pale and resigned.

Her hips shaking like a willow in a gentle wind, Hana walked to the living room where Emi was standing and bowed slightly so that her peacock crest would not fall.

"I'm sorry to have let so much time pass before coming to meet you, Madam Emi," Hana said in an affected high-class lady's tone of voice. "I've been thinking of visiting you for a long time since Taku-san always tells me you are a very sweet lady. I wanted to be your friend. I know this is your birthday and Taku-san's away in Hokkaido, so I thought it's a good opportunity. How are you today? You are looking splendid. I brought you some *mochi*-cake. I asked the best sweet shop in town to make it for you with mugwort grown in my garden."

With a self-confident smile, Hana unwrapped a silk *furoshiki* cloth with her long fingers and presented Emi with a wooden box filled with dainty little green cakes. Emi saw each of Hana's five fingers glitter with jade, emerald, opal, diamond and sapphire rings.

Hana looked all around the room and breathed a sigh of relief, obviously satisfied to see there was absolutely nothing luxurious about it. The room looked empty, as it had been made accident-free to protect against Emi's falling. It had no furniture except for a plain round table. A faint smell of incense came from the little Buddhist temple placed at a high corner of an alcove.

Hana noticed an oil painting hung on a wall opposite the temple and asked, "Emi-san, where does the painting come from?" It was an evening scene of farmland with a peasant woman walking home carrying a basket of vegetables and a child following her with a load on his back.

"Taku-san bought it on his first trip to England, because it reminded him of his childhood in Nogami where his mother worked hard on her farm and he followed her around," Emi said.

"It's sentimental, isn't it? Typical Taku-san," said Hana dismissively.

Then she scrutinized Emi from top to toe and noticed her new *obi*. Hana's wild cat's eyes flared with jealousy, suspecting that it was a birthday present from Taku. She praised it with extravagant words before prying from Emi whether it was indeed his birthday present. "What a gorgeous brocade *obi* you are wearing. You look so elegant in it, Emi-san. Do you know how expensive that *obi* is? You see that those phoenixes are embroidered in pure gold thread. It's the kind only princesses wear. It's brand-new, isn't it? Emi-san, is it a birthday present from Taku-san? It must be."

Emi did not want to hurt Hana's feelings and just smiled. Hana pouted her lips and said, with a spiteful grin, "Look at my *obi*. Isn't it very similar to yours? Mine has cranes instead of phoenixes, but is embroidered in pure gold, too. Undoubtedly woven by the same artisan. Our man has a nerve to give us both the same present. I know all men are heartless. Our man's no exception, is he?" Hana emphasized the words, *our man.* Taku was no longer Emi's man, but *our* man.

Hana added, "But he gave me this kimono and this purse as well as the *obi* on my birthday."

"It's a beautiful kimono and purse," Emi said calmly. "They gleam like a peacock's feathers."

Hana looked offended and said, putting her chin up, "This is more special than a peacock. The whole kimono was dyed with an extract from the iridescent wing cases of those jewel beetles, *tamamushi.* Taku-san ordered this to be made specially for me." She continued proudly, patting her purse decorated with wing cases from the beetles, "Don't you see the lovely sequins on this purse? The beetles get this magnificent color by feeding on highly scented tansy chrysanthemums."

Emi felt stung at the sight of the wing cases on Hana's purse. Hundreds of beautiful jewel beetles had been killed for it. And thousands of them to dye a whole kimono, if dyeing with the iridescent extract from beetles was a true story.

Jewel beetles or not, however, Taku had no doubt bought the kimono and the purse for Hana either for her birthday or some other occasion. He must have bought her those rings on her fingers, too. Why did Hana have to decorate herself all over with Taku's presents if she really came to make friends with Emi? Did Hana visit Emi just to torment her? She saw Hana's spidery fingers crawl on her husband's body and her dark-red lips kiss his face. She could tell that Hana could get Taku to buy anything for her with her foxy flattering and her cobwebby stickiness.

Suddenly Jun ran into the room, saying, "Mama, I'm b-back from s-school." Surprised to find a guest, he said, "E-excuse me," and tried to leave, when the guest said with a purring voice, "Is this Jun-san? So nice to meet you, Jun-san. What a lovely boy. I've heard all about you."

As Jun managed to escape from the room, he heard the

purring voice say, "It's a shame he stutters so badly. Is he well? He looks pale."

"He's very well, thank you. He's a sweet boy," he heard Emi snap.

By this time Chiyo was back from the pilgrimage to her religious institutions. She stood pasted to the sliding door, just as Yoshi had been, in order to listen in on the conversation between Hana and Emi. Chiyo even peeked through the gap and saw Emi and the bewitching woman wearing the same golden *obi.*

Enraged, Chiyo went to the kitchen to ransack the spice shelf all over again to look for the powdered seeds of Chinese hackberry she had misplaced. If she put the powder in tea and served it to the witch, her relationship with Taku would cool off. But she could not find it.

Usually when Emi had guests, Yoshi would serve tea and sweets promptly. But today no tea was brought to Hana. Emi tried to open the sliding door to the kitchen in order to remind Yoshi to do so. It was unusually heavy to pull and it derailed when it finally opened, obviously because Yoshi and Chiyo had been leaning against it. Even before Emi opened her mouth, Yoshi said loudly, "I will not bring tea to that malicious sorceress, Emi-sama."

"Shhh. You are so rude, Yoshi-san." Emi pressed her finger on her mouth, suggesting silence. Yoshi reluctantly made tea and brought it to Hana.

Eventually Hana stood up and said in a cheerful voice, "I'm glad I finally met you, Emi-san. It's better to be a friend than a rival or an enemy, isn't it, when it's a lifetime relationship? I hope you'll have a nice birthday with your family."

"Thank you. I was happy to meet you, too, Hana-san," Emi said politely.

Hana walked out of the room with an affected gait. As Emi said *sayonara* to her and was about to close the door, Yoshi dashed out from the kitchen and spattered salt all over Hana's back.

Hana turned around and screamed at Yoshi, "Shit! What a bitch! You try to soil my jewel-beetle kimono Taku-san gave me on my birthday. If you did that to wish me ill luck, I have big news for you. Wait and see what my man's going to do about you, bitch." She shook her head so violently with rage that her immaculate hairdo became disheveled and her peacock crest came askew.

While Emi apologized to Hana and patted her on her kimono trying to shake the salt off, Yoshi said, her eyes rolling with mischief, "In my country, spattering salt on a guest is wishing good luck. Too bad, if it's wishing ill luck in your book."

Hana left bristling and growling, and Yoshi said triumphantly to Emi, "I know you'll scold me, but I couldn't help it, Emi-sama. I didn't want her to come here again. Do you know that in some regions it's a custom for a geisha mistress to visit her man's wife regularly for every season's greetings? Do you want to see that malevolent witch four times a year? I hope I buried her out of your sight for good."

"But Yoshi-san, she was visiting me, not you. It's up to me to decide if I want to see her again or not."

"Then do you want to see her again?" Yoshi said, defiantly.

"I'm not sure," Emi said, and everybody laughed.

"Now let's all have tea and cake," Chiyo said. "Jun and Lee-san, there's this cake Yoshi-san made."

Emi added, "There's this green *mochi* with mugwort Hana-san brought us."

"Oh, no. Don't ever touch the sorceress's cake. You never know what kind of deadly poison's in it. Look at this slimy green color," Yoshi said and threw the whole box of cake into a garbage pail before Emi could do anything to stop her.

"Good for you. Who wants to eat that? You are naïve if you think it's not poisoned," Chiyo said, still chagrined at not having given tea with hackberry powder to Hana.

"Don't be so spiteful about Hana-san. She said she wanted to be friends with me," Emi said hesitantly, as if trying to believe in her own words.

"You are hopelessly naïve, Emi," Chiyo said in a burst of anger. "Would any mistress who wants to be your friend visit you, clad all over with gifts from your husband and boast to you about them? Would she tell you she received more gifts from him than you, and spoil your birthday? Why would she irritate you with words like 'our man,' 'my man,' and 'lifetime relationship'? She's a cobra in a green kimono."

"That's because she's jealous of me just as I am of her. She has a sharp tongue and wants to humiliate me, but she's just as vulnerable as I am," Emi said.

Chiyo stretched both her arms high and said, "You are too much of an angel. Or a hopeless martyr, Emi."

One day Taku came to Emi, his heavy eyelids red and tears rolling down his cracked cheeks, and asked her to attend Fukuzawa *sensei*'s funeral with him.

Emi walked with him on a silent march with 15,000 other mourners, following the coffin from his home to the family cemetery. Normally buoyant Tokyo was silent, mourning the enlightened thinker they had lost. Even the piercing February wind hushed for the procession. During the long hours of the walk and the funeral, Emi feared collapse, and was glad she made it safely. Indeed, she worried more about her husband who could not walk straight and often staggered, overcome with sadness.

"*Sensei* was the spirit of young Japan. I feel the good old days have died," Taku said.

The night they came home from the funeral, Taku was still mournful. As Emi patted him on his back, he slowly collected himself and sat in front of Emi. He said, "One of the reasons I'm so sad is that toward the end of *Sensei*'s life, I wasn't as loyal to him as I should have been. I didn't live up to his example. Particularly his teaching about women. Tonight I'd like to apologize for what I've done to you, Emi."

He kneeled with his legs folded, placed his hands on the floor, and bowed to Emi until his forehead reached the floor. As he sat back, he looked into Emi's eyes and clasped her hands in his.

"You must have suffered so much, Emi. I'm really sorry. I know that a thousand words of apology would do nothing for you. I don't understand why I betrayed such a lovely wife as you, and no excuse justifies what I've done. I don't know if I'm even allowed to say this, but I love you, Emi." He spoke in a hoarse voice, tears flooding his eyes.

"I love you, too, Taku-san," Emi said, but she added, "but you love Hana-san, too, don't you? Aren't you going to keep her and her children?"

"I've thought of giving them up," he said hesitantly, "but I can't, Emi. I love them, too. I know I'm selfish, but I love all of you in a different way."

"I used to believe that you were different from all the other men," Emi said, her voice quivering with smothered anger.

"I'm sorry, Emi."

"This is a man's world. Lots of men seem to do what you've done to me, although in my mind that doesn't justify it. Anyway, the situation is at a point of no return." Her voice gradually dropped to quiet resignation.

Emi could tell how sincere his apology was and how deep his remorse. Since his second family would not disappear from the surface of the earth, there was nothing she could do but forgive him. After all, no matter how much one loves another person, one cannot possess his or her entire being. One can only take what the other gives, she told herself. One should cherish the special quality of the person, the special love and the special time they share with you.

Once Emi decided to forgive Taku, suddenly she felt as if she had finally climbed out of the murky quagmire of jealousy and resentment, and in front of her spread a clear field shimmering with sunlight. A sweet melody sprang up in her and she wanted to fill the sky and the field with songs.

Having met and talked to Hana helped, too. Hana might be beautiful, but she was just as vulnerable as Emi, insecure under the haughty façade of superiority. Probably that was why Hana came to see her anyway. Emi put herself in Hana's place and felt sorry for her for the same reason Emi was sorry for herself. Hana had stolen her husband, but she was no winner, since Emi still existed in Hana's life as Hana did in hers. It was a stalemate.

Taku came back much more often than before. He played games and read books with Jun. He talked about books and world affairs with Emi. World affairs were easier to talk about than their own affairs.

One evening in September 1905, Taku dashed home, laughing loudly. "Can you believe it, Emi and Jun? Japan won the war with Russia. Our navy sank the entire Russian fleet in a single day," Taku said, his slim eyes beaming. He hugged Jun, now almost as tall as he was, and danced around on the floor.

"Aren't you happy, too, Emi?" Taku asked Emi, who stood quietly by the father and son. She did not look happy and said, "When we won the war with China ten years ago in 1895, you were also euphoric, Taku-san, and said, 'Now finally, my dream will come true. Korea will be an independent country.' On the contrary, the Japanese murdered Queen Min a half-year later in the most brutal way. And there's been no sign of its independence ten years later. Now we've got Russia out of the way and we're likely to gobble up Korea. And you seem to be ecstatic. What happened to all your idealism about Korean independence, Taku-san?" Emi was unusually bitter.

"I still hope Korea will be independent some day, Emi." Taku sighed like a drunken man suddenly sober. "I was naïve and simplistic when I was young. It's easy for the young to dream of fixing up the world. Now the militants are taking over Japan. I found myself powerless and absorbed myself in the business in Hokkaido, trying to forget about Korea. But you are right, Emi:

the Japanese have been terrible in Korea, particularly about Queen Min." Taku sat in deep thought, reflecting on the assassination of Queen Min, masterminded by the Japanese Legation minister in Seoul, Miura, who called this event a fox hunt. A group of Japanese men had burst into her bedroom at dawn and killed her. "The queen was no angel, but her murder was despicable." Taku sighed out loud at the barbarism of it all.

They often talked till midnight. "There's nobody I can speak my mind to so openly as you, Emi," Taku said. But he wanted to be more than friends with her. He looked at Emi with the tender and affectionate gaze of many years before. When he hugged her, he clasped her to his chest so ardently that she could not breathe. Emi could tell he really loved her again.

Emi had forgiven him in her mind, but it was still not easy to do so physically. The vivid image of Hana in the emerald kimono stood in front of her and Emi found her limbs frozen in Taku's arms. His passionate embraces gradually softened her limbs, but she still felt more like talking with Taku than anything else.

They talked about Jun. "I wish Jun had more friends," Emi said. "After he comes home from school, he reads books, or sits by the pond, watching tadpoles and beetles swim. The only friend he has besides me is Lee-san. They work together in the garden. With Lee-san, Jun doesn't stutter. He's relaxed."

"He's been wrapped in silk floss and pampered by all the women around him, that's why he stutters," Taku said. "He's also too thin and sickly. It's my fault because I haven't been home often enough. Now let me do something about him. By next year he'll be speaking like a normal boy and looking as healthy as I do."

From then on whenever Taku was home, he threw his son off the futon at six in the morning, took him out in the cold, half-naked, and said, "Jun, draw two buckets of water from the well." When Jun pulled two buckets up, Taku emptied one all over Jun who screamed from the shock of the icy water. Taku did the same to himself with the other bucket and said, "This's our morning shower." Then Taku showed Jun how to rub and dry his body with a twisted towel until the skin was red and scraped.

Taku gave speech lessons to Jun with great enthusiasm, but quickly gave up. He was too impatient to sit and watch his son suffer from pronouncing simple words. "Keep doing this with your mummy," he said. Jun smiled happily.

On Sundays, Taku played ball with him and taught him sumo wrestling. He invited Ken from the second house and they played together. Ken was a year younger, but he beat Jun at whatever sport they played. Jun liked him anyway.

After a year, Jun's speech problems were not cured, but he looked taller and healthier. Taku looked at the pencil signs on the hall pillar where Jun marked how many centimeters he had grown each month and boasted as if it were all his doing. "After all, the Spartan lessons your father taught worked miracles, didn't they?"

The usually quiet Jun smiled and said, "I'm th-thirteen now. It's only natural I grow taller. All my friends are shooting up like b-bamboo shoots."

Emi was delighted to see her son spend more time with his father. She was also happy that Jun got along well with his half-brother. Emi met not only Ken, but also his two sisters at Mariko's dance studio where they took dance lessons. They were all such lovely children that Emi felt better about the second family. If the children were brought up so well, Hana could not be such a bad person, she thought.

For the first time since she had found out about Taku's second family, Emi felt she could cope with reality. It might not be ideal, but it was not worth wasting her life trying to deny it.

She no longer worried so much about her son's stutter, either. Jun was such an intelligent and sweet boy that it did not matter if he stuttered a little. Recently he had grown as much in mind as in body. He read avidly and seemed to absorb everything. Often deep in thought and reluctant to open his mouth, he did not readily explain what was on his mind, but whatever he told Emi surprised her. His mind was exploring faraway places which hers had never reached. He seemed to be able to imagine things she never had, such as abstract ideas in science and mathematics.

Emi cherished every moment she spent with her son and feared that time was ticking away too quickly. Her health was deteriorating and an inner voice was telling her that her time in life was limited. She wished that the short time she shared with Jun could stretch, deepen and enrich to eternity.

Every morning she woke up with her head clouded in heavy fog. She got up, but was so weak and dizzy she often had to lie down again. When she had an attack, she did not recover from it so easily as before.

One afternoon, she took a walk with Jun to the field behind the nearby Akashi Temple where wild parsnips and white Japanese pampas grass grew. She picked flowers while Jun watched the bees and butterflies.

When he saw a mayfly perched on a leaf, he called his mother who was a few steps back, "Look, Mother, how th-thin and lacy his wings are." His mother did not answer. He looked back, but she was nowhere in sight. The thought of her having fallen on the ground flickered through his mind and frightened him. He ran back and looked for her. He heard a rustling noise in the pampas grass and pushed his way through the thicket.

His mother was lying in the grass, her limbs shaking violently, face contorted. He had seen her collapse many times, but this was the first time he had to cope with it alone. He sat by her, put part of her kimono sleeve between her teeth so that she would not bite her tongue, and cleared the prickly grass out of her reach. Then, putting his palms together, he prayed fervently, as never before to the eight million gods of Japan and asked them to save his mother from this horror as soon as possible.

The sun was going down and Jun shivered with chill and fear. His mother must be cold, lying on the muddy ground helplessly shaking. He wondered if he should carry her home on his shoulder, or run back home and call someone to come and help. She was kicking too hard for him to carry. But how could he leave her unattended?

"Jun-saan. Emi-saan. Where are you?" A voice was calling in the distance. It was Lee's. It sounded to Jun like a voice from heaven, which his prayers must have reached. He dashed out of the thicket and waved at Lee, shouting, "We're here, Lee."

"I was worried because you've been away for a long time," Lee said, running. By the time he arrived, Emi's eyes were open, nervously looking around. At the sight of Jun and Lee, tears welled up in them. Lee carried Emi all the way home, since she was still feeling too sick to walk. She did not feel well for two days. She collapsed again two days later and this time did not regain consciousness for three hours.

When Taku came home, he was shocked to find how emaciated Emi had become in the short time he had not seen her. He consulted the best doctors in town, who examined her and found nothing particularly wrong. They all suggested she rest more, eat more and maybe go somewhere nice for a change of air.

"Unfortunately, I have to go to London this summer to sign the contract to start a steel mill in a joint venture with the British companies, Armstrong and Pickers. So I can't be in Japan to be with you all the time, Emi, but wouldn't it be nice if you and Jun spent the summer on some nice beach while I'm away? Fresh air may make you feel better," Taku said, his thin eyes full of concern.

"I would love to be on the beach with Jun, Taku-san," Emi said.

Several days later, Taku returned, and said, "I've rented a villa on a hill overlooking a quiet bay. I went to see it. From the three windows you can see the blue sea extending to the horizon. The beach is right down the slope from the house. I'll come and stay with you for a while before I leave for England."

The thought of Taku coming to stay with her in a summer house cheered Emi. How lovely it would be to walk on the shore hand in hand with him. She might indeed feel better sitting on the sand with Taku and Jun like a real family, watching the blue sky and sea. The image of Hana did not bother Emi so much any longer, and once she was there, the wind, the sun and the waves would wash away the last scraps of ill thoughts about Hana. Then Emi would be the happy person she used to be before she had been dragged into this morass.

The summer house Taku had rented for Emi stood at the tip of a promontory. The smell of the sea and the sound of the waves filled the house when the windows were open. The heavy fog in her head disappeared. She walked to the beach and watched Jun run into the water, splash and swim away.

When Taku visited them, Emi took him outside and they walked hand in hand down a road leading to the beach. Pink and yellow portulacas dotted both sides of the road and the air was fragrant with fruit trees arching over them like rows of lacy parasols. The white sand sparkled in the shimmering light.

"Isn't it strange that all these fruit trees are here, Taku-san?" Emi said, reaching for a young peach hanging from a branch. "Look, Taku-san. This must be Momo who has turned into a peach. Here is a *ume* tree. Maybe this is a gate of heaven and they are welcoming me there."

"Oh no," Taku shook his head. "They just came to see you here."

They walked along the shore. Since Jun was reading in the house, tired of swimming, nobody was in sight and it was as if this was a desert island. As she walked, holding Taku's hand and watching white ripples glitter with the sun, Emi was so happy she felt as if she were ripples herself, dancing on the water. When had she last felt as lighthearted as now?

"I feel like a young lover again," Taku said, his cheeks glowing pink. "Do you remember the day when we walked along the rice paddy of Nogami, Emi? You were hopping and skipping like a girl and I felt like a bird out of the cage, just freed from prison. I feel the same way again, madly in love with you." He stopped and clasped Emi in his arms. He whispered, "I love you, Emi," and kissed her so passionately for such a long time that she almost fainted.

When Emi got tired of walking, they sat on the sand. "I've never seen the sea so blue and the sky so crystal clear, Taku-san. I wonder if I'm seeing through the world beyond this life. Is this the color of heaven? The air is so endlessly transparent," Emi said, squinting her eyes and looking far away.

Taku looked at Emi with foreboding. "Oh, please, Emi. The sea is blue and the sky is crystal clear to me, too. You should stop talking about the other world. You are only thirty-six. This fresh air will make you feel all better soon. You must live for Jun. And for me—until we grow old together." Taku looked eagerly into her eyes.

Because the sun seemed too bright for her, they moved to a shady spot under the pine trees, where a thick bush grew. It was deathly quiet except for the sleepy sound of waves. Taku laid her on the soft sand under a thicket and stroked her hair gently, keeping time with the rise and fall of the waves and gazing at Emi with dreamy eyes. Time traveled backward and she was a young girl, newly married to a young man, Taku.

Taku was indeed like a young lover who did not know how to stop himself. At first Emi was hesitant, but soon she felt so passionate herself that she forgot all her worries and thoughts of Hana. Was she already in heaven that had been enticing her so often in recent dreams and where there was only bliss? But she must still be on the earth because her husband's heavy body was crushing her on to the grainy sand and above his shoulder was a warm light scintillating through the leaves.

Lying on the sand, she watched a white cloud slowly swim

from one pine branch to another. Then the most heavenly music flowed into her ears, at first like little birds chirping in the distance, but louder and louder and suddenly in a resounding chorus. From the fluffy cloud, dozens of birds with white wings flew out and soared higher and higher into the sky until they became the shining particles of the sun. Emi wished time would stop and this very minute would last to eternity.

They went to the shore with Jun, too. Emi sat on the beach and watched father and son swim together far into the sea until they became two dots bobbing in and out of the waves. She watched them sumo wrestle and throw balls on the sand. Taku proudly listened to Jun read books aloud without much stuttering.

Finally, happy days are back, Emi said to herself. Or maybe this is my last honeymoon.

But the time came when Taku had to leave. On the day before he left, Taku and Emi walked on the beach and sat at the place under the pines where they had made love on the first day. White flowers were growing in the sand, hidden in the shade. They looked plain, thin and insignificant under the vast sky and in front of the endless stretch of the sea.

Emi picked a flower and gave it to her husband, saying, "This is me. I'm small, weak and helpless, but thank you very much for loving me, Taku-san."

Taku looked at the little flower admiringly. "Do you know the passage in the Bible, 'Consider the lilies of the field, how they grow. . . . I say to you that even Solomon in all his glory was not arrayed like one of these'? You are so modest like this flower, Emi, but you are the sweetest person I've ever met. Thank you very much for loving me in spite of my unfaithfulness to you that you didn't deserve." Taku's eyes were moist again, and gazing eagerly at Emi.

In the morning Taku left for Tokyo, Emi said to him, "I feel so much better, Taku-san. Can I come to Yokohama Harbor next week to see you off to England?"

"Oh no, Emi," he said, "You'll be sick again if you travel so far in this heat. Please stay here. I'll be thinking about you during the long trip over the ocean and I'll come and see you as soon as I'm back. You must stay well and take care of yourself and Jun." Emi saw his small eyes overflow with tears.

She continued feeling well even after he had left, her illness cured or lulled by her regained happiness. Seized with the desire to see her husband one more time, she hired a horse carriage and rode to the harbor with Jun and Yoshi, in spite of Taku's advice.

It was a long trip and the road was bumpy. At first she enjoyed the ride along the shore and in the quiet countryside, but soon she felt sick, as the sun was too hot and the air muggy.

When they arrived at the harbor, Jun and Yoshi took Emi to the waiting room where she could rest. The room was upstairs and from a window she could see the harbor where many people were gathering. In the center of a crowd, Taku in a silk hat and a high-collared suit, looking like a penguin with an oversized hat, was busy bowing and chatting with well-wishers.

Among the crowd was a tall woman in an emerald kimono standing like a peacock with its feathers spread. She was surrounded by people who came to admire her, like those who circle the beautiful bird in a zoo.

Now four children, a boy of Jun's age and three little girls, all in fancy kimonos, ran to Taku and eagerly talked with him. They hugged him and romped around him. Taku was all smiles, looking very happy and proud.

Emi was glad she was in the room, away from the scene. What if she and Jun had been there? How would Taku have dealt with his two families? No wonder he had not wanted Emi to come to the port. She was certain that he had been feeling genuinely concerned about her health, but he must have also wanted to avoid a confrontation.

Jun kept looking with a pout at the children talking happily to his father. He already knew Ken well and also had met Hana when she had come on Emi's birthday several years ago. But it was the first time he had seen his half-sisters.

"Mother, I see Ken there with Father, but I also see three girls. Are they all his second family? D-does it mean that I have a half-brother and three h-half-sisters?" Jun whispered into Emi's ear. Emi nodded in silence. Jun whispered again, "It means I have to sh-share my father with four other children, but you are mine only, Mother."

"Why don't you go down and say bye-bye to your father, Jun. Just don't tell him I'm here. He'll be worried about me," Emi said.

Jun hesitated for a moment, but went down the stairs. From the window Emi saw her son run all the way to his father and shake hands with him. Taku's face broke into a big smile. She saw them talking animatedly together. Emi was happy.

As the ship was leaving the port with the melancholy howl Emi had heard so many times in the past, she was still sitting at the window. Jun stood not too far away from his half-brother and sisters and watched the boat slowly slide away to the sea.

Hana was holding the pink paper tape connecting herself to her lover. Emi had done the same with Taku when he had left for America. She remembered feeling sad when the ribbon was torn. Hana's was inevitably cut, too, as were the hundreds of other colorful ones held between the departing voyagers and their families and friends. Even the bondage of lifetime love would eventually be severed.

Emi had a fever when she returned from the port. Her temperature went down in a few days, but her head was heavy as if it contained a damp rag. Yoshi told her to stay in bed, but, as soon as she felt better, Emi went to the beach with Jun, saying, "The fresh air will clear my head." They sat on the beach and read. Emi read Taku's old Bible and Jun read Emi's old Russian books.

"I also read those books at your age. It was around the time I married your father. I was a child bride," Emi said to Jun.

"You must have been very p-precocious," Jun said.

"Because I read Dostoevsky at fourteen and a half?"

"No. Because you were married at f-fourteen and a half." He smiled.

When they were tired of reading, they watched the crests of the waves break into white splashes and gigantic white clouds in the sky slowly merge and separate.

"Those two cu-cumulo-nimbus clouds are a man and a woman. Now they are getting m-married and making l-love," Jun said.

"You've been reading love stories, haven't you? You are precocious too, Jun," Emi said, smiling. The other day she had seen Jun in a trance watching butterflies make love on a mimosa, one restlessly on top of the other.

They sat there the whole afternoon until the sun went down beyond the horizon, dyeing the sky crimson. A dragonfly flew into the flaming sun, his wings all red and glittering.

"*Yuyake koyakeno akatombo. . . .*" Jun sang, but he stopped in the middle since his voice sounded like a punctured drum. He was no longer the boy soprano he used to be.

"Don't worry," Emi said. "You'll be a great tenor soon, Jun." After a pause she asked, "So what are you going to be when you grow up, Jun?"

"I'm thinking of becoming either a d-doctor or a medical scientist," he said. "I've seen you s-suffer from epilepsy and from s-sicknesses the doctors don't know what to name. So, I'll be a doctor and cu-cure your illnesses."

"Whatever you choose to be, I'm sure you'll do well. I wish I live long enough to see what you'll be, but I have a premonition I may not live that long."

"Oh no, Mother," Jun said, staring at his mother with fear-stricken eyes. "You must live. Don't ever die. What would h-happen to me if you weren't here?"

"I'll try, Jun. I'll try to live for you," Emi said, beaming sadly at her son.

What would happen to Jun if she wasn't there anymore? Wouldn't Taku most likely bring him up with his other children?

It meant that Jun would be raised by Hana. The second family would become the first and Jun would be Hana's stepson. Hana might make a good mother for him. You never know. But no matter how good a mother she made, Jun would miss Emi, or so she hoped. Hana was going to take her son away from her as well as her husband. I'll live for Jun, Emi said to herself.

She looked at the vast sea and sky. It was strange that Taku who had been sitting here next to her last week was so far away beyond the distant horizon. But his sweet words, dreamy eyes and his passionate embraces had not left her. As she watched the waves dance, reflecting the pink sun, she was flooded with the forgotten joy of life. Taku might love Hana, too, but the time Emi had spent with him was her own. Nobody could ever take that away from her. The jealousy that had tormented her for so long had been washed away with the wind and the waves. On what trivial emotions had she been wasting her precious life?

The summer days were waning. The long shadows crept up the slope in the late afternoons. The *momo* trees drooped with heavy pink fruit and their leaves were yellow. Some of the fruit fell on the ground and fattened voracious crows.

Emi had fewer falls during the summer than usual, but then she started to have frequent bouts again. She had an attack during dinner and was rescued by Yoshi and Jun. Once she found herself alone on her bedroom floor, and another time in the bathroom. After each attack, Emi woke up feeling much better than before the collapse, as if she were a new person. Her head was as lucid as a clear sky and wherever she turned, the world was filled with beautiful melodies. Emi had left her *koto* in Tokyo and wished she hadn't, but she kept humming or even singing loudly what she heard in her mind.

One evening when she was walking with Jun on the beach, Emi had another attack and collapsed on the wet sand. By now Jun was used to it and did not panic. Fearing that she might catch cold, he tried to pick her up on his lap, which was as difficult as picking up a child in a tantrum. By the time he finally managed to get her on his lap, she was calming down as if out of exhaustion, but she did not regain consciousness as she usually did. Jun kept calling, "Mother, wake up. Mother," but she lay lifeless on his lap, her face ashen. The evening breeze was chilly. Jun took off his jacket and shirt and wrapped them around her. He put his palms together and prayed to the gods.

As dark shadows crept over the beach, Jun became worried. "Help! Help!" he called, but his voice was swallowed by the waves which were getting louder and closer with the high tide. Nobody was in sight on the beach. He wished Lee would come running to the rescue as he had done in the field behind the Akashi Temple. But Lee was in Tokyo tending to the house and the garden.

Jun managed to hoist Emi on his back and staggered toward the house. She looked light to him, but she weighed him down like a heavy sack of rice. He was fearful that she was dying or dead since her limbs were cold and dangling like frozen icicles on his back. But he felt her shiver from time to time. They were tremors like the aftershocks of an earthquake.

"Hello. Hello. Do you need help?" A faint voice was approaching between the roars of the waves. Jun looked back and saw a man running after him. Where did he come from? He must be a fisherman. His face was tanned and he was wearing tattered clothes. He put his fishing pole and a bucket down on a rock and held Emi in his arms. The man started to run, asking, "Where's your home?" Jun ran with him, pointing in the direction of the house. The man carried Emi all the way to her bed in the house.

While Yoshi took care of his mother, Jun ran with the man to get a doctor who lived in the next village. They saw an empty rickshaw on the way and the fisherman said to the rickshawman, "Take him to Dr. Sakai. Run like *kamikaze*." After Jun climbed on, he turned to thank the fisherman, but he was nowhere in sight. He had disappeared as fast as he had come, like a *ninja*, the samurai's legendary agent who could fly.

Emi developed a high fever and had difficulty breathing during the night. Dr. Sakai, whom Jun had brought back with him, said that Emi had not only had a severe epileptic attack, but also had developed pneumonia. He gave her a Chinese herbal medicine and Yoshi brewed tea. They bundled Emi up in layers of down-quilt futons.

Jun sent two telegrams, one to Chiyo and the other to Emi's doctor in Tokyo, and asked them to come down right away.

Emi was in a delirium. In front of her stretched the sea of crystal blue and the sky endlessly transparent. "So this is the color of death after all. I kept seeing this color that nobody else has seen. Where are Taro, Ume, my unborn baby who died in the pond, and Momo? Where are the eight million gods of Japan? Is God somewhere in the sky? And where is Buddha?

"What about Jun? Do I have to leave Jun at the mercy of Hana-san? Please be nice to him, Hana-san. Somebody in heaven, please protect Jun. He's a sweet and intelligent boy. Taku-san, please take good care of him.

"Taku-san, I'll remember forever all the happy times we shared together. I know you love me. I love you, too. I'll take with me to heaven the memory of your gentle eyes gleaming with tears I saw on the beach. I wish you could be with me when I die. I'll miss you. I hope you have a happy life with Hana-san. The Bible says, 'Love your enemies.' Hana-san, you aren't even my enemy. You tried to be friends with me. We are friends. Hana-san, please be kind to Jun."

"Mother, Mother." Jun's voice was catching up with Emi on the long, lonely flight to the sky. She looked back and saw him far below climbing a long, thin ladder toward her. But the ladder was not long enough to reach her. His figure as small as a bird in the midst of a vast sky, he stopped at its tip, crying desperately, his arms stretching out to her.

As Emi opened her eyes, she saw Jun's teary eyes looking intently into hers. She smiled at him and his eyes suddenly lit up like the brightest stars. Emi was so happy she tried to stretch her arms to him, crying. Tears blurred everything and she found herself in delirium again. She floated back and forth over the North Pole and the tropical desert, shivering and sweating in turn. The air was so thin that she kept panting for breath.

"Mother." Jun's voice woke her again. She felt his warm hand clasping her icy one. "I love you, Jun," she said. But the words halted with hiccups like the ones Taro had before he died. "Emi. Don't die. You must live, Emi," Chiyo's crying voice came from far away.

"Where are you, Mother? I'll miss you. I was lucky I had a wonderful mother like you. Please take good care of yourself and of Jun, Mother," Emi said in a voiceless whisper, as she felt her mother's trembling fingers on her cheek.

Now and then, Emi saw in front of her dimming eyes Lee and Yoshi with their eyes brimming with tears. "Why are they looking so sad? Oh, yes. They're here to say the last *sayonara* to me," Emi said. "*Sayonara,* Yoshi-san and Lee-san. Thank you very much for having been so kind to me. Cheer up and don't be so sad," she whispered and closed her eyes again. The doctor from Tokyo gave her an injection of a modern medicine, but it did not wake her.

The crystal sky was inviting her again. Emi floated among the birds with white wings she had seen on the beach when she had made love to Taku for the last time. She flew with them into a transparent sky where the only things she could see were shining bubbles. Were they the particles of the sun? Or were they the souls of the dead? Then she saw herself turning into a bubble, floating in an eternally silent, fathomless, weightless, colorless and timeless sky. Is this death? Is death nothing? Nothing but eternally transparent air? But if only I could see Taro, Ume, my unborn baby and Momo.

"Please give me back Jun and Taku-san. And give me back music," Emi cried out, but her voice was swallowed in a vacuum. The bubble she had turned into popped in the dark. Emi fell into a deep sleep from which she never returned.

"Mother, Mother," Jun cried. "Don't die. Please don't die. I'll be all alone without you." He patted his mother all over, kissed her cheeks and touched her hair, clasped and shook her hand and body, but she did not move. He hugged her futon, buried his face in it and burst into tears.

Chiyo cuddled Jun with her arms from behind, patting, stroking and crying, but soon she crouched over him and fell with him on the floor. Yoshi wailed with the loudest screams, shaking with convulsions, her hair flying all over. Lee tried to help Chiyo and Jun up, but his bony body collapsed on to the floor as if broken into pieces.

The night wind carried wails of sorrow through the windows into the dark sea. They were heard for hours over the waves and then absorbed into silence.

CHAPTER 5

For days and months after his mother died, Jun had sleepless nights. The slightest sound of rain woke him. His heart ached imagining his mother wet and cold in the grave. The sound of a *koto* woke him and he sat up on the bed. It was the wind hissing through the crack of a window.

His mother often appeared in his dreams. Once she came in from the front door and called him. He got up and dashed to the door, but she was gone by then. Another night she came and dropped a letter in the letterbox. At dawn he rushed to the mailbox but found no letter from her. After those dreams, he rushed to the door every time the doorbell rang. He stood in front of the mailbox, every morning with the strange expectation of receiving a letter from his mother.

Some afternoons he climbed up an oak tree behind the house, the branches of which touched the roof. He made sure that nobody was watching and hopped to the rooftop from a big branch. Once Chiyo saw him jump and screamed. She told her grandson never to do that again. But he did it anyway. On the roof, the sky was big. He sat and read on the tiles, or just watched clouds go by. Here he was closer to heaven where his mother was. He felt her in the air. Once he saw her floating on one of the clouds. "Mother," he shouted, "*Okasan, Okasan.*" She did not answer.

Loneliness found him strange companions. He sat by the pond in the garden and watched hundreds of insects swim on the water's surface. It was like watching an ice-skating party. Some slid in circles, some in zigzags, others jerked at dazzling speed in random directions, and one never collided with another.

On the ground, ants were carrying a dead praying mantis in a long funeral procession, which brought Jun back to the day of the long ride from the beach to Tokyo on a horse-drawn hearse, sitting next to his mother's coffin in a drizzling rain.

Insects fascinated Jun about the mystery of life. What made them live and what had made his mother die? He envied them their vitality. But he understood the transience of their life. One day everyone's life would end.

Somebody patted him on the shoulder. It was Lee, his triangular eyes looking sad. He had stopped whistling since Emi died. "Guess what? I brought you a present," Lee said with a smile, and opened his fist. On his palm was the cast-off skin of a cicada. "I found this on the oak tree there. Isn't it beautiful, Jun-san? No seamstress could sew such perfect overalls."

Every day Lee came up with a new idea to cheer up Jun. "Let's go to the field by Akashi Temple, Jun-san. This is the last week before the dragonflies and crickets die out," Lee said. He took Jun to the field of the pampas grass bush into which Emi had fallen. Its white ears swayed in the autumn wind. Lee and Jun ran all afternoon among wild parsnips and thistles, catching insects with a butterfly net. Jun caught a red dragonfly that reminded him of the one he had seen with his mother on the beach. Its body was the deepest hue of the sunset, its wings as thin as air itself.

Jun wanted to take him home, but Lee insisted he let him go. "He has to die soon, Jun-san. Let him die in nature." He flew off Jun's fingers and into the air. "Your mother up there is happy to see him live one more day," Lee said, squinting his eyes, and looking up at the sky so that the tears would not overflow.

Taku visited Jun almost every evening after his return from England. Jun wished that he had done so while his mother was alive. He seemed to be coming to console himself as much as Jun. He threw his arms around Jun and cried like a child.

He told Jun about the day he had received the telegram on the final leg of his voyage from England. "I was convinced it was a mistake. Emi would wake up again just as she always did. If she must die, I wanted to see her before she went. It was only one day before we were to land in Yokohama. The ship was hopelessly slow, like a swimming turtle. I could jump in the ocean and swim faster. Like a flying fish." Jun had never seen his father so feeble. He suddenly looked like an old man; his hair had turned gray. He had probably shriveled because he had cried so much and the water had run out of him.

Taku cried shamelessly at the *koto* concert that Chiyo and Mariko organized in memory of Emi. Chiyo and her students played the music Emi had composed and Mariko danced to it.

Taku was happy about his son's fascination with miniature creatures and bought him a microscope. Jun felt as if he had discovered the secret of life, unknown to anyone else, when he first saw unimaginable living things in a drop of pond water. He found identical creatures in a book the teacher lent him. Jun showed his father the wriggling things under the lens, saying proudly, "These are called p-paramecia, vorticellae and s-stentor. I've developed a d-double vision about everything in the world, Father. It's f-fascinating that there is a different truth under the surface of things. Beauty is s-skin deep, they say, but there is a totally different b-beauty under the skin."

"You seem to be a born scientist, Jun." Taku beamed at his son.

Taku and Jun visited Emi's grave in Azabu, Tokyo. On a holiday, they went on a trip to Nogami together. On the long train ride to their family graveyard in the village, they carried an urn that contained half of Emi's ashes. Another grave was built for Emi between Taro's and Ume's small tombstones. There was an even smaller one behind theirs for the unborn baby who had died in the pond.

"Emi, now you are happy to be with the babies you've missed so much," said Taku, patting the shining new granite stone.

On the train ride back to Tokyo, Taku said to Jun, "You've met Ken before, but have you met your half-sisters, Yumi, Tami and Kana? Will you come and meet them? They are all lovely children."

Jun suspected that his father was going to make one family out of the two, now that Emi was gone. By getting him acquainted with the other siblings, Taku was trying to get Jun used to the idea. He pictured in his mind the pretty girls he had seen at the port when his father had set off for England. He remembered the strange excitement he felt, realizing that they were his half-sisters. So he did not mind getting to know them, though he was not sure whether he liked that tall lady in the green kimono.

"I don't mind m-meeting them. But Father, are you thinking of marrying their m-mother?" Jun asked his father.

Taku studied his son's face carefully and said, "Eventually, though not soon. Not until we observe the first-year memorial service for Emi. Then I'll buy a big house and I'd like you to move in with the rest of the family. The current houses won't be big enough."

Three months after his mother's death, Jun visited Taku's second house. At the entrance of the house, he heard running footsteps and loud shouting from inside. "It must be Jun-san." The noise stopped at the two hall pillars and two girls peeked at him, one behind each pillar, giggling. Silky hair, pink ribbons and kimono sleeves flickered in and out from the pillars. Then the taller girl came out, put on a prim face, sat down and bowed.

"Welcome, Jun-san. My name is Yumi," she said shyly, and

smiled, a dimple on one cheek. She had quiet eyes and straight hair which opened like a fan over her shoulder. She looked like a girl from an ancient storybook.

The younger one followed her sister and said in a loud voice, "*Konnichiwa,* good day. My name's Tami." Tami was not shy and did not even sit down to bow. To show him a welcome, she jumped three times like a bouncing ball with a big smile on her round face.

The sight of pretty girls bowing and bouncing made Jun feel like jumping, too. But when he tried to say "*Konnichiwa,*" his tongue tangled up and he was only able to say, "*K-k-k-k.*" He swallowed the word and bowed his head down so that the girls would not see his quivering lips and flushed cheeks.

"Who came in without even saying hello? Is it a burglar?" A woman's harsh voice came closer from the back of the house. Yumi winked at Jun and apologized, "It's our mother, Jun-san. She's like that when she has a headache."

A tall lady with lowered eyebrows stood in front of Jun. Somehow she did not look like an impeccable peacock as she had seemed when she had visited Emi on her birthday, or at the harbor where he had seen off his father. Something was loose about the way she was dressed and the way she slurred her words.

"Oh my, poor boy," she sighed loudly, as she examined Jun from head to toe. "You're as thin as a nail and look as naked as one. Did you walk in the cold with no coat on? And nothing on your feet but those wooden *geta* clogs? No wonder your toes are like strawberries with frostbite. Yumi and Tami, he doesn't know how to look after himself, so take good care of him. I must go and rest. I have a terrible headache." She disappeared quickly.

"Don't worry about what Mother says. She is like that to everybody," Yumi whispered, tilting her head to look into Jun's eyes as his mother used to do.

"Mummy has a fierce tongue," Tami said, smiling to cheer

him up. "Our maids call her Ice Queen of the North Pole. But she isn't as bad as she sounds."

The girls led Jun to the living room. In the center of the room a *kotatsu* heater was hidden under a table covered by a quilt futon.

"Stretch your legs under the futon and relax," Yumi said. When he did so, his toes tingled with sudden warmth. Tami sat on the opposite side of the table and also put her legs under the quilt. She wiggled them and said with a playful smile, "We always have toe-fights under the futon."

"Behave yourself, Tami," Yumi scolded her younger sister. But Tami kept wiggling. When her small toes touched Jun's, she said, "Excuse me," and giggled. It was ticklish and her giggle was as pleasant as a bird chirping. Jun laughed, too.

"Tami is so excited to have you here, Jun-san. After all, she is only ten," Yumi said, embarrassed.

"Yumi's only twelve, but she thinks she's a big boss." Tami pouted.

It was true that Yumi looked grown-up for her age, although her cheeks were as soft as a baby's, while Tami was still a child, frisky and with a smile full of mischief. Everything about Tami was round. Her eyes were as black and round as tadpoles, her nose like a button and her hands plump as a *mochi*-cake.

"Will you play flower cards with us, Jun-san?" Tami said coquettishly. Jun tried to answer, but his tongue quivered and he stuttered heavily. "I-i-if you t-t-teach me h-how." It was the first time the sisters had heard Jun speak. Tami turned pale, gazed at Jun and slowly stood up saying, "Excuse me, I must go to the toilet." She tiptoed out of the room. Yumi seemed sympathetic and looked down at her fingers. She hesitated for a while, but she said, "I'll go and look for my brother. You know Ken-san, don't you? Maybe he can teach you how to play cards better," and left, too.

Jun sat alone in the room. Tears welled up his eyes. He crept under the futon cover and said, "Mother, why did you die and leave me alone?"

He soon wiped his tears with the tip of the futon. He sat up straight and whispered what he used to repeat with his mother: *"A, i, u, e, o, ka, ki, ku, ke, ko, sa, shi, su, se, so."*

Jun saw his mother sitting and watching in front of him. "So you haven't stuttered at all, Jun," Emi said with a smile.

"*Konnichiwa,* Jun-san," Ken said, coming in with his two sisters. "I've been playing *shogi* with a friend and didn't know you were here. Are you sure you want to play flower cards? That's for girls. Wouldn't you rather play *shogi* with me?"

"I'd like to p-play both. But T-Tami-san asked me first. So I'll play f-flower cards first." This time everybody pretended not to notice his stuttering.

"You don't have to play flower cards unless you really want to," said Yumi.

"Do you prefer to play house? You can be our father," Tami said with her bird-chirping voice, patting Jun on his shoulder with her chubby hand.

But before they played anything, Taku came home and everybody was called for dinner. Hana sat next to Taku looking like an impeccable geisha, her face newly powdered and her hair done into a high-fashion oval chignon. Jun sat next to Ken facing the girls. They looked like ladies with hair freshly combed and kimono creases straightened. The third sister, four-year-old Kana, was sitting restlessly beside Hana, making constant noise, knitting the eyebrows of her irritated mother. Kana had a nose pointing upward. From time to time, she stared at Jun with hostile eyes like her mother's.

Taku was in good humor, sipping saké from a little cup and looking over all the children lined up around the table. "Jun is new here," he said. "So can everybody be nice to him?"

"We are very nice to him," Tami said proudly. Hana nodded and feigned a smile, but her face twitched and the powdered cheeks cracked a little. Jun suspected she did not want him here. When their eyes met, she did not smile.

"Jun likes to see insects under a microscope. It makes a fly's leg look as fat as a bear's. His microscope makes things look twenty times larger," Taku said.

"T-twenty-f-five times," Jun said.

"He speaks funny," Kana whispered aloud to her mother. Yumi closed one eye and winked at Kana. Tami shook her head at her baby sister. But it was too late.

"Some bright boys stutter sometimes," Taku said. "He'll grow out of it soon." But Kana kept staring at Jun like an animal determined to catch its prey. Finding the vinegar-marinated seaweed cucumber left untouched on his tray, she pointed at it triumphantly and said, "Mama, he doesn't eat that dish."

Jun nicknamed Kana "woodpecker" for picking holes in others. He hated her nostrils looking upward in the center of her face.

"Jun-san, you'd better eat that marinade," Hana said, sounding as happy as Kana, now that she had an excuse to pick on him. "No wonder you are so scrawny; you don't eat good food. In this house you aren't allowed to leave any food."

"Leave him alone. Jun's a guest today, Hana," Taku snapped.

"Some people are born thin," Yumi said.

"You are thin, too, Mother," Tami said with a smile.

"He doesn't know the rules of this house yet, Mother," Ken said.

"Shut up. Don't contradict your mother." Hana's face quivered with rage.

Jun gulped the marinade. He was not so upset by Hana's comments as touched by the chorus of sympathy from the rest of the family, which made the marinade taste like a sweet and sour seaweed cucumber.

Since that day, whenever Yumi and Tami invited Jun, he visited them gladly. They taught him how to play flower cards. When he played *shogi* with Ken, he was determined to win. But he was not serious about cards and often lost. "Are you stupid or playing stupid, Jun-san?" Tami kept asking.

Jun liked both Yumi and Tami. Tami was an adorable child, while to him, Yumi was a lady. She had dainty lips, tapered fingers and a slender body. Yumi resembled her mother, but her features were quieter, her nose not as angular as Hana's and her eyes not wild like a cat's, but with a gentle shine. When Yumi tried to grab a card and covered Jun's hand with hers by mistake, he felt as if he had an electric shock. It was like the warm hand of his mother that he missed, but younger and softer. He wanted to feel it again and touched it, pretending to grab a card. It was a dangerous game, but he was happy he had done it. Every time he relived the sensation, he trembled with joy.

Tami kept after Jun to play house with her. "Ken-san never plays house with us. Can you be the father, please, Jun-san? Yumi's the mother; I'm the big sister, and Kana's the baby sister."

Jun said half-heartedly, "Well, all right. Just once," though acting was the last thing the shy Jun liked to do. It was a mistake to agree. Yumi turned out to be a talented actress. Saying, "I'll start," she put on a sober look, came up to Jun, shaking her hips right and left as her coquettish mother often did, and knelt down.

"Welcome home, my dear," she said and bowed, smiling with a dimple. "How was your work today? Now, sit down and relax. I'll bring you a drink." His face flushed red, Jun burst out laughing and ran out of the room.

"Oh, Jun-san. A father doesn't behave like that," Tami said, pouting, terribly disappointed by him. Kana sneered, saying, "He's a bad actor."

Lonely in the house where he saw only his mother's shadow, Jun did not much mind when the time came to move into a new house after Taku's informal wedding with Hana.

Chiyo insisted on staying on in the teahouse where she had been. Taku built two additional rooms and a kitchen for her.

Lee moved with Jun to the new house. But, feeling sorry for Chiyo, and sad about leaving the garden he had cared for, he promised Chiyo to come back regularly to attend to it. "That way I'll keep Emi-san's memory alive," he said.

Yoshi was worried about leaving Chiyo alone. But Chiyo told her to leave. "I'm healthy and I can live alone. Obviously, you don't want to work for Hana-san. You'd better find a job at a shop or a factory and you'll meet a nice man, Yoshi-san."

"I will, Chiyo-sama. I'm perishable goods. If I don't rush, I'll soon be a rotten peach left on a grocer's shelf. But I'll come back to help you any time you need me and we'll talk about our Emi-sama together."

The new house was enormous. The main house was built of wood in the Japanese style. Fourteen *tatami* rooms surrounded a rock garden. But Taku assigned a separate western-style wing to Jun and Ken, saying, "Boys must live in austerity unspoiled by decadence." But there was nothing austere about the western wing, as the rooms were spacious with high ceilings and each boy had a desk, a bookcase and a bed. "Father means to protect us from Mother's abuses," Ken said, smiling.

Jun got along well with Ken, who was athletic and rowed in the regatta at his high-school rowing club. When they played ball or sumo, Jun had no chance against him, but he was a little stronger than Ken in *shogi* as well as in the game of *go*.

The girls seldom visited the western wing, but one day, Yumi came there to ask about her algebra homework. Ken was not in. "I'd rather ask you anyway, Jun-san," she said with a shy smile. "Ken-san refuses to give me the answer and just tells me to think."

Alone with Yumi in his room, Jun pretended to be calm, though he was far from it inside. He wrote down an answer and took a deliberately long time to explain it. Yumi sat next to him, looking at the equation, her fingers playing with a strand of her hair. The downy hair on her forehead shimmered, reflecting the sun from the window and her cheeks looked as tender as the petals of the magnolia blooming in the garden. His head swirled and the letters, a, b, c, and y danced in front of him.

Bored with the equation, Yumi looked around the room and her eyes stopped at Jun's drawings of wiggly creatures on the wall. Then, noticing the microscope on the desk by the window, she said, "Can I look into your machine, Jun-san?" He focused the lens on a dead spider he had left on a tray and told her to look. She closed one eye and bent over it. Yumi shivered, but she kept looking, saying, "It's a monster, but fascinating."

"Are you going to be a scientist when you grow up, Jun-san?" Yumi asked, taking her eye off the lens. When he said, "Maybe. Or a doctor," she smiled and said, "That's nice. Do you know what I want to be?" She paused for a while and said proudly, "A storyteller."

"Do you? What kind of stories will you write?" Jun asked.

"Now I write fairy tales in my mind and tell them to Tami and Kana, but someday I'll write stories for grown-ups," Yumi said with a serious expression on her face. Then she stood up, thanked Jun and left.

Some afternoons when Jun came back from school, he went around the azalea bush in order to pass by the girls' playroom before he reached the western wing. One day he saw Yumi through the window, standing and talking, her arms crossed over her chest, her eyes dreamy and her cheeks pink. Tami and Kana sat, gazing at their elder sister, a captive audience in a trance. Jun could not hear well as the window was only partly open, but from the words he heard, such as "elves," "devils," and "the princess born out of a bamboo joint," it was clear that Yumi was telling fairy tales.

One day, Tami saw Jun standing outside the window and said, "Oh, Jun-san. Come in. Come in. Yumi is about to start her fairy tale." But just when he sat down in the room, Hana peeped in and sneered, "What are you doing in the girls' room listening to sissy tales, Jun-san? You should be playing ball with the boys outside."

That ended Jun's visits with the girls. But at least he saw them at dinnertime. It was a pleasant time, particularly when Taku was home. Though feared outside as "Thunder and Lightning," he was a good sport in the family and so sweet to his daughters that they called him "bean-paste Daddy." They often teased him.

Kana said, "Daddy, you are spilling rice like a baby. Is it because your eyes are so slim that you can't see?"

"No, Kana," Tami said. "He can't see because he's getting old and poor Papa has a bird's eyes. But he spills mainly because the way he holds chopsticks isn't correct and because he eats too fast. Slow down, Daddy, or else you'll wear a bib."

Taku laughed and said, "Oh, Tami. You inherited your mother's sharp tongue."

"I didn't inherit it. But I'm getting one, listening to it everyday."

On special nights, such as birthdays, the girls danced in pretty kimonos or played a skit. On Hana's birthday, Yumi arranged a fairy tale called "Tongue-cut Sparrow" and let Kana play the wicked woman who cut a sparrow's tongue out of malice, and in the end was chased by a one-eyed demon played by Yumi and a gaping-mouthed monster that was Tami. Kana did not have to act a wicked woman. She made everybody laugh being her naturally wicked self.

Sometimes they had dinner guests. Taku considered entertaining a waste of time, but he succumbed to it since Hana loved to have company, particularly important men. Then her knitted eyebrows melted into radiant smiles and her harsh voice tuned up to a purring one. Her quick wit made men laugh. She could engage in sophisticated conversation, quoting ancient poems and improvising *haiku*. No man could help falling in love with Hana.

For one guest, a politician Hana liked, she did a mock *kabuki* performance. She walked and danced in an extravagantly coquettish way, as a well-known female-impersonator did, swaying her body like a mermaid and caressing someone in the air with her spidery fingers. Casting a flirtatious glance at the politician, she whispered, "I love you," in the impersonator's weeping soprano voice.

The guest was mesmerized. When Hana came back to her seat, he came to sit next to her and kept pouring saké in her cup. He gradually inched up to her and put his face close to hers. When he whispered something into her ear that made Hana giggle, a thundering voice fell from Taku, "Stay away from my wife, will you?"

"Sorry, Taku-san," the politician apologized. "I meant no harm. Hana-san was such a good impersonator, I was confused. I thought I was talking to an actor." But still he did not move away from Hana, his eyes glued to her as if by a magnet.

When Hana had no dinner guests, she played mah-jong at night. Taku, who found mah-jong boring, did not play, saying, "I have no time." So Hana forced Ken, Yumi or the servants to join when they would rather sleep. Now Jun was added to the list. Ken, who also found the game boring, was relieved when Jun replaced him. Jun was curious about the game and did not mind it, particularly when Yumi was playing.

Once during the game, a maid chuckled and gloated over beating her tyrannical mistress. Hana's face grew red with rage and she threw an ivory tile at the maid. Yumi turned pale, stood up, took the maid's hand and left right away, saying, "I'll never play again with you if you are so abusive, Mother."

Jun left with them, too. Yumi tried to soothe the maid, patting her face with a cold towel. But the maid said that she had had enough and left the next day with a swollen cheek. She never returned.

Being a *kabuki* devotee, Hana went to all the shows of the season. Since Taku was seldom available, she wanted to take the children along. Ken had recently refused to go, saying, "There're better things to do." Tami did not want to go either. "In the last show a man committed harakiri. He cut his belly open. It was ghastly," she said. "In the other one, the lovers committed double suicide," Yumi said.

Hana found out that Jun had never been to *kabuki* and was happy to invite him. Yumi saw Jun turn pale at the thought of accompanying Hana alone and said, "I'll come and keep company with you, Jun-san." Her sympathy made his heart leap.

That night, Yumi looked like an evening primrose in her yellow kimono. Jun wore a student uniform that was all black except for the brass buttons, making him look as plain as a crow. But he walked with his chin up, proud of escorting a beautiful lady. He noticed people's admiring eyes on Yumi and had an urge to advertise to the crowd: "She is my half-sister!"

But he noticed that the admiring eyes went first to her mother. Hana walked as haughtily as a peacock, creating an aura of grandeur. Everyone stopped and stared at her. They stole another look back at her as she passed. Hana obviously enjoyed the sudden halt and hushed silence she caused.

Sitting next to Yumi in the dark theater, even as high drama was unfolding on the stage, Jun stole quick glimpses at her face absorbed by the play and her dainty hands crossed on her lap. Since he was watching Yumi as much as the stage, Jun had difficulty answering, when Hana asked, her eyes glowing from the excitement of the show, "Wasn't it wonderful, Jun? Did you like it?"

He replied evasively, "It was very i-interesting, but to me the acting was too s-stylized."

Jun was taken aback when Hana so adamantly defended the stylized acting. "Jun-san. Isn't that why *kabuki* is unique? Art doesn't have to copy life. Over the years they have found, through simplifying and exaggerating, the essence of acting. The lines are deliberately refined and stylized." Jun realized that Hana's superb mimicking of the stylized acting of the female-impersonator was no accident.

Hana remained an enigma to Jun. She could be extremely gracious on some occasions and wayward and abusive on others. She was often so nice to Jun as to make him believe that she did not hate him, but even liked him a little. Yet, out of the blue, her cruelty could fall with the vengeance of a bomb.

When Hana happened to be in the western wing, Jun tried to entertain her with the wiggly creatures under his microscope. She took a quick look into the lens, jumped away from it and scoffed, "What are you, Jun? I don't understand a boy who enjoys chopping up the ugliest creatures in the world and then tries to magnify their ugliness."

Another time she said to him, "Jun, say that again. I don't understand you because you speak so badly. When are you going to stop stuttering? They say if you eat acorns, you'll stutter. Your mother must have fed you lots of them."

Yumi overheard her mother and rushed in to confront her. "Mother, that was a terrible thing to say. You owe an apology to Jun-san, and to his mother in the grave." Jun saw tears in Yumi's eyes and found himself about to cry. Not because of what Hana had said, but because of what Yumi had said for Emi. His mother did not deserve to be made fun of.

Hana looked pale and pensive for a while. Then she spoke in an unusually reflective tone. "Jun, I'm sorry. Yumi is right. It was a terrible joke you and your mother didn't deserve. Do you remember I visited Emi-san once, when you were a young boy? She was very nice to me even though I was the source of her grief. I respected her. I apologize to your mother. I must be nice to you for her sake. Sometimes my tongue slips and says what I don't mean to say. I've grown an axe on my tongue." Her voice was tender.

"Th-thank you for your apology. My mother would be g-glad in heaven to hear what you said," Jun said.

He knew well this would not be the last time Hana would insult him, but he felt closer to her after this incident. He thought that Hana might not be as bad as the Ice Queen she pretended to be. She was perverse, but not wicked at heart. Her meanness was a capricious way of asserting her power over others.

She was the same with her husband. They did not hate each other, but Hana was wilful and bitchy, which often provoked Taku. They tried to avoid arguing in front of the children, but their voices became so loud in the end, that everyone in the whole house heard them.

Taku complained about Hana's spending. "I try not to be mean, Hana, but there's a limit to everything. I've received another huge bill from your tailor today. You already have a museum-size collection of kimonos. With the amount of money I've been paying, I could have founded a bank."

"If you don't want to spend money on me, I can easily find another man. The other night at the *kabuki* theater, I was proposed to by a good-looking man. He said he owns a bank. I told him I was married. He said he'd wait for me forever and, in the meantime, he wouldn't mind being just a friend. He gave me a business card."

"His bank would go bankrupt right away if he married you," Taku snorted.

He talked about the antiques that were still creeping into the house every week. "Pretty soon this house will look like a warehouse. What are you going to do with all this furniture? Why don't you open an antique shop and sell some, Hana?"

"Don't you love them, Taku-san? I'm my father's daughter. I'm only interested in buying, not selling," Hana said.

"But you don't want to end up like your father, do you, Hana?" Taku said. "There are better things to collect than material possessions."

"Such as?" Hana asked.

"Such as good friends, good deeds and memories of good times, or of making people happy. Knowledge, truth, skill . . ." Taku went on.

"I'm my father's child; I'll collect antiques just as you collect good deeds."

Their bickering increased in frequency and fierceness as time went on. More or less the same problems, Hana's compulsive shopping and her abuse of servants were the triggers, but mere trifles sufficed as well. They could start quarreling over mostly groundless accusations of who had flirted with whom. Taku would accuse Hana of flirting with a certain politician, or Hana would belittle Taku for his receding hairline, drooping eyelids and bumpy skin making him look and feel like a crocodile and, therefore, giving her goose pimples when she touched him or even looked at him.

Once Taku said to Hana, "You used to be so sweet to me. Why did you grow a tongue like a scissors?"

"As a geisha I had to make a living from the art of flattery and I hated it. So when I got free, I decided to avenge myself," Hana replied.

After their arguments, a dismal silence oppressed the whole house. At dinner, Tami often said something to crack open the suffocating air. "When we played house before, we used to play a happy house. Now, we play an animal house, barking and yelling."

"I thought the parents are supposed to worry about their children. In this family children worry about parents. It's an upside-down world," Yumi said.

"When I don't behave, you scold me; so now I scold you," Kana said, pointing her fingers at her parents. The parents looked sheepish and the whole family laughed.

Obviously there was more to their relationship than firecracker fighting. They had happily produced four children. Being graceful and witty, Hana was an added asset to Taku as his business grew and his political power increased. Though she had a venomous tongue, Hana was a faithful wife to her husband, except for occasional flirting. With so many children around, she had no time to stray. No intention, either. The only men she was really interested in, except for some politicians, were female-impersonators. And she liked their femaleness rather than their maleness. For Hana was a narcissist. She said to Taku, "My childhood dream has come true. I always wanted to become a queen. At least I'm a queen in this house."

Now it was five years since Jun had moved in with the family. His secret love for Yumi had not abated. Yumi was no longer the innocent-looking girl he had first met. She was growing up to be an attractive young woman. By her occasional alluring smiles and by the way she blushed when he bumped into her in a corridor, Jun suspected that she had special feelings for him as he did for her, but he did not know for sure. Living in the same house, he could not even talk with her freely or listen to her fairy tales for fear of the unpleasant remarks of Hana and Kana. Kana acted as if she were a spy and reported to her mother that Jun still stood in front of the girls' room listening. Hana then told Jun not to be a Peeping Tom. Hana must have said something to Yumi, too. Lately Yumi went to Ken to ask about homework. She looked somber and did not smile at Jun.

One day, Yumi announced to everyone at a dinner, "I'd like to be a Christian. From now on I'm going to church on Sunday."

Taku, looking surprised for a minute, responded with a benign smile. "It's not a bad idea, Yumi. I'm a Buddhist, but I respect Christianity. I read the Bible while I was in prison. It's a good book."

"So our idea of sending Yumi to an America-san's 'amen' school was a disaster after all," Hana sighed and grumbled, half at herself and half at Taku. "She may have learned a few words of broken English, but she has been caught by the 'amen' religion."

"Mother, my school is not called 'America-san's amen school.' It's a Christian school run by American missionaries," Yumi said proudly.

"Yumi, I used to know a Christian man," Hana said. "He

said 'amen' at the end of every second sentence. He said religion had saved his life. But he was baptized in vinegar and looked like a shriveled pickled cucumber. He was a failure."

"He may not have been shriveled inside. He may have been a happy cucumber. 'Judge not according to the appearance,' the Bible says," Yumi retorted.

"I think it's all right to believe in any religion if it's a good one," Ken said.

Hana said with a sigh, "This is a nation of imitators. A nation of pickpockets. From the West, we stole dynamite, steam engines, bloomers, skirts, and high heels. I'm a traditionalist. Look at me. I don't wear dresses or high heels. We've borrowed Buddha from India and Confucius from China. Our altar is overflowing with Buddha, his disciples, our family Buddhas and eight million Shinto gods. How many more gods do we need?"

"Just one," Yumi said.

"I don't think God minds if a Japanese borrows Him," Taku said.

"Buddha was an Indian man. Confucius was Chinese. Amen-san must be British or American. Why do we need so many foreign saints?" Hana said.

"You are wrong. Jesus was a Jew. We don't know who God is," Ken said.

"British, American, French or Jewish, they all look the same to me," Hana snapped.

"If we go to church, can we meet God?" Tami asked.

"If you believe in Him, you might," Yumi said.

Tami looked confused, but said, "Can I come with you to church on Sunday?"

"I'll come, too," Kana said.

Jun borrowed the Bible from his father's library. If this was the religion Yumi believed in, Jun wanted to know what it was like. Some parts were familiar to him because his mother had read them to him in the last days of her life. Emi's face had shone, reading some passages. But she said to him, "I like what the Bible says, but I'm like a person at the bottom of a high mountain who doesn't know how to climb."

Jun also felt like that. Worse: he had a basic doubt about the existence of God and walked with helmet and armor on, and with his eyes closed, so that he would not be persuaded if God appeared in front of him on a shining comet. Scientifically oriented, Jun would not easily believe what he could not logically ascertain. He had learned about the theory of how life had evolved from single-cell creatures he had seen under his microscope. The existence of God had not been proven scientifically, although that might not exclude the existence of God.

On the other hand, there was the fisherman who had suddenly appeared on the beach on the day his mother had fallen ill and carried her all the way home. Was he a Good Samaritan or a holy spirit?

On Sunday morning, Tami and Kana were as excited as if they were about to go on a picnic. Ken surprised his sisters by saying, "I'll escort you girls to church." He said apologetically to his mother, "Mother, you may be right about us being an imitating nation, but I'm really curious about this religion. Some of my friends talk about it as if they had caught scarlet fever. It is probably only a fad, but I want to find out."

Jun said, "I'm cu-curious, too. I'd l-like to come with all of you."

The church was a great disappointment for Tami. Expecting it to look like a palace or a castle, or at least a gingerbread house she had seen in a picture book, she found a simple white structure with a pencil-top spire and a round window that was not even the multicolored mosaic of precious jewels she had heard about. The inside looked like the auditorium at her school, except for candles on the altar and a big cross on the front wall.

A big Western man with blue eyes, and a thin man with wavy brown hair smiled at Tami at the entrance and said *"Konnichiwa,"* in a funny accent. They wore black gowns and crosses round their necks. Neither one looked like the God she had expected to meet. The pastor who gave the sermon was not even a Westerner, but a small, bespectacled Japanese. She did not understand what he talked about even though he spoke Japanese and she was struck with a fit of yawning eight times in a row.

"I won't go to church again, Yumi. I believed in God, but I didn't see Him," Tami said, coming out of church with a pout. Kana, who had also been bored and restless, ran out, letting out the happy shriek of a woodpecker.

"I didn't see Him either," Ken said to Yumi.

Ken went to church once again and decided not to go any more. He said to Hana, "Mother, you should go to church and learn a little from them. Their teaching, 'Keep thy tongue from evil, and thy lips from speaking guile' is a good lesson for you, but it's not for me. Too many miracles happen for my liking. I'm hopelessly agnostic." Hana smiled triumphantly.

After several weeks, Jun arrived at the same conclusion as Ken. But he kept going to church mainly because he wanted to be with Yumi. She seemed to look happier outside the home. "How nice it is to breathe in the free air." She sighed and smiled at Jun affectionately, which she had stopped doing at home.

One day after church, Jun said to Yumi, "I h-hesitate to say this, Yumi-san, but I'm still walking in the dark s-searching for God, even after all these weeks."

Yumi gazed into Jun's eyes in the gentle way that reminded him of his mother and said, "Jun-san, to tell the truth, I'm not too different from you. The minute I believe I've seen God, I lose him. But I have a wonderful teacher, Miss Thomas, at school who says to me, 'He is up there and He loves you. Just relax and listen to what Jesus says in the Bible.'" Yumi's words had not cleared his doubts, but the kind way she had said them lightened his heart.

"I have a good idea. It's a beautiful day. Let's go there and sit down for a while," Yumi said to him, pointing at the corner of the churchyard.

"Yes. Let's," Jun said, his heart leaping.

They walked to a cool spot under a chestnut tree. She undid the *furoshiki* cloth in which she had wrapped her Bible and stretched it on the grass, wet from earlier rain. She told him to sit on half of it and she sat on the rest. Her kimono sleeve touched him and made his whole body shiver with joy.

"I used to lie down with Tami in our garden and look up at the sky through the leaves of a beech tree," Yumi said, lying down like a child, but then sitting up right away. "I shouldn't lie down on the ground any longer. What a nuisance it is to be a lady."

Then she opened the Bible and said, "Do you mind if I read my favorite psalm? No matter how often I read it, I still like it."

It was the psalm about a shepherd, green pastures and still waters. Yumi's voice was low and soothing. As she read it, the sun and shadows flickered on her hair, on her cheeks and on her pink lips. Jun thought she was the most beautiful creation of God, if He had created everything on the earth as the Bible said. She was a miracle, just as the sun, the sky, light, and shadows were. All the phenomena around him, prickly chestnut burrs, weeds, ants and even a speck of dust were fathomless layers of miracles even the strongest compound microscope or the highest powered telescope could never figure out. It did not matter whether Jun had seen God or not. Maybe the whole world was the manifestation of Him. Maybe.

When it was time to go, Jun offered both his hands to help Yumi up. He had been afraid to touch her, but now it felt like the most natural thing to do. Her hands clutched at his and felt heavy and warm. When he pulled her up, he did not let them go and kept clasping them for a minute longer until both of their fingers were sweaty. Yumi smiled at Jun and it was the sweetest smile he had seen.

He was blissfully happy for days after. The light and shadows on Yumi's face kept flickering in front of him. Her soft voice kept reading the psalm in his ears. He relived every moment of the afternoon countless times. It was like floating among clouds made of happy dreams.

Then his euphoria was shattered. Jun and Yumi were summoned by Hana to her room. She sat in front of them with lowered brows and asked in a stern voice what they had been doing in the churchyard last Sunday afternoon.

"We just sat down on the *furoshiki* cloth together and talked like a brother and a sister. I read him a psalm," Yumi said in a calm voice.

"I don't believe that was all. What else?" Hana said with the cold-bloodedness of a reptile and looked like one. Jun shuddered

"I s-s-sat down on the g-grass and listened to Yumi-san read the p-psalm. It was a b-beautiful one. I offered Yumi-san my h-hands to help her up."

"Kana said you were holding hands together. A neighbor saw you together, too. She said to me with a wry smile, 'Isn't it nice that your daughter and stepson get along so well.' You are much too old to sit together outside, even if you were a real brother and a sister. And you aren't. If a rumor spreads about you two, it'll affect Yumi's marriage prospects. There have already been some *miai* proposals for you, Yumi. So you shouldn't go to church either. Being Christian is detrimental to marriage prospects. There aren't too many men who want to marry an 'amen' woman."

Jun was like a happy bird shot to the ground—shot and stabbed by Hana's piercing eyes and icy tongue. He saw Yumi tremble with anger. His heart bled for her. He wished he could say something to Hana to defend her, but he knew that talking back was not allowed.

That evening he overheard Hana say to Taku, "Did you notice the way Jun looks at Yumi? He has the hungry look of a dog in heat. I noticed it before, but I had pity on him and kept my mouth shut. I've been too generous."

"I've never noticed it." Taku said. "You may be imagining it, Hana. It's puppy love, if anything. I assure you he isn't the kind who would do anything to hurt Yumi."

"Kana said that Jun stood outside the girls' room and peeped. I don't want funny rumors to spread before Yumi gets married."

Jun ran to his room and shut the door. He wanted to run out of the house and go far away. Far, far away to where his mother was. He wished he could talk to her. She would understand.

He decided he should move out of this place in order to protect Yumi from problems. It would be sad not to see her. He would miss his other siblings, too, particularly ever joyful Tami. But he would visit them from time to time.

The next night, Jun was asked to come to his father's study. He had expected some talk concerning the matter with Yumi and braced himself. But when Jun came in, his father looked at him, his small eyes full of affection.

"Jun, why don't you come with Ken to Hokkaido this summer and stay with me for a while?" Taku said. "I'll show you my new factories and you and Ken can go hiking and fishing."

"Father, it would be nice to go to H-Hokkaido with you and Ken, but I was about to tell you that I'd like to m-move out of this house because of the rumor," Jun said.

"Don't worry about that. It's nonsense. I know you haven't done anything wrong, Jun," his father said, patting Jun's shoulder.

"But I'll move out in order to p-protect Yumi-san."

"Let's forget about it and prepare for the trip. We'll talk about it after we come back, if you still want to move out."

Taku put his arms around him. Jun leaned on his father's chest, which was big and warm as he had remembered it as a child. He stayed there to hide his tears. His father's heartbeat was steady and soothing.

CHAPTER 6

Jun left for Hokkaido with Taku and Ken, leaving Yumi bereft. Her stomach churned with anger at her mother and she confined herself in her room. When Kana came to play with her, she asked Tami to take her away. Yumi tried to write stories, which she normally loved to do, but she had trouble writing. She had a magic wand with which she killed demons, punished wicked witches and brought happy endings to her fairy tales, but now as she wrote her own story, her wand lost its magic. Fairies and elves would not help her out of this crisis. No goddess seemed to know how to bring a happy ending to her love story with Jun.

Yumi tired of writing and opened the drawer of her desk. She kept a photo there inserted between two notebooks. It was the picture of her in the yellow kimono and Jun in his school uniform at the *kabuki* theater. Jun was looking intently at Yumi, his eyes gleaming like stars in love.

Her thoughts wandered to the day Jun had visited her house for the first time. She was excited to meet a half-brother who was coming to live under the same roof. "I wonder how I would feel if I were this poor boy who had lost his mother and had to live with a mean stepmother who had stolen his father from his mother," Yumi had said to Tami.

Yumi liked Jun's gentle countenance, his dark gleaming eyes, thin nose and soft, brownish hair. Though not as handsome and well built as Ken, he seemed sweet and sensitive. When she saw his lips quiver and cheeks flush red as he stuttered, she felt terribly sorry. She thought his stutter might have come from growing up in a lonely family without a father.

At first her feelings for him were sisterly, or even motherly. Though younger than Jun by two years, she felt older and wanted to protect him from her sharp-tongued mother. As time passed—she did not remember when—she started to think about him at night with a shiver she had never before experienced. Perhaps it was the night Jun had sung for Taku's birthday. He was shy and his face all red at first, but once he began singing, he had forgotten stuttering and bashfulness. For a normally quiet boy, introverted and bookish, his singing was surprisingly expressive. He had a clear, lyrical voice and his songs remained in her ears long after the music had ended.

Jun did not talk much, but his eyes spoke loudly. They were as dark as the bottom of a deep well and looked at Yumi with an entranced gaze. Sometimes they looked sad. She wondered if he was sad because he was in love with her, but could not express it, just as she could not speak about her feelings for him. Other times they looked far away. They might be scientist's eyes, seeing what she did not see. Were they reflecting the mystery of the universe, counting the light years from a star, or picturing the anatomy of bees and frogs? Or were they seeing his mother who was in heaven, and cherishing her memory?

Yumi had met Jun's mother only twice, but she remembered her vividly. One afternoon Yumi and Tami had stayed at Mariko *sensei*'s studio after their dance lesson was over, because it was raining heavily and they had no umbrella. After the class, *Sensei* practiced dancing herself and allowed Yumi and Tami to watch her. Mariko *sensei* usually danced to a gramophone, but this time a lady named Emi-san played music she had composed called *A Winter Tree*. At times the music was so calm that Yumi could hear snow falling on a bare tree in a dark field. Other times it was so fierce that she felt swept away by a stormy wind. Emi-san was so thin and her fingers dancing on the strings looked so frail that Yumi wondered from where the power and the passion of the music came. Emi-san was bending down over the instrument, tilting her head to listen to the sound, but when she looked up from time to time, Yumi saw a sad and intense glow in her eyes. Mariko *sensei* was trying to choreograph the music, her arms swinging like shaking branches and her fingers quivering like leaves in the wind. As the music ended, Mariko *sensei* fell on the floor with a thump like a winter tree toppling with all its strength gone. Emi-san's eyes brimmed with tears. Yumi did not realize who Emi-san was until the maid who had come with an umbrella said that she was her father's wife.

The next time Emi-san was at the studio, Yumi and Tami stayed again to watch *sensei* practice with her. Afterward, Tami dragged Yumi to Mariko *sensei,* pulling her hand. With her usual innocent audacity, Tami said to *sensei,* "Could you please introduce us to Emi-san?"

Sensei hesitated for a moment, but then said to Emi-san, "You know about Taku-san's daughters, don't you, Emi-san? These are Yumi-san and Tami-san."

Emi-san opened her eyes wide, looked at Yumi and Tami with an affectionate smile and said, "How do you do? I've seen you dance and was wondering who the lovely girls were. I'm so happy to meet you, Yumi-san and Tami-san."

"How do you do, Emi-san. I like your music," Yumi said.

"I like your music, too." Tami giggled happily, bouncing three times.

Those were the only two occasions Yumi had met Emi-san, but she had not forgotten her music and her warm-hearted smile. Yumi was angry that her mother had stolen her father from Emi-san. How would she feel to have her husband taken away by another woman? What a cruel thing Yumi's father had done, leaving a sweet wife like her and starting another family.

One day, a few years later, Mariko *sensei*, who looked as if she had been crying, told Yumi, "Emi-san has died. She was such a sweet person and a very talented musician, but so modest. She was my best friend." The sad music of *A Winter Tree* and Emi-san's tears came back to Yumi. She was the winter tree that had died after a desperate struggle.

Somehow Yumi blamed her mother more than her father for having betrayed Emi-san. Of course, it was her father who had betrayed her, but for many years after Emi-san died, Yumi often saw him sitting and praying fervently in front of the family altar that contained a small lady Buddha who looked like Emi-san. Yumi saw tears roll down her father's cheeks. Emi-san Buddha must have forgiven him by then for what he had done, Yumi thought.

It was the resentment Yumi felt against her own mother that made her think about Emi-san. How nice it would have been to have a gentle mother like Emi-san. Deep down, Yumi was often angry at her mother. Since she was the oldest, she was expected to be a model for her sisters. She pretended to be an obedient daughter, but she was not so inside.

As a small girl, Yumi wanted her mother to play with her, or at least to care about what she did and thought. Whenever Yumi wanted her mother's attention, or wanted her to listen to the new fairy tales she had made, Hana said, "No, not now, Yumi. Later," because she was either trying on her new kimonos, sitting in front of a mirror with a maid doing her hair, or in bed complaining of a headache.

Not that Hana did not care about her daughters. She was eager for them to grow up to be cultured, upper-class ladies. She took Yumi and Tami to the dance studio. She took them to piano lessons. She took them to a tea ceremony class. Every time she took them to lessons, she said, "You'll be cultured ladies and marry rich men." Everything she did for them was to prepare them to marry rich men.

Hana had chosen the American Missionary School for Yumi, because, as she said, "The knowledge of English will help in finding a rich man." But Miss Thomas, who taught Christianity, had opened Yumi's eyes. The world was not all about being beautiful, cultured, well bred and well mannered so as to marry money. Blessed are the poor in spirit. Blessed are the meek and the merciful. Jesus praised the salt of the earth and the light of the world. The Christian value system that treasured love and forgiveness, generosity and spirituality were the last things Hana would teach the children. They were not written in her book.

The idea of God was new to Yumi. At first she was interested in God as a concept rather than as an object of religious belief. One God instead of eight million, and instead of Buddha and her ancestor buddhas. And she just hoped that, if God was an almighty savior, He should somehow save her from the anguish and the dilemma she was in, being in love with her half-brother. It might be taboo, but Jun was the first man in her life for whom her body flushed and her heart pounded. Her fairies and witches hadn't solved her problems. Perhaps God would give her spiritual elevation.

When Yumi announced to her family that she would like to be a Christian, her faith was not at all firm, but God would come soon and lead her, she thought. It was also a rebellion against her mother. Yumi knew Hana would not like her daughter to be a believer of a foreign religion, but she did not want to be just an obedient daughter any longer.

Yumi thought God was another supernatural being like elves and angels who made life rich and imaginative. But He was even more elusive than her little fairies and goblins. He never came to lead her with a firm grip, as she had expected. Her love for Jun showed no sign of abating despite her prayers.

After Jun left for Hokkaido, Hana asked a *miai* agency to find a dozen of the most suitable young men in Tokyo for Yumi to meet. Hana was possessed with an urge to marry off her eldest daughter, though she was only seventeen, before she became involved with the wrong man, such as Jun, became a fanatic about the "amen" religion and got wrong ideas into her head about love and marriage.

Hana said to the head of the *miai* agency, "The man must be healthy, rich, intelligent, good-looking and kind. Have a detective find out how much wealth the family has. And each man has to be followed around to see what kind of life he leads and what reputation he has among friends and elders. Make sure he is a hard worker, doesn't go to disreputable places at night, consort with indecent women, or drink too much."

Hana showed Yumi the pictures of the young men the agency had brought her. Hana said, "Pictures tell a lot. The nose of this man isn't straight; he may have a crooked mind. The lips of this man are too thick; he may be promiscuous. This man is a little skew-eyed, but he looks shrewd; he may be a successful type."

"Oh, please, Mother," Yumi said. "You are like the worst kind of fortune-teller who looks at your hand and face, and says anything that randomly comes to mind. You can't judge a man from his looks. When you met Father for the first time and saw his droopy eyes, did you think he was a brilliant man?"

"Oh, yes. Under the heavy lids, his eyes twinkled like the beads of an abacus. I knew he was good at counting money. But what I didn't see was that he doesn't count money for himself and his wife, but only for his company, his country and for fellow humans." Hana sighed. "But I didn't do badly otherwise. Although your father was ugly and touching his skin gave me goose bumps, he was rich and famous, and yet honest to a fault and naïve as a country bumpkin. I used every possible trick to seduce him so that I could get out of the geisha house. The only thing I felt bad about was stealing a husband from a good woman like Emi-san. But after all, it was Taku-san's problem. Yumi, you have to be as determined as I was about finding the best possible man for your life. I'm just helping you."

From the candidates Hana had selected, the agency set up *mi-*

ais for Yumi. Her heart preoccupied with Jun, Yumi was reluctant to meet any man. On the other hand, in her sane moments, she knew that marriage with a half-brother was out of the question and even contemplating it a waste of time. If she met a man she liked reasonably well, it would be better both for her and Jun. Yumi could continue loving Jun as much as she wanted in the fantasies of her fairy tales. And it was consoling to think that Jun would not disappear from her life because he was her half-brother for life.

Mr Arai, the first man she met, was not as good-looking as in the photo, which showed him with impeccably smooth skin. In reality, his face was covered with acne and dotted with moles, big and small, like stars in a clear night sky. He had a pug nose that had been skilfully modified in the picture. He was tall, but his back was permanently hunched, and as a result he constantly looked down when he talked. Even when he looked up, Arai was so shy that he avoided looking into Yumi's eyes and only stole swift glances at her face from time to time.

"I understand you work at the Japan Bank. It must be interesting to deal with all that money," Yumi said, because Arai did not say anything for two minutes and she wanted to kill time.

"It's not really that interesting. For us money is only numbers. Unfortunately, we aren't allowed to talk about what we do or how much money we deal with, although, of course, what we do is absolutely fair and square and a mistake of one yen is not tolerated," Arai said, nervously blinking his eyes a few times, as if he had already violated the rule about his work. Yumi remembered that the report from the agency said that Arai had a reputation of being serious and honest. She realized that being serious and honest could be utterly boring. The conversation stopped there and he looked down at a grain of wood on the table. Yumi studied the constellation of moles on his face and found the Big Dipper on his forehead.

Yumi decided that it was a waste of time to spend more time with him. She said politely, "Excuse me, but I'm not feeling too well. I must leave now. It was nice meeting you, Arai-san." She bowed and left.

The second man Yumi met was Mr. Seki, a well-built, good-looking man with lively eyes. A descendant of an old samurai family, he looked self-confident and proud. He stared boldly at Yumi and asked all about her, what she did at school and at home. At first Yumi liked his audacity and his curious eyes, but she noticed that he was not interested in what she said and just mumbled, "Hm, hm, is that so?" while his eyes roamed all over her. Yumi squirmed, feeling as if every square inch of her body had been licked.

Mr. Seki sent a messenger to propose to Yumi. When she said no, he sent various agents to persuade her to change her mind. Yumi confided to her mother what she had thought about him and Hana asked the agency to investigate his private life one more time. It was discovered that Mr. Seki had a child from a woman he kept in town.

Yumi met two more candidates, but she managed to find fault with both. Although they liked Yumi and pestered her, she did not change her mind.

Luckily for Yumi, Hana's search for a suitable husband for her daughter had to be interrupted for a while because of an unexpected crisis concerning Taku's business. This happened shortly after Taku returned with his sons from Hokkaido and before Jun had time to move out of the house.

Both the coal mine Taku had run for seventeen years and the steel mill he had founded three years before were in danger of being taken over by the Mitsui conglomerate that had been buying big blocks of their shares. Without warning, Mitsui Bank cut off its financing to the coal firm, demanding payment of half the loan in ten days. They also terminated all loans to the steel mill.

Behind this were Uno's connections with Mitsui. Uno was Mitsui's self-appointed director, and had a hand in all their big deals. The old wounds had never healed and Uno's anger had flared up when Taku had recently refused his request to give exclusive rights to trade coal and steel to Mitsui Trading Co.

Uno's man in Mitsui spread a rumor in the financial community that Taku's financial statement was not clean. Anybody inside and outside the companies knew Taku was not the kind of man who would cheat, and that he could prove that nothing was wrong with the statement.

Perhaps Mitsui's takeover of Taku's companies in this manner would not have happened if former Prime Minister Ito had been alive. But recently Ito had been assassinated by a Korean. Just two months before his death, Ito had visited Taku's companies in Hokkaido and had praised Taku for his work.

Somehow, Taku lacked his usual fighting spirit and seemed strangely resigned. The locomotive that had been running nonstop for all its life appeared to be out of steam and he looked haggard. He returned from an emergency directors' meeting and said that the directors were indignant.

"They were determined not to let this outrage be forced down their throats. They suggested we switch financing to Yasuda Bank and fight against Mitsui." Then Taku sighed and mumbled to himself, "I'll repay all the loans by borrowing under my name. After that I'll give the company to Mitsui."

"Taku-san," Hana exploded, jumping up and stamping her feet, "don't forget you have five children and a wife to look after."

Hora came and tried to talk Taku out of resigning. "Taku, what happened to your courage?" Hora said, his normally pale face fiery red. "You who are notorious for your hot temper and quick counter-attacks, quietly resign at the first sight of wolves? Everybody knows that without your farsighted vision and painstaking efforts, this first steel mill wouldn't have been realized in Japan. Will you let the wolves devour the sweet feast you have prepared during years and years of work?" Nobody had ever seen Hora so passionate. His hands were shaking and his eyes glaring.

An old colleague came and banged the table in rage. "Don't

let the bastards roll over you. I worked with you in the early years of your coal mine and know how honest you are, how you turned it around from a miserable failure to a giant firm. It's outrageous to give your life's work to the cock of the street as a reward for bullying."

Tami, who had been sitting behind them with the rest of the family, came up to her father and patted him on his shoulder with her chubby hands. "Father, when bullies beat you on your stomach, do you just let them beat you to death? Let's not give up so easily." Taku looked at Tami affectionately and smiled for the first time.

"Father, you are only fifty-five. What will you do for the rest of your life?" Ken said.

Taku looked weary and said, "To tell the truth, I'm too tired to deal with these virulent blackmailers. Recently I've been surrounded by too many crooks, warmongers and the power-hungry. I worked nonstop to this day, believing that I was doing something good for the country. But I wasn't. The navy and the army have been fighting over my steel mill. I realize that the mill is only going to be used to build war machines to kill people. I feel as if all the efforts I've made in my life have ended badly. When I was young, I worked hard for Korean independence and you know what happened? This country has turned into a Leviathan, gobbled up Korea and made a colony out of it. Now my mill will create war machines. Maybe I was just a hopeless idealist. I want to spend some time in meditation and think about better things to do."

Veins appeared on Hana's forehead like lightning streaks. "Taku-san, meditation won't bring money," she said, her voice trembling. "You and I, we'll fight like cats and dogs if you stay home all day."

"Don't worry, Hana. I won't stay home and listen to your barking. There are things I still want to do in my life. I'm proud of what I've done for my companies. It's time to pass the baton on to other people. *Sensei* used to say that the big *zaibatsu* conglomerates like Mitsui that are protected by the government aren't all bad. They can compete with foreign firms. Let's see what they'll do."

Hora jumped up and shouted in fury, his eyes popping out. "What an old-fashioned idea. This is the age of free competition. A plutocracy will only breed evil. Don't you see, Taku, you are the very victim of it, threatened by the big bullies."

In spite of the ardent pleas, not only of the people close to him, but also from the financial community, from the coal-miners and office workers, Taku did not change his mind. He was strangely calm as if this were all happening to someone else. He resigned from his two companies as soon as the loan was paid off.

Taku stayed home for the first time in many years, and meditated in front of the family altar all day. On the second day, when he sat in the same place, Hana came into the room with a feather duster and started to dust the shelves and the altar, something she had never done before. Dust like white mist fell on Taku's head.

"This room is filthy. It's no good for you to breathe in dust all day," Hana said, her brows knitted and her patience about to blow. "Why don't you go out for a walk with Yumi while I'm cleaning, Taku-san?"

Yumi was glad to take her father out for a walk. This was a rare occasion to have her father all to herself. It was a warm autumn day and Taku walked leisurely, often stopping to pick up a fallen leaf to show Yumi how colorful it was. They came to a small muddy pond and stopped. On the pond covered with fallen leaves, one white lotus was blooming out of season. "Look how white that lotus is, even though it grew in mud," Taku said, gazing at the flower. "It looks lonely, doesn't it? Buddha was like that."

He resumed walking and said, beaming at her under the benign sun, “Yumi, I heard you’ve met a couple of young men. How did you like them?”

“I didn’t like any of them,” Yumi said.

“You have plenty of time, Yumi. Don’t rush. Once you make a mistake, it’s not easy to undo. I’ve made many mistakes in my life. I was not kind to Jun’s mother.” Taku paused and looked far away in the sky. Then he said, his face haggard, “This country is making a big mistake, too. I feel really bad about Korea. Too bad, Prime Minister Ito was assassinated. He told me he wanted Korea to become a strong country on its own. Right after he was killed, Japan annexed Korea.”

“It’s a shame, because you worked so hard for Korea,” Yumi said.

Taku did not stay home and meditate too long. The locomotive was quickly refueled. “Now I can put more energy into the Diet and work for the issues that will directly affect people,” he said.

Hana, who had been barking at Taku for having stopped being a money-making tree, was calming down. She now looked like a wise fox, scheming. “Don’t worry, Taku-san,” she said. “I’ll make money myself. I’ll start an antiques business. I’ll be rich. The other day I asked a few dealers to come here. They all said I have a fantastic collection. I obviously have an eye for it. Some of the things I bought several years ago are eight times their value now.”

Jun stayed at home and tried to be supportive of his father while he was having a difficult time. But as soon as Taku looked happy again, Jun rented a room near the university he had entered. The day he moved out, Taku patted his shoulder and said, “I wish you would stay, but I suppose every child must leave home sooner or later. Come back often and tell us all about university life.” Jun promised to do so.

He looked forward to living alone. No woodpecker would

lurk behind him. Nobody would call him a dog in heat anymore. He had actually often been like that inside, with a fiery passion for Yumi, but he hoped living away from her would quench the fire and he might feel like a monk.

But it was not as easy as he had hoped. In the solitary room, he found himself talking to Yumi. The small room was filled with Yumi; her soft, dimpled smile, her passionate voice telling a fairy tale. When he saw a butterfly dart about outside the window, it turned into Yumi in the yellow kimono, looking like a nymph in one of her stories, and she flew away, her hair flowing and her wings flapping.

Occasional visits with Chiyo did not dispel his loneliness. Jun decided to move into a dormitory in the university. It was a good decision. The constant bustle of roommates, lewd conversation and boisterous parties, though he hated them, did not leave him time to be alone. Finding Jun inexperienced, friends cajoled him into going to bars and cabarets to introduce him to saké and women. He was too shy to do anything with women, but they distracted him from his morbid obsession with Yumi, at least a little.

For some reason, he found himself stuttering less and less except when he was extremely nervous. Jun often looked at the sky and whispered, "Mother, aren't you proud of me? I can finally speak well." He saw Emi smile happily in the sky.

He found passion in the study of medicine. He spent so many hours in the laboratories scrutinizing bacteria under a microscope that, even when he wasn't, he saw funny-shaped creatures wriggling in his eyes.

One autumn afternoon, when he came out of the laboratory, the deadly S-shaped spirochaete bacteria were still dancing in his eyes. As the bright sun eventually killed them, he saw in front of him hundreds of fan-shaped yellow leaves falling off the gingko trees that flanked the road leading to the gate of the campus. Jun caught one of them that had landed on his shirt sleeve and looked at it through the sun. Golden light shimmered through thin fibers. In his eyes, the leaf turned into Yumi's hand, delicate and soft with pale veins showing through.

He had an acute desire to see her. It was more than half a year since Jun had been back. He had deliberately put off visiting the family, having promised himself to get over his obsession with Yumi before he returned.

He remembered well the last time he had visited them. Overcome with homesickness, particularly for Yumi, he had walked over. Hana must have been in an unusually educative mood. From a half-open window, Jun saw her teaching her three girls how to be beautiful women. "Being beautiful is an art. Think of painting yourself on a canvas. When you dress, you pay attention to color, shape and texture, just as when you paint a picture. All of you have natural beauty thanks to your mother, but a gem won't shine without daily polishing. You must walk, act and think beautiful." Saying that, Hana walked back and forth in the room, pursing her lips, casting a pensive sidelong glance, her hips swaying. "Geishas exaggerate this even more," she said. "But you shouldn't overdo it. You are the daughters of a high-class family. The act of enticing must be subtle."

Kana followed her mother, walking on tiptoe, mimicking her mother. She saw Yumi and Tami making faces at each other behind their mother. "Mama, they aren't serious," Kana said, pointing her finger at her sisters.

"Yumi, you must be a good example to your sisters," Hana scolded Yumi.

Now all three sisters put on a wistful face and mocked their mother's way of walking. Yumi noticed Jun outside the window watching them, blushed red and winked at him. Hana greeted Jun, saying, "Hello, Peeping Tom."

"Oh, Jun-san, come in. Come in," Tami cried out, happy to have an excuse to stop the silly lesson. Dashing out and pulling Jun by the hand into the room, Tami bombarded him with questions. "Oh, Jun-san, we missed you. What is your university life like? Is it so much fun there that you've forgotten us?"

Yumi gazed at Jun quietly. When her eyes met his, she blushed and looked down. The corners of her eyes were wet and gleaming. She had her hair up in a bun called a split-peach style, which was a softer, rounder version of Hana's oval chignon. The hairstyle made Yumi look grown-up and very much like her mother, but prettier. Her youth and sensitivity shone on her face.

But she was somewhat different from the Yumi Jun used to know. She looked more like a pretty doll than the determined, independent-minded young woman he knew. She looked like a perfect lady a man would like to have as a wife. Maybe she was resigned to the destiny of every young woman and was ready to be married. What alternative did she have? She must have been persuaded by Hana in spite of her inner rebellion.

But he was sure that it was only the surface. The Yumi Jun had admired was there, hidden under the perfect façade. He had no chance to talk to her then, but as he left the house, she tilted her head as if wanting to say something. Then she smiled a sad smile. That had been more than half a year ago.

As he walked out of the campus, Jun put the gingko leaf that had reminded him of Yumi's hand in his pocket, and tried to get her image out of his mind. He deliberately looked at women passing by, hoping to be attracted by someone else. It was a busy street. There was a walking tofu vendor, pushing a cart of tofu in water, calling in a sleepy voice, "Tofuu. Tofuu." There was a man dragging bamboo poles, shouting, "A big bargain for laundry poles." Jun was so absent-minded that he stepped on one of the poles and nearly fell forward. The smell of sweet potatoes baking on burning red stones in the middle of the street did not entice him today. He found himself on a tram that would take him to his father's house.

Jun entered the front gate, his heart throbbing with the

expectation of seeing Yumi. Lee noticed Jun and ran to meet him. "Oh, Jun-san, nice to have you back," he said. Then he added hesitantly, looking sorry for Jun, "They seem to have a guest, Yumi-san's friend, but I'm sure they'll love to see you."

Who would be Yumi-san's friend? Jun looked at the window of the living room where guests were often entertained. The glass reflecting the afternoon sun made it difficult to see. But looking from an angle, Jun saw the face of a handsome young man with a charming smile sitting next to Yumi.

The whole world blackened in front of Jun and he feared he was experiencing an epileptic attack like his mother. He stood trembling in front of the door regretting the visit, but it slid open and Tami was there smiling her sweet, round smile.

"Jun-san the stranger! So lovely to see you. I've been cross because you never come home. Are you all right? You look so pale. A poor, starving student. We'll have dinner soon and we'll feed you well. Guess what? Yumi is engaged. Her fiancé is visiting her. He'll be happy to meet you."

The ground he stood on shook and Jun had difficulty standing straight. He tried to smile, but his face contorted. As soon as Tami cried out, "Yumi, Jun-san's here," Yumi was there with a tall man with broad shoulders behind her. Yumi looked pale for a second, but she introduced Hisao to Jun.

"Nice to meet you, Jun-san," Hisao said and bowed politely. "Yumi-san has talked about you so much. You are the one studying medicine."

"C-c-congratul-lations." His tongue tangled up and Jun stuttered again, a habit he had been convinced he had finally conquered.

"Come in. Come in. Can you stay for dinner, Jun-san?" Yumi said.

"I can't s-stay today. Maybe some other time."

"Oh, come on, Jun-san. At least you must have tea with us, please," Tami pulled his arm and led him into the house.

Yumi sat close to Hisao, looking striking in a white kimono with blue irises painted on it. She was as fresh as an iris herself. Jun felt intoxicated with the faint fragrance that emanated from her. Her hair was put up high in a spiral fashion like a snail shell and decorated with a blue bow looking like an iris. Her cheeks and lips were rosier than usual. Were they painted to look pretty for Hisao? Were they so pink because Yumi was in love with him?

Over tea, everybody asked Jun what he had been studying. "What are you cutting up to see under the microscope now, Jun-san?" Yumi asked.

"Are you chopping up people's dead bodies to study atoms?" Tami asked.

"Anatomy, you mean, Tami-san," Hisao said, smiling.

"Yes. I've done that. But lately I've been studying bacteria that cause deadly diseases. I'm in love with them." How sad he was to be in love with deadly bacteria rather than Yumi, Jun meant to say.

"Aren't you going to get diseases, if you are in love with bacteria?" Tami said.

Yumi and Hisao were looking into each other's eyes as if they were not interested in what Jun was talking about. It was the intimate gaze of lovers, enraptured by each other and oblivious to anyone else in the world. Jun kept telling himself he must feel happy for Yumi. What business do I have being jealous? She is my half-sister.

Hisao seemed to be an intelligent man, although he was proud and tried to trump Jun with the degree in mechanical engineering he had earned in America. His sentences often started with, "When I was in America . . ." and he dropped names. "I'm sure you know Professor So-and-So who has received a Nobel Prize. When I was at Johns Hopkins, I used to live near his house and often saw him walk by. As you know, it's a famous place for medicine. You should consider going there, Jun-san, if you have an opportunity." Or, "Thanks to my father's cousin, Iwasaki, who owns Mitsubishi, our family has a machine-tool company. My father is getting old and I'm virtually in charge."

Jun was not interested in a name-dropping contest. He could not bear being exposed to more evidence of the lovers' infatuation. So he begged to leave before dinner. Everybody asked him to stay, especially Yumi. Probably because she felt sorry for him, but then she would understand why he did not want to stay.

As he left, Tami saw him off outside. Seeing him shudder with a sudden chill, she said, "Don't catch cold," and helped him put on his jacket from behind.

"Are you all right, Jun-san? You look so pale." She had a worried look in her big tadpole eyes. Then she patted him on his shoulder with her round hand and said, "Jun-san, how did you get rid of your stutter? You spoke beautifully today."

Jun was grateful to Tami for trying so hard to cheer him up. She must know that he was broken-hearted about Yumi. He had always liked Tami, but her kindness touched him deeply this evening. He wanted to cry on her shoulder.

Preoccupied with his obsessive love for Yumi, he sometimes forgot how wonderful Tami had been to him, how much joy and happiness she had brought into his life since he joined her family, with her sense of humor, bird-chirping laughter and innocent coquettishness. Being so sweet and warm-hearted, she pretended that she had never noticed his special feelings for Yumi. If she had known, she had not shown any jealousy. She had not complained or tattled on him to her mother as Kana had done.

"Come and see us even after Yumi is gone. Come back more often, Jun-san," Tami said with a full moon smile, patting him again on his shoulder.

"Of course I will. I'm happy you are still here to come back to, Tami-san."

Jun felt like crying and quickly walked away into the dark.

CHAPTER 7

Jun was in his laboratory looking into cultured bacteria under the microscope. It was an inauspiciously dark morning with the wind rising from the west. He looked up and out of the window for a moment, then said to his assistant, Sayo, "Look at the sky. Doesn't it look ominous, Sayo-san?"

"It's the first day of September, the typhoon month, Dr. Jun. I wouldn't be surprised if we had a storm," Sayo said.

His eye had again been glued to the lens when suddenly it slid away as if a devil had played a trick. Then the array of test tubes, beakers and trays, the desk itself, the shelf, the filing cabinet and everything else slid to the end of the room, falling all over the floor.

"An earthquake. All the bacteria devils are out. . . ." Jun's head reeled, as he fell on the floor and was taken on a seesaw ride, while the whole room waved back and forth like a boat tossed over a gigantic wave.

"Goodness, no earthquake was written on the calendar today," Sayo said, as she fell over Jun, her arm bleeding from broken glass. "This is a hellish one. Get that pillow and cover your head, Dr. Jun."

Jun crawled sideways like a crab to grab the two cushions

from the chairs. He gave one to Sayo and took the other himself, as the books, lamps, the windows and doors fell over them. "Shut your eyes and mouth. Pinch your nose under the cushion, Sayo-san," he said. Loud rumblings and the voices of people screaming roared in through the broken windows.

When the tremors lessened a little, Jun crawled about until he found an unbroken iodine bottle in the wreckage of the room and poured some on Sayo's arm. He looked in horror at the damage, precious research data ruined, experiments smashed to pieces and wondered what to do about the spilled bacteria, when Sayo shouted, "Fire. I smell fire, Dr. Jun. We must get out of here quickly. Everything will burn. All the germs and devils will burn."

He tried to collect some of his research data before he left, but Sayo pulled him out of the room by the arm and he ended up picking up only his usual doctor's bag without which he would have felt his right arm was missing. The corridor was filled with smoke. They rushed out to the balcony and came down its stairs, when another tremor bent the iron steps into an S-shape and shook them off on to the ground. Luckily they were already halfway down from the second floor.

"My bottom is permanently flattened. It might've been cracked, too," Sayo said and frowned, but she managed to get to her feet and pulled Jun up. His left leg was in acute pain and he fell on the ground again. "This leg is broken." He grimaced as he was jolted again by a tremor.

"Let's go to the bamboo forest behind the shrine there," somebody shouted behind them. "The tough roots have made the ground firm."

"Let's do that," Sayo said and gave her shoulder to Jun. It was a sturdy one for a woman and he hung on it and hopped. The street was full of people, mothers with crying babies on their backs, men carrying a safe, women holding pots of rice and people pushing a cart piled up with futons.

Hundreds of people were already in the forest clutching

bamboo stems, or crawling, crying out each other's names. As Jun sat down and looked back, he saw his laboratory and the adjacent university building in flames. An acute sense of loss stung him as he thought that the precious data was ash by now. He was primarily a doctor specializing in infectious diseases, but he had been lured into research. He had returned to Tokyo last year from Germany where he had studied for three years at a medical institute. He had just finished setting up a laboratory with funds from the university.

A man nearby was moaning. A child was lying with a cut on his forehead. I'm a doctor: I should be saving lives, Jun said to himself, but the pain in his leg made it difficult even to crawl.

"Do you mind if I borrow this?" Sayo snatched his bag and walked away without even waiting for his answer. He could trust her because she knew more about medicine than most doctors. He saw her run from crying children to moaning men. People raised their hands, calling out to her, "Please come here, Nurse. Please."

The sky was covered by yellow smoke. A young man was running around, shouting, "The artillery factory is on fire. The clothing factory, too. People are being burnt to death, or buried alive. This is Doomsday." Jun thought about Yumi, his father, Hana, Ken, Tami and Kana. Were they all right? How were Chiyo and Lee? What about his apartment, where some of his research papers were stored, as well as all his belongings?

Sayo came back with an empty bag, saying, "I used up all the supplies. We can't help anybody any more. But what about you, Dr. Jun? You can't move."

"Don't worry about me, Sayo-san. Why don't you go home and see if your mother's all right? Walk carefully. There will be aftershocks."

"I can't leave you here like this, Dr. Jun. Oh, I have a good idea. You know that medical supply store down there? If it is still standing, I can get crutches for you. Then we'll find a hospital somewhere."

"Nobody would bother with an ambulatory man at a hospital now. I'm a doctor. I should be treating patients if any hospital is still standing."

"Anyhow, I'll go and see if I can find crutches for you." Sayo was fearless and left before Jun could stop her. He watched her totter and run on the trembling ground.

Jun had known Sayo for two years before he went to Germany. She was working at the hospital where Jun had done an internship. He had been so impressed by her quick action, good judgment, and kind care of patients that he begged her to work with him when he returned to Tokyo. She helped him both at the university hospital where he worked and at his new laboratory.

Sayo was a single woman of twenty-six. She called herself a *fuki,* a thick stalk of a wild vegetable, butterbur, which, unless it is picked early in the spring, quickly becomes too large and too hard to eat. She meant she was no longer eligible for marriage. Indeed she was not the willowy beauty that men in Tokyo seemed to admire. She had a short nose on a pink, round face, but she did not look as overgrown as she described herself. She was so good-natured and her laughter so contagious that she was always surrounded by people, men and women. She enjoyed making fun of herself in order to amuse the patients. They laughed when she talked about her unrequited love for a popular sumo wrestler.

"Don't you think he is gorgeous?" Sayo took out the fat wrestler's picture from her wallet and showed it. "His skin is smooth and has no sag. He attacks like a polar bear." And she lowered her hips, stuck out her big upper body and posed a ready-to-attack position, looking like a bear herself.

"I wrote a letter to him. I waited and waited, but he never wrote back. So I wrote to him again. I hope he'll answer this time."

Sometimes Sayo brought in sick people wearing rags from the street. She cleaned them and brought them to Jun and said, "I know you are generous enough to see them for free, Dr. Jun.

You know I'm a socialist. I believe that the poor have the same human right to see a doctor as the rich." Jun smiled at her and saw them without charge. Thanks to Sayo, a few lives had been saved.

Sayo was so pleasant that, no matter how busy he was, Jun found a few minutes to talk to her between patients or after hospital hours. Even after he had gone home and cooked himself soup in his kitchen, he found himself talking to her as if she had still been standing by him.

One weekend, he rowed a boat with Sayo on the Sumida River. Sayo almost invited herself, saying casually, "I love rowing, but it's something a woman doesn't do alone." That day she looked so much prettier than usual, in a flowery dress, an entirely different woman from the nurse in an antiseptic white gown smelling of medicine. Every night since, he saw in his eyes her skirt flutter with the wind and felt the fullness and warmth of her breast, which had pressed on his arms when he caught her as she tripped jumping off the boat onto the dock.

Jun enjoyed working with her even more than before. He was already thirty and was becoming a *fuki* himself. The thought of marrying Sayo frequently occurred to him. How happy he would be living with her not only during the day, but also during the whole night.

Watching Sayo run at the risk of her life to get crutches for him, Jun decided to ask her to marry him. It was a bit strange to propose marriage in the middle of an earthquake. Maybe the shock of the destruction, the loss of his research and the pain in his leg made him vulnerable and lonely, and gave him a sense of urgency. It was very possible he would die at any moment from an aftershock that would cut open a gaping hole under his feet and bury him alive; fire could sweep him to death; debris might fall on his head and finish him off. How sweet it would be to spend a few intimate moments with Sayo, talking about marriage before he died.

If he did not die, it was a good time to marry. Over the years, he had met several women as candidates for a wife, introduced by his friends and professors. Taku and Hana had also arranged a couple of *miai* for him. For one reason or another, none of them had worked. Whenever he met a beautiful lady, his stutter came back and he spoke badly. After the meeting, a polite rejection was sent by messenger. When the first meeting went well, something prevented him from falling in love with the lady. He found himself comparing her with Yumi. Yumi had been married to Hisao for several years. She had had two miscarriages, but she had finally had a son. What was the use of thinking of her even as a point of reference? But Yumi still lived in him as a part of his body.

Jun had gone to Germany for three years, beginning in 1920, partly because he wanted to sever the past, forget Yumi and make a fresh start. But he suffered from severe homesickness.

German words were long and guttural, and his stutter returned. Jun could never finish pronouncing a word like *Sehenswüurdigkeiten* if he could ever begin. He did not understand why the word meaning "places of interest" must be so difficult, but of course Japanese must be just as hard for the Germans because it involves unfamiliar characters. Medical terms were long whether German or Latin. Jun had to write the names of the diseases such as *Hirnhautentzündung,* meaning "meningitis," and *Bauchspeicheldrüsenkrebs,* meaning "pancreatic cancer," because he did not want people to wait for three minutes for him to finish the words.

His colleagues were kind, but his shyness and unwillingness to talk prevented him from making close friends. He frequented concert halls alone. It was a delight to listen to live performances of the music he had known from Emi's records. Beethoven, Schubert, Brahms. . . . He tried to read Nietzsche whom everybody was admiring as a god, even after he had declared God dead. Reading was more enjoyable for him than speaking. Professionally, they were productive years. He studied bacteriology with top professors and worked hard. But Berlin was cold and dark in winter.

Yumi and Tami sent him food parcels from Japan: green tea, seaweed, plum-pickles, dried persimmons. Yumi wrote him letters, too. When he found her letters in the mailbox, his fingers trembled as he opened them, even though he knew they were just sisterly notes written to cheer him up.

She gave him news about the family: "*When the Diet is not in session, Father is working with Ken-san at a hydroelectric power company, building a big dam. He's ecstatic, saying, 'Electricity lights up the world, not like steel that builds military ships.' Otherwise he's becoming more and more a devout Buddhist, almost a mystic, and gives away to charity more money than he makes, which does not please Mother. Do you know that Ken-san married the daughter of a baron and Tami a businessman in Yokohama?*"

Tami also wrote to him: "*We're proud of Mother having turned into a shrewd businesswoman, buying and selling antiques. People in town call her 'that eccentric antique woman.' She forgot who provided the money to buy her antiques and said to Father, 'Don't even touch the dust on my antiques, Taku-san. It's all mine. When you touch it, it's dust, but when I touch it, it'll turn into gold.' But now she's been bedridden for two months, moping with acute pain in the knees. We are afraid she might become a real antique woman. We are all waiting for you to come back and make her better, Jun-san.*" Jun read the letters over and over until they disintegrated.

Yumi appeared frequently in his dreams. In one dream, Yumi came to visit him in Berlin and he showed her *Sehenswürdigkeiten* all around the city. In another, he sang German *lieder* for her. Those were happy dreams with nothing sexual about them. But in the cold bed in Berlin, he was often haunted by the contorted faces and figures of Emil Nolde's and Kirchner's paintings which he had seen in an Expressionist exhibition. One strangely beautiful nude painting by Kirchner kept appearing in his dreams. As he looked at it closely, the face was Yumi's. He started to indulge himself in the dreams. They were Freudian dreams, according to his own analysis. It was a time when Freudian psychology had invaded the medical field as the newest vogue and crept under people's skin like an infectious disease. Suddenly people became neurotic with sexual fantasies. Jun caught the disease, too.

When he returned to Tokyo, the practice of medicine kept him busy and, in his spare time, he immersed himself in research. He only saw Yumi, Tami and the family occasionally. Yumi did not appear in his dreams any longer.

One of the reasons Jun's obsession with Yumi faded was because he had had an affair with a woman named Mitsuko. He met her at a card table on the boat returning from Germany. She was a musician who had studied violin at a German school. Weary with the boredom of the long journey, Jun played bridge every night. Mitsuko had been flirting with another man, but somehow Jun caught her fancy, perhaps because he was a better cardplayer. Mitsuko often asked Jun to be her partner. She winked at him over the table with her mysterious eyes. It was not clear if she was sending a signal about the cards or a more alluring hint. When she was dummy, she came to sit next to him and offered him drinks, while she chain-smoked. She was slender and not unattractive, dressed in the latest Berlin fashion. But her skin was tired and sallow. She might not be as young as she was dressed to look.

They played cards until the wee hours. One night when Jun was walking to his cabin, Mitsuko followed him to the door and handed him a handkerchief, saying, "Did you drop this, Jun-san?"

He said, "No. It's not mine." But she did not leave.

"I don't feel like sleeping tonight," she said. "You know, when we play cards, we don't have a chance to talk. I'd like to know you more, Jun-san." So Jun invited her into his cabin. She sat next to him on the couch and talked a little, smiling with her dark eyes and inching up closer to touch him. Soon they started to play with each other. She taught him how to make love.

They made love every night after playing cards and sometimes during the day, too, in the dark cabin. Time passed quickly. They were sad when the ship arrived in Yokohama and they promised to see each other again.

The affair continued for half a year. But it was not the same as it had been in the dark cabin on the boat. Mitsuko often stood Jun up. Sometimes she was passionate, other times cold and distant.

One day when he was waiting for her at a café, she was late. When she finally arrived, her face was painted thick to hide her tired skin. She was dressed in a blouse with deep décolletage.

"I'm terribly sorry, Jun-san. I've been wanting to tell you this for a while, but I'm engaged now. I've enjoyed your company, but this'll be the last time. . . ." She walked out of the café and a moment later, Jun saw her arm in arm with a man.

It was strange to think about Mitsuko in the middle of a major earthquake. He had few regrets about her. Her memory returned like an aftershock and woke him up to physical sensations. She was a temptress. Thanks to her, he had rid himself of his obsession with Yumi.

Now he was only interested in Sayo. Sayo was blithe and gay, unlike Mitsuko who was secretive and mysterious. Sayo was the ever cheerful sun, while Mitsuko was the moon in dark shadow, with waves of passion swelling and waning. Sayo had a sun-drenched supple skin, unlike Mitsuko's sallow one.

Another aftershock. Everybody squatted down, hung on to the nearest bamboo or even grabbed grass. Jun worried about Sayo. She had been gone for a long time. As usual, she must be involved in helping people, having forgotten about herself. But was it possible that some wreckage had fallen on her? He wished he could get up and look for her.

As the tremor subsided, Jun looked in the direction from

which Sayo should come. To his happy surprise, there she was, hopping with crutches under her arms and wearing a wide smile. Jun laughed through tears and said to himself, It's something only she would do—hopping on crutches in the middle of a quake just for the fun of it.

"Sorry, Dr. Jun. It took so much time," Sayo said, out of breath. "The roof of the shop had caved in. The owner's child had a concussion and the wife had bad bruises. I helped them a little and they gave me these crutches and plaster."

Sayo squatted down and tucked up Jun's trousers to see his leg. Saying, "This part is hot and swollen," she quickly applied the wet plaster she had brought in a bag. It felt cool and soft on the aching leg. She bundled up his leg with a bandage.

"It's so soothing. The bones feel put together. I must break my bones more often to be treated by you. By the way, Sayo-san, I should kneel before you like the men in the American movies, but I can't with my broken leg," Jun said, his face all red. "But I wonder if you wouldn't mind m-m-marrying me?"

"What did you say, Dr. Jun?" Sayo opened her eyes wide and laughed aloud. "As if breaking a leg wasn't enough, you've lost your head, too?" Sayo laughed again, convinced that she had heard a joke.

"I'm serious. I wonder if you could m-marry me," Jun said.

"Just because I've brought you plaster and crutches?"

"No, no. Because I love you."

Sayo stared at Jun with a suspicious look, as if it was a sentence too incredible to believe. It occurred to her from his serious look that he might have meant what he said, and her cheeks changed color from pink to fiery red.

"But let's not talk about it now," she said shyly. "I suspect the quake has affected your brain a little, Dr. Jun. There are more important things to do now. Let's find out how your family is. I must see how my mother's doing, too."

"Yes, of course."

Sayo helped Jun stand up. He put the crutches under his arms and walked. They went first to her mother's place, which was on the way to Jun's father's house. It was a slow and painful walk. Destruction had made the streets unrecognizable. The appalling reality blew away the fantasy of marriage and they walked in silence.

Civilization that had taken hundreds of years to build had crumbled to nothing in a day by nature's flip of a finger. The town that had looked neat and proud only this morning, had turned into piles of rubble. Had they as a nation done something so wrong as to deserve this? Did heaven punish Japan for getting too proud and aggressive?

When Sayo saw her tiny terraced house in a small alley half crumpled up, she dashed in, calling, "Mother?" A stocky lady, a smaller and older version of Sayo, crawled out of the collapsed roof. As she saw her daughter, her distraught face wrinkled up and tears rolled down her cheeks. "Oh, Sayo. My goodness, you lived. I knew you'd have the wits to survive the worst of crises. Well, I've been digging from the mess here whatever could be saved. There isn't much. We didn't have much to start with. It doesn't matter if I lost everything because you are alive, Sayo."

Sayo wanted to accompany Jun to his father's house, but he thanked her and left. The ill-fated day was turning into a gray evening. There was a long way to go. His leg was hurting, but there was no choice but to walk since obviously no transport was available. Red flames were rising from the center of black smoke that covered half the sky. Roofs, poles and debris were dancing in the flames. The scene reminded Jun of the Kandinski paintings he had seen in Germany. This was a grimmer version painted in dark colors.

His father's house was on the periphery of the smoke. As he came within three blocks of the house, the smoke blocked his sight like a dense fog and his heart throbbed with anxiety. Choking with smoke, rising heat all around him, he barely managed to reach the corner where the house had been located, when he saw a black skeleton of the house that had once been the marvel of the neighborhood. About a quarter of the house, including the western wing where he used to live, was still standing, though badly scorched.

Yumi's husband Hisao, Honda and a group of men were pouring water from buckets on the smouldering remains. Their faces were black with soot.

"Where are the family? Are they all right? Where is Yumi-san?" Jun asked.

"Oh, Jun-san. They are inside," Hisao said. "Look at our heroic effort. Without us the whole house would've been burned. The water pipe is broken and there's no running water. So we've been scooping well-water. Did you break your leg, Jun-san? Too bad." Hisao led Jun to the western wing.

Jun saw Yumi running out with a baby boy in her arms. Lines of worry and fatigue were drawn on Yumi's face, there were dark circles under her eyes and her hair was unkempt, but she still looked beautiful to Jun. He was sure he had no more special feelings for her, but he found himself blushing again at the sight of her.

"Oh, Jun-san, you are alive," Yumi said, her eyes flashing. "You've broken your leg, haven't you? It looks painful. You know, it was lucky that most of the family were away. Father's at Ken-san's place in Nagoya. Kana's been traveling in Kyoto. The only one I'm worried about is Tami. She and her husband have just moved to a new house in Yokohama. They say Yokohama was hit badly."

Jun had a sense of foreboding. "There's no way to find out about them, is there? The phones are cut. Trains aren't running."

In the corner, Hana was sitting like a dead bird, her normally impeccable hair disheveled, her peacock hairpin bent askew and her shoulder slumped.

"Are you all right?" Jun said to Hana. "I'm sorry you've lost your b-beautiful house. But we're lucky everybody is all right so far. I hope Tami-san is safe."

Hana bawled out, in an unexpectedly loud voice for a dead

bird, "We aren't lucky at all, Jun-san. All my antiques and my beautiful kimonos are gone. Someone in heaven has been so cruel. You know, they should have destroyed this wing. This place has only junk like your old books and microscopes. Damn it." Hana scowled at Jun and then scratched her scalp. Her hair stood up and coiled like Medusa's. She picked a book out of Jun's old bookcase and threw it on the floor.

Then she laughed and said, "Sorry, Jun-san. I'm not cross with you." Then she started to cry like a baby, shaking her whole body as violently as the earthquake itself. But she suddenly stopped crying with a frightened look on her face. "I hope Tami is all right," she said, and gazed outside at the dark.

Yumi brought a bowl of rice to Jun and said, "Sorry. This is the only thing we can give you for dinner."

"This is the most wonderful feast I could think of. Thank you, Yumi-san." It was true. Jun had not eaten for the whole day.

Yumi sat next to Jun. "Jun-san, I'm worried not only about Tami, but also Lee-san. He went out to see how your grandmother was doing and hasn't been back yet. It's rather late. I hope nothing has happened to him."

Hisao spoke in a loud voice, as if to announce to everybody there, "There are rumors that the Koreans are responsible for some of the fires. They put poison in the wells. I hope Lee hasn't been involved in such things. Don't drink the well-water, anyone."

His face all red, Jun stood up quickly, forgetting about his leg, and collapsed on the floor. "W-who t-told you such stupid nonsense, Hisao-san?" Jun said, trying to sit up. "Who spread such groundless rumors? And you think Lee's involved, Hisao-san? He's the last man in the world to do anything like that."

"How can you say it's groundless, Jun-san? Somebody in the street told me he had seen a Korean throw an oil can and start a fire. I saw a notice on the bulletin board, '*Do not drink well-water because of possible foul play by the Koreans.*'"

"Who'd ever think of p-poisoning others when you are on the brink of death? Neither a Korean nor a Japanese. I have to g-go and find Lee now. I must go to my grandmother's house anyway to see how she is doing. She may be able to tell me where Lee is," Jun said, his voice trembling. The whole room hushed, shocked by the fiery eruption from the normally quiet Jun.

"I've never seen you so angry, Jun," said Hana, opening her eyes wide. "You have your father's temper after all. I like it. You've gained dignity since you became a doctor. You used to be so shy and tongue-tied; now you can shout. Good for you."

"You are right, Jun-san," Yumi added. "People were so panic-stricken today that they probably wanted to blame somebody for what had happened."

"Yumi, you always take sides with Jun-san. Go out and read the bulletins yourself," Hisao shouted, his eyes glaring. Yumi looked away, her eyes darkening.

She came to see Jun to the door. Handing a bag of rice balls to him, Yumi whispered to Jun, "I hope you won't overdo it tonight, Jun-san. Take care of your leg. Can you take these rice balls to your grandmother, please? I'll be praying for Lee-san."

Jun suspected that Yumi might not be happy with Hisao, who sounded like a jealous husband who did not want his wife to have a mind of her own. Tami had told Jun they were not getting on with each other. The lines under Yumi's eyes might not have been etched just by the tensions of the day.

It was drizzling and dark outside as if black poison had been thrown into the sky. The electricity was out and there was no light except for the smouldering fires flickering out of the embers in the rain. Jun almost stumbled over the half-burnt body of a three- or four-year-old boy. His arms were lifted halfway up in the air as if asking for help. Nobody was near. Even his mother's body was not there. Jun felt the boy's chest and wrist just in case, but he was as hard as clay. Jun stroked the boy's hair with his fingers and wept.

It was a short distance to Chiyo's house, but it seemed interminable for Jun whose leg was hurting. Around the corner, he saw the roof of the house he had grown up in. Part of it had collapsed and slid into the garden. Debris filled the pond he used to sit by to watch the insects swim. Where were Chiyo and Lee? He noticed that the extended quarter Taku had added for Chiyo was unscathed. Seeing candlelight flickering in it, Jun was so happy that he rushed and tripped on a stepping stone. He fell on the moss garden and just sat there, too exhausted to get up.

The sliding door opened and Chiyo came out, her hair in disarray just like everybody else's that day. "Hooray, you broke your leg, but you're alive, Jun. Thank gods, Buddha and Christian God, they made you survive," she cried out. Jun noticed that her back had bent like a cooked shrimp in the few years he had not seen her.

"It's too early to say that. I might die of exhaustion if I'm not buried alive in the next aftershock," said Jun in a faint voice, still sitting on the moss.

He crawled into the house and collapsed almost on top of the *koto* in the middle of the room. "Oh, oh, careful," Chiyo said. "This is the only thing I've saved intact from the teahouse. I carried this out all by myself."

"It was pretty impressive for an old lady to have done that," Jun said.

"I'm no old lady. I survived this horrible quake with flying colors," Chiyo said, raising her arms up to stretch her back. It did not straighten, as a cooked shrimp's wouldn't. Jun smiled for the first time this evening, happy at his grandmother's spirit. Watching her gobble the rice balls Yumi had sent, he thought again about Lee.

"Did Lee happen to come here?" he asked.

"Yes, he did this afternoon. He was happy to see me alive and well. He brought these candles to light up the house and a thermos bottle, thank goodness, the only drinking water I now have. Then he rushed to your house with another thermos for you, saying he must find out how you were," Chiyo said.

"Then I'd better go home and find him," Jun said, standing up.

"Oh, no," Chiyo said, "You'd better stay here tonight. You don't even know if your place is standing, do you? You must rest your broken leg after such a long day. The bedroom is undamaged and I have enough futon for you." Chiyo's voice still had the authority that used to frighten the young Jun.

"But I don't want Lee to wait for me all night. My place is only a few blocks away from here, as you know. I'll be back if it's not there any more." Jun insisted, in spite of further warnings from Chiyo. She made a fuss and covered him up from head to toe with a heavy hood and cape for protection from falling objects.

It was quiet out. People were either dead or asleep. Even the earth was silent, at least for the time being, probably thinking it had done enough work for the day. As he walked, an unbearable sense of loss came back again to him about his data and facilities that could never be restored. Tears kept rolling down his cheeks.

For some reason, his house and the whole neighborhood was untouched. It must have been a small region the devils had overlooked. At the doorstep to his place, he found two candles and a thermos with a piece of paper under it. The paper said: "Jun-san, I hope you are all right. I'm glad your house looks good. I'll come back tomorrow morning. Lee." The note worried Jun. Did Lee make it back home safely despite the rumors Hisao had talked about? But Jun was so exhausted that the minute he touched his futon, he was asleep like a dead man.

The sun was way up in the sky when an aftershock awoke him the next morning. The tremor brought him back to the nightmare of the day before. Unfortunately, it was not just a bad dream. There was no more laboratory for him to go to. He wanted to get in touch with his colleagues, but he did not know how without any communication system. He thought of Sayo and wanted to see her. And what about Tami? He prayed to heaven for her safety. Then he remembered Lee and the note he had left at the door. Wasn't he here yet? A clock said it was already eleven. Lee was a man who would never fail to keep his word.

Jun had a breakfast of dried biscuits he found in the kitchen and drank water from the thermos Lee had left. Then he went out to look for Lee, carrying over his shoulder the doctor's bag, refilled with medical supplies. Everywhere people with sooty faces and muddy hands were busy clearing rubble and constructing shelters with burnt tin and pieces of wood. With tremors coming back like hiccups, barracks shook like faltering tops and fell as soon as they had been propped up.

Men were standing at every corner with swords, hatchets, bamboo spears or pieces of wood. They outnumbered the policemen in uniform. "Who are they? Why are they there with dangerous weapons?" Jun asked a man cooking rice in a burnt pot on a hibachi at the roadside.

"They are a self-appointed vigilante corps watching out for Koreans. Haven't you heard about them? They are burning houses, dropping bombs and pouring poison. You see, the socialists organized the Koreans to join an uprising they had planned for this week and somehow this quake coincided. So it was a divine blessing for them. They've been wreaking havoc."

"H-how do you believe such a ridiculous rumor?"

The man stared at Jun with suspicious eyes: "Are you a socialist or a Korean yourself? Watch your tongue. The vigilante corps will catch you," he said and went back to stirring rice.

Tramp-tramp. Heavy bootsteps came from the distance, sounding like another approaching tremor of the earth. An out-of-tune military call of a trumpet screeched into Jun's ears and tore at his already racked nerves. He looked back and saw a regiment of the army marching toward him like a tsunami, causing a dust storm in the air already filled with smoke. He felt as if the soldiers' bayonets were stinging his back. Why were armed soldiers marching instead of rescuing the buried and helping the homeless? Why were they frightening people in this fear-ridden city punished enough by nature's anger? The marching boots suddenly came to a halt. An officer shouted into a megaphone.

"Citizens! Three thousand Koreans are said to be marching from Osaki region. Our authority asks your cooperation to keep peace and security in this city. Act with discretion and you will not be blamed for your activity."

Goose pimples ran down Jun's spine. Staggering on crutches, he headed for his father's house to see if Lee had come back. In the fire-ravaged ruins, Honda and a few servants were cleaning up the debris. But there was no sign of Lee. When Jun asked about him, Honda looked sulky and said, "I don't know why he's taking so much time coming back. Lee should be working here. I have a suspicion he might be involved in the sabotage people're talking about."

Jun ignored him and asked the servants where was the most likely place Lee could have gone the previous night. "Before he left yesterday, he was talking about Oh-san in Fukagawa. His daughter is Lee's girlfriend. Oh-san works at the arms factory there. I'm sure he went there," one of the servants said.

"Thank you for telling me," Jun said and left.

Fukagawa was a hard hit industrial area at the east end of the city and tens of thousands of people were said to have been burned or buried to death. It was at the other side of Tokyo and a whole day's distance to walk, particularly on crutches. Jun was weary. It would not be good for his leg. Sayo's treatment was good as a temporary measure, but the cast had to be reset quickly. Besides, even if he were to look all over Fukagawa, how much chance would he have to find Lee?

Jun dragged his heavy feet. He wanted to say hello to Sayo and decided to stop by her house. Just seeing her might cheer him up. But only her mother was there. "Sayo was worried about you, Doctor Jun. But a nurse friend stopped by this morning and told her to come to the hospital. The hospital hadn't been damaged so badly. Thousands of people are thronging there."

It made Jun feel guilty that he was not working. If he went

there, his leg could be reset right away and then he could help patients, sitting down. He could probably save more people's lives that way than looking hopelessly for Lee.

As he set out to walk to the hospital, Jun heard a menacing voice at his back. "Halt! Stop!" He looked back, fearing he had been called. A middle-aged man with an eye-patch was running after a young man in a white Korean gown, a symbol of purity. Though he looked as meek as a sheep, wearing Korean clothes today was a death sentence. The eye-patch thrust a sword at the back of the young man. A red splash ran down his white overalls. With his face grimacing in pain, he reeled. Jun stumbled, feeling pain as if he had been stabbed.

"You are a Korean, aren't you?" the eye-patch barked.

"No, I'm Japanese," the young man said, his face as white as his gown.

"A liar." The eye-patch put a rope around the youth and shouted with a triumphant grin, "Walk!" Passive as a stabbed sheep, the boy tottered at gunpoint. The red blob on his gown got bigger by the minute. Jun followed them, blood oozing from his heart as from the boy's back. His crutches shuddered as he walked.

They came to a square where a dozen other men had been tied in a row like a string of beads. The eye-patch and his fellow vigilantes, all of whom looked like rabid dogs, joined the sheep boy to the string. A few of the men on the beads were wearing white gowns, but most of them were in the *happi* coats Japanese workers wore. Any of the captives could pass as brothers or relatives of the captors, except that the latter looked ten times more beastly and demonic.

The eye-patch and his fellow rabid dogs shouted dirty words, and kicked and beat the newcomer. The boy fell on the ground, causing the rest of the captured men to fall like dominoes. The dogs trampled on them and poked them with bamboo spears.

An officer with a long, flipped-up beard, which he had been

stroking, strode on to the scene and shouted, "Enough." Then he indicated with his chin that the men should throw the captives into a truck that was waiting. Cans of oil and split wood were also loaded in the truck. An onlooker said loudly, proud of his secret knowledge, "Do you know why they need those oil cans and wood? They'll take those Koreans to Fukagawa, burn them in oil and throw them into the river."

Shocked, Jun stumbled to the truck, shouting, "W-wait. Please t-take me with you. I'm a doctor." Jun showed his identification card to the bearded officer, who looked at this crippled stutterer with disdain and sneered, "What's the use of a doctor? We don't need a doctor for Koreans."

"I may be useful. I hear there are thousands of wounded people in the east end of the city. I could be of s-some use."

The officer looked at his card and stared at Jun. "All right. If you promise to save my daughter's life. She was burned on her face and is seriously ill. It's strange because she wasn't in the fire."

"I can't promise, but I will try," Jun said.

Jun was hauled into the back of the truck with the rest of the men. He sat by the sheep boy who lay motionless, his gown crumpled with blood and mud. Jun opened his bag to get medicine for him. The officer yelled from the front, "Doctor, I'll throw you out of the truck if you touch them." He wanted only his daughter's life saved.

The sheep boy curled up, as gentle as a sacrificial lamb, his eyes looking far away in the sky. Had Lee been walking in a street, caught like this boy, tied up and carried away in a truck? All around Jun, there was silence. Some of the prisoners were shaking violently, others half dead and listless. They bore their pain, sadness, anger and despair silently, except for the one who kept pleading with Jun, "Doctor, I'm no Korean. No Korean. I just couldn't read what they told me to. Tell them that, Doctor, please. I've got five children and a wife. I can't die."

Jun's heart cried for everybody, Korean or Japanese. But he

could not promise anything to anybody. He did not know why he had volunteered to come with them on the truck. Particularly if he was not even allowed to treat their cuts or bruises. The truck would take him closer to where Lee might be, but finding him would be more difficult than locating a button fallen in the ocean. If I can't find Lee, I will at least save this boy's life, Jun said to himself.

The truck crawled through a wasteland piled with ruins. Tens of thousands of burnt bodies were strewn about, blackened and swollen like bronze Buddhas. A girl in a scorched kimono was running among the sea of the dead, crying with the piercing sound of tearing silk, "Mama-a, Papa-a."

The *kabuki* theater he had visited with Yumi, the department stores he had been to with Emi, and other impressive-looking buildings had crumbled or burnt. Red-hot wires were dangling in the air, coiling like angry snakes. The burnt leg of a man was hanging, caught between a crushed roof and a window.

Nature had satanic power. But who had thought up the sinister idea that any of these buildings had been destroyed either by the socialists or by the Koreans? Who had the enormous scientific or financial resources to create such powerful bombs? Certainly not poor socialists and Koreans. If some of us were evil enough to create a rumor like that and most of the citizens were crazy enough to believe it, we deserved what we had received, Jun thought. Just as Babylon had fallen from excess, so had Tokyo from paranoia.

The truck came to a sudden stop on a bump that made Jun and the other riders jump. When he got off the truck, he saw a body and a pool of blood under the front wheels. Why had the truck purposely run over the body? But then, the whole ground was littered with them so that it would have been impossible not to drive over one. His blood froze as he looked closely. These were different from the scorched bodies in the ruins; they looked fresh as if they had just died. Their faces had been tormented with pain. Their white Korean gowns were soaked red.

Those tied had been taken to the riverbank. The sheep boy was looking up at the sky as if to pray, trembling. The bearded officer and two vigilantes with guns stood in front of them. Jun staggered on crutches to the officer and said, "P-please, Officer, don't kill them, please. They haven't done a-anything."

The officer shouted angrily, "Don't interfere, Doctor. I'm acting on orders. They are Koreans."

"K-Koreans or Japanese. Look at the faces of these people. They wouldn't have thrown bombs. They are as weak as sheep."

"Are you a socialist, Doctor? Then I must arrest you, too."

"I'm no socialist. But I don't believe they have plotted any scheme. L-let me save your daughter first before you do anything with these people. We might not be able to save her, if we don't rush."

The officer looked down at the ground as if thinking of his daughter who was wasting away. The doctor was right; the Koreans could wait. His daughter might not. He shouted at the men, "Put them in the warehouse for now. Leave them tied up."

The officer and Jun went back to the truck. It stopped at a half-burned house and the officer carried out in his arms a little girl with a swollen red face. Jun held the girl on his lap. She was pleading in a feeble voice, "Give me water. Water, please. My face hurts. My head hurts." Jun examined her face, part of which was covered with blisters, and said, "This is not a burn. It might have been caused by a small burn, but it must be erysipelas, an acute febrile disease." He suggested they drive her right away to the university hospital where he worked.

The hospital was a solid throng of quake victims, but Jun managed to take the child into the emergency room and put cool compresses of magnesium sulphate solution on her skin.

As he asked around for an empty bed for her, he bumped into Sayo in a corridor. Her cheeks blushed pink. "Oh, Dr. Jun. I've been worried about you all day. Where have you been? How's your leg?"

"Sayo-san, can you find an empty bed for my patient,

please?" Sayo ran off, saying, "They are hard to come by, but I know of one." In a minute she came back and smiled. "Ready," she said and carried the girl to the bed.

Finding Sayo and seeing her smile, Jun felt as if the sun had lit hell. He breathed deeply and told the officer, "I hope your daughter will be all right. It was lucky it wasn't a burn. It won't leave any scar on her face."

The officer smiled for the first time. "I'm really grateful, Doctor Imura. Please call me Kuroda," he said, taking off his cap and bowing to his knee. Before Kuroda left, Jun said to him, "Could I ask you a big favor, Officer Kuroda? Please don't kill those men I rode with on the truck. And can you make sure that the wound of the young man who was stabbed in the back will be taken care of? You can bring him here if it looks bad."

Kuroda looked into Jun's eyes and said, "Yes, I will spare their lives and take care of the young man for your sake."

Jun saw the gentle eyes of the sheep boy, and smiled. "I appreciate it very much, Officer Kuroda. And can I ask you one more big favor? Could you please find out about a Korean man named Lee, who works as a gardener at Taku Imura's? He's a gentle-looking man of fifty-eight with a broad nose and triangular eyes like Mount Fuji. He is a very special man."

Kuroda thought for a moment, stroking his beard. "Trouble is so many are named Lee. And we haven't kept the names of the men we've caught, but I'll try my best to look for him."

Between treating quake victims, Jun saw a bone doctor Sayo had arranged for him. Luckily, his leg did not look bad in spite of its heavy use. Sayo's temporary treatment had worked. After a new cast was set, Jun went back to see more patients. Sayo worked with him until dark and then by candlelight.

From then on Jun and Sayo worked together every day. They had no time to talk to each other. But she often smiled at Jun in a way she had never done before. She blushed burning red when he touched her fingers by mistake, while handing her a syringe.

Jun judged the new reaction as a positive answer to what he had asked her about on the day of the quake. Though physically exhausted, his spirit lifted.

Kuroda stopped by to see Jun two days later. He took off his cap and bowed down to his waist. "Doctor Imura, I must thank you again. My daughter looks much better now. My wife asked me to tell you how grateful she is. Please don't worry about the Koreans. They aren't going to be killed. The young boy lost a lot of blood and is weak, but the cut isn't infected and he'll be all right. They are still kept in the warehouse because, if I let them go, other vigilantes will catch them. You know, Doctor Imura, to tell the truth, I'm ashamed of myself for what I've been doing. You are saving people's lives and I've been only killing them, even though I was just doing my duty under martial law.

"You were right, Doctor Imura," Kuroda continued. "The rumors turned out to be groundless. Three thousand Koreans were supposed to come from Osaki and only sixteen came. A Korean caught on suspicion of carrying bombs had only a can of pineapple and a bag of rice. We killed several prominent socialists, but there was no proof any of them had done anything suspicious. I thought I was doing the right thing, but you made me think differently. Ninety thousand people died overnight from a natural disaster, why do we have to kill more? Now the authorities who started the rumor, have admitted to having gone too far and have posted notices all over town: '*Do not persecute the Koreans. They are harmless people just as you are.*'"

"Thank you very much for saving those men," Jun said, smiling. "I'm so glad about the young boy. Were you able to trace Lee?"

"I came here to apologize for it. It was difficult to trace him because there are no records. If anybody looked like a Korean, he was killed. We didn't even ask their names because they'd never tell you Korean names anyway. I remember an older man with sharp eyes whom our men shot. But, of course, he may not have been Mr. Lee. I hope not. It's difficult to locate any of them now, because lots of Koreans are hiding. I'll keep enquiring about him, Dr. Imura," Kuroda said, lowering his head.

"Thank you for being so honest. I hope he's hiding somewhere."

"Dr. Imura, please listen to one word of advice. Don't say anything sympathetic about the socialists. The government and the police are out to kill them."

"I'll be careful. Thank you."

Jun was saddened about Lee. There was little chance of his being alive. Lee had been so sweet to Jun. He never forgot the afternoon they went together to the field behind Akashi Temple and caught dragonflies with a net. He remembered the tears in Lee's eyes as he let the red one fly back to the sky so that it could live one more day. What had the Japanese done to such a sweet man?

At the end of the day, Jun dropped in at his father's because he wanted to find out about Tami and just to see, if by any small chance, Lee had come back. The place was strangely quiet. Lee was not there. He would have dashed out to greet Jun, whistling Korean tunes. Jun stood in front of the western wing, the scorched façade of which looked eerie in the dark.

A maid came out and whispered in a teary voice, "There's sad news about Tami-san. She was buried under the roof of her house. She was such a kind lady."

Inside the room, Hana was crouching on the floor in a heap of sorrow, hitting and shaking her head on her thighs. Her kimono was all wet and crumpled with tears. She looked tiny. Overnight she had diminished into a bag of bones. Jun came up and hugged her shoulders from the back. He had never done that before, but he could not help doing it because he was sad himself. They stayed there and cried together for a long time, Jun and Hana.

"It must've been terrible to be suffocated to death," Hana said, her voice trembling and her red eyes gazing in the dark.

"She yelled for help, but no one came. Then it got harder and harder for her to breathe. How desperate she must have felt."

"It might not have taken so long." Jun tried to console her as well as himself.

"She was my favorite child, although, of course, every child is, in some ways. She was an angel. I don't know how such a sweet child was born from me. She must have come from heaven. She brought laughter to the entire house. The gods take away their favorite children, don't they?"

"It seems so, doesn't it?" Jun was thinking about Lee, too.

Jun could not believe that Tami had really died. He felt as if she would run into the room any moment, laughing with her bird's chirping voice and her innocent black button eyes shining. He remembered the happy sensation when she touched her toes with his under the *kotatsu* heater, and her disappointed pout at the time he could not play father; how she came out to console him when he had been heartbroken about Yumi being engaged to Hisao. She had put his jacket over his shoulder with her chubby hands and said, with her full moon smile, how happy she was that he didn't stutter any longer. She was a grown lady then, but she remained in Jun's mind an eternal child. She was indeed like an angel. Or a sweet imp at times. It was hard to believe she would never come back.

"Her husband came here. He was so shaken I wasn't sure he'd survive. Yumi went with him to Yokohama. I hope she's all right. She was as devastated as he was. Yumi was so close to Tami, you know. They were best friends to each other. Taku-san will be back tomorrow. I wonder how he'll take all this. All his piety has done nothing, but I bet he'll become even more of a monk after this," Hana said.

The maid came in and said that Hana had better rest because she hadn't slept a wink since last night when she heard the news.

Jun worked hard at the hospital in order to bury his sadness. For if there was a free moment, tears welled up in his eyes. As he saw so many patients with swollen eyes, he realized that he was not the only one hiding sorrow. After 90,000 deaths and 152 aftershocks, the earth was finally quiet and the autumn air crisp, but life was not the same.

One chilly evening, Jun came down with a high fever. He must have caught an infection from one of his patients. Working with one leg in a cast, seeing so many deaths in the family and in the hospital, and suppressing an acute sense of loss about people and about his research had pushed him to the end of his tether.

As he lay at home, Sayo came to visit him in the morning, at noon and after work. She nursed him hand and foot as if he had been a prince. "You are lucky you have professional service free," Sayo said. She pretended to act just professionally, cleaning his body and limbs as if they were sticks. But then, at times her face flushed red at the touch of his fingers. She worked with amazing efficiency, all the while humming and whistling, putting cold towels on his forehead, making medicinal tea, squeezing apple juice, cooking soft rice and feeding him with a spoon, and cleaning his clothes.

Jun waited eagerly for her visit. His temperature soared and his whole body trembled at the sing-song voice, "Doctor Jun. I'm here." Though moaning with headache, he was deliriously happy at the slightest touch of her hands on his forehead and limbs. He thought he would die of pleasure when she washed his body with a warm towel.

His proposal to Sayo remained unanswered for some time with the commotion of aftershocks. He did not feel it appropriate to talk about marriage after so many sad things had happened. But he could not wait too long. On the day he was recovered and back at work in the hospital, he said to Sayo, "Let's go out for lunch today. Some lunch places must be open now."

Out in the street, the rubble had been cleared and barracks were shooting up like bamboo shoots after rain. People with diehard business spirit had set up temporary shops and restaurants.

Jun and Sayo had lunch at "Creative Tempura," where anything edible was thrown into the half-burned pots and cooked. They had been so starved that even the bitter leaves of chrysanthemum and overgrown *fuki* tasted good.

They walked up the hill past a barber and a kimono shop, amid the workers putting up electric poles and digging water pipes, and found a quiet place behind the ruins of a house.

"Let's sit down," Jun said. "I'm so tired of walking with these crutches." As he sat on a rock, he saw a gecko scurry away from under it. It was an ugly, fossil-like creature, but it made him happy to see another sign of life among the ruins. "Did you see him, Sayo-san? A little gecko."

"No, I didn't." But she said in a loud voice, "Look, a wild rose is blooming under the rubble," and pointed at a small bush with one little pink flower on it. She said, "Maybe the gods haven't abandoned us after all."

"This rose is blooming for all the dead," Jun said to Sayo. "Tami-san, Lee, and all the rest."

"It's the bleeding hearts of all the Koreans and socialists," Sayo said.

"Do you know Schubert's song of a wild rose, *Heidenroeslein*? Let me sing it for you," Jun said, and sang the song he had learned in Germany.

Sah ein Knab ein Röslein stehn,
Röslein auf der Heiden. . . .

"I didn't know you had such a beautiful voice, Dr. Jun." Sayo looked at Jun, her eyes shining.

"Do you remember w-what I asked you on the day of the earthquake, Sayo-san?" Jun said to her, looking into her eyes. "I've been waiting for your answer."

Sayo's cheeks blushed as pink as the wild rose. Her high cheekbones softened with a shy smile. "It made me very happy that you thought of me as a candidate for your wife," Sayo said hesitantly. "But then I wondered if it was an aberration that occurred in a shaky moment. I'm not from a good family as you are. I'm not beautiful, not well educated and I'm only a nurse."

"Only a nurse? I often think a nurse is more important than a doctor. I thought it over and over again to make sure that this wasn't a decision I made in a panic. No earthquake can shake it off, Sayo-san. You are the woman I love and I want to m-marry."

Sayo's eyes flashed, reflecting the bright autumn sun. She started to cry and laugh at the same time. "If that's the case. . . ."

Overjoyed, Jun tried to hold her hands and kiss them, but Sayo stopped him and looked down as if something else bothered her. "I must tell you something," she said, in a low, determined voice. "I hate to tell you this because you may change your mind about me. But I must tell you." Sayo looked pale. She sighed and said, "I'm afraid I'm a socialist."

Jun looked around to see if anybody had overheard her. "Don't talk so loudly, Sayo-san. But it doesn't surprise me. You've often said that before. What kind of a socialist are you?" he whispered.

"I don't even know what kind. I'll tell you how I became one. I used to go to night school to study English. There was a young student named Fumiko. She was the brightest woman I've ever met. She was quick-minded and made a joke out of everything. She invited me to the *oden* shop where she worked. I had a delicious *oden* she had cooked. But the place looked different from an ordinary restaurant. Men talked in low voices. They argued about a man named Marx. They talked about the Russian Revolution and how people had killed the king, the queen and the entire royal family. I found out this place was called 'Socialist's *Oden*' and some of the men who went there were Communist Party members. Fumiko was in love with a Korean man there and left me alone. I talked with a man named Yasuo. He told me that socialism was an idea to try to make society equal for everyone. I liked the idea." Sayo stopped, and breathed heavily, looking nervously at Jun.

"I liked Yasuo, too." She looked down at her fingers and continued, "Soon we became lovers. Yasuo is the only man I've ever known. He was organizing an artists' club for the proletariat. I helped in his activities, drew propaganda posters and pasted them on billboards. I went out with him for a while, but he often frightened me because his views were so violent. He cheered when someone talked about making bombs to throw at the Emperor. I hold no brief for the Emperor, but I don't like any idea of violence. Besides, I found out he was a womanizer. So I broke up with him. I've had nothing to do with the socialists since then. So this is about my past. You may not like me any more after this story, Dr. Jun."

Sayo kept looking down, as if prepared to hear a rejection from Jun. Then, before Jun said anything, she looked up and said, "The other day I read in the paper Fumiko and her Korean boyfriend had been arrested. It really frightened me. I may be arrested because I've been to the Socialist's *Oden* place." Her eyes sank.

"Do you think you are a socialist because you went to the restaurant and because you had socialist friends?" Jun asked.

"Also because I liked their ideas. I haven't read Marx or anything, but they say we must correct the system. The poor are exploited by the rich. I think they are right, though I don't like the violent path the Russians took."

"I also agree with most of the things the socialists say," Jun said. "But it doesn't make me a socialist. I wouldn't mind if you are a full-fledged party member. You are free to believe in anything. The only trouble is that the government and the military police are out there now trying to catch every single socialist and their sympathizers. So for your safety, don't speak as if you were one."

Sayo gazed at Jun. Her eyes gleamed under the puffy lids. "You are so fair-minded, Dr. Jun, but don't you mind about Yasuo?"

"No. I also had a girlfriend named Mitsuko for six months."

They smiled at each other and kissed. Jun held Sayo in his arms and felt happy for the first time since the quake. Sayo said, "I feel guilty being so happy while you are mourning for Tami-san and Lee-san."

"They would all have loved to see me happy. My mother, too. They must be smiling at me from heaven," Jun said, looking up at the sky.

"Do you think your family will accept me? A nurse from a terraced house?"

"Of course, they will. If they don't, so what? It's my decision." While saying that though, Jun remembered that Ken had moved to Nagoya, his wife, Ayako, having been tormented by Hana. "My stepmother is a little difficult, but I'm sure you'll win her over with your charm," he said, stroking Sayo's hair.

Jun did not think it appropriate to bring up the subject of his marriage to Taku and Hana so soon after Tami's death. He did not talk about it when he visited their house to see his father whom he had not seen for a long time.

The wreckage of the fire had been cleared. The shrubs were overgrown without Lee to trim them. From the window of the western wing, Jun saw his father sitting with his palms joined in front of a bronze Buddha. Hana hovered around him, shouting. She had been a heap of sorrow the last time he visited; she was back to life and shouting again.

The minute Hana saw Jun, she yelled in a louder voice, happy to have a new audience, "Jun-san, how long do I have to put up with living in this pathetic matchbox? Your father tells me he doesn't have money to build a new house since the insurance companies are bankrupt and can't pay for our lost house and treasures. Instead of doing anything about it, he's busy fighting in the Diet for the dead Koreans and socialists. He's collecting money to build houses for poor people, but not for us. As usual his priorities are mixed up."

Taku was looking outside the window, his eyes as small and sad as an elephant's. "Tami was such a special person, wasn't she, Jun?" he said, ignoring Hana. "I don't feel like talking about a new house Tami will never come and visit."

Rubbing his prayer beads, Taku continued, "Oh, Jun. What happened to our country? Poor Lee. The bastards must have killed him. You know, Jun, as I was coming back to Tokyo by train, policemen got on board with guns. They looked at the passengers and picked out three men who looked like Koreans. I argued with the policemen and they menaced me at gunpoint, accusing me of being a socialist. They dragged the three men out at the next station. As the train left, I heard three gunshots." Jun told his father what he had seen on the first few days of the earthquake, more frightening than the earthquake itself.

Jun found it difficult to talk to Taku and Hana together. They were as incompatible as a whimpering dog and a growling cat. So he left soon, but since he could not wait any longer to tell them about Sayo, he visited them again a week later.

"I c-came to tell you today about my plans for m-marriage. I'm going to m-marry a woman named Sayo Komai. We won't marry during the period of mourning for Tami-san. Sayo is a nurse and my indispensable colleague."

They had been arguing about something as usual, but as soon as they heard Jun stutter this out with his cheeks flushed red, they forgot all about it.

"Well, well. Germany has made a modern man out of you," Hana said, her eyes shining with curiosity. "You didn't like any women your father and friends introduced you to and now you choose one yourself without even consulting us. Then you talk about her as if it's a *fait accompli*. What's she like? Is she pretty?"

"Probably you won't call her a great beauty. She has a s-short nose and heavy eyelids. But she has a beautiful smile. She is warm-hearted and has a healthy mind and body. She's funny, too."

"She sounds good. The best wife should have those qualities," Taku said.

"The best wife should have a short nose and heavy eyelids? You have them, too, but they haven't made the best husband out of you, Taku-san," Hana said.

"I'm talking about the latter part of the description: a kind heart, a healthy mind and body. And she's funny."

"I'm the best wife, then. I'm kind to myself. I'm healthy and funny, too. Anyhow, what kind of a family is she from? Well, this is a stupid question. The rich don't send their daughters to a hospital to change linen for the sick," Hana snapped.

"She lives with her mother in a terraced house. She came from poor country in the north. Her father was a c-carpenter, but he deserted his wife and young daughter. Sayo came to Tokyo, became a nurse and supported her mother."

"Jun-san, you are marrying down," Hana declared. "A famous politician-businessman's son and a doctor who's studied abroad could marry a millionaire's daughter. What a shame. You know Ken is married to the daughter of a baron, an ex-minister of the army. Yumi is married into a rich family. Kana isn't married yet, and she can't marry well if she has a half-brother whose wife is a nurse."

"Is it all right for Kana to have an ex-geisha as a mother, but not all right to have a nurse as a half-brother's wife?" Jun wanted to ask, but he didn't.

"If you think you'll be happy with her, I'll be happy for you. Can we meet her sometime soon?" Taku's elephant eyes beamed.

Next Sunday Jun visited them with Sayo. She wore a light-green cotton dress that made her look more plump than she really was. Sayo had three good kimonos and two flowery dresses she had sewn herself for special occasions. But they had been put away since all she wore every day was a nurse's white gown. When she crawled under the rubble and managed to pull them out for this special occasion, they were soiled and torn.

Since there were only two chairs and they were occupied by Taku and Hana, Jun and Sayo sat on a *zabuton* cushion on the floor. As Sayo sat, with legs folded and feet beneath her bottom, her tight skirt slipped up and her bare knees popped out. They looked like two enormous squashes. She pulled down the skirt, bowed her head to the floor and said in a stiff voice, "How do you do? This is Sayo. Very nice to meet you."

Taku stared at her face and said, "Do you know you look like my mother, Sayo-san? She was a very good woman."

"He's very partial to his mother. It means he likes you," Hana said.

It was a good start, Jun thought. Then Kana came into the room with a tea ceremony set. Jun had seen Kana only a few times since he came back from Germany. Even before then, he had not seen Kana as often as her older sisters, Yumi and Tami, because she was much younger and they did not always play together. Actually, Jun had tried to avoid Kana because she was spiteful to him.

Now Kana was nineteen and her nose was still pointing upward. Primly dressed in a black and red kimono, she looked like a perfect woodpecker. Glancing at Sayo's squash knees and bulging thighs with a reproachful frown, she said, with an affected air, "Nice to meet you, Sayo-san. I am Kana. Well, it was so lucky this tea set has survived the earthquake. We need something to make us feel calm in this terrible wasteland and in our sad circumstances, don't we? I have an urge to transcend this sordid reality and feel Karma. Do you know what this teacup is, Sayo-san? This is Imari."

It was a beautiful teacup as big as a soup bowl with exquisite texture and patterns, but Sayo could not tell Imari or Satsuma from anything. She was afraid she was in trouble because she hardly knew what one was supposed to do in a tea ceremony. In her life, Sayo had never had the luxury of drinking tea in a ceremonial fashion. She led such a busy life in the hospital that if she had any time to drink tea, she would pour it from the kettle into a cheap hospital cup and gulp it. No tea ceremony had existed in her childhood when they had lived in poverty.

After she became a nurse, a friend took her to a tea ceremony lesson once, convincing her that she would find serenity and become a civilized woman. She found the ceremony so boring that she almost fell asleep. Her legs went to sleep, too. Every joint of her body hurt for two days from the stress. She certainly had not attained serenity, nor had it made her a civilized woman.

Sayo did not understand why one must make a ritual out of a simple pleasure like drinking tea. There were enough ceremonies in life such as funerals and everyday greetings to bosses and colleagues. For serenity of mind, she would drink as much tea as she liked in the kitchen and take a nap, or go watch sumo.

Kana did the preparation of boiling water in an iron pot, cleaning and wiping the tea bowl in such punctilious fashion that it took an eternity. The whole process was like watching a film in slow motion. Pursing her pouting lips with utmost intensity and moving her long fingers like her mother's with elegant dexterity, Kana scooped dark green tea powder from a lacquered container with a tiny bamboo spoon as thin as an earpick, put it into the bowl, poured boiling water over it with a dainty dipper and whisked it with a fine-feathered bamboo brush. Her fingers holding the brush shook like a spider quivering on his net in the wind.

Sayo had to admit the whole process was a refined art, but found it too time-consuming. Her main attention was paid to her legs folded on the floor that had been squashed and tingled as if stung by hundreds of bees.

Kana presented the bowl to Sayo. In the bottom, green bubbles of water were simmering. Sayo tried to remember how she was supposed to drink it, but her tingling legs paralyzed her brain. Even her left hand started to tingle with nervousness.

Sayo decided to ignore the rules, received the bowl with her right hand and drank it in a gulp to everybody's dismay. Kana stared at her in utter disdain and Taku had a big smile on his face. Hana burst into laughter.

"You obviously don't have manners. I like your boldness, Sayo-san. I'm glad you didn't drop the bowl." Hana kept laughing loudly.

"You did n-nothing w-wrong. Next time, you must hold the bowl with two hands and drink it in three sips," Jun whispered to Sayo, who was on the verge of tears.

"Sayo-san is a nurse. She had no time to drink tea in such a slow fashion," Taku said. "The tea ceremony is for ladies who have nothing better to do."

"Oh, Father." Kana stuck out her nose and said haughtily, "Tea ceremony is an art everybody should appreciate. It makes one a cultured person."

"I'm an uncultured person, then," Taku said. "Because I don't know how to drink it properly either. I enjoy tea, but I drink it the way I like."

"Yes, you are an uncultured person, Father," Kana spoke aloud as if to insinuate the same to Sayo. "Zen monks in the Middle Ages hid from the turmoil of the civil wars and tried to transcend sordid reality by drinking tea in a quiet teahouse. That was how the tea ceremony started. In the time of the earthquake, isn't it the best thing to do to seek solace?"

Hana was bored with Kana's lecturing and changed the subject. "Sayo-san, do you play mah-jong?"

"No, I'm sorry. I don't." Sayo knew Hana liked to play mah-jong.

"Too bad. But I'll teach you how."

"What is your hobby, Sayo-san?" Kana asked.

"Let's see: I can't dance; I can't sing; I can't play piano or *koto;* I can't write poems; I cook a little and I sew well. Oh, yes. I watch sumo and write letters to the wrestlers. And I go to Chaplin films."

Kana frowned, but Hana smiled and said, "They say Chaplin is funny. I like *kabuki* actors, but not sumo wrestlers. Their sagging skin gives me goose pimples."

"Oh, no. Some of them have beautiful skin. Their skin doesn't sag." Sayo was so adamant about defending them that both Hana and Taku laughed.

Jun had a feeling that Hana liked Sayo in spite of her unculturedness. She did not attack Sayo with her usual venom. Had Hana softened a little after all the tragedies? Or did Hana appreciate Sayo's honesty and sense of humor under her clumsiness? Or was she trying to restrain the verbal abuse that had sent Ken and his wife to Nagoya?

Jun did not want Sayo to be tormented by Kana anymore and said they must go. Before they left, Hana said to Jun, "Maybe I'll visit your hospital one of these days, Jun-san. The knee problems I had while you were in Germany are back again. Can you help me?" Jun made an appointment for her and left.

As soon as Sayo came out of the house, she squatted down behind a shrub. "Oh, Jun-san, I'm a disaster," she said and burst into tears. "I'm not good enough to be your wife. I don't belong here. Hana-san and Kana-san look down on me."

"Hana-san liked you," Jun said, pulling her up and kissing her wet cheeks. "You don't know how vicious she can be. This was the nicest I've ever seen her. And you know my father liked you very much. Never mind about Kana-san. She's like that to me, too. We love each other. That's the only thing that counts in the end."

Taku brought Hana to the hospital before the day of the appointment. "This morning she woke up with a high fever, chills and acute pains in every joint of her body. Hana's still mourning for Tami. Her illness was probably triggered by sadness. Can you take good care of her?" Taku asked his son.

Hana was there for ten days. The fever went down, but the pains remained.

"Jun-san, hurry up and cure me. I can't stand staying in this terrible place filled with the smell of the sick and the dead. I'll get sick if I stay here too long," she said, as if she had not been sick already.

"You must stay here a little longer until we determine what you have."

"I know what I have. It is the same problem as before; I have neuralgia."

"Your blood sedimentation rate indicates you have arthritis."

"Arthritis? That's what old women get. I'm only forty-eight."

"Yours is rheumatoid arthritis, not osteoarthritis that older people tend to have."

"When can you cure it?"

"I'm afraid I can't c-cure it."

"What? You kept me in this unpleasant place for ten days and all you've done is switch my illness from neuralgia to arthritis. And you can't cure me. You must be a quack, Jun-san. But if you can't cure me, will I be crippled for life?"

"If you are lucky, it won't be so bad. You might even have remissions. It's a strange disease we don't yet understand. It's like a chimera for us."

"What is a chimera?"

"It's a fire-breathing Greek animal with a lion's head, a goat's body, a tiger's limbs and a snake's tail."

"You are trying to say that I'm a chimera." Hana laughed loudly.

"Your disease is as mysterious as that," Jun smiled, "But we'll try our best to make you feel better. They say acupuncture is good for it."

"What? You went to Germany for three years and learned Chinese medicine?"

"Twenty-five hundred years of Chinese medicine brought good wisdom."

Sayo came in with a smile that lit up the room. She had been tending Hana.

"How do you like your nurse?" Jun asked Hana.

"Oh, she's my best friend," Hana said and beamed. "She is the only person who treats me like a human being in this slaughterhouse. You doctors strip me naked, prick me with needles, steal blood and make me feel like a plucked chicken on a cutting board. Sayo-san cleans me, dresses me, pats me, powders me and treats me like a queen. She tells me funny stories like how Chaplin was so hungry he cooked his old shoestrings and ate them like spaghetti. I'm thinking of stealing her and taking her home with me as my nurse."

"Don't steal her; she is my nurse." Jun smiled.

"When are you going to get married?" Hana asked.

"We'll wait until next year," Jun said.

"Don't put it off because of Tami. She'd have been so happy to have a sister-in-law like Sayo-san. They would have been best friends, Tami and Sayo, chirping together like two birds. So hurry up and marry before Sayo-san runs off with a handsome patient." Jun saw tears shine in Hana's eyes as she talked about Tami.

Jun and Sayo got married in the New Year. They decided to do so while Sayo was still in high favor with Hana, for the wind could change its direction unpredictably. A quiet reception was held because Jun's family was in mourning. They were glad it was that way since Jun was too shy to have a fancy affair and Sayo did not see any point spending time and money on a mere ceremony. They had attended too many funerals after the earthquake. The newlyweds lived in Jun's tiny apartment and were as happy as two clams in a shell.

CHAPTER 8

"Yumi-san. I'm here. Sayo's here. I brought you dried persimmons. Let's have tea together," Sayo called from outside Yumi's house. She called in almost every afternoon at Yumi's since she and Jun had moved to a house two blocks away. Sayo had stopped working at the hospital to take care of her son, Shun, and her mother who had suffered a stroke. Often too bored to stay at home, she made excuses to visit Yumi: to borrow a cup of flour or a few carrots, or to use the sewing machine, because Yumi's was better than hers.

Sayo came into Yumi's kitchen and they drank tea and ate dried fruits, while watching their children play with each other. Yumi had failed to conceive for four years and had had two miscarriages, but she finally had given birth to a healthy boy, Masao, rambunctious and full of mischief. He was two years older than Shun and was bossy, but took good care of his younger cousin who was shy and bookish as his father used to be. Sayo wanted Shun to be more boyish and outgoing like Masao. Yumi wanted Masao to read more books and to be more interested in his schoolwork. Yumi tried to teach English to both boys, but Masao was so restless that she ended up teaching only Shun.

Yumi was fond of Sayo. After she had lost her favorite sister, Tami, and was left with the sour-tongued Kana, she thought God had sent Sayo to her in place of Tami. Sayo was funny and warm-hearted like Tami. She was always ready to help people and knew how, having been a nurse. Yumi did not call a doctor any longer; Sayo solved all the problems, and, if not, Jun was there. Sayo was also clever with her hands and sewed new curtains for Yumi's kitchen.

Despite Yumi's affection for Sayo, a tinge of jealousy stung her from time to time, because of Sayo being Jun's wife. Whenever Sayo mentioned Jun, Yumi listened with special attention even if it was a trivial matter. When Sayo said casually, "Last Sunday Jun-san took us for a boat ride on the Sumida River and we had a lot of fun," or when she showed a little shopping bag and said, "Isn't this lovely? Jun-san bought me this," Yumi felt a touch of envy. She thought of her own marriage and felt sad.

For a while after Yumi married Hisao, she thought the fervent young love she had felt for Jun was a thing of the past. It was a girlish affair and she had decided to draw a curtain on it.

Yumi had thought Hisao was a blessing from God. Bright-eyed, intelligent and engaging, he made a good first impression on her. This time love was open, encouraged and welcomed by everyone. The professional agency that had arranged the *miai* had persuaded Taku and Hana that he was the right man for their daughter. The agency wanted to arrange the match quickly before Yumi started to find faults in him, as she had done with all the other men. Yumi was engaged to Hisao after one date and married after two rendezvous. The agency said they had met twice too often.

But somehow the marriage had not brought happiness as Yumi had wished. She had to live with Hisao's parents since he was their only son. Though they had built a detached house for the young couple, she had to spend a lot of time with her mother-in-law who was critical of Yumi and whatever she did. Hisao's father took a liking to Yumi and defended her whenever she was blamed, but this made his wife jealous and aggravated the situation.

When Yumi wore a kimono with thin green and blue stripes, her father-in-law said, "Yumi-san, those are such refreshing colors. I thought a sweet breeze had come into the room." Later, Yumi overheard her mother-in-law say to her daughter, "That kimono is too flashy for a married woman. Well, she is the child of a geisha, after all."

"Yes, she is. Don't you think her red hairpin is too young-looking, too?" Hisao's sister replied.

Hisao's father fell ill with TB and was bedridden for three years before he died. Yumi was grateful to him for having been kind to her and every day she cooked nutritious foods for him, tofu, vegetable soup, shiitake mushrooms and flounder, hoping he would be better. He was so happy when Yumi came into his room, he started to talk and did not let her leave. As his illness became worse, he even cried when she visited. Although she was fond of him and felt sorry for him, she became wary of keeping company with him every afternoon in a room haunted by germs.

Those were dark years Yumi would rather forget. She was worn down not only by her father-in-law's illness, but also by her mother-in-law and Hisao's constant nagging: "So, are you pregnant?" Yumi heard her mother-in-law refer to her as "a stone woman," meaning "a childless one."

"Yumi is too tense, or it's possible that she has soiled blood, because her mother was a geisha and had too many men." There was never a question whether her son was a stone man. When Yumi finally became pregnant, she had two miscarriages, again because "she was too nervous." Yumi's fairies, angels and elves had long since died, squashed and shriveled in the dark house filled with reproaches and nagging.

Hisao was kind to Yumi in the earlier years of their marriage, but he usually came home late and did not know what Yumi was going through. He did not want to know about trivial happenings at home. When Yumi complained of something about his mother, he said, before Yumi had finished her story, that it was a typical, mean, mother-in-law attitude and Yumi should not take it seriously. Gradually her resentment grew against Hisao who would not listen to her.

Yumi was offended by Hisao's view of her religion. He sounded like Hana. "Don't we already have enough gods without catering to a foreign religion? How can a modern woman like you believe in a virgin birth or the Resurrection?" He did not want Yumi to go to church and said, "Sunday is the only day I'm home. Who is more important, me or Christ? A woman shouldn't have two masters."

Once the relationship soured, Hisao's whole personality began to seem undesirable to Yumi, just as once a perfect peach has a bruise, in no time the whole fruit becomes discolored and rotten.

Hisao was hardworking and ambitious like Yumi's father, but Yumi found her husband lacked the qualities that had made Taku a special man—vision, idealism and a social conscience. A demon in business, obsessed with money and power, Hisao was a tank that would run over anything in his way and had no conscience to check his drive. Hisao might be a great success if luck was with him, while Taku was a Don Quixote who had fallen short of success because of too much idealism. Yumi admired her father for that reason and she could not respect Hisao for trying to be a ruthless winner and a conqueror.

One day, Hisao came home, his face glowing with excitement. He stood behind Yumi, covered her eyes with one hand and thrust something cold and metallic in her back. She shuddered.

"Guess what this is," he said in an animated voice.

"I don't know, but I feel as if the mouth of a rifle or a gun is pushing me," Yumi said, pale and in a trembling voice.

"You've got it," Hisao said, taking his hand off Yumi's eyes and showing a shining rifle. "Isn't this beautiful? This is my company's newest product."

Yumi's chest hurt, as if she had been shot. Hisao had been evasive about what he had been producing at his father's machine tool company that he had inherited. Now Yumi understood why he had been that way.

"Doesn't it bother you that you are making products to kill people?" Yumi said in a hoarse voice, her heart still throbbing from the shock.

"It's business," he said irritably. "I only worry about how to produce arms with the best killing power in the most cost-efficient way. Japan is about to go to war with China again. We need more weapons; I'm doing a service to our country."

"Why do we have to fight with China again?" Yumi asked.

"If we don't take China, the Communists will," Hisao said. "Or America and Britain will. It's better if Asia is united and fights against Western imperialism. Once the whole of Asia unites, we can even beat America."

"Why do you have to beat America?"

"Because we have to revenge ourselves on America. Do you remember how they made a law to prohibit the Chinese and the Japanese from buying land there? My uncle was a dreamer and went to California, believing that America was a land of democracy, a land of freedom and of opportunity. He reclaimed wasteland and bought it with the money he had saved for twelve years. The Americans said he was the yellow peril, took his land away and kicked him out."

"My father went there with some emigrants," Yumi said. "He didn't stay, but the others did and bought land after many years of hard work. Their land was taken, too, and they weren't allowed to become citizens. It was a shame. But then, what have we done in Korea? We took their land and made their people our slaves."

"I don't know anything about what's going on in Korea," Hisao said fretfully.

"Whatever the reason, I wish you wouldn't make murdering machines," Yumi said, with a sigh of despair, knowing it was already too late. "I don't like to be the wife of a man who promotes war." Yumi covered her face with her palms. This was the final blow, adding to the long, pent-up resentment against Hisao. Tears welled up from deep down in her body and gushed out like water in a pond that could not contain any more after a heavy rain. She was mourning the death of her love for Hisao.

Hisao was taken aback by Yumi's emotional response and exasperated by it, thinking that she was after all a woman who used tears as a weapon. He patted her shoulder and said, "Think this way, Yumi, someone must make arms. It's a necessary evil. I'll make a lot of money and make your life easier. You are a beautiful and intelligent woman, but you have too much of your own mind for your own good."

When the long-awaited baby was born, Yumi was grateful God had finally been kind to her. Masao brought so much joy that her heartache about Hisao and his factory, and the problems with her mother-in-law did not seem to matter as much as before. She told her fairy tales to the baby who did not understand a word.

Although Hisao's mother had reproached Yumi for many years for being childless, when Masao was born, she did not like him much. Masao was a baby with a high temper and he disturbed her peace. "The commotion and rumbling coming from your section of the house remind me of that terrible earthquake," she said to Yumi.

As Masao grew older, his mischief did not please his grandmother. One day, a crayfish with long whiskers and fierce scissor-claws that Masao had kept in a basin found itself in his grandmother's bedroom. Her hair bristling with anger, she dashed to the detached house to scream at Masao and Yumi. Instead of screaming, Grandma almost fainted when she found in his room two more crayfish, both of which were about to crawl out of a basin, three beetles with enormous horns, and stinking guinea pigs in a box.

Yumi defended Masao, saying that it was accidental that the crayfish had visited her mother-in-law. But, after she had left, Masao confessed that he had left the creature in front of Grandma's room, because, "She is so nasty to you, Mama."

Although Yumi dared not tell that to her, Grandma's patience had already short-circuited and she told Hisao that either Masao got rid of his collection, or they must move out right away. Hisao, who had not been keen on living with his mother, gladly took the latter option.

How liberated Yumi felt to live in a new house where Masao could let all his animals crawl in the garden, and she could stretch her limbs and the wings of her fairies. She was overjoyed when Jun and Sayo moved into a new house two blocks away.

The two families often spent evenings together. They did so even when Hisao stayed overnight in Kawasaki at his factory, unwilling to waste two hours commuting. The boys played games and everybody talked and sang. It was an innocent family gathering centered around children, but Yumi looked more radiant than usual, her eyes shining and her cheeks rosy.

Yumi knew that Jun was happily married to Sayo; it never occurred to her to steal him. But living in the neighborhood with more occasions to see each other, the old feelings crept back. The smothered embers caught fire and Yumi's body felt warm when she saw his dark eyes gaze at her cheeks, or cast a sidelong glance at her fingers. Yumi felt like a young girl in love.

Jun often brought Yumi books or records he thought she might like. He enjoyed talking about them with her because Sayo preferred Chaplin or sumo to classical music or literature, which she found boring. Yumi felt she shared some secrets with Jun, playing the music or reading the books he had given her. He satisfied the cultural yearnings that Hisao did not fulfill.

When Hisao was home, the two families went on outings together. On an early summer morning, they went to Chiba beach to gather shellfish at low tide. Sayo planned the trip so well that they arrived there at the lowest tide.

"What happened to the sea?" Shun cried out. There was only muddy sand where there was supposed to be water. Far away near the horizon, the silvery water was glimmering under the early morning sun. Shun was convinced a disaster had happened to the sea and was not easily comforted when Jun explained the ebb and flow of the tide and the waxing and waning of the moon.

Watching a seagull soar across the misty sky, Yumi felt like flying, free in a Western dress instead of the usual tight kimono. She breathed in a deep breath of the salty and slightly fishy air and said to Jun, who was walking next to her, "I knew this smell even before I was born, because I was a seagull before this life." Yumi said it with such a serious face that Jun gazed at her and smiled.

"You look like one in your blue dress," he said.

She took her shoes off and walked with bare feet on the wet sand. "Oh, it's heavenly," she said to Jun. "It's like walking on the finest carpet. Why don't you take your shoes off, too, Jun-san?"

He did as she had suggested. "Oh, I love it, too," he said. His feet sank in and out of the sand, splashing mud with each step he took. She remembered seeing him walk with bare feet in her father's house. But what she saw now were a grown man's feet from which bones and blue veins protruded. They were pale, long and masculine.

The waves had carved layers and layers of furrows on the sand as they receded, leaving faint bubbles on their curvy shapes. They were like a lover who, as he left his mistress in the morning, etched the signs of his lovemaking deep in her body. Although Yumi had never made love to Jun, layers of thoughts of love and stories she had written for him had been engraved on her body, as on this sand, she thought.

The sand was dotted with white clams and black mussels that were sticking orange tongues out of their mouths. Small bivalves were crawling in and out of their holes and crabs were scurrying sideways, bubbling like angry men. In no time, each family collected a bucketful of shellfish for dinner. But Masao and Shun kept picking up everything they found; seaweed, pebbles and broken shells.

As Yumi arched her back from too much bending, she saw Shun trip over a rock and ran to rescue him. She almost reached him, when something sharp stabbed her toe, a shard of glass. Instead of helping her nephew, she fell on her knees.

"You take care of Yumi-san and I'll look after Shun," Sayo shouted to her husband and ran to her son who was staggering to his feet.

Jun ran up the beach and came back with his medical bag. He told Yumi to sit on one of the rocks nearby and placed her wounded foot on his folded thighs. The warmth of his thighs was transmitted to her foot like an electric current. He bent down closely to her toe, saying, "I want to make sure no pieces of glass are left in there." Then his skinny fingers carefully patted her toe with cotton wool soaked with iodine. As he finished wrapping her foot with a bandage with professional efficiency, he stood up and said, "Go and rest in a dry place with Shun, Yumi-san."

Yumi and Shun sat on the dry beach, keeping their wounds away from water and sand. She cuddled her nephew in her arms. Shun resisted being treated like a baby, but he giggled. To Yumi he was a miniature Jun.

The sun was already high, suffusing the horizon with golden light. The tide had risen. From where she sat, Yumi could see that water was up to Masao's knees, where it was at his ankles before. They were heading back to the beach, Sayo and Masao hopping and splashing water and Hisao and Jun wading slowly, talking to each other. It was a happy day.

That night, when Yumi was half asleep in bed, she saw herself sitting on a beach. Jun came wading through water toward her. All of a sudden, a big blue wave swallowed her, the sky, the sea, Jun and all. Millions of water bubbles flooded her eyes and she was drowned under the deep ultramarine blue. As she struggled to surface above the water, Jun came to rescue her and she was tangled up with him.

After a time, she found herself on the sand, drenched with sunlight. Next to her was Jun, lying on the sand, his eyes dreamy, his cheeks wet and rosy. As they watched the innumerable bubbles slowly soak into the sand, another wave attacked and she was knotted with him again, laughing and panting, until they were thrown back on the sand again.

Yumi spent more time now not only with Jun's family but also with her own parents. She found Hana's open explosions more refreshing than her mother-in-law's nagging and backbiting. Hana was as ferocious as ever, but the sorrow of losing Tami and debilitating arthritis had somewhat diluted her venom. She was facing her own vulnerability. Yumi found her mother more human and felt closer to her than before.

Yumi remembered the day Taku gave Hana a walking stick out of his collection, since her knees hurt and she wobbled. Hana thought it an insult and said to Taku, "You are trying to humiliate me. This is a symbol of old age. I used to stand like a flamingo on one leg. How would a flamingo feel if she stood on three legs?" She threw it on the ground and then faltered. She would have fallen if Taku and Yumi had not caught her.

Taku picked up the stick and gave it back to her, saying, "It looks nice on you. It's a good weapon to hit a ruffian with. Look at all the pictures of English gentlemen. Look at me and my colleagues. Every man has one. It's a status symbol. We could walk together like an old couple now."

"It's no status symbol for a woman; I don't want to be mistaken for an old man," Hana snapped.

She looked into the mirror and said, "Not only my illness but also my age is catching up with me. Oh, Taku-san, I'm no longer a beautiful young woman. I have wrinkles, gray hair and my skin isn't as supple as it used to be."

"You are still a nice-looking woman, Hana."

"What? Only 'a nice-looking woman'? I'm not beautiful or stunning, but only 'nice-looking'?" Hana let out an outraged howl.

"No, no. You are still a beautiful woman."

"What do you mean, 'still'? You mean I'm over the hill, but 'still'?"

Taku threw his arms up and sighed.

The next day Taku came home with tickets for *kabuki,* hoping that would cheer her up. Hana looked forward to going to the theater. She stayed in bed till late in the morning that day so that she would look her best in the evening, for she had discovered that the two wrinkles she had acquired under her eyes would disappear and her joints did not hurt so badly after a good rest.

Looking chic in a blue and silver crèpe kimono, Hana left for the theater happily. Her knees hurt and she wobbled, but she refused to take a stick and walked hanging on Taku's arm. The theater was filled with beautiful people, but Hana was sure she was still the most beautiful one. She enjoyed the sudden halt and hushed silence she caused among the passers-by.

Then she noticed their eyes invariably shifted from her face to her wobbling knees. They watched her stumble in pity. She heard a woman whisper to her companion, "She may be beautiful, but she walks like a duck."

Hora and Mariko said, "Poor Hana-san, what happened to your legs? They must be hurting." They had forgotten to mention how stunning she looked.

It was utter humiliation. Hana did not want to be an object of pity. But it came home to her that she was now only a wounded peacock. Or a duck. She was defective: a beautiful but flawed piece, like a prized antique depreciated because of a crack; a thoroughbred horse put away because of a limp; a bird who cannot soar into the sky because of an injured wing.

"My days are over," Hana said to Taku.

"Cheer up, Hana. Nobody is young forever," Taku said.

It took a long time for Hana to admit that. When it had finally sunk in, she asked herself, What can I live for if I can't live for my beauty?

One day Hana said, her eyes having regained the old glitter, "I've found something permanent to live for, Taku-san. This could give joy to myself as well as to others, as my beauty used to. Guess what? I'll make a garden, an eternal garden that rejuvenates itself. Rather a collection of gardens: a rock garden, a moss garden, a mound, a maze, a flower garden, a topiary garden, a foliage garden, a pine forest and a bamboo forest. I'll make a stream flow among the gardens and let *koi* carp, ducks and swans swim. The gardens will outlive me and be my eternal symbol. I'd love to collect antiques again, but they'll burn. I could collect men, but they get old, stupid and boring. I'll find a new life in a timeless arboretum."

Taku opened up his small eyes and beamed. "What a good idea, Hana. You can use all the insurance money that we are finally getting, and some more."

"Let me be in charge of the whole project because you are too busy building poor people's apartments, Taku-san. Since we have no children living with us except Kana, who I hope will marry away soon, we don't need a big house any longer. I hate this Western box, but I must admit it's good to live with chairs since it hurts my knees to squat on *tatami* floors. So, we'll just add a teahouse that will look like the Silver Pavilion in Kyoto, and in the rest of the empty plot I'll make gardens."

"I look forward to enjoying your gardens, Hana." For the first time in years, Taku and Hana were in perfect agreement.

Hana made a blueprint of the house and gardens. She hired builders to make a teahouse. She invited various master gardeners, told them her ideas and listened to their proposals. She sat outside on a wicker chair and ordered workmen to do this and that, flourishing her stick. She thrived on watching men sweat and toil, carrying rocks, digging holes and crawling on the soil like slaves.

She exploited not only the gardeners, but the entire family. Each time Yumi or Jun's family visited, Hana would say, "Yumi, pluck that giant thistle there. Jun, can you move that rock forty-five degrees toward me? O-oh, you messed up the sand, Jun. You must comb it back with a rake. Oh, that terrible bird shit on the stone. Can you remove it, Sayo? Masao, kill that slimy worm there, and Shun, pour salt over that slug and let it melt."

Masao rebelled. "I won't kill worms. They are good for the soil, Grandma." The rest made faces at each other behind her, but they did what they were told.

Taku, who had been happy at the thought that the gardens would not be as costly as a big house, was astounded by the huge bills arriving from the various gardeners. He complained to Hana one day, "You can sell antiques, but you can't sell gardens. All the money is down the drain with each pebble you put in the stream."

Hana just smiled and said, "You and your descendants will get priceless pleasure out of my gardens."

When the initial work was completed, Hana invited families and friends for a garden party and guided them through her arboretum, saying, "I don't expect to go to heaven after I die, but this is my heaven on earth." Though the shrubs and trees were still young, the fountain too new and the stones not yet covered by moss, the place was indeed heavenly. As the guests strolled the meandering pathways along the stream, a new scene at each turn surprised them like a new page in a fairy-tale book.

"Hana-san," Hora said, "you should name this rock, 'Taku Rock.' When Taku meditates, he's as boring as this rock."

Yumi suggested, "Let's call this English garden 'Tami Garden.' She'll watch flowers from heaven all year round."

"Mother, this is almost as elegant as the new dam my company has built," Ken said, looking at a miniature waterfall.

The guests laughed when they found in the topiary garden caricatures of Taku made out of dozens of potatoes and of Hana made out of peacock feathers.

One day Kana said to her parents at dinner, "While you were preoccupied with your arboretum, I've found a wonderful man to marry."

Hana looked at her daughter with cautious curiosity. "What kind of a man is he? Did you pick up a stranger from a terraced house like Jun-san, after you turned down all the nice candidates we had introduced to you?"

"But you love Sayo very much, Hana," Taku said, and turned to Kana. "Anyway, what kind of a man is he, Kana?"

"I'm no Jun-san. A sensible woman like me wouldn't pick a man from a terraced house. His name is Isamu Kato. He has just finished the Army Officer's School and is already a second lieutenant," Kana said. Then she put her fingers under the layers of the *obi* binding her chest and took out a photo of a young man in army uniform. Showing it off, with her nose up, Kana said proudly, "Isn't he handsome? His nose is as straight as a pencil. His eyes as big and black as a goldfish's."

Hana received the picture and said, "Oh, my. This photo is melting with your body heat, Kana. He looks handsome, but every man looks handsome in a soldier's outfit. That's about the only good thing about soldiers. What possessed you to fall in love with a professional killer, Kana?"

"Mother, soldiers are peacekeepers. They are heroes who secure peace and prove the strength of the great Japanese Empire to the world."

"You sound very right-wing, Kana." Taku's thin eyes blinked.

"Isamu-san's father is a lieutenant general and a very influential man," Kana said proudly. "He's a close associate of Prime Minister Tanaka, Father."

"A close associate of Prime Minister Tanaka? That's bad news. You shouldn't marry such a man's son, Kana." Taku grimaced, wrinkling up his pocks.

"My goodness, Father. I thought you would be understanding about a love marriage. You were so generous about Jun-san's marriage to a lowly nurse; you can't order me not to marry a bright man from a prominent family just because his father happens to be a friend of somebody you don't like. Particularly when that somebody is the head of your political party and the prime minister."

"He became the head of our party because he brought in lots of money. I never wanted an army man to take over our party. Military men tend to disregard democratic processes. But, worst of all, there's a good reason to be suspicious about the money he has brought to buy up power."

"Even if there is a reason to be suspicious about Prime Minister Tanaka, it has nothing to do with Isamu-san's father."

"I hope that's the case, but close associates share secrets. Who keeps company with a wolf will learn to howl."

"I'll never change my mind about my man no matter what you say. He's crazy about me. And I'm crazy about him. Can I invite Isamu-san on Sunday?"

On Sunday Isamu came into the foyer and stood to attention, straight as a T-square in a khaki uniform, his goldfish eyes and pencil nose pinched with nervousness. When Hana came out to greet him, he still remained like a wooden soldier.

Hana laughed and said, "Well, well, Isamu-san, nice to meet you, but you've been in the army school too long. Is it beneath an army man's pride to bow to a woman? Is your uniform so stiff that you can't bend? Are you afraid of wrinkling it?"

Isamu turned pale under the brim of the cap and bent his head forward to bow clumsily like a block of wood. Kana, standing behind him, cried out in a rescue attempt, "Mother, what kind of a welcome is that for a future son-in-law? He didn't know whether to salute or bow to a lady. Right, Isamu-san? He was taught by the army that making a mistake is death, so he had to think for a minute."

"You have no chance of survival in a war if it takes a minute to make a trivial decision," Hana said.

"Yes, madam. Army discipline has trained one to tolerate verbal abuse." So saying, Isamu abruptly stopped talking and stood at salute as he saw Taku coming. Taku copied Isamu's salute, raising his shriveled old hand to his wrinkled cheek.

"Taku-san," Hana said with a smile, "it's very becoming for you to salute in your defenseless cotton kimono. You've been a brave old soldier all your life. Pathetic and vulnerable, but it's exactly you."

Taku was so shocked to hear Hana praise him even in a measured way that he adjusted his glasses on his dented nose to see better if something was wrong with her.

"Thank you, my dear. I take it as a heartfelt compliment. This is the best comment I've received from my wife in many years, Isamu-san. She isn't always as sweet as this, as you've already noticed, but there's hope for you."

Isamu smiled for the first time. His smile revealed a timid but good-natured boy concealed under the awkward automaton of a soldier.

Hana led everybody to the new teahouse that looked out on a garden with rocks and a pond full of *koi* carp. Hana talked about the garden, expecting words of praise from Isamu. But he sat fearfully and responded to her as briefly as possible so as not to be chided by her again, saying, "Is that so, madam?" or "That's lovely, madam."

Taku changed the subject and asked, "The army is invading China, but isn't it a mistake? China is a huge country. We won't win so easily."

"We have a mission to defeat Chang Kai-shek and the Communists in China. The Emperor is behind us. We'll win," Isamu replied, his face rigid again.

Taku breathed heavily and stopped talking. Nobody talked anymore and Isamu left soon.

"He's an Imperial Army puppet," Taku sighed.

"But he's right: we have to fight against Communism," Kana said.

"He's a stone head. A rock in my garden is ten times more interesting than he is. I'm not sure if he's good enough for you, Kana," Hana said.

"No matter what you say, my mind has been made up," Kana said.

Both Taku and Hana knew it would be as difficult to change Kana's mind as to tell a woodpecker not to peck. Three months later, Kana married Isamu. The wedding was a grand affair at Kana's behest.

Isamu's father and his guests came in army uniform, decorated with glittering medals. Clad in white gloves, a white uniform with a long sword at his waist and a gold-rimmed white cap with a feather sticking up, Isamu stood shyly next to his bride, who was looking as prim as a splendid woodpecker in a red and black kimono with chrysanthemums embroidered in gold. Her eyes shone with excitement and her pointed nose stuck high with pride.

That night, Hana had a temporary remission of the pain in her knees and she walked as elegantly as a peacock again. In her silvery ceremonial kimono she was as beautiful as she used to be, or even more so with the added dignity of age.

Prime Minister Tanaka, who had dropped in between other parties for a whirlwind of bowing, shoulder patting and glad-handing, came to a sudden halt in front of Hana. Looking Hana up and down and all over, he said with his heavy Kyushu drawl, "Taku-san. Many congratulations, not only on today's happy event, but also for such a precious pearl of a wife you have.

Aren't you a lucky man? We would've been better friends if I had known you had such an absolute jewel of a wife. Well, of course, it's not too late. Let's be good friends again, Taku-san." He smiled jovially at Taku and bowed many times to Hana, beaming his admiration at her between bows.

"It's too late for me, but it depends on what your administration will do for the country. I'm cautiously pessimistic," Taku said bluntly.

"Oh, don't be so critical, Taku-san." Tanaka patted Taku on the shoulder, sneaked a wink at Hana and rushed into the crowd.

After the reception, Hana invited the family to her teahouse. This was the rare occasion in which the whole family was gathered in one place. Kana was not happy since the men of the family had forgotten who was the star of the day and talked more about politics than about the wedding.

"I thought Prime Minister Tanaka made an aggressive speech," Hisao said to Isamu. "Does he really want to colonize Manchuria, Isamu-san?"

"He thinks it's our mission to do so. We are a special country governed by a living god and destined to rule and protect all of Asia." The Imperial Army puppet was speaking again.

Listening to their conversation, Sayo interrupted, with a look of childlike innocence, "Isamu-san, I'm sorry to ask you a naïve question, but I wonder if you really mean that the Emperor is a god? Maybe I am not allowed to ask such a disquieting question, but it has been bothering me for a long time."

Jun pulled the sleeve of Sayo's kimono at her back, but it was too late.

Isamu stared at Sayo in shock. He said, his face blushing red with rage, "Indeed, you aren't allowed to ask such a blasphemous question, Sayo-san. The history books tell us that the Emperor's family were the direct descendants of the sun goddess, Amaterasu, who originally created the nation."

"Beware of the new law of the Tanaka government, Sayo-san,"

Hisao said. "If the authorities hear you talk like that, you'll be put in prison. His new law will wipe out anarchists, communists, socialists and dissidents."

Hana was sympathetic to Sayo. "Sayo meant no harm. It's a question everybody hides inside and doesn't dare ask."

Yumi turned to Sayo's rescue, too. "From a Christian's point of view, it may be blasphemous to say there's more than one God."

"Yumi." Thunder fell from Hisao. "Mind your tongue. Christians aren't loved by the authorities either." Yumi pursed her lips and lowered her face.

"Why has this country become a place where one is not allowed to say what one thinks or believes?" Jun said, feeling sorry for both Sayo and Yumi.

Taku nodded and said, "When I was young, this country—"

"Oh, please, Father. Always 'when I was young.' Now all of you are ruining my wedding day." Kana stood up, pulling Isamu's hand. "Let's go to our new home, Isamu-san. We must leave early for our honeymoon tomorrow."

On the way home, Sayo asked Jun, "Does Isamu-san really believe that the Emperor is a god? I remember some of the socialists used to laugh at the idea."

"He sounds like it," Jun said. "The army has adopted the German method of propaganda. They tell you the same thing a hundred times and you believe it. If you say you don't believe it, you'll be punished. Fear keeps people silent. Sayo, you tend to be outspoken, which is a good quality, but be careful of what you say in this political climate. Think of your friends, Fumiko and her husband, who were sentenced to death for having said that they had contemplated killing the Emperor."

"Poor Fumiko. I keep thinking about her," Sayo said. Fumiko had hanged herself ten days after she had been pardoned.

Soon after this, Taku lost the election for the Diet for the first time in thirty-six years. His political opponent, an extreme right-winger, accused Taku of being unpatriotic, citing his speeches deploring the direction in which the country was heading and his voting record against the increase of military budgets.

Not only was his political career over, but his latest venture was hit by the Great Depression in America that invaded Japan like a tsunami. By the time he paid off his debts, he had little money left.

Taku apologized to Hana for having lost his fortune. He sat on the floor in front of her and was braced for a thunderstorm. Hana's face was pale, but surprisingly serene. Her eyes did not have the raging glare he had expected. "We lost most of our possessions in the earthquake, and that was nothing compared with Tami's life," Hana said calmly. "We don't need much money now, since we can't take it to our graves anyway. Well, I still have my garden. The money tree has lost its fruit, but all the other trees are growing."

Taku opened his small eyes as wide as he could to see whether Hana was the same woman who had been called the Ice Queen of the North Pole. Did ice melt and the queen blossom into an all-forgiving goddess? He had often been bewitched by Hana's beauty or wit, but this was the first time he had been charmed by her generosity of spirit. "You never cease to surprise me, Hana. Thank you for being so understanding," Taku said, so touched that his eyes started to blur.

"Don't get carried away, Taku-san. I'm no saint," Hana said and laughed. "I won't suddenly turn into a goddess of frugality. I'll go on living like the proud rich woman I deserve to be. All I'm saying is that I have everything, and don't need much money to live on. I've already acquired dignity and I don't have to earn it by buying another ring."

Taku and Hana got on better with less money.

One day, Isamu came to see Taku and stood like a wooden soldier, both hands straight down at his sides. He declared solemnly to Taku, "I came to report to you that the army has posted me to China. This is the first time my training is to be put to the test."

"How long will you be gone, Isamu?" Taku asked, looking worriedly at Kana, who stood near her husband looking anxious.

"It won't be long. We'll beat them quickly. They are only Chinese."

"How do you know it'll be easy, Isamu-san?" Kana said.

"Don't worry about it. I'll be back soon," Isamu assured Kana.

"It may not be so easy. Take care of yourself," Taku said in a resigned voice.

After Isamu left, Taku shook his head and said to Hana, "They colonized Korea and Manchuria, now they are trying to conquer China. Isamu so believes the army propaganda that he thinks it'll be easy."

Yumi and Sayo accompanied Kana to the station with their sons to see Isamu off to war. "Poor Kana will be lonely. She has no baby yet after three years of marriage," Yumi said to Sayo.

At the station, the departing soldiers in khaki uniforms stood in files on the platform. They looked exactly alike, with their faces half hidden by the visors of their caps. An important-looking man stood in front of them, raising his arms and shouting, "*Banzai!*" three times.

A young soldier stepped forward and raised his right hand to salute. Yuki and Sayo could not tell who he was, but Kana cried out, "Isamu-san." Whether Isamu heard Kana or not, he did not look in the direction of the voice. He turned his heels from left to right awkwardly like a toy man worked by a spring, all the while giving an honorable salute to everyone, with his right hand seemingly nailed to his car.

Then he stopped, stuck out his chest and opened his mouth so wide that his face looked torn, a burning tongue showing from the gaping hole. He roared in a thunderous voice, "We will beat the Chinese. We will spread the Emperor's message and come back for a victory march."

A big cheer rose from the crowd. Yumi whispered to Sayo, "Don't pout, Sayo-san. Put on a patriotic face. I know the socialists are against the war; the Christians are, too. But we must cheer up Kana."

"Of course, I'm a patriot. Hooray for Isamu-san," Sayo shouted loudly.

They sang military songs with the rest of the crowd, waving the rising sun flags they had made with paper and chopsticks, as the heavy door of the train opened and swallowed the soldiers into the dark hole that would take them to a faraway land. Inevitably, some of them would not come out of the door of the returning train.

"Didn't Isamu-san look brave, Masao and Shun? I'm so proud of him," Kana said, sticking up her nose.

Masao nodded and said, "He was a shining model of a soldier." Shun nodded, hesitantly.

After Isamu had gone to war in China, along with thousands of drafted men, Kana went back to her parents to live in the teahouse.

She irked Hana with her preaching. "Mother, do you know that luxury is our biggest enemy? You are wearing an expensive silk kimono. In order to win the war, we must change our attitude. We must be frugal."

"Kana, I never asked my country to start a war. Conquer China to make her a colony? A stupendous idea like adding an elephant as a tail to a monkey. I bet nothing good will come out of provoking an elephant. The war is the biggest waste. If you don't like luxury, stop fighting," Hana said with defiance.

Tired of arguing with Hana, Kana went out and joined a women's group organized to support the war effort on the home front. Most of the women there had husbands who had gone to war. They were lonely and talked about their husbands, while making food parcels together, with pickled plums, seaweed, tins of sardines and tuna.

One of them asked, "How often does your husband write to you? Mine only writes to me once a week."

"You should be happy: mine writes to me once in two weeks," another said.

"Mine writes to me twice a week," Kana bragged proudly, although it was not true. At first Isamu wrote often, but lately less and less.

Then they gossiped about a wife who had taken a lover in her husband's absence. It made Kana indignant. She stood up and made a big speech. "It is the duty of the wives to be absolutely faithful in our minds and bodies to our husbands on the front line. Let us be vigilant so that nothing like adultery will ever happen. Anybody found guilty must receive a reprimand." It was the epitome of Woodpecker Kana.

"Isn't that infringing on private life?" Some women voiced doubts.

"This is a special time," Kana argued passionately. "Husbands are not here to watch their wives; we must save our poor husbands who are dying for our country from being cheated."

So the next meeting became a censoring session. One member said she saw a neighbor who had gone out the previous Saturday evening with a suspicious-looking man. Another saw a friend walking, with heavy makeup and with a fancy hairdo, wearing a dress that looked too provocative for a woman on the home front.

Kana was a self-appointed judge. She said that the first woman had to be watched carefully and that the second must be advised to wear something more suitable, which meant to wear something gray and drab.

Kana made more enemies than friends. People nicknamed her the "Secret Police." At the third meeting, they voted not to continue the tattletale practice.

One day, Kana received a notice from the army informing her that Isamu was back at the army hospital in Yokohama because of an injury he had suffered to his knee. The news made Kana worried and excited at the same time. She would finally see

Isamu after a year and two months. No matter how serious the injury, she would cure him with love and devotion. Kana went to visit him right away.

Isamu was in bed in a room with five other wounded men. His leg was bundled up and hung from the ceiling. He looked tanned, but gaunt and weary. Hollows were carved under his eyes and their former intense glow was missing. How could a man change so much in a year and two months?

He stared at Kana from head to toe and said, "You are wearing a fancy dress. You look sexy in it, Kana." He winked at her with a lewd smile, as if he were a shameless man in the street. Kana was shocked because she had never known him to be salacious. It was understandable that Isamu desired her, coming back from a long campaign, but she wanted him to be romantic and passionate about her as he used to be before he went to war, just as he had been about the mission of the war. He had been as loyal to Kana as he had been to the Emperor. Isamu had been like a young tree, shining bright and green; now the tree looked sick and smelled of decay, leaves wilting and yellowed.

Tears of joy that flowed at the first sight of him froze on her cheeks. But maybe Isamu was bashful about expressing his feelings in front of the five other soldiers. It must be unmanly for an army man to show emotions.

Kana asked gently, "How's your leg, Isamu-san? Does it hurt badly?"

Isamu's lips did not move. It was as if they had been sealed with lead. Kana kept asking, "What happened to it? Will it heal completely, or will it leave any problems?"

Isamu finally opened his heavy mouth. "I was hit in a skirmish. It isn't too bad. They say it'll heal soon and I can go back again. It's too bad. I should've been hit badly and permanently crippled, so that I wouldn't have to go back."

Kana was surprised at his cynical tone of voice. She wanted to know more about his leg, about the war and about the life he had been leading.

"It's boring for you; it's not worth talking about. I'm too tired now even to think about it," he said wearily and yawned.

So Kana talked about her family and about what she had been doing. Isamu snickered cynically when she talked about the club she had run.

Isamu might be lethargic from fatigue. So Kana left, promising to return soon.

The next time she visited, the curtain was drawn between the door and the beds. Kana thought the sick men were changing or being cleaned. She sat on a bench near the door and waited. She overheard them talking.

"Do you know how easy it was? When I went into this farmhouse, there was this Chinese woman all alone. I pushed her to a corner at gunpoint. She was so shaken that she fell into my arms like a hot cake. I felt guilty afterwards, but after a few times I was addicted to it. I did the same thing in every village I went to."

"Yeah, the first time I got frightened when a woman fainted just at the sight of me with a sword. But it made things really easy. I felt sick later, but I got used to it."

"When we were stationed near a mountain, I went down to a creek to get water." This was Isamu's voice. "There was a pretty girl doing her washing. I smiled at her and she smiled at me. She must've liked me. She didn't refuse me at all. We met each other every day while I was there. Too bad it was only five days."

"Ho, ho, ho. What a romance. But I bet you it won't happen again. The word has spread and they hate us so much that they try to kick you and bite you."

Kana stood up, rushed out the door, discarded the flowers, the *sushi* and the sweets she had brought for Isamu in a bin and ran as fast as possible to get away from the place. She did not remember how she got home, but she found herself back in the teahouse and collapsed on the floor, crying. So was this the holy war? What a farce it was that Kana had been on vigilant watch to keep herself and other wives faithful while their husbands were raping women left and right.

Kana did not want to visit Isamu again. She was so enraged that she wanted to shut his image out of her eyes and mind. She did the tea ceremony for herself in order to calm down. She used to feel peaceful sitting in the quiet tearoom, listening to the sound of boiling water and whisking green tea to fine bubbles. But the sound of water, normally so comforting, turned into the torrent of the creek in China and in front of her eyes was a young girl smiling at Isamu.

After several days of silence, Isamu phoned Kana and asked why she was not visiting him any longer. "The other day I came to see you and I overheard an unpleasant conversation from behind the curtain," she said, her voice suppressing anger.

"What unpleasant conversation?" Isamu asked, but Kana did not answer.

"I'll be allowed to come home soon," he said in a hoarse voice. "I'll explain things better there."

Isamu returned to the teahouse on crutches. Kana did not talk to him. There was a long silence between them. After a while, he opened his leaden mouth. "I don't know what you overheard. If something I said hurt you, I'm sorry. War is a terrible thing. Life is so unbearably lonely there. And it's a dog-eat-dog world where you might be killed any day. What you heard was soldiers' talk. We brag and entertain each other because there's nothing else to do."

"So did you love the girl who had fallen in love with you?"

"Which one?"

"The girl you found by the creek; the one doing the washing."

"I liked her. But I'll never see her again."

"Did you rape many women?" Kana said in a throaty voice.

"Three. I don't know why I raped them. I suppose I was lonely. It was all a passing event and didn't mean anything," he said, his eyes as gray as the winter sky.

Kana crouched on the floor and sobbed. Between the sobs, she asked, "Oh, what happened to the romantic and idealistic Isamu-san I used to know, fanatically devoted to the nation and to me?" Isamu stayed silent, tears trickling down his cheeks.

"So is this a sacred war?" Kana asked, still weeping, but in the harsh tone of a prosecutor.

Isamu burst out crying as if the hard shell that had been tightly shut had cracked open and a soft, naked heart had oozed out.

After a while he stopped crying and said, uttering words like a sick man vomiting, "Nothing sacred about it. It was the hardest revelation I had to face over there. The army deceived me. They are devils. I sold my soul to devils. A holy war for the Emperor? No. It's a dirty, brutal, interminable war. Why are we fighting? Why are we killing each other and innocent villagers?"

"Do you have to go back again?"

"As soon as my leg is better."

"Are you going to rape women again?" Kana asked, her voice trembling.

He thought for a while and said, "Probably not. Not only for your sake, but for my own sanity. I've been haunted by the women I raped. Every time I close my eyes, I see their eyes glaring at me with hatred and their cheeks twitching with shame. They called me, 'Don Yan Gguei.' Do you know what it means? 'Devil from the East.' I don't want any women to hate me as much as to call me devil, bite me, spit at me and curse at me."

Then, Isamu gazed at Kana for a long time. Tears brimmed in his eyes again. "Do you know, Kana," he said, "I love you? You don't know how much I thought about you, sitting in the trenches, walking endlessly in the mud and hiding in the bushes. Reality was so sordid I felt like a beast and started to behave like one. I'm sorry, Kana. I'll promise to behave myself for your sake."

Isamu looked at Kana with loving eyes and tried to hug her,

but she flinched. She was not sure she could forgive him. His eyes sank in despair.

After a while Kana felt sorry for him. The war had soiled him. But at least he was honest. Under the muddied skin, she could sense the unspoiled Isamu crying in despair, longing for love. It was the war or the army she should blame. Not him. Maybe she should forgive him this time. She kissed him and they became lovers again. Color came back to his cheeks and light back into his eyes.

As his knee healed, he wanted to walk with Kana around the neighborhood. They visited a small museum five blocks away, sat on a stone step and fed soybeans to the pigeons. Isamu was as proud as a child when a pigeon perched on his palm. "Look, Kana, he likes me. How nice to make friends rather than enemies and kill each other," he said, gazing at the bird's eye, his own brimming with tears.

They climbed the stone steps that led to the museum hall where giant statues of a benign Buddha and Satan Emma of the Hell Empire stood side by side. The dark bronze Satan was exploding with rage. His eyeballs were popping out, the mouth roaring and spouting venom, the jagged teeth ready to bite like a shark's, and the pumped-up muscles steaming with hatred.

"Don't you think this Satan Emma is far more exciting than the pale, effeminate Buddha next to him, Kana? The sculptor who carved the Satan was more successful stirring emotion in a viewer, even if it's a diabolic emotion. Or am I doomed to be captivated by Satan who will take me to hell? When I was a child, my father read a description of hell from a Buddhist book and said, 'If you are a bad boy, that is, if you are dishonest, unkind, lazy, stingy, call others names or act with malicious intent, Satan Emma will cut off your tongue and send you to his hell Empire after you die.' I tried very hard to be a good boy, but I've been sent to hell even while I'm alive. The war in China is worse than the hell my father described to me."

"What is hell like according to the Buddhist book?" Kana asked.

"At hell's gate, the guard pierces you through with a skewer and throws you on a burning fire. Or you'll be put into a pot and cooked, bobbing up and down, in boiling lava. After you are cooked, he picks you up and pounds you with a hammer. Then you'll be taken to the abyss that is stretched to eternity, until you reach the stinking River Vetarani. You have to cross the river, the ripples of which are made of razor blades. On the other side of the river, wild dogs and foxes devour you. Hawks and other birds peck at you," Isamu said, smiling as if he was amused by his own story. "I'll skip the worst part because you look bored, Kana. But no matter how you repent, there's no escape from this hell. The number of years you must stay there are as many as the sesame seeds on a cart. According to the wise man who counted them, it was five thousand trillion and twelve hundred times ten million years."

"Is the war in China worse than this hell?" Kana asked.

"Definitely," Isamu said and stopped talking.

As the day neared when he had to go back to war, he slipped back into his dark mood, his eyes gray and cheeks haggard. One afternoon when they were strolling in Hana's garden, Isamu sat on a bench under a bamboo bush and bent his head on his lap, covering his face with his hands. Implored by Kana, he talked about the real hell he had been in, which was worse than the Buddhist hell.

"I was assigned to be a prison guard at the place where we had trained. A sixteen-year-old boy, Wang Sho-yin, had been kept there. He was a Communist guerrilla who, like the other captives, fought to protect his village. He was just a peasant's son, no soldier. He had such innocent eyes that I couldn't bear the thought of him being used for target practice. My fellow guard said that he would probably be saved because he was a minor. I was glad.

"In the night, I stood with my bayonet in my hand and

watched as Wang slept leaning on the wall, with his hands tied behind his back. In the middle of the night, he woke up and wept, letting his tears stream down his cheeks. He whispered, '*Muchin.*' It means mother. He wept until no more water was left in him.

"Before I left next morning, I picked up a rice cracker I had in my pocket. I opened the wrapping and brought it to his mouth. He opened his mouth and accepted it without resisting. When our eyes met, his sad eyes gleamed.

"In the afternoon, we marched in ranks outside, all armed for a drill. When we halted, I saw Wang in front of us lining up with several older captives. My heart stopped and I had a terrible foreboding. My friend was told to dig a hole in the ground and put a stake in it. Wang was bound to the stake. I averted my eyes and looked at the sky. Cotton-wool clouds looked like big teardrops. Heaven was crying.

"'Attention. Second Lieutenant Isamu Kato. Step forward,' the commander called.

"'Yes, sir,' I popped forward like a shocked toy.

"'You are the first one. Remember, if you can't carry out your task, you'll get the same punishment you received the other day. The target is the boy.' The commander's eyes glared at me. I couldn't kill the target the last time and I was thrown on the ground, kicked and pounded by his boots.

"'Charge. Go.'

"I kicked the earth, my bayonet in my arm. Growling like a bull, I ran toward Wang. Just when I lifted my arm with the gun, I heard the saddest voice seep through Wang's mouth, '*Muchin.*'

"My feet froze and I collapsed on the ground. The boots kicked and thumped my back, hips and my helmet, until my whole body became numb.

"'Stand up, coward,' the devil shouted.

"When I stood up and looked at Wang, his eyes were gazing at me, the sad eyes that had shed streams of tears the night before. I burst out crying. Wang closed his eyes.

"'Ready. Charge!' the devil screeched.

"I dashed to Wang with tears splashing all over. Like a heartless bull I pierced young Wang's chest. His head nodded forward without even a cry."

Isamu nodded his head forward as if acting out the boy's death and wept until the afternoon passed into dark evening.

CHAPTER 9

Taku got up with the first rooster's crow as he had done all his life. As soon as he washed his face in cold water, he was wide awake and his head clear. He put on a blue cotton kimono and went out for a walk. The town was still asleep and shrouded in mist. Except for the sound of his cane and slightly uneven footsteps, all he could hear were early birds chirping.

Recently a pain had developed in his left leg, but this morning it was worse than ever before and by the time he walked nine blocks to the Shomanji temple, he was limping badly. So far he had not told anybody about the pain. If he did, Jun would insist on examining it. Whatever it turned out to be, he would likely tell Taku not to walk so much. For Taku, walking was his lifeline. He had a dozen unfinished works and another dozen new ideas to carry out, and nothing would be accomplished if he could not walk, except maybe for writing books and his memoirs that were among his two dozen items. But being an activist, writing came last on his list. "I'm only seventy-eight. It's too early to retire to a chair," he snorted, enraging Hana who, sixteen years younger than he, had trouble walking.

He arrived at the temple, but he paused at the gate. There were fourteen stone steps to climb to the altar. He used to run up all of them in one breath. This morning they looked like Mount Fuji. He sat down on the bottom step and waited for the pain to go away. A few minutes later it was still there. Impatiently he stood up and climbed the steps slowly. Patience was a waste of time even in his old age.

Taku bowed to the familiar face of the benign Buddha on the altar. Every morning he came here and prayed for every member of his family. While he was grateful most of his family were doing well, Taku's heart ached with anguish as the faces of Kana and Isamu appeared before his eyes. He prayed fervently for them.

Isamu had been stationed off-and-on in China since 1932 where there was almost constant war. Each time he returned, either on leave after campaigns, or for recuperation from injuries, he looked more and more tormented.

When Taku met Isamu for the first time, he was the perfect specimen of a military education—rigid, patriotic, and ready to die for the Emperor's horse. Behind the façade though, Isamu looked vulnerable and fragile as if he were made of thin glass. Each time he returned, he seemed less and less like the shining hope of the army. The glass had been chipped and a naked, wounded man with a frail soul revealed within.

Kana had also been torn to pieces. Before her husband went to war, the world was either right or wrong for her, and she was always right. She was eager to peck at people in the wrong, but when her husband came back, her clear-cut view of the world was shattered. In the so-called sacred war, he had raped women and killed a prisoner.

On his recent visit, Isamu had been like a man who had lost his soul. He just sat, his eyes unfocused like two empty holes. Occasionally he bellowed, "Yeow . . . ," his face contorted in agony and tears gushed from his eyes. He often let out a shriek like a parrot's mock laughter. He was on the brink of madness, if not already mad. Asked by the desperate Kana to deal with her husband, Taku talked to Isamu, but Isamu was cautious and hardly responded.

Every day Taku sat and talked to him with patience and gentleness, two qualities he was not born with. Isamu finally started to confide in Taku.

"I'm a failure. I'm the laughing stock of my troop, because I still can't kill enemies. Ever since I killed the sixteen-year-old Wang Sho-ying, I freeze in front of them. I've been harassed by my commander. He said, 'Coward. What's a soldier for, if you can't even kill? I'll give you a lesson.'

"The commander dragged out a Chinese soldier who had been tied with a rope like a dog on a leash. He said, 'Execute this dog who shot Lieutenant Asai to death.' I asked my commander if he was certain that the soldier had killed Asai. He slapped me three times on the cheek for having talked back to him.

"Pushing and kicking the poor man, who was wan and trembling as a weed in the wind, my colleague made him kneel on the bank of a creek. He sat facing the water shuddering, his body and arms tied up. He was made to sit that way because when the neck is cut, the body then jumps itself into the water.

"I had a sword ready, but the minute I stood up, I cowered again. I couldn't kill him. The commander kicked me in the back, threw me on the ground, stamped on me with his boots and chided, 'Lieutenant Isamu Kato, aren't you supposed to be a grandson of a samurai? Isn't your father a lieutenant general?' He laughed aloud.

"I got up and did it for my honor. 'Ay, Yahhhh. . . .' The sword glittered, cut the neck and flew back to my feet. The head rolled down on the ground, bounced like a ball a few times and fell into the creek. Out of the headless neck, a column of dark blood spouted, drawing a tall arc like a fountain. As it subsided, the body flew up in the air by itself and jumped into the water as if chasing its head.

"Ten minutes later, Asai, who was supposed to have been shot by the man I had killed, came back smiling. He said he had lost his way."

As he finished telling the story, Isamu stood up and let out a screech again, "Yeow. . . ." Then he fell back into the chair and said, "The war is mad. You become a brave soldier only when you've killed your humanity and innocent fellowmen."

Taku sat next to Isamu, put his arm around his son-in-law's shoulder and said, "The newspapers never write about such atrocities. Have you thought of leaving the army? It's no dishonor to leave such a war, Isamu."

"The thought has often occurred to me. I mentioned it to my father. He yelled at me and said he would disown me. He said, 'We are a special samurai family. You were born to serve our Emperor and our holy nation. We are no quitters. You'd scar my name permanently if you leave. No war is easy. A tiger's mother drops her cub into a thousand-foot valley. Only when he makes it back to the top, will he become a tiger.' So I'm not allowed to leave the army, sir," Isamu said and pursed his lips, looking away into the distance, at the wilderness of China to which he had to return. His once innocent, youthful face was haggard.

Kana had said that Isamu was in agony, but Taku had not realized how profound it was until then. Something had to be done quickly. Without telling Isamu, Taku visited his father. A big man, Lieutenant General Kato, with a flipped-up mustache counterbalancing his slanted eyes and eyebrows, he sat proudly in a room with walls covered with glittering medals. He was terribly offended, his face red with anger, at Taku's suggestion that Isamu was on the brink of madness and that it was of critical importance for him to leave the army.

"Isamu must overcome his cowardice. It's good discipline for him to be in a war, as it was for me, although I admit this war seems more bloodthirsty than the war I fought with the Russians in 1905. I never killed a single civilian," he boasted.

"They should fight the way you did, Lieutenant General Kato. Why is the army ignoring international rules and coercing young men into killing captives? Please use your power to stop this random killing, General Kato," Taku pleaded.

"We are trying to stop the practice, but they're out of control," Kato said and pursed his lips. No matter how passionately Taku argued that Isamu should leave the army, Kato kept shaking his head. In the end he refused to talk and sat like a rock.

Feeling desperate, Taku came home and told Isamu that he should ask for sick leave and stay home. Isamu did and stayed for a few months. But under pressure from his father, he went back to China again.

Taku was sorry for Kana, too. She had no child to take care of. What was she supposed to be doing during her husband's long absences? For a few years she had been teaching a tea ceremony class in the teahouse. But it had not healed her wounded soul. Kana said she wanted to do something more exciting to absorb herself so that she would not think about her husband and the war. It had never occurred to Taku that something exciting meant for her to have an affair. How did Kana dare think of it after she had led the tattletale committee? But Taku had to be suspicious, since she often went out with heavy makeup and a tight dress—the very look that had earlier caused her to accuse others of unfaithfulness. It was possible that Kana, with her vindictive personality, would not feel justified until she had balanced Isamu's disloyalty with her own. Taku, who had kept another woman while his faithful wife waited for him at home, was in no position to accuse his daughter. He advised her in vain to do something better like going to school, doing charity work or taking up a religion.

As Taku finished his early morning prayers at the temple and began walking home, enjoying the flowers on the roadside shimmering in the morning sun, a recent troublesome event flitted across his mind. It had happened on the day the family had gathered to view the cherry blossoms in Hana's garden. Taku had taken Kana and his grandsons, Masao and Shun, to a nearby shrine. The others stayed behind, Hana talking with Jun about her arthritis, Yumi wrapping cherry-blossom cake with cherry leaves, Hisao watering the garden, and Sayo weeding.

It was a balmy Sunday. As Taku strolled outside the shrine, Kana frantically ran up and down its corridor, praying for Isamu's safe return from the deadly Nanking campaign in which he had been fighting. If she ran back and forth there a hundred times, her wish was supposed to be granted. Masao and Shun joined their aunt, sorry that she looked so distraught.

"The noisier we are, the better they hear us up in heaven," Masao said.

"Please let Uncle Isamu return safe and sound," Shun chanted, running.

When they were done, Masao proposed they try their luck by drawing an *omikuji* fortune-teller. "After all this running, heaven must grant us good luck."

Kana would not dare consult her omens. The two boys ran to the shrine house where *omikuji* fortunes were stashed in a sacred chest. Each one put in a coin and chose a folded rice paper out of hundreds packed in a wooden drawer. They opened the folded little paper with happy expectations, as most people seemed to find in it a message like "A Good Omen" or "A Great Fortune." Their chances of good luck must have been multiplied after having made such an effort running.

As Shun read the omen, his face turned gray. Without saying anything, he put the paper in his back pocket. Masao opened his and clucked his tongue. He crumpled it into a ball, clenched it in his fist and looked away.

"What's the matter? What did you get?" Kana asked the two boys, anxious about their pale faces and silence. She took the paper out of Shun's pocket and opened it. A big black word, "Misfortune," appeared on it and she shuddered. The character for the word was a picture image of a sword in a box. You were thrust into a box with a sword.

Kana forced Masao to open his palm, took the crumpled paper and smoothed out the wrinkles. It said "Great Misfortune" in even bigger letters. There was hushed silence all around them. Even the birds stopped chirping. A passerby peeked at the ominous letters and skulked away, shaking himself as if trying to beat off ill luck.

Taku said with a forced smile, "These are just make-believe."

"This is supposed to be a sacred oracle," Masao said, in a husky voice.

"You know very well that they weren't written by gods, but only by men," Taku said. "Believing an *omikuji* fortune-teller is like reading bad luck in a passing cat. Just forget about them, Masao and Shun." Taku tore their papers and threw them in a garbage can with pretended nonchalance, as Masao and Shun stood dazed. Taku tried to cheer them up with jokes and happy stories all the way home, but the boys did not laugh or smile.

Kana, who had almost been in tears, said, "Masao and Shun, don't worry. They aren't your misfortunes; you were betting my luck: so they are mine."

"No, they are ours, Aunt Kana. Ours. I got 'Misfortune' that was probably only one out of a hundred fortunes. Both of us together, we got one out of ten thousand chances. It's pretty bad," Shun said, trying to laugh.

Although Taku refused to believe in such a superstition, as he had told the boys, the black letters remained vividly in his eyes and kept annoying him. Since that day, Taku had been fervently begging Buddha, "Spare the boys, Kana and Isamu from any misfortunes, Buddha. If ill luck must fall on anyone, let it fall on me. Give the young ones a bright future."

As he clutched the cane and walked, trying to push the black letters from his eyes, Taku had unbearable pains in his leg and sat down on the pavement. The leg was purple and swollen. After a few minutes, he tried to stand up with his cane as a support, telling himself, only two more blocks home. He almost succeeded in rising, but then reeled and fell backwards.

A tofu vendor, who had just finished delivering breakfast tofu to customers, was on his way home when he saw a bamboo cane lying in the middle of the road and a bundle of a blue cotton kimono on the pavement. He came closer and saw a man lying, his eyes shut and his face bluer than his kimono. "It's Mr. Imura," he cried out. "Mr. Imura, Mr. Imura. Are you all right?" he called, feeling Taku's forehead and cheeks.

Seeing that Taku did not respond, the tofu vendor left his cart on the spot, ran to Taku's house and shouted at the entrance, "Please, somebody come out quick. Mr. Imura has fallen on the road."

Honda rushed out, crying, "Where? Where?" Before he followed the tofu vendor, Honda told a maid to call Dr. Jun to come right away and to wake up Hana.

Honda felt Taku's heart. It was warm and ticking. "Thanks to you, he's still alive," Honda thanked the tofu vendor. At the touch of Honda's hand, Taku opened his eyes and squinted at the sun. He looked puzzled, but recognized Honda.

"What're you doing here, Honda? I don't need help." Taku struggled to get up.

"I know, sir, but it's a good idea to see Dr. Jun. He's on the way here now," Honda said, trying to keep Taku quiet.

The color came back to Taku's face, as did his impatience. "I don't have to see Jun. He's busy. Let's go home," he said and lifted his head. But it fell on the ground.

Jun arrived with an ambulance. He told his father not to resist, but Taku was still trying to get up by himself. In the end, he was tied on a stretcher, carried into the ambulance and taken to the hospital.

After examining the test results, Jun told his father that he had an embolism. "The blood vessels have been obstructed by a clot, that's why your leg has been hurting. If it travels to an important organ like the heart, lung or an eye, it'll be troublesome. So you should rest and lead a quiet life for a while."

"So this is the disease I may die of, isn't it, Jun? Before it happens, I have a lot of things to do. Time's running out. Let me go home now," Taku pestered his son.

Jun made him stay at the hospital against his will until the pain and swelling of the leg disappeared. Then he sent his father home with Nurse Kei. Taku had never been ill in his adult life and was irritated that he was. But he had to admit that he was old and that death would catch up with him sooner or later. Maybe, Buddha had listened to his fervent prayers and made the fortune-teller's sign of misfortune fall on him rather than on his grandsons, Isamu or Kana, he thought.

Taku reorganized his life with the help of Honda and Nurse Kei. Instead of going to meetings, he talked over the phone or sent his ideas in writing. He prepared letters to be read after his death for Hana, his children, grandchildren, friends and politicians. He finished the book on his interpretation of Buddhism.

The blood clot disappeared from Taku's leg and his illness appeared only a temporary sign of a misfortune. But further ill luck visited the family. Kana received a notice from the army hospital that Isamu had returned there with an illness. It was the beginning of 1938, twenty days after the newspaper had announced the news of the Japanese Army's conquest of Nanking, then capital of China. "I hope that this'll be the end of the war. At least Isamu will return here for a long leave," Taku had been telling Kana.

Kana rushed to the hospital. A nurse who led the way to his room said to Kana, looking sorry, "Don't be shocked by the way he looks. I hope he'll get better soon."

Kana braced herself for the worst, but when she opened the door and saw him, she burst into laughter.

"Hup two three four, hup two three four, lef right lef. . . ."

Isamu was marching around the room in a white hospital gown. Kana cried out, laughing, "My goodness, Isamu-san, you are so lively. I thought you were ill."

"Stay away. This is no place for a woman," Isamu said, still marching with a stiff gait, without even glancing at Kana.

"Oh, stop joking, Isamu-san. I brought you sushi, your favorite seaweed-wrapped sushi," Kana protested.

With the word, sushi, Isamu tramped over to Kana and

peeked at the colorful assortment of sushi in a box. Marking time, he bent down and snuffled like a dog.

"You've been starving, haven't you? Please have one, Isamu-san," Kana said.

Without eating it, Isamu put his palms together, and bowed to the sushi as if to worship. Then he climbed up on a chair by the bed and stood up straight, his eyes glaring. They had not glanced at Kana yet.

It finally sank into Kana there was something seriously wrong with Isamu.

"Fall-in. Come on, quick now, men. Atten-shun," he shouted from the top of the chair and looked around the room. Then he gave a speech in a solemn voice.

"Today is a victory day. His Imperial Majesty has been greatly pleased about our conquest of Nanking, and particularly the bravery of our Unit 52. Therefore, His Majesty graciously bestowed upon us seaweed-wrapped sushi. Accept it with tears of gratitude. After this ceremony, you'll be discharged for five weeks. Mind you, never tell anyone at home how many villagers you've killed, how many women you've raped, how many pigs you've stolen and how many houses you've burned. You'd be gravely punished for the disclosure of top military secrets. After five weeks, you are required to report to the port of Yokohama again. Remember at all times that your duty is heavier than the mountains and your life lighter than a feather. Be ready to die at any time for a horse of His Majesty."

Isamu stepped off the chair and, looking pale, collapsed on the bed, flat on his stomach and breathing heavily. Kana sat on the bed and patted him gently on his back. "You must be exhausted, Isamu-san," she said. "It must've been a hard war to fight."

Isamu looked at Kana for the first time. He stared at her with a puzzled look and said, "Who are you? Let's see. Are you Shunming?"

"I'm Kana, your wife."

"Oh. You are Kana. Did you have a baby? I want to have a baby."

Kana stared into Isamu's eyes and burst into tears. Isamu saw her cry with icy indifference and said, "I don't need a crybaby; I want to have a happy one."

Kana turned away from Isamu and crouched on the bed, covering her face with her hands, tears spilling through her fingers. With hollow eyes, Isamu watched her shoulders heave up and down.

With no more tears left, Kana stood up, combed her hair, straightened the wrinkles of her dress and left the room without glancing back at Isamu. She went straight to visit a doctor on duty.

"He's in a manic state with an element of schizophrenia," the bespectacled doctor said with professional coolness. "Let's hope he'll be better soon. This war has been a rough one and we have other cases like him here. I understand he has been discharged from the army, so we can't keep him here too long. There's not much we can do for him anyway. We'd like you to take him home whenever you are ready."

When Kana talked about Isamu's condition at home, Taku was distraught. "Shame," he said. "He should have left the army earlier. Any man with a slice of heart would go mad there. Anyway, bring him here, Kana. Let's take good care of him and he'll be better again."

Hana did not agree. "Taku-san, you are overconfident about curing an insane man. I've known a few mad men in my life including my own father. They'll make you go crazy before you cure them. Kana, don't you think Isamu-san should go home to his parents? Two invalid parents and a crazy husband will be too much for you. I didn't build the teahouse as an asylum. I don't want that tranquil place to turn into a rattle-box. His family must have a big house. His father can afford to hire a doctor and a nurse."

Kana nodded eagerly. "I'll go and ask his parents. They

certainly have a big house. I'd be more than happy to return him to them," she said with a sigh.

"It won't work that easily, Kana," Taku said sternly. "Once you were in love with Isamu; you can't abandon him just because he has fallen ill. Poor Isamu had a bad time." True, Kana used to moon over Isamu, but each time he returned, the moon was a little more chipped and her love for him had waned.

Though Kana was sorry that he had had to fight a terrible war, still she could not forget or forgive the way he had talked about women when he returned for the first time. He had never mentioned women again; he had probably kept his promise to her about not raping another woman, but Kana had been determined to revenge herself on him.

Kana had an affair with a married man. He was a heavy drinker and she, too, had learned to drink. The affair had ended because his wife had found out and he was not willing to ruin his family life. But the experience had taught Kana that it was possible to have a life other than being a virtual war widow, or an insane husband's nurse. The sweet taste of a secret love, like the intoxicating taste of wine, was not easily forgotten.

Isamu had not even remembered Kana's name this time. A mental patient often forgets the names of the family, the doctor on duty had said. Kana wondered whether that meant that she did not exist even in his subconscious. Isamu was not even interested in looking at her. The only thing he wanted from her was a baby. Kana craved a baby, too. But now she was glad she had no baby from him. Who would want a baby of a man who does not even know its mother's name?

On his previous leaves, Isamu had been depressed or sad, but not coldhearted. At first, Kana had been baffled and deeply wounded by his chilly demeanor. Then she became angry and was not sure she wanted to take care of him. She did not know how to be a nurse for a mental patient anyway. Isamu's parents should share the burden. His father was responsible because he would not let Isamu leave the army when it was obvious he was at the end of his tether.

Kana visited Lieutenant General Kato. He was polite to Kana. After all, he must have felt a little guilty that his son had left her joyless and childless for so long and had returned a madman. He said he was sorry that his wife, upset by what had happened to her son, had fallen ill and could not see Kana.

"We admire you for having waited faithfully for Isamu for so many years, Kana-san," Kato said gently, pinching his mustache and combing it upward with his fingers. "It's been a difficult war. We thought the Chinese would surrender when we conquered Nanking. No sign of it. But we'll go on to spread the Emperor's message, no matter how hard it is. You deserve a medal just as much as Isamu. Do you know that they have just bestowed on Isamu the silver medal of courage?" The father held up the shining medal on his palm and showed it off to Kana as if it mattered more to talk about it than about his son's illness. The medal was a small token given to Isamu in order to discharge him, seemingly graciously, from the army.

"I wish they hadn't discharged him for only a temporary illness," Kato said, knitting his slanted eyebrows. "He would have gone back to service in no time and would have a great future in front of him. I could've stopped it, you know, but I didn't want people to think I'm twisting things for my son, using my important position. It's a tough world, the army. The survival of the fittest. But don't worry, it was an honorable discharge and he'll be paid a lifetime pension. I'll find him a good job. You see, Isamu was too excited about this last patch of fighting. He'll be better in no time when he has rested."

The father was trying to make light of his son's illness perhaps for his own comfort. He fidgeted restlessly, playing with the silver medal in his hands, the empty token of glory. The medals hung on the wall behind him were mostly bigger and shinier than the one in his hands. In the center was the gilded-framed acknowledgment of Lieutenant General Kato's bravery and leadership in the Japan/Russia War, embossed with the Emperor's golden chrysanthemum seal. Bigger and more strongly built than Isamu, his father was usually an impressive presence, but today he looked small and old. He was trying to look brave and philosophical, but his eyes revealed disappointment and sadness.

When Kana asked about the possibility of Isamu coming back to his house, the father said quickly, "I'll talk with my wife about it. The trouble is that she is as ill as Isamu. I'll phone you tomorrow, Kana-san." It was clear that the answer was negative. He rang the next day to repeat the same words, but he said he was willing to send a nurse to help Kana. He would find a doctor, too. Kana suspected that the father could not bear to be reminded constantly of the failure of his son. Probably he did not want the neighbors to know that his son had gone mad.

So Isamu returned to the teahouse. A nurse named Tama came every day. Nurse Kei, working for Taku, helped, too. Even so Isamu was a handful.

Isamu liked the teahouse. "This is by far the best camp we've ever been stationed at," he said, inspecting the house with a meter ruler at his hip instead of the bayonet and the sword Kana had taken away. He trampled in his jackboots on the *tatami* mat, tearing its fibers. He poked holes in the paper screens with the ruler and said, "We need look-out holes." He pounded the walls and said, "They're rather thin."

Kana and Tama managed to put him to bed, but while they were busy in the kitchen, he sneaked out and disappeared. Kana found him in the pine forest, wearing leaves and twigs for camouflage and lashing the trunk of a tree with the belt he had taken off his pants, until the bark peeled, exposing the white wood. Isamu howled like his old commander at the naked tree, "You're too naïve. War is about killing. You won't be a soldier until you can kill. Understand? Say yes. I'll beat you until you say yes."

Panting for air, he kept whipping the tree like the madman that he was. The resin of the pine dripped like teardrops.

The next time Isamu disappeared, Kana found him in the thicket of the azalea bush. His head in the camouflaged helmet was poking in and out of the bush. When he spotted Kana and the nurses, he screamed, "Shoot, men. Shoot." He stuck out his ruler above the bush and aimed at Kana. "Bang. I got her." He smiled.

"We have no food left. Let's go to the village and pick up rice, potatoes, chickens, pigs or whatever is edible," he shouted. "Then we'll burn the village. Remember, we have no time to have women today." He ran and stooped to avoid imaginary bullets. He stopped in front of the pond and said, "Good. The bridge is still standing. Follow me," and hopped across the bridge to a bamboo forest.

Tama and Kei caught Isamu in the bamboo and dragged him back to the teahouse, but he did not stop talking gibberish. His head was like broken clockwork and his words skidded, slurred and were mixed up with secret codes and Chinese. His stories disconnected from one sentence to another and spun off at random. He started to talk about a soldier who had contracted venereal disease. In order to cure his disease, the soldier cut off a farmer's head to eat his brains. That was supposed to be a miracle cure. But, before he finished telling if the soldier had really eaten the farmer's brains or not, Isamu was talking about a young comfort woman who had been taken from Korea to satisfy the soldiers' needs and had died of exhaustion after taking eighty men a day for three months.

Isamu had no appetite. Kana had to push food into his mouth with a spoon. At night he was delirious, but kept telling more stories, his eyes wide open and glaring. When Kana dozed off, he shook her awake. "Kana, you ignore me and treat me as if I'm a madman," he said. "You really think I'm insane, don't you? You are wrong. I'm lucid and the world is insane. True, I was mad once like the rest of the world. Do you know how I was cured of it? I refused to kill; I refused to rape; I didn't steal; I ate lizards, toads and worms. One day when I ate wild berries, I got poisoned and almost died, but then my madness was cleaned out of my system. Those who ate the stolen food had cholera. Some died and those who survived became insane."

Indeed Isamu often sounded lucid, and looked perfectly sane and serious. He talked again about the comfort woman who had died of exhaustion. "After the girl died, I made a big fuss to my commander about her and the plight of women like her. The commander said, 'It's too bad they are abused, but you can't help it, since they are whores, after all.' I was furious and said, 'They are not whores. These poor Korean girls were abducted from their villages to serve in the Patriotic Volunteer Corps. Are they volunteers? Are they patriotic to Japan? Ha, ha, ha.' The commander slapped me on both cheeks and demoted me one rank for talking like that."

The rest of the world was definitely madder than Isamu.

Isamu had no physical lust; lunacy consumed all his energy. He boasted of conquering women so as not to seem as if he was not interested in them. What was sadder than that was that he was devoid of emotion. He did not want to hug Kana or laugh or cry with her. When Kana held his hand, it felt as cold and hard as the metal fingers of a man from a different planet.

Early one morning, Kana found Isamu digging a hole with a garden shovel in the moss-covered mound Hana was so proud of. Two bonsai trees were uprooted and turned over. She heard him mumbling in a sing-song voice, "This is the twenty-fourth. The twenty-third was a woman I raped. Twenty-fourth, her husband."

Kana screamed and tried to put the fallen trees back into the hole when Isamu grabbed her by the arms and said, "Get away, woman, or else you'll be the twenty-fifth. We must bury the dead quickly so that the villagers won't find out." When the two nurses tried to grab Isamu, he raised a shovel in front of their faces and said they would be the twenty-sixth and twenty-seventh.

Kana went to tell Taku and Hana what Isamu was doing. They came out in their nightgowns, dragging their feet and holding their canes. As soon as Isamu saw them, he stopped digging and stood at salute.

Looking at the upturned mound, Hana bawled, "What have you done to my beautiful mound and trees, Isamu-san?"

"I'm digging a shelter for you, madam. The enemy's coming."

"More importantly, what happened to our precious Isamu, a brave soldier who went to fight a holy war?" Taku said gently, looking at Isamu with sad eyes.

Something happened to Isamu when he saw tears shining in Taku's small eyes. He dropped the shovel, fell on his stomach in the dirt and burst out crying. He bellowed like a child, flailing and kicking the earth with his arms and legs.

Taku squatted down and patted his back, saying, "You are exhausted, Isamu. Why don't you rest for a while and you'll feel better. Then let's talk, you and I."

Isamu looked up at Taku with blurred eyes, and calmed down. He staggered to his feet. Kana and the nurses brushed the dirt off his face and his pajamas, and removed his camouflage leaves and twigs. Then they led the way to the teahouse. He followed them as obediently as a child who was contrite about excessive mischief.

Taku said to Hana, "Let's ask the gardeners to fix your mound right away."

"I'm sure he'll do it again. He'll ruin the whole garden," Hana said sighing.

When Isamu was back at the teahouse, he went to bed and slept through a day and a night. Contrary to Kana's wishful thinking that he would be better after a good rest, when he woke up, he was as sick as before, though in a different way. His mood had swung and now he wept like a monsoon. His tears made his bed so damp that mushrooms could grow out of it. He looked like one himself, grown so pale and limp. He did not want to get up, talk, eat or drink. The savage glare in his eyes had been replaced by gray film, lifeless as a stagnant swamp.

He often screamed at night and stood on the bed. "The Chinese are coming here to attack me," he said. "Order my Unit 52 to come right away and guard the teahouse, Kana."

Kana patted Isamu on his shoulder and repeated every time, "Yes, I already did. They'll be here soon to protect you."

Jun and Sayo came to visit Isamu. Jun thought that even though he was no specialist in mental illnesses, he could be of some help. Sayo brought him a sumo magazine, thinking that gossip about the wrestlers might cheer him up. He might even laugh if she pantomimed all the exciting matches she had watched recently.

Yumi and Hisao came, too. Yumi brought Isamu's favorite seaweed-wrapped sushi. Hisao wanted to talk about weapons with Isamu, as he might have some good tips, being an experienced user of arms.

But none of them was allowed into his room. Isamu said to Kana, "They are foreign agents. They're pretending to be relatives, but they're spies."

When his own father came to visit, Isamu had the most violent reaction. As he heard his father's voice, Isamu suddenly got out of bed, closed all the storm shutters despite it being the middle of a sunny day, and locked every door with the double locks he had recently had made to order. Pale and shaking, he went back to bed and lay in a fetal position, holding his legs tight with his arms, with a futon cover over his eyes.

The doctor Isamu's father had sent said that Isamu had depression and paranoia and that he should be watched carefully so that he would not kill himself. Kana had already cleared Isamu's room not only of his guns, rifles, swords and belts, but also of any rope, string, knife, nail, pin, needle, scissors and match.

One day, Taku walked to the teahouse. He said aloud from outside, "Isamu, it's a lovely day. Let's take a little walk. I'm no foreign agent; I'm just your father-in-law. Why don't you come out?"

Kana came out with a big smile on her face and whispered to her father, "He's coming. He's dressing up in his army uniform."

Isamu came out squinting his eyes against the sun that he had not seen for months. He looked like a bean sprout even in the uniform and faltered when he stood to attention and saluted. Taku shifted his cane from his right hand to his left and returned his salute.

"How nice to see you, Isamu. Let's go to the bower and sit. The sun is too strong here," he said beaming, his pocked face wrinkled like an elephant's.

Taku winked at Kana and took Isamu for a walk to a small arbor in the bamboo where the thatched roof kept out the boiling heat. When Taku sat down, Isamu was wobbling, still trying hard to stand. Taku laughed and said, "Isamu, this isn't the army. Sit down."

Isamu sat down timidly. He was fidgety and changed his position a few times. Then he looked at Taku and said, "General Shogun Taku, I should not talk to a high officer like you from a sitting position, but I must report to you about the situation of the war. Nobody of sane mind would believe what's going on in China.

"The biggest problem is that not too many food-carrying units reach the frontline soldiers because the Chinese place land mines and destroy the bridges, the roads and the trucks. So headquarters tell the soldiers to supply their own food. It means going into villages and stealing from the houses. When the soldiers find women there, they rape them. In order to cover up their crimes, they murder them, often their husbands, too. Sometimes they burn villages. The army office has belatedly prohibited lawless activity, but the soldiers keep looting because they're hungry and resentful, having been kept in the endless, aimless 'holy war' for years on end."

Isamu looked wan and anguished. Panting for air, he continued, "After a while, you get used to the savageries, they say. But I never got used to them. I started to hallucinate, scream and laugh. I was told I had gone mad and was sent back. I didn't think I became insane from just screaming and laughing; those boys who are raping and killing, they are madder than I. They all should be sent back before they kill more innocent Chinese."

Taku was horrified by Isamu's descriptions of the war, but he was at least glad his son-in-law was not as ill as he had expected him to be. Taku even wondered if Isamu had not been feigning lunacy all this time. Or was this just a lucid interval?

But the first outing after a long illness, in a stiff army suit on a hot day, was too much for Isamu. He stood up, gasping for air. Fearing that he might faint, Taku rushed to his son-in-law just in time for his head to fall in his arms. His head was as heavy as a big rock and it almost stopped the old man's heart. Taku staggered back on the bench and let Isamu lie on his lap, feeling dizzy himself, his heart beating loudly, but happy he had caught Isamu, who would have fallen on the hard ground.

Isamu's face looked as serene as a child's on his lap. How could this innocent-looking young man have committed rapes and murders? Can a civilized man become a beast in different circumstances? Why had the Japanese, who had recently struggled so hard to become enlightened, turned into hideous demons? Had Taku's lifetime toil of trying to contribute to his country's modernization only helped turn it into a Leviathan with a monstrous face?

When Isamu opened his eyes, he saw the benign smile of an old man and thought he was in heaven. "But there's no chance I could go to heaven," Isamu mumbled, "after having committed such gory crimes." Getting up slowly, he saw the smile spread wide on his father-in-law's wrinkled face.

"Do you feel better, Isamu?" Taku said to him. "Do you know that you fainted in my arms? I was lucky to catch you. I'm always lucky with a fainter. My first wife, Emi, fainted in my arms in the middle of our wedding. Anyhow it was a terrible war you've been fighting. You are so right. They're mad, the officers and the soldiers. We must do something to stop it, you and I. We have to talk to your father again."

With the word, "father," Isamu flinched. His eyes turned gray and his face returned to its madman look. "It was nice talking to you, sir," he said to Taku and stood up. "Thank you very much, Shogun Taku. I must rest for a while." Taku walked Isamu to the teahouse and parted. Isamu stood at salute until Taku disappeared into the trees, limping slowly with his bamboo stick.

Taku felt sick during the short walk back to the western wing. He barely made it and lay down on the floor of the foyer. The world went dark in front of him. Is this my turn to faint? Or is it death? I can't die yet. I have so much to do. I want to do something about the war in China. . . .

When he opened his eyes, the world was covered with fog. Something had happened either to his eyes or to the world. He saw a blurred image of Hana watching him with a worried look. With his back and arms feeling a hard surface, he must be lying on the floor. He tried to get up and couldn't.

"Taku-san," Hana said with a sigh, "are you all right? You shouldn't have gone out for so long. You disappeared as soon as Nurse Kei was gone. I have sent for Jun-san to come right away. Honda-san suggested putting you to bed, but I was afraid of moving you."

As Hana was talking, Jun ran into the house, almost stumbling over Taku. "My goodness, Father, you must be cold lying there. Where's Kei?"

"She has a holiday today and Taku-san sneaked out and took a long walk."

As Jun started to examine him, Taku whispered, pointing to his eyes, "Jun, something's wrong with. . . ." And he lost consciousness again. The embolism was on the move. One of his eyes must be blocked by a blood clot. Some other blood vessels might also be obstructed. His breathing was not normal. His lungs did not sound right. Jun decided against taking him to the hospital. It would be too risky to move an old man almost in a coma. With the utmost care, he and his assistant carried Taku to bed. Jun told Honda to call all the family to come and say *sayonara* to Taku. It might take days before he died, but he would eventually.

Sayo arrived with Shun. Yumi and Hisao came with Masao. One day later, Ken and his wife Ayako came with their three daughters from Nagoya. Each family took turns and visited Taku on tiptoes. Looking as if he were in a coma, his eyes half open, he mumbled a few words to each whenever someone was near him, though what he said was mostly unintelligible.

Ken's daughters folded origami cranes. "If we make a thousand of them, his illness will be cured. Grandpa will live for a thousand years like cranes," they said. Masao and Shun joined them. Sayo, Yumi and Ayako also helped. They folded paper while singing quietly. They saw Grandpa smile faintly and his eyes brim with tears. With each hundred cranes done, they threaded them with a string and hung them from the ceiling above Taku's bed.

Hana, normally irreligious, picked up the Buddha's sutra and read a passage that Taku had recited every day of his later life:

"Let us honor the almighty, enlightened Bodhisattva.

In this world, physical phenomena have no substance. For that reason, they are physical phenomena.

In the same fashion, senses, images, will or knowledge have no substance.

In this world, nothing that exists has substance.

There are no eyes, no ears, no nose, no tongue, no body, no heart, no form, no voice, no aroma, no taste, no object to touch or to feel. No suffering and, therefore, no end to suffering. There is no old age nor death. Therefore, no disappearance of old age nor death. Nothing to know and nothing to gain. Therefore, nothing to fear.

The enlightened live in the achievement of wisdom and in eternal peace.

The enlightened. We wish you happiness."

Hana took Taku's hand and stroked it. She said, "I always thought this prayer refers not to the world we live in but to the next world, though it's my ignorant guess. So you'll live peacefully in this nirvana, Taku-san. Thank you very much for everything wonderful you've done for me and thank you for having put up with my willfulness. I'll see you up there, if Buddha lets me come." Taku smiled and Hana cried.

Kana was sitting there alone. She said that she had not yet told Isamu about her father's condition. Isamu loved and respected Taku so much that he would be too upset if she told him about it. She told everybody that Taku and Isamu had talked at the bower that afternoon just before Taku had fallen ill.

"When Isamu-san came back, he was a different man. He was bright-eyed and completely sane for the first time since he had fallen ill. He said in a happy voice, 'Your father doesn't think I'm a madman. He understands me. He cured my illness. Do you know that he caught my head when I fainted and fell? I've finally found a real father, Kana.' So how can I tell him that our father is dying? He'd be so sad, he might go crazy again."

But Jun saw signs that the end was near with his father. He told Kana to tell her husband about it and bring him here before it was too late. Isamu would be even more upset if he was not given a chance to see Taku before he died.

Isamu came in his uniform and cap. He bowed to everybody politely and went directly to Taku's bed. He took off his cap and kneeled down.

"Shogun Taku, I'm forever grateful to you for understanding me so well. But I have so much more to talk about with you. We have so much to do together, you and I, to stop the war. So please don't die. Please . . ." he said, and burst into tears.

A feeble voice came out of Taku's throat, "Stop . . . the. . . ."

Jun whispered to everybody to come around Taku. He gazed at his father's eyes, now unseeing, and touched the still-warm eyelids to draw them closed. Taku was smiling.

"Our father worked so hard, fought so hard, did so much for his country and his family. At least he didn't have to fight hard to die. He went gently into heaven," Jun said, his eyes brimming with tears.

Isamu put on his cap and stood up to salute, tears rolling down his cheeks like a flood, while all the rest sat, bent their heads, or crouched down to cry.

Nine hundred and eighty-six multicolored paper cranes hung from the ceiling of the room where Taku was lying.

CHAPTER 10

After a protracted struggle with her nightly insomnia, Yumi was just beginning to slip into a dream about her late husband when a siren blew. It hooted as if it were a gigantic owl: *tu-whit tu-whoo, tu-whit tu-whoo*. She sat up wearily in the dark, put on a hood as thickly padded as an Eskimo's, and staggered outside to hide in the underground bomb shelter dug in the garden.

A searchlight was shooting a fan-shaped light in half-circles over the black sky. Yumi wished it were a magic wand a fairy was waving, but this was no fairy tale. The searchlight was tracing American B-29 bombers led by P-51 Mustang fighters, rushing on to assault the sky over Tokyo like a vast swarm of locusts. They were frequent visitors these days, dropping bombs all over the city, incinerating people and houses like innumerable piles of garbage.

It was becoming increasingly difficult for Yumi to remember that a mere year and a half ago Japan had been winning all of the major battles in the Pacific. Pearl Harbor was a literal bomb from the blue in December 1941, only three years after Taku died. Despite his last wish, the war with China had not stopped, but had spread over the Pacific like an epidemic. Yumi's son

Masao, then a patriotic high-school student, bought a map of the Pacific and, as the days passed, pinned little rising-sun flags on the sites Japan came to claim as its own: Malaysia, Singapore, Hong Kong, Manila, Indochina, Indonesia and Burma.

Yet, in less than a year, the news from the front had become far from glorious. Although the newspapers played down the extent of the defeats, Sayo, whom the government had sent back to the hospital as a nurse, heard the soldiers' stories. Passing those tales on to Yumi, Sayo concluded, "We'll be lucky if we die in our beds. Thousands are perishing every day—in the jungle, in the air, and on the sea."

Except for the searchlight, the night was black; with the first warning of a raid, all the lights of the region had gone off. Yumi carried a candle and a matchbox, but she was not allowed a light, lest a plane spot it. With the ease of long practice, she felt her way to an underground shelter in the garden, touching first the wooden wall of the house, then the rugged bark of three pines, and next the smooth trunk of the myrtle. Her mind strayed to Taku, as it often did when she made this journey: her night-blind father had also groped trees when he walked in the dark. She saw him sitting in heaven like a Buddha, and growling with rage as he watched his country destroy itself in the war.

Three steps from the myrtle, a wooden cover, roughly the size of a manhole, rested on the ground: it was the entrance to the shelter. As she began to descend, another siren wailed, this time a more high-pitched, hysterical *tu-tu-tu-tu*—a warning of imminent danger.

The shelter was a hole Masao had dug in the ground, covered with boards and a mound of dirt: a space barely large enough for three people to squat in. For Yumi, stepping into the cave was more frightening than either the B-29s or the bombs. She always imagined that a rat, a fox, a badger or a homeless tramp was waiting down there to jump on her, even though the only animal she had ever encountered in the hole was a lost little mole, who had blundered his way over her foot.

With her fears once again proved groundless, she breathed a deep sigh and crouched in the dark, her arms clasping her knees. The hole smelled musty and the chill seeping through from the earth made her shiver.

Suddenly she felt a tickle on the sole of her left foot. Maybe it was another mole. She lit a candle and found an inchworm busily measuring her foot. It was a seven-millimeter creature with black dust specks for eyes. She did not mind tiny creepy crawlers like him. Since she had become a frequent inhabitant of this cave, ants, spiders, and even hairy centipedes were her friends. She even envied them; they were not about to fight, go crazy, or die like people involved in this terrible war.

The inchworm suddenly stopped inching and, standing on his last two millimeters, stretched his antennae and wiggled them left and right. The wall of the cave had begun to vibrate faintly; a few grains of earth slid off the muddy walls. Then the trembling grew to a rumbling, just as at the onset of the big earthquake of 1923 that Yumi remembered all too well. But this time the sound was coming from the sky. The inchworm squirmed, fell on the ground, and disappeared.

Yumi peeped outside through a hole and saw a swarm of winged things like locusts approaching with great speed, their eyes blinking in the dark. They were dropping torrents of red-hot fireballs, dozens and dozens of spear-headed demons of death. They were the same messengers of death who had taken Hisao's life in an earlier bombing in Kawasaki.

Then a deafening thud lifted Yumi off the ground. She wondered if she had died, but two seconds later, she found herself still alive. Through the crack, she saw the upper half of a tall building sliding to the ground like molten lava. Millions of sparks showered on the neighborhood, lighting it up as if it were day.

Yumi was shaking from horror rather than chills. Her arms and legs were wet with cold sweat. She had decided some time ago that it did not matter much if she died—not with her husband dead, her mother about to die, her son taken to war. But it was still not easy to face death, no matter how often she was close to it.

After a few minutes the roar died down, and the night grew strangely silent. But the silence only made her wonder who had died, who was missing, and how loudly their families were crying out for them.

When the sleepy siren came on to lift the alert, Yumi crawled out of the hollow. Flames were still raging where the building used to be; as she looked up, a huge chunk of wall dropped with one last resounding thump.

Stars had replaced the searchlight. Yumi had noticed that the stars always hid themselves during air raids, perhaps fearful of being shot down. They came back after the raids, filling the sky with the tears of the dead. They seemed to have grown in numbers as the victims had multiplied. The brightest ones were the most recent dead. Which one was Hisao's? Was it the silvery one orbiting Mars, the god of war? Her late husband had always been so much of a martial spirit. Yumi thought that when or if peace came, she would write a fairy tale of those who had died in the war and turned into stars.

Yumi remembered how excited Hisao had been at the news of Pearl Harbor. He clasped his son, Masao, with his arms and danced around on the *tatami* floor, saying, "Fighting with China was like a sibling's quarrel; finally, we are facing the right enemy and we'll fight a real war. The whites have been conquering the world and when we tried to do the same, they condemned us as the yellow peril. We have a mission to protect Asia from the threats of the white peril."

"Do we have a chance to win?" asked Masao. "America is a huge country."

"Of course we do. Holland and France have been beaten by Germany. It's the right time to go south and get Dutch Indonesia and French Indochina, while their mother countries are on fire. Do you know what it would mean to have Indonesia in our hands, Masao? It means we'll have oil, iron ore, sugar and rubber, all the things we don't have in Japan. If we have enough natural resources, we can beat America."

Hisao had quadrupled his production of arms. His uncle's financial company had fattened so much over the years that it could lend the capital for Hisao's plant. He worked harder than ever before and boasted that the bombs, machine guns and bayonets he was making were the best in the country. Yumi squirmed every time her husband mentioned the deadly weapons his factory was producing, but she kept her mouth shut, because whenever she said anything against them, he scolded her. "How can you be so unpatriotic? Don't you want our soldiers to win the war?"

Even when Yumi said, "You must come home and rest more, Hisao-san. You are working too hard," he reproved her.

"Everybody is working for the nation now, Yumi. Even students of Masao's age are mobilized and work at my plants all day. How can I be lazy?" He insinuated that Yumi was lazy, not working for the country's war effort. Hisao was a fireball of patriotism.

When he was home, men wearing decorations on their military uniforms often visited him at night. Even those who usually strutted and swaggered took off their caps and bowed humbly to Hisao. Sometimes a group of them came and drank too much saké. Yumi did not like them because they made rude jokes in vulgar language and sang military songs. She stayed in the kitchen, recollecting with nostalgia the evenings she had spent with Jun's family, and how they had talked about books, sang peaceful songs and played games with the children. Now Jun and Sayo were so busy at their hospital that, though they dropped in to see Yumi, they did not stay long.

A regular visitor, Captain Suzuki, often stared at Yumi. Once, in the corridor to the kitchen, he coiled around her and kissed her on her cheek. She managed to push him off and rubbed the cheek right away with hot water and a generous slab of soap, but for long after she felt as if the stench of his heavy breath had not come off.

Suzuki did not come again after she told her husband about the incident, but the others kept coming. Once, she overheard one of the group say to Hisao, "The six-chambered revolver your company makes is very impressive. I had very good use of it in China." Yumi wondered how many people had been killed by the products of Hisao's factory. She felt like a mass murderer, living off the earnings of her husband. Hisao worked even harder as Japan's fortunes in the Pacific war began to wane. He often stayed overnight at an inn near his plant in Kawasaki in spite of Yumi's pleas, "The arms factories will be the first target of the air raids."

The first bombings were indeed aimed only at the munitions plants. Hisao planned to move his factory far away into the countryside, but the plan remained only that, for, in one of the earliest raids, his plant was hit. Not too many workers were around, but Hisao was still in his office. Japan was not fully prepared yet for air attacks and the warning came too late. As soon as the siren blew, he ran out of the door, just as the bomb hit the plant with an ear-splitting explosion. A worker saw Hisao blown two meters high.

Yumi was devastated by the news of Hisao's death and felt guilty that she had not admired him more while he lived. Since she did not like the idea that her husband made weapons, she had not given him enough credit for his devotion to his work and to the nation. In every dream she had since then, he haunted her. She had not been a good wife to Hisao, nor had she been a patriotic citizen.

Soon after his father's death, Masao received the inevitable pink card in the post. With soldiers dying off, boys of eighteen were being drafted. "I'll be as good a soldier at the front as my father was at his factory," Masao said proudly. "Do you remember that I hit a 'Great Misfortune' in the *omikuji* fortuneteller, Mother? It might mean that I'm destined to die young in the war. But I don't mind dying for the Emperor." He turned away from Yumi to look outside, his bluster hiding his tears.

Masao was destined to go to war. Every day at high school he had been taught that fighting and dying in the holy war was the most glorious mission in life. He did his morning calisthenics, shouting, "Exterminate America and Great Britain. One-two-three. Annihilate America and Great Britain. One-two-three." The favorite pictures he drew were those of Japanese fighter-planes and battleships. He played the "Destroyer-Torpedo" game with his cousin Shun, and he read accounts of each battle in the Pacific avidly, counting up how many enemy battleships had been sunk without ever doubting the veracity of the quoted figures. He learned about all the exotic battlegrounds in the Pacific that sounded like distant guns: Guadalcanal, Kolombangara, Gorontalo, Kuala Lumpur.

His school days started and ended with a deep bow to the Emperor's photograph and the recitation of words of allegiance to him. If a student failed to take off his cap and bow to the Emperor's picture even from across a room, he was slapped on both cheeks, just as a citizen in the street was taken to jail for failing to bow to the gate of the Emperor's residence.

Education had succeeded in molding Masao into a war machine, a pawn called "a foot soldier" in *shogi,* one that could be used and discarded to protect the king. Masao had taken to heart the lesson that his own life was a trifle and worthwhile only if he died for this glorious country governed by a living god.

A brave mother was supposed to be happy to give her son away to her nation. Yumi had pretended to be stoic and merely wished Masao luck, but she kept asking herself, Did I raise my son only to kill and be killed in the war? Since Masao left, she had prayed daily to God, "Please, don't let him die for the Emperor. Let him come home safe and sound."

Yumi was now alone. Almost every day she visited her mother who needed special care. Her sister Kana was living in the teahouse, separated from Hana's wing only by a garden and a pond. But Kana had never been a dutiful daughter, and now that she drank so much and sometimes even sneaked out at night with heavy makeup and her hair up in fancy rolls, Yumi could not count on her at all. On those days and nights Kana was not home, Yumi also looked after Isamu whose mental state had become precarious again after Taku's death.

Caring for her relatives kept Yumi busy and distracted her from mourning for her husband and worries about her son fighting in the Pacific. Hana and Kana had asked Yumi to move in with them thinking she must be lonely, but she refused as she thought it would be too much to be a full-time nurse for three people as difficult as Hana, Kana and Isamu.

Jun and Sayo suggested that all four evacuate to a safer place in the country, as lots of families had. "It's really dangerous to stay in Tokyo," argued Jun. "Sayo and I have to stay here because the hospital needs us, but all of you should leave here. How about Nogami? Father's relatives are there. Or how about the village north of Nagoya where Ken-san's family have been evacuated?"

Hana was an invalid, but she was still stubborn. She insisted on staying where she was. "I'd rather not be uprooted to a strange place when I'm just about to move to heaven." Kana did not want to move because her lover was living in the neighborhood. Isamu did not want to lose the job in the clothing factory he had just started.

Yumi also preferred to stay in Tokyo. More specifically, she wanted to stay in her own house, which was a short distance from Jun's. She could not bear the thought of moving away from Jun and Sayo. Sayo always made a fuss over Yumi, saying, "I'm frightened of bombs even with Jun-san around. How scared you must be, Yumi-san, being all alone." She sewed an extra thick hood for Yumi and a jacket filled with layers of silk floss for nights when there were air raids.

Jun was quieter about his concern, but Yumi knew he was worried about her, too. Ever since Yumi had lost her husband, Jun took every excuse to visit her even when Sayo could not. "With Masao gone, you can use a man's hand," he said, and helped her repair a shutter, fix a broken lamp, or carry a heavy bag of charcoal.

The last time Jun visited, he cleaned a gutter clogged with dead leaves. After he had washed his hands, he sat down and sipped the tea Yumi served, gazing at her face and fingers, his dark eyes gleaming.

"Have you heard from Masao recently?" he asked.

"No, I haven't heard anything for more than three months since he wrote to me he had landed at Lae, a port in eastern New Guinea. So far, he has sent me only two cards, this faded, yellow one from the ship going south on the Pacific and this soiled one from New Guinea," Yumi said, picking up the two cards from the table in front of her.

Both were brief notes, written in a rush. The first one said only: *It's been a long and boiling hot trip on this ship. We'll soon stop over in Manila. Don't worry about me because I'm doing well. Take care. Love, Masao.*

The second one was difficult to read because the letters were blurred: *It's going to be a difficult war. Rain is rushing down like a waterfall every day and we haven't had much to eat. The enemy is lurking in the jungle.*

"Do you see how this card was wet once, Jun-san?" Yumi said, looking at her son's warped card. "I wonder if it was wet in the rain, or with his tears. Masao was never a good letter-writer, but I wish he weren't so brief. But, of course, he must be cautious of the army's censor. Maybe he is purposely uncommunicative. The more he writes, the more worries he'll give me. Anyway he hasn't written again so I don't even know if he is alive or not." Yumi put the cards to her chest and hugged them, her eyes frightened, picturing the jungle of New Guinea.

"In the jungle it's not easy to write and send letters," Jun said, feeling extremely sorry for Yumi and not knowing what to say to comfort her.

"What a terrible age we are living in, Jun-san," Yumi said, breathing a deep sigh. "Do you remember what peaceful evenings we used to spend, singing and laughing? I never dreamed then that in a few short years, I would have no husband and Masao would be taken to war in New Guinea."

Jun gazed at Yumi, his eyes wet and shining like stars, and his lips pressed tightly together. He was trying hard not to cry. Slowly he stood up and said in a muffled voice, "Good night. Take good care of yourself, Yumi-san. Eat well and don't catch cold." He turned around, trying not to show his tears.

Sometimes, when the siren blew, Sayo and Jun ran to Yumi's and stayed with her in her shelter. When they were there, the ominous hours became intensely happy ones. Yumi would not have cared if a hairy animal were hiding in the hole, or even if a bomb hit her.

The first time they came, Sayo missed a step while descending into Yumi's shelter, and tumbled in, landing on her knees. Trying to stand up, she hit her head on the low ceiling. "Yumi-san, this isn't exactly a masterpiece of a shelter, is it?" she laughed. "And it's freezing. We'll have to sit close together to get warm."

"Is there a way for us not to sit close together here?" Jun asked, rubbing his wife's head and knees to feel if they were all right.

"Jun-san," said Sayo, "sit in between us and hold hands with both of us. At least we won't die lonely." Normally just a brush of Jun's arm made Yumi's heart leap. Now they sat holding hands and pressing their sides against each other. She was glad it was pitch dark since nobody could see how her face and body had flushed red.

"It's a funny time to be happy, but I feel as content as a sweet potato growing underground with her sibling potatoes," Yumi said, smiling in the dark.

The rumbling of the planes approached overhead. "Oh, Jun-san, they might drop bombs on top of us. Can you hold us tight in your arms?" Sayo said to Jun. The tight clasp of his arm around her shoulders made Yumi so warm that she almost fainted. How often had she dreamed of being held by Jun like this. What a sweet woman Sayo was, trying to share her husband with Yumi who had no husband, and knowing that Yumi had always had special feelings for Jun.

Since that night Yumi had waited for them to come whenever the siren blew, but she was usually disappointed. Sometimes they had to be at the hospital; other times danger was so imminent that they had to stay in their own shelter.

But, as the siren wailed and she heard the running footsteps and whispering voices of Sayo and Jun, Yumi was so overjoyed that she wiped away tears in the dark. With the rumbling sound overhead, Yumi found herself pressing tighter against Jun. Fear and darkness made her daring and she felt for Jun's fingers and held them tightly. His fingers clasped Yumi's in return as hard as hers did his. His hand was warm and slightly wet. But so tightly interwoven were their fingers that she could not tell if the warmth and wetness came from her hand or his. She held on to his hand long after the enemy planes were gone.

When he was not there, she forced herself to seek the threadbare comfort of dreams about her dead husband on cold nights alone in the bomb shelter, but it was the memory of her half-brother's fingers that kept her warm.

Yumi had long been tormented by the idea that Hisao had died because she had not loved him enough. The lack of love and warmth at home had driven him into a passion for work and then for war. It was God's way of punishing Yumi for her lukewarm feelings for her husband and for her secret love for Jun. Didn't the Bible say that whoever looked at the other sex with lust had already committed adultery? God must be disappointed with Yumi. She might not be called a Christian any longer, but she wanted to go to church once and pray so that Hisao would rest in peace in heaven.

Yumi walked to the church she used to attend. Since half the city had either been burned or destroyed, she was apprehensive it might no longer be there. So she was both delighted and surprised when she spotted it from a distance, its pencil-thin steeple a forlorn point in the flattened wasteland. After all, the Americans would not dare destroy a church. Or was it proof of divine grace?

As she came nearer, however, she realized that the whole place was a mere ghost of what it once had been. The white paint had peeled off, the stucco was chipped, the windows sooty or broken and the door locked shut with a heavy bolt. The chestnut tree under which she had once sat with Jun was there, but it looked thin and droopy, half its branches gone. The yard was overgrown with weeds.

Yumi asked a passerby about the church. "You don't expect the enemy's religion to survive this war, do you?" he said. "Some pastors are in jail, others pretended to renounce their faith. The blue-eyed pastor has long since gone home."

Feeling at a loss, Yumi walked to the school she used to go to as a young girl, wondering what had happened to the chapel and the missionary teachers. The school seemed to have escaped destruction. But on the stone gate, the brass plaque engraved "St. Mary, American Missionary School" had been replaced by a wooden plaque, the calligraphy on it proclaiming "The Cherry Blossom School for Girls."

Yumi stepped closer to the chapel by the gate where the American teacher Miss Thomas used to speak about Jesus. The door was open, but the interior was gloomy; gray curtains covered the windows and neither candles nor flowers adorned the chapel. As her eyes became used to the dark, she was shocked to find a photograph of Emperor Hirohito above the altar where the cross had once hung. The Emperor's eyes were sleepy and uninspiring in the shiny frame decorated with a puffed bow of a purple ribbon. Yumi ran out, angry with herself for having been so unaware of what war had done. Not only were peace and people dead, but so was freedom. Socialists, liberals, anti-war dissidents and Christians had been put in prison or sent into exile.

In the playground where Yumi had once played volleyball, young girls in black-and-white uniforms were standing in files with bamboo spears in their hands, each one twice as tall as the stick Taku used to carry, and sharply pointed at the top.

"You must be serious," a woman teacher was saying. "When the enemy lands, you have to fight for your lives." With solemn faces, the girls watched the teacher fling her spear upward and then, with a screeching shout—"Yay"—bring it forward as if to stab somebody. After that it was the girls' turn to try.

Yumi could not bear watching the girls innocently fling the spears, left quickly and started to drag her heavy feet back home. She decided to stop and see how her mother was. Hana was on hunger strike. Out of disgust for the war, its ugliness and privations, she had made up her mind to die. Yumi no longer blamed her. She secretly admired her mother's courage.

After Japan's sneak attack on Pearl Harbor, the entire country had been awestruck. The news inspired a sense of mission as well as a curiously humble sense of pride that their country, tiny as it was, had the guts to challenge the strongest nations of the world. Everybody knew very well that without total commitment, cooperation and a spirit of self-sacrifice, the war could not be won. But even at that time Hana had remained aloof from the clamor and the glamour of war.

"When they started the war with China," she said, "they told us it would be over before the next day's breakfast. So they didn't even declare war. We've been bogged down there for ten years. And look what happened to Isamu. If we can't even fight the Chinese without going crazy, what chance do we have against the Americans and the British?" She snorted, sounding like the contrarian she had always been.

At the beginning of the war, at least, it seemed she was wrong. In the evenings, Sayo came to visit and tried to cheer her up. "We take care of the soldiers returning from the war. Even those who are seriously wounded or those who are dying, are optimistic about our eventual victory. So you should be, too, Hana-mother." Even ex-socialist Sayo seemed to have been convinced by the war propaganda.

But Hana refused to be cajoled. A few things had happened that persuaded her that she was right to despair.

One day, two women in glasses, representatives from the National Women's Defense Committee, had visited Hana to suggest that she wear peasants' cotton pants as they did, and not the luxurious silk kimonos that were her normal attire.

"These pants are so much more practical and comfortable," said the larger of the two women. "In case of an enemy attack, you could run and save your life. They're easy to make—we'll show you how to sew them. This is a time to be frugal, as you know; any luxury items you have should be donated to the country."

Hana drew herself up haughtily and said, her chin up, "I appreciate your advice, but I have arthritis and cannot run, whether in peasant pants, bloomers or flappers' skirts. About your second suggestion, if I donate my old silk kimono, what could the government make out of it? They can't make an airplane or a ship out of silk. It's more of a saving if I wear what I have." Then Hana slammed the door in their faces.

When Kana heard her mother growl about this interference, she laughed. "See, I was a little ahead of my time. They're doing what I started many years ago in my club, meddling in other people's affairs. But you know, Mother, these pants are the newest fashion now. They are comfortable. Why don't you try them on?"

Kana made her mother angrier. But the peasant pants had indeed become the fashion. In every neighborhood, women taught each other how to cut their kimonos to sew them into pants, and tie them with a string at the ankles. Sayo, a good seamstress, made pairs for Yumi, Kana, and also for Hana. They all joined forces to coax Hana into trying them on. "With your long legs, you'll look like a fashion model, Mother."

Hana only made a sour face. "Why can't I wear what I like? Why do I have to follow orders? There's no more freedom in this country." She wore a silk kimono again the next day.

A week later, the silver-haired president of the Neighborhood Association came with a workman and asked Hana if it was all right to remove the wrought-iron door from her front gate and the iron lattices from the outhouse in her garden.

With a face as red as a burning iron, Hana shouted, "What? What for? Are you burglars? Or crazy? What utter impudence to suggest such a thing."

The old man bowed politely. "Didn't you read the notice we distributed the other day? The government ordered everybody to donate anything made of iron and steel from the house. They'll be turned into guns and *kamikaze* fighter planes. So it's a good thing to do for the nation."

"I've never thought it a good thing to make guns or *kamikaze* planes," Hana fumed, standing tall and defiant. "What a waste of precious young lives. The fewer planes and guns, the fewer deaths of young men, ours and the enemies'. I won't allow my gate and lattices to be taken."

The old man left, saying, "You give me no choice but to resort to a last measure," and came back later with a policeman. They removed the wrought-iron gate, a showy piece that had cost Taku a fortune, and which he had eventually come to cherish. The association replaced it with a raw wooden gate. Not only did they take the lattices of the outhouse, breaking a window pane in the process, they also inspected the whole house and removed iron latches from the doors and the chest of drawers. From the kitchen they took all the pots made of metal except one.

This was the last humiliation Hana could swallow. When the association asked that she collect recycled articles, rusty nails, wires, beer-bottle caps, tin plates and cans, she gathered them and buried them in her bonsai mound out of sheer spite. Kana laughed and said, "I heard the neighbors gossip about this real eccentric Hana-woman, but I didn't realize how right they were, Mother. You are perverse."

The Women's Defense Committee came again. This time they offered to buy her expensive rings, gold hairpins and ornaments for the price of trinkets. Boiling with rage, she took all of her jewelry to a nearby creek and scattered it in the bottom of the water. "Let them call me an eccentric. I'd rather have fish eat them," she said.

This made Kana furious. "What kind of a mother are you? It's one thing not to give them to the government, but don't you love your daughters enough to leave some for them?"

"No," retorted Hana. "If I leave anything for you, it'll only disappear. Some of my kimonos have gone missing lately; I know they've been drunk."

Kana took Isamu to the creek. After wading in the water for hours, they managed to retrieve some of the beautiful stones and pins Hana had scattered, but the bottom was full of rocks and it was not possible to find everything.

One day, Hana decided she had to have shark-fin soup for dinner, having been bored with the nightly supper of rationed potatoes. She asked Yumi to cook it for her, but there was barely a sardine to be found at the fish store. Yumi went all the way to the Tsukiji fish market near the harbor. An old fisherman there told her, "We have to send more than thirty thousand tins of sardines next week to the starving soldiers. All the young fishermen have been taken for the war. We have no time to go fishing sharks to satisfy the taste of some spoiled rich woman. If we do, we'll either be eaten by them, or hit by a torpedo."

After that, Hana refused to eat. "Nothing worth eating is available," she said. "Do you expect me to eat potato porridge every day? All the good things in life are gone. The *kabuki* theater is closed; the Americans burned down my favorite antique shops; one shouldn't wear a silk kimono; one can't buy rice or matches without lining up in a queue for rations. Do you see any point in living? It's better to be dead than to watch my country destroy itself."

At first Yumi tried to coax Hana from her hunger strike and cooked her mother's favorite dishes, vegetable sushi or stir-fried tofu and shiitake mushrooms out of her own meager supplies and brought them to her, because Hana always yielded to temptation when faced with what she really liked.

Kana objected. "Mother's like a spoiled child. Why do you cater to her every whim, Yumi-san? People are dying of hunger. They're bearing all sorts of hardships. You shouldn't force food on a person who doesn't want to eat."

In one of the last conversations Yumi had with Hisao, he said, "I think your mother is serious about what she's doing. Why don't you respect her last wishes?" At the time she did not follow his advice, because Yumi could not bear to watch her own mother kill herself. But after Hisao's death she thought she should respect her husband's last words.

Hana, too, protested. "Leave me alone, Yumi," she said. "I don't want you to fuss over me. I don't have much freedom in the way I live—shouldn't I at least have freedom in the way I die? I'm doing this not only because I don't like what this country is doing, but also because I'm good for nothing and I'll only make myself as well as other people miserable if I live any longer."

Hana felt she was good for nothing because arthritis had damaged all the joints of her body and she lived in pain. The lion-headed, snake-tailed and fire-breathing chimera had run all over her once beautiful body and ravaged her till she felt half dead. Just as this mysterious monster was an unlikely combination of various animals, he attacked her body in totally unforeseen ways. Some days he tortured her knees. They swelled like balloons filled with vile liquid. Then he attacked her feet and her every step was like walking in shoes with thousands of nails sticking up. Later, he moved to her shoulders and elbows, and relentlessly banged them with a hammer. He had crept silently into her hands and managed to transform her once graceful fingers into twisted old hooks. Her soft and slender arms and legs were now as thin and brittle as knotted branches of an old tree. Cartilage in the joints had worn away and the bones rubbed against each other. They made creaky sounds like rusted hinges.

One day, Hana was locked in the outhouse because she could not open its door with her crippled fingers. She screamed for more than half an hour and, when Kana found her, she barked as ferociously as the chimera himself, blaming Kana for not having found her sooner.

Being a proud woman, Hana did not talk much about her pains. The thought crossed her mind that she had been punished for being too haughty, but she was too haughty to admit it. She would rather die proud in pain than admit her sins and wait for forgiveness from Buddha, millions of gods or an alien God, each of whom seemed to be as undependable as the weather and as willful as herself.

Though not religious, Hana was superstitious. If something fell on her toe or a needle pricked her finger, her first reaction was, "What did I do wrong? What am I being punished for?" Any misfortune was retribution for something she had done wrong in the past. Arthritis could, therefore, be karma from her past. It occurred to her that she might be receiving punishment for having been a geisha. But it was what she had been forced to be by her father. She had hated being a geisha and had seduced Taku into buying her out. She should not be punished for it because there was nothing else she could have done in order to be freed. So Hana did not find any reason to repent.

Hana would rather die than live in pain and deprivation. She would not even eat the special dishes Yumi cooked. Now there was no more special food for Yumi to cook, anyway. Forget shark fins—sardines, rice, flour, fruit and vegetables had all disappeared from the shops. People waited in long queues for rations, and the portions shrank with every passing season.

"It's funny that after putting all the socialists in prison, the government has now turned this country socialist. With food handed out equally to everyone, there's no more rich or poor," Sayo said to Yumi with a bitter smile.

One afternoon when Yumi visited Hana on the way back from her unhappy church and school visits, Nurse Kei, who was there to help Hana at Yumi's request, was giving Hana a back rub in bed. Yumi had to turn her eyes away: Hana's back was all ribs, with what looked like ditches dug in between. The skeleton Yumi had seen in Masao's science class looked fatter. For a second, the supple, youthful body of her mother returned to her eyes and she sighed. Years ago they had bathed together in a hot spring, and when Hana stood up in the tub, misty white with steam all around her, Yumi was awestruck. She thought this must be the very vision of Venus rising from the sea.

Once Hana was dressed in a kimono, she looked better. Her cheeks were sunken, but her eyes shone with the alertness of a wild animal's and her face showed the strong will of a woman courageously facing death. "I'm still alive, Yumi," Hana said. "Do you know what? Since I started fasting, I've been feeling ecstatic. This may be the Buddhist nirvana Taku-san always talked about. But death comes so slowly. I wonder when it'll be here."

Yumi knew why her mother was not dying, because Jun had confided the secret to her. Hana, still vain about her looks, wanted to die, but only gracefully. "Jun-san," she said to her stepson, "how can I die beautifully? I hear people starving to death lose their hair and nails and grow a paunchy tummy. I don't want that kind of death. Is there a miracle pill to keep me beautiful until the last day?"

Jun, who like the other family members had been worried about Hana, used this opportunity to help her live. He prescribed glucose pills, cod-liver-oil tablets and vitamins, saying,

"These will keep you as beautiful as ever until you go." He visited Hana regularly at night to give her an injection of glucose— "An added medicine for what you wish."

Lulled into a feeling of well-being from her back rub, Hana soon fell asleep. Sitting in the kitchen over tea, Kei told Yumi she would have to leave for her hometown in order to take care of her own mother. "Then I have to move in with my mother," Yumi said. She wanted to take good care of her mother during her last days, anyway. It would be better than living alone, sleepless at night, worrying about Masao and waiting, usually in vain, for Jun and Sayo to visit during the raids.

After tea with Kei, Yumi roamed the garden, which had been neglected since Hana stopped bothering about it. Trees and bushes were overgrown and reminded Yumi of the jungle where Masao might be fighting a terrible battle.

Masao had not sent any more cards, but Yumi kept reciting the two letters she had received, imagining all the possible things that could have happened to her son. The jungle of New Guinea did not seem to be on a paradise island or in a fairyland where benign miracles took place as in the stories Yumi used to write. What if he were bitten by a snake, poisoned by wild berries, caught by the natives or shot by an enemy gun?

On the way back from the walk to Hana's bedroom, Isamu came into view. Today he was folding paper planes out of newspapers and flying them outside Hana's room, saying, "I must keep Hana-mother amused so that she'll forget about dying."

"Do you see how this plane flies better than the last, Hana-mother?" Isamu said loudly. "I'm experimenting to see which shape of plane flies fastest. Soon paper will be used to make a *kamikaze* plane, you see. We're about to run out of metals."

"Isamu-san, it's a good idea to make a *kamikaze* plane with paper." Hana's sleepy voice was heard from her room.

"Oh, this one staggers like Kana when she's drunk—which is, of course, pretty much all the time these days. Maybe it isn't a bad idea for a *kamikaze* pilot to plunge into an enemy ship, happily intoxicated—what do you think, Yumi-san?"

Isamu folded more planes with newspaper, saying, "We must prepare for the enemy's landing. Yumi-san, do you know that those hairy monster enemies will land really soon, unless *kamikaze,* the god wind, blows and sinks all of their ships, just as it did when Kublai Khan came to invade us six hundred years ago?"

Coming across a picture in the paper of the Emperor on his white horse, he said: "*Ah so*. I'll be put in jail for folding the Emperor into half and making him into a *kamikaze* pilot. But then he'd be a real hero, not like the phantom god he is, ha, ha."

"Oh, here's a photo of General Tojo. Let's fold him into pieces and make him charge into an American carrier. He must be a role model for all the young men, not through his pompous words, but with his heroic deeds. Let this narcissist die in a *kamikaze* plane as he tells millions of youths to do in his self-righteous speeches. 'You are the chosen ones who are born to die to help the nation's crisis. You are the saviors to liberate the world from the demons of the West. Die for a great moral cause and you'll live to glorious eternity!' Let him be a shining example for the chosen ones who are born to die. Let him die for a great moral cause." Isamu spoke so loudly that Yumi had to hush him for fear someone might overhear. But he did not stop.

"Ah, here's my father being quoted in yesterday's paper," Isamu smiled and continued, "'We the hundred million will die together for His Majesty the Emperor. We will never surrender if the last one in the land dies.' Oh gods. What nerve to use 'we,' as if all of us agree with him. Let's fold him into a *kamikaze* and let him be the first one to go. He won't mind dying since there's nobody at home waiting for him any longer. His son has gone mad and his wife has died of grief. All the old men like him order the young to die. Why don't they go first? They're the ones who started the war. They are old and evil, and deserve to die. Don't you agree, Yumi-san?"

Isamu often startled Yumi with his stinging sarcasm, or his speaking the naked truth. Just the other day, Hana had said to Yumi, "Do you think Isamu is mad, or only feigning? If he's insane, I must be, too, because he thinks the same way I do about many things, particularly about the war."

"You and Isamu-san are a good match," Yumi said. "He's so much more lucid than most of us, just as you are. You both have courage to say what others wouldn't dare to and get away with it, because you're eccentric and because he's supposed to be mad. It's not a bad way to stay sane in these crazy times."

"Poor Isamu's left alone by Kana. He may be a failure as well as a cuckold, but he's lovable," Hana said. Yumi thought Hana had become more human in her old age.

After Taku died, Isamu had been sad, but he acted like a man reborn. Isamu had not forgotten his mission to stop the war in China. He had promised this in the last minute of Taku's life. As if it were the only reason to live, Isamu spent his days writing protests against the war to newspapers, the army office and the government. When nothing came of them, he went directly to the prime minister's office, and the army headquarters where his father worked. Everywhere he went, he was dismissed as a dissident, or a mental case, or both, and turned away at the gate.

Once he refused to leave, and ended up in prison. The police beat and kicked him so severely that once again he really seemed to have lost his sanity. He was found bellowing out commands, "Fall in. Come now quick, men. Atten-shun," and marching around the cell all day. He woke the other inmates in the middle of night, shouting, "Let's go to the village and rape women." It was not clear if he was really insane or pretending. Eventually his father consented to use his influence to free his son. In exchange, Isamu had to promise never to visit the offices again.

At home, Kana found him a nuisance and pressured him to find a job. This was not easy, since Isamu had no intention of working for anything remotely connected with the military, even if that was his area of expertise. Fearing for his own reputation, his father also did not want his son, with his disgraceful record, to work anywhere in his orbit. Finally, Yumi found a job for him at a clothing factory run by her late husband's relatives, but the factory made only military uniforms. Isamu could not stand seeing thousands of military uniforms every day; it brought back in full force all the memories he had learned to suppress. He went to his boss and told him that the war was a lost cause, that he should stop making military uniforms and switch instead to women's underwear. When his advice was not followed, he organized an anti-war campaign and a strike, and was fired.

Once again he was back at the teahouse full-time, driving Kana crazy. Irked by her good-for-nothing husband, she went out one night heavily made-up and did not come back until midnight. The next morning Kana was humming, her hair limp and tangled, but her eyes alight and her cheeks rosy even without rouge. She said to Isamu who was seething with jealousy and anger, "If you don't behave, I'll leave you. I have a better man than you to take care of me." Isamu bit her, beat her, and threw books at her, kicking and howling. He was confined in a mental hospital for a while, but since he acted like a perfect gentleman the whole time he was there, he was quickly released back to the teahouse.

Kana's affair ended when her young lover was drafted and sent to the Philippines. "I'm always a war widow," Kana lamented wistfully. But in hardly any time at all she found a new lover. After acting the role of faithful wife for years, Kana had become shameless, as if she were a different woman altogether.

"Being an adulteress is more fun than catching one out," she said to Yumi. "You know, Yumi-san, you've lost Hisao-san, and Masao is far away; why don't you get yourself a man? You won't feel so lonely all the time. You may not be so young any more, but you're still beautiful enough to attract any man you want."

Kana's new lover was fifty years old. "Old men are better," she said, "because the upper age limit of the draft is forty-five. Besides, this man has a slight heart condition, so there's no chance he'll go to war." She did not stop drinking, though. More kimonos disappeared from Hana's chest. Her *obis* had also gone missing. Empty saké and wine bottles piled up in the garden.

Once Kana was found asleep on her stomach in the moss garden, her head dangling in the fish pond. Isamu said to Yumi, "Kana must have been looking at her reflection in the pond like Narcissus. Good thing she didn't fall all the way into the water."

Hana was exasperated with Kana and scolded her. "What happened to my self-righteous daughter, the one who used to point her finger at others for anything suspicious? Why don't you point your finger at yourself and stop drinking, or whatever you are doing? I know things haven't been easy for you, but one's strength can be measured by how one copes with difficult situations. You haven't shown much, so far. I don't want my daughter to be an alcoholic and a tart."

"It runs in the family," Kana said, sticking out her nose.

"I never drank much, and I was never promiscuous. All I did as a geisha was my professional duty," Hana said proudly.

"Professional duty, I wonder what it is?" Kana said and laughed. "Anyway, don't worry, Mother, I'm a grown woman: I'll take care of myself."

Despite Jun's pills and injections, Hana gradually grew weaker. In the morning she was alert, drinking tea for breakfast and cracking a few jokes, but she did not always make sense; her venomous tongue had lost its sting. For the rest of the day she slept. One night, the air raid siren blew at midnight, but Hana slept through its howls. Yumi wondered what to do. She knew that Isamu could carry Hana to the shelter under the bonsai mound. But it might not be such a good idea to move her to the cold hole in the ground. Yumi thought she would take a chance and stay with her mother in the room.

But Isamu was already standing in front of her. How had he arrived here from the teahouse so quickly? Had he flown over the mounds and the pond like a *ninja,* a secret agent for a samurai? He said, "Let's go. It's so easy, Yumi-san. I've been carrying her in every raid."

Hana opened her eyes halfway and said wearily, "I'm too sleepy. This might be my chance to die. Let me stay here, Isamu-san."

But Isamu covered her up with a hood and a thick blanket. He said, "Shogun Taku is dead. I don't have a father. My mother died, and Kana might as well be gone. You're one of my few friends. So, for my sake, Hana-mother, please don't die." He did not exactly fly, but ran through the dark gardens as fast as a soldier in a guerrilla war, carrying Hana in his arms as easily as if she were a rag doll. Yumi ran as fast as she could, too, and when she got down into the shelter, a candle was already lit and Hana was bundled up on a cot.

This shelter Isamu had built was an underground palace compared with Yumi's primitive cave. It was spacious and its ceiling high; one could stand up straight in it without bumping one's head. Isamu asked Yumi to sit on a chair and served tea which was kept in a thermos on a raw wood table he had made. He gave a cup of tea also to Hana, but she was too drowsy to drink. The hot tea made Yumi warm and cozy. "This is so civilized, Isamu-san, that I almost forget about the enemy planes," she said, although her thoughts were on the whereabouts of Jun and Sayo. Were they in their shelter at home, or working at the hospital, taking care of the injured? Yumi closed her eyes and prayed for their safety.

This hole was so deep in the ground that the drones of the planes could only be heard as distant thunder. Isamu sat with his arms crossed on the table, candlelight flickering on his gaunt face. While he was not on hunger strike, he was, like most people, not getting enough to eat. The rings around his eyes were dark, and from them his eyes protruded like a goldfish's. His pencil nose was now razor thin.

"Yumi-san, we have no more hope, other than the divine wind, *kamikaze*. But can you believe this?" Isamu said, rolling his eyes. "My father tells me that they are making the Koreans dig a gigantic secret shelter in the mountains of Nagano so that Hirohito-san, Tojo, and the likes of my father can hide when the enemy comes to catch them. Isn't it a laugh that they are trying so hard to save themselves, while they've been busy telling millions of men to die honorable deaths for their country? I hope the enemy will catch them and hang them upside-down as the worst fiends in history."

"Aren't the Americans going to kill us all, as the leaders say?" Yumi asked.

"We don't know. But whatever they do, we'll go down in history as the most unholy nation; we've committed despicable crimes against China, Korea and the rest of Asia. We were indoctrinated by the military and lost our senses. They say there are eight million gods in Japan, but don't you think there are just as many demons among us? We were driven by our own demons. My sin will never be atoned even after I die. That sixteen-year-old Wang Sho-yin I killed in China will never come back to life." Isamu gazed into the flickering flame of the candle.

"But you know, Yumi-san, think of those American pilots who are dropping bombs over us right now. They are killing innocent civilians by the thousands, all with one shot. The only difference between them and me is that they kill people *en masse,* instead of one individual at a time. Perhaps such mass killings are sinless according to their merciful Christianity, because you are not killing, the machines are. You can hide your face behind those B-29 bombers and P-51 fighters; you're guiltless because you fly away and forget about everything you've done. You don't see the faces of the maimed, the dying and the dead, and therefore you don't suffer. Those Americans are faceless and nameless murderers. And they are self-righteous because they think they are here to punish our savagery and arrogance. They go home and will be welcomed as the heroes who exterminated the hideous dwarf demons. They've got it only half right—

I should definitely be killed—but how about the thousands of innocent children?"

He looked at Hana, who was suddenly alert and listening, gazing at Isamu with her penetrating eyes. Isamu continued, "But relax, Hana-mother. Some day soon peace will come. It's a rule of nature: the sun comes out even after the most terrible typhoon. Time will solve all your problems. Everything is both tentative and relative. The war criminals will be hanged and the dissidents will take over the world. Once again we'll have freedom, kabuki, sumo and shark-fin soup. If not tomorrow, then in a few years. So don't rush into killing yourself, Hana-mother," he rambled on, unaware that Hana had gone back to sleep.

Suddenly Isamu let out a sob and shook his head. "Where's Kana now? Well, it doesn't matter. We don't know if we're going to be alive tomorrow or not. She has a right to enjoy her life." He covered his face with his hands, his whole body shaking.

Yumi moved to sit near him, put her arm around his trembling shoulders, and cried with him in the silence of the dark. By the time Isamu stopped shaking and sat up, the distant roar had died down and the candle had burned out. The hole was black and cold. Isamu turned on a flashlight, picked up Hana, and slowly walked with Yumi back to the house.

The next morning, when Yumi brought tea and medicine to Hana and called out to her, she did not answer. She called her again. Hana's face was serene and beautiful, but when Yumi touched her hand, it was cold and hard.

Hana's wish had been granted. Before she called anybody, Yumi washed her mother's body, put on her favorite dark blue crépe kimono, and tied it with a brocaded silver *obi*. Hana had grown so thin that the *obi* had to be wound around her waist five times. Yumi tied her mother's hair in the elegant oval chignon she had always worn, and put a peacock pin in the knot. She touched her cheeks and lips with rouge, and sprayed her with perfume.

Yumi alternately cried and smiled throughout these preparations. She was certain her mother must be content, happy that she was so stunningly beautiful even in death, and relieved that she was finally dead and did not have to complain about the stupid war and its privations. Taku would be pleased and surprised when she appeared in heaven looking every bit as elegant as she was in her youth. Her gardens would thrive for generations, just as she had planned, with lilies, irises, and roses blooming as a reminder of her own beauty.

She was buried next to Taku in Shoman-ji temple, on the other side of Emi.

Isamu blamed himself for Hana's death, having taken her out in the cold the night before, and was distraught. But Jun convinced him that it had been inevitable; it was her time to go. Yumi told him how Hana must have appreciated his devotion and his philosophical remarks on the last night of her life.

After Hana's funeral, Yumi found herself once again preoccupied with Masao. She studied a map of New Guinea, which lay between the equator and Australia like a giant bird stretching its wings. She went to a library to read about the land. The second biggest island in the world after Greenland, it rained heavily there, just as Masao's card had said, and its lower regions were covered with thick jungle and often flooded by mile-wide muddy rivers. The coastline consisted of rugged cliffs, some of them the highest in the world. Dangerous crocodiles, flying foxes, and poisonous snakes abounded; the natives ate not only fish, but also lizards, dogs, and even humans. Even without a battle, Masao's life was in danger.

At night, Yumi waited with impatience for the morning, when the sun and the chores could distract her from her anguish. When the morning came, the picture of her son dying on a faraway island still tormented her.

Yumi went to the army office and enquired about her son. A man there answered her politely. "One of the harder battles was fought in eastern New Guinea and across the sea, in Guadalcanal. The casualties of the latest battle were sixteen thousand seven hundred and thirty-four, and there is no way of knowing about the fate of individuals. I'm surprised that you have even received a card from your son. You should consider yourself fortunate in that regard." He went away quickly, as if to escape further questions. For him, finding out about an individual was like singling out an ant in an anthill. Men were just numbers, like 16,734. By the way he professed surprise that she had received a card, it was obvious that for him her son was but a dead man on a forgotten island.

With a candor unusual for the government, the radio gave a report of the battle in New Guinea: "It is extremely difficult to supply ammunition and food to this formidable island. Our soldiers are left with weapons unimaginably inferior to the Australians' firearms, the quantity and quality of which are overpowering. But our soldiers are bravely fighting to their death, eating berries off the trees." The news ended with a theme song, as it did after every report on a battle:

Umi yukaba, mizuki kabane, yama yukaba, kusamusu kabane . . .
(In the sea, corpses float in the water,
In the mountains, bodies lie in the grass,
We want to die near our Emperor, and won't look back.)

It was an ancient poem set to new music, a reminder that this was not the first time in history that soldiers had died like dogs. But it was a cruel song to a mother whose son might number among the dead who lay in the grass.

Chances were that Masao had died as one of the 16,734; if not in battle, then from starvation, malaria, fatigue—perhaps from a scorpion or snakebite. He could have fallen from a cliff, or drowned in a flood; he might have been eaten by a crocodile or the natives. What an abundance of choices. Whatever death he had faced, had it contributed anything to the war? Was it an honorable death and had it been worth its cost? Maybe it would be a blessing to die rather than to keep living in the midst of such a battle. Even so, how could a mother give up hope for her son's life?

Yumi found herself increasingly angry. She was angry at the government, the military, and the Emperor. Yes, the Emperor. Admittedly he was a figurehead, used to mobilize the nation, but he was no phantom. He had the ultimate power of veto. How could he just sit there, watching his people obediently give up their husbands, fathers and sons, knowing very well that so many of them were destined never to return?

Yumi was also anxious about her nephew, Shun, who had recently been drafted. She had visited Shun on the day he left. He said he would play the piano for the last time. "After all, when will I next be able to play again?" he asked, lovingly stroking the keys. He chose a Mozart sonata. Once he began to play, he looked intensely happy, his fingers, his ears and his mind absorbed in the sound. The way he tilted his head to listen to his music and the passionate glow in his eyes reminded Yumi of the time she watched his grandmother Emi play her music on the *koto*. His sadness at his imminent parting from his family, his fear of war and of death, poured into the music and each key he pressed had a different color, texture and feeling. Jun sat behind him, gazing at his son's back and listening to the music, tears rolling down his cheeks.

Until the moment he left, Shun was speechless and lingered at his parents' side, strained with emotion. He was not like Masao, who had swallowed his fears and declared he would dedicate his life to his country, just as his father had done. Shun, although exposed to the same propaganda, had not turned into a passionate patriot like Masao. Sayo hugged Shun and cried uncontrollably, while Jun placed an arm around each of them and buried his head in his son's shoulder. Yumi put her arms around Shun, too. He was another son to her—she had known him since he was a baby, and she loved his father.

Since that day, Yumi had prayed for Shun as well as for Masao. While the *omikuji* fortune-teller's sign for Masao was "Great Misfortune," it read only "Misfortune" for Shun; with any luck, he would not have to go to a place as deadly as New Guinea.

Isamu often distracted Yumi from morbid thoughts about Masao as well as the added worries about Shun. "Yumi-san, come out to the bomb site two blocks south," cried out Isamu, coming up to the house, his goldfish eyes popping. "We're going to have a fire drill. Make sure you bring a bucket."

At the special request of the silver-haired president of the Neighborhood Association, Isamu had begun working for the local Vigilance Corps. The old man knew that Isamu had been discharged from the army as a mental case, but going on the evidence of an occasional chat, he had come to the conclusion that Isamu, though sarcastic, was perfectly sane and extremely intelligent. He thought it would be a waste for the country not to utilize this able-bodied former army lieutenant.

Isamu thrived at the job. Every time the siren blew, instead of hibernating in the cave like a dormouse, he went out with his old iron helmet on his head and his haversack on his back. Like a child on a forbidden adventure, he ran quickly from corner to corner, guiding anyone left on the street into the nearest shelter. With his military training, he was as nimble and alert as a *ninja* and was ready whenever anyone needed help.

One night he rescued a baby from a burning house. He raced through the flames, bundled her inside his army jacket, took her to a water tank and plunged her inside it to cool her burns. On another occasion, he saved a boy whose shirt was burning by catching him and rolling him on the ground. Since then, the neighbors had taken to calling him "Ninja-san."

Behind Isamu's almost suicidal actions was a secret: his indifference to his own life. With Kana having virtually deserted him, there seemed little reason to go on, and he continued to blame himself for Hana's death. Yet while there had been a time when he talked about killing himself, either through hunger strike as Hana had done, or by hanging himself on a tree, his job took away the need for such plans. He said to Yumi, "This may be better than hanging. Do small good things as penance for my sins, then die under a bomb."

Full of both beans and ideas, he spent his days walking around, studying the best evacuation routes in case of a fire. "It's an ironclad rule that one should go upwind in a fire," he explained to the neighbors. "This is an alternative route in case there's an east wind." He salvaged a few large tubs from the ruins of a factory, cleaned them and set them up as extra water tanks at street corners in the neighborhood.

He organized fire drills for the residents—mostly women, left to guard their houses in the absence of men. Isamu, looking serious, said to them, "You are firefighters. Don't think this is only a game, ladies." He made them line up and gave them military commands. "Advance. Take your positions. Charge." Under his orders, they relayed bucket after bucket filled with water scooped from the tank.

He even taught the residents how to march, saying, "It's important for you to be in good physical shape for an emergency." Yumi had a hard time synchronizing her left hand and right foot, but most of the women seemed to enjoy walking like soldiers.

Those women who did not come to the drill at first, scoffing at the idea that a few buckets of water could ameliorate the consequences of a bomb, came the next time, as the word had spread that not only was Ninja-san young, good-looking, and crazed, but he saved lives, too. Young men were rare sights those days. Some women brought him rice balls, others sweet potatoes, and they all implored him for help. "In case my house gets burned, can you help me, Ninja-san?"

Even Kana joined the drill, boasting to the women, "Do you know that he is my husband?" She was a little jealous of the attention Isamu was getting from the ladies, and she started to spend more nights at home.

Yumi was happy that Isamu had finally found something useful to do. His wounded ego had been healed a little by the attention he was receiving, and he no longer talked about dying.

One afternoon, Kana, sober and pensive for a change, came to see Yumi and said, "My lover has gone to his relative's place in Nagano for safety. He wanted me to go with him. He said, 'If you go far away from Isamu-san, you might forget about him and then we could be married.' I seriously thought about it, but somehow I can't do it. I had fun with my lover, in part because I was only half serious, but when it comes down to it, I can't leave Isamu-san, because he is, after all, such a sweet man. He's had hard times and we've gone through so much together. I've already hurt him enough. So I told my lover I'll stay here. Yumi-san, do you think I made the right decision?" Kana was melancholy, still wavering between the two men.

"Will you stay because you love Isamu-san, or because you feel guilty?" Yumi asked.

"I do love Isamu-san, but I can't forget my lover so easily, either."

"Isn't it time to make a commitment to one man?" Yumi said. "The war made Isamu-san crazy and you had a hard time, but he's all better now. He's a lovely man and deserves to be loved and treated better. You could make him really happy if you go back to him, and you'd be happy, too. So I think you've made the right decision, Kana."

"That's what I think. I hope I'll forget my lover in just a little while."

Yumi was so happy, she said, "Let's celebrate at a candlelit dinner tonight."

Food was so scarce that there was not much to celebrate with. Yumi cooked a soybean porridge; Kana picked plantains and dandelions in the garden and sautéed them with used tea leaves and pounded egg shells. Isamu caught two frogs and a grasshopper and barbecued them with soy sauce on the hibachi. The candlelight made the food look elegant, and everything tasted fine; they all ate well for a change.

Isamu was proud of his grasshopper. "It's such a delicacy, isn't it? So crisp and delicate. Particularly the whiskers and eyes."

Kana said, "They tell us to donate used tea leaves for the provision of horses, but they're too delicious to give away. And the crushed egg shells are good for bones."

"People sell kimonos to the farmers in order to buy food in the black market," added Yumi. "But we won't ever have to do that if we eat like this."

Isamu laughed and said, "Our kimonos are all gone: not eaten, but drunk."

It was a cold evening for March. A north wind had been blowing all day. Isamu said, "They might visit us tonight. The B-29 steel typhoon. Have you noticed that they pick windy nights so that the incendiary bombs will burn more effectively? So don't drink too much, Kana. We have to stay sober."

"I would rather die intoxicated," Kana said, sipping more saké. Becoming more and more flirtatious with every swallow, she fondled Isamu's fingers, and kissed his cheeks. She pushed her saké cup to his mouth and forced him to drink. Isamu was red, from happy bashfulness as well as drink.

"It's time to stop drinking and go to bed, children," Yumi said.

After they retired to the teahouse, Yumi smiled, feeling happy for Kana and Isamu. It had been years, but now, finally, they would be happy together.

At midnight, Yumi was about to go to bed when the siren blew, just as Isamu had guessed. As she walked out to the shelter, wrapping herself with her hood and her silk floss jacket, she saw Isamu rush out of the gate in his helmet. Kana was shouting after him, "Don't be reckless, Isamu-san. Protect yourself."

Isamu called back, "Don't worry, Kana. I'm a *ninja*."

It was an unusually long and heavy raid. Like animals sniffing for every sign of danger, Yumi and Kana sat in the shelter, straining their ears. Hundreds of planes must be passing overhead and the droning sound only increased. Yumi was anxious not only about Isamu, but also about Jun and Sayo. She prayed that God would protect them wherever they were.

"I'm going out, Yumi-san. I can't stand staying here like this," Kana said.

"It's suicidal. Are you still drunk, Kana? We can't help anybody anyway."

"I'll find out what Isamu-san is doing. I've got to tell him to come back here for his own safety," said Kana. She was already climbing up the steps.

Yumi followed Kana, saying, "If you're going, I am, too."

Outside, the roar was so overwhelming that Yumi and Kana had to plug their ears with their fingers. The sky over to the east was all red. Half of Tokyo was burning.

Whiz. The air reverberated with a great flash of light, and Yumi and Kana drew back. A deafening explosion followed. They lay on their stomachs on the ground, their fingers covering their eyes and plugging their ears and noses. When the drone finally faded in the distance, they slowly got up and resumed walking, cowering down each time they heard a blast.

As they came to the square, they saw that an entire cluster of terraced houses was in flames. Kana spotted Isamu shooting water from a hose. Coming as close as she dared, she screamed at him, "Isamu-san, come back to the shelter. It's more important to save your life than the houses."

Isamu shouted, "What are you doing here, Kana? Go into a shelter. Quick."

One of the men fighting the fire also ran up to Isamu. "Ninja-san, I see the planes coming in at an unusually low altitude. They look like P-51 fighters. Let's go and hide." The man scurried toward the trees for cover.

Isamu looked up at the sky, and then he, too, started to run. Suddenly, a monstrously heavy plane appeared; it dived low, an eagle swooping down for its prey. Her arms outstretched, Kana watched Isamu dash toward her.

With a sudden flash of light and crackling sounds, rat-tat-tat-tat, Isamu jumped up in the air like a jack popping out of his box, and then fell to the ground, on his stomach. The plane vanished into the night sky as fast as it had come.

Kana shuddered as if she were having a convulsion. She crawled out of the bush, ran over, and crouched beside Isamu. She touched him all over, crying out, "Isamu-san, Isamu-san, Please don't die." Trying to hold his body in her arms, she felt the blood well up from under him. She lifted his face and saw one of his eyes was blown out. She hugged him, kissed him all over and cried, burying her head in his body.

Slowly people emerged from their hiding places and surrounded Isamu's body. "He saved my baby's life," a woman said, bursting into tears. "He died because he was trying to save my house," another woman said, lowering her head.

The fire continued to rage at the back of the square.

CHAPTER 11

The train chugged along the shore of the Pacific, coughing with each seam of the rails and creaking at every curve. Jun was sitting next to Sayo, who was asleep, bending her head and nodding. Each jerk of the train tossed her head toward Jun's arm like a volleyball, but, worn out by the night shift at the hospital, she showed no sign of waking. They were taking two days off to see their son Shun, who was at a training camp prior to being sent off to war abroad.

Jun felt sorry that Sayo was so overworked. He put his arm around her shoulder so that she would not be shaken too much, and looked at her face that had once been full, sunken now from the woes of war and poverty of diet. The cheekbones jutted out sharply, her once smooth skin was weathered, but still red and ruddy. Jun liked Sayo's face. It was not pretty in the classical sense, rather resembling the earthy face often seen on peasant women, but Jun found it infinitely more beautiful than a painted doll's face like that of a geisha. It was the face of a nurse who, after years of service, still cried for her patients, the face of a mother whose son had been taken to war. It was a face in mourning for the nation that had lost its soul.

Jun and Sayo were dutiful wartime citizens: neither liked the war, but they were aware there was nothing they could do about it. They knew very well that showing even a trace of dissidence would only bring trouble. They were chained in a prison called war, just like everybody else in their generation.

These days Jun had also been working hard, so much so that he thought he might die of fatigue. He was one of the very few doctors left at the hospital. The main units and their long-term patients had been evacuated to a remote town in Gumma prefecture and the hospital building in Tokyo had been leveled down to two stories so it would not be an easy target for bombs. Many of the other doctors had fled dangerous Tokyo, opting instead for Gumma, and most of the younger staff had been sent off to war. The Tokyo unit was about to be closed down, but in the event of a fierce raid, where would the emergency patients go? Jun had decided he had no choice but to stay and take care of them.

His hospital was a battle zone after each raid, particularly after the night of the most recent one—10 March 1945—the one in which Isamu died. Tens of hundreds of wounded had been jammed in. It was the very picture of hell, with people moaning everywhere, their bodies burned black, their intestines pushed out, legs and arms missing. Jun felt like the captain of a ship sinking because it was overloaded with dying bodies, and his heart sank, too, with the unbearable weight of his helplessness. It seemed to him that in the scene before him he could read the destiny of his country.

He was immensely thankful that Sayo was with him. Without her he would have resigned from his position long ago, unable to bear the faces of agony and death. Sayo dreaded the raids and was terrified by the bombs, but once she saw people in dire need, she did the right thing at once, forgetting about herself and her fears. She always did as much as or more than the doctors, but since the March raid, Jun felt doubly aware of her value, just as in the aftermath of the great earthquake. She saved many lives by virtue of her quick actions, her thorough care and even just her kind words, and she cried bitterly for those who died.

Jun, too, was grateful that he had been able to save a few lives. But he was very sad that he hadn't saved his grandmother. The other day he received a notice asking him if he was related to Chiyo Yamato who had died in a fire started by an incendiary bomb. He reported to the ward office. The clerk told him, "Probably fast asleep with the storm windows shut, the old lady did not hear or smell anything until it was too late." Chiyo had insisted on staying in Tokyo, in spite of Jun's urging her to evacuate to the countryside.

He went to see his old home that was now a black skeleton. The pond where he used to watch bugs swim was covered with ashes. A red camellia and a few spots of deep green moss peeping through the blackened ground stung his eyes. Those were the only signs of life in the place where he had once lived with Emi, Chiyo, Lee, and Momo, none of whom were in this world any longer.

Jun looked outside the window at the ocean, where white waves were dancing in the sun. The sea was beguilingly peaceful. It was hard to believe that somewhere on the same sea, fierce battles were being fought and thousands of men were dying every day. A seagull flying low on the shore reminded Jun of the day his and Yumi's families went low-tide shell fishing. Yumi had hopped like a young girl alongside him on the beach, saying she felt like a seagull, and looking like one in her blue dress. She was a happy young woman then, at least outwardly so, in an intact family with her husband, Hisao, and Masao, a rambunctious boy. She had cut her toe on a shard of glass on the sand, and Jun remembered the shiver that had run through him when he held her wounded foot on his thigh. Her foot was so dainty, her little toes lining up like lima beans, and the blood so pure red on the big toe. She had watched him raptly as his fingers touched her wound with cotton, her cheeks almost as red as her blood.

Yumi might not have been as happy as she looked, for she

and Hisao had been ill-suited. But at least she had not been alone then. The war had deprived her of her family. Caring for Hana, Kana, and Isamu had distracted Yumi from her loneliness and worries, but with both Hana and Isamu dead, and Kana off to Nagano to join her lover after Isamu had died, Yumi had been left alone. How dreary her nights must be now, with only the air raids to interrupt the monotony of her solitude.

Over the past few weeks, her brother Ken had come often to try to persuade her to move to the village north of Nagoya, where his family had been evacuated. Yumi was initially reluctant. Jun had strongly urged her to go before leaving on this trip, although saddened by the prospect of her moving so far away. Tokyo was much too dangerous now. So, by the time Jun returned to Tokyo, Yumi would not be there. He missed her already.

After leaving the shore and meandering among the mountains, the train halted at a small station with its name written shyly somewhere, tucked away out of sight. Even at this little station, though, Jun encountered the familiar sight of a departing soldier surrounded by well-wishers.

But this scene was different from the usual one. Here there was no boisterous group singing military songs, shouting out "*Banzai*" in an all-too-clearly staged show of excitement. The boy who stood surrounded by the quiet group of peasant women was sickly thin; his new military uniform hung on him like the baggy outfit of a scarecrow. It was obvious from his muddy, tired-looking boots that he had walked a long way to reach the valley. By the way his hands were stained with dirt, he might just have finished planting seedlings in his rice paddy.

Timidly he bowed to all the women around him. Suddenly, a tiny woman, his mother or perhaps his grandmother, hugged the small boy and burst into tears. In flagrant disregard of the demands of both convention and patriotism, which called for stoicism in the face of this parting, the woman sobbed freely, her white hair flying around her, her worn-out face wrinkling like a plum pickle. The boy bit his lip and stroked her disheveled hair, but soon he, too, succumbed to tears.

The station-master's whistle shrieked. The boy gently disentangled himself from the embrace of the woman, and ran up the steps of the car behind Jun's. The morose group of women waved a white flag with his name written on it in black. It dangled like a funeral flag, or one of surrender. Through Jun's window, the small station became a dot and then disappeared into nothingness as the train chugged away, belching out black smoke.

Badly shaken, Jun leaned his head against the coolness of the window. Just three months earlier, Shun had wept like this boy before he left home, hugged by Sayo who cried, writhing like a madwoman. How well was Shun faring in the navy? He was not cut out to be a soldier. He was not like Masao, who had worshipped the Emperor and practiced with a bamboo sword at home. Shun had preferred reading about the constellations, scribbling equations on a piece of paper or playing the piano, to talking about the war. He played war games with Masao, but only as games. He so dreaded being drafted that he had nightmares. When the notice arrived, he secretly hoped that he would fail the physical, for he was skinny, wore heavy eyeglasses, and he did not have the animal instinct, toughness or nimbleness that would enable him to survive on the battlefield. But the desperate military had passed him with a B grade.

One afternoon before Shun left, Jun had taken him to the beach in Chiba, near the place where they had gone with Yumi's family. They walked on the endless stretch of sand, father and son.

"I feel as if I've received a death sentence for some crime I don't know about," Shun said. "I'm eighteen; my life may end before I reach twenty. There's so much I want to do still in this life—so much to read, and so much music to play. They say it's a beautiful thing to die for the Emperor. Is it really, Father? I'm not allowed to say it aloud, but I don't know. They say that the Americans and the British are monsters, but are they? Aren't they human beings, too? I go to war unprepared to fight. I'm not ready to kill anybody and I don't want to be killed either. I'm scared of dying." Shun stopped to look at the horizon. His wet eyes reflected the sunset over the sea.

"I don't want you to die," said Jun. "Try your best to live, Shun. Don't obey the battlefield order to kill yourself for the Emperor. It's wrong to glorify death. If you live, someday the war will be over. Unless the captors kill us all, you'll do all the things you want to do in life: watch the stars, play the piano, read books, fall in love and get married. Someday yet, we might be able to laugh at the stupid war."

"We'll never laugh at this stupid war. We'll only cry for all those who died meaningless deaths, as Masao might have. I might die, too, and then I won't even be able to cry." He squinted his eyes, watching the sun going down over the horizon, and added, "I thought Japan was the land of the rising sun, but the sun is falling from us."

"We're falling from the sun's grace. Amaterasu, the Sun Goddess, will shut her cave door and hide herself, letting the black night fall on us, as she did when she was enraged by her brother's mischief," Jun said.

It seemed to Jun they were walking in the twilight of history, in the calm before a dark night fell on their nation. A shadow had crept on to the sand as they walked. Jun remembered the beach he had walked on with his mother on the last day of her life. On that evening, too, the shadow of death had crept on to the sand.

He looked back and saw two long parallel lines of footprints. Then the rising tide washed away some of them, leaving only one line of the prints intact. As Jun was walking closer to the water, it was his that had been erased. If it were only he who had to go, rather than his son, he would be grateful.

Waking from her sleep, Sayo rubbed her eyes. She looked around and saw her husband. "Oh, Jun-san, where are we? Are we still on the train? I had bad dreams. I was dreaming about that night again. That night of 10 March when Isamu-san and so many others died. It was just sheer luck we didn't." She looked away to the window, her eyes weary.

Jun took her hand in his, the hand that had grown gnarled from overwork at the hospital. Sayo smiled at him, and the tenderness in her glance soothed him. Her eyes were small, but sweet and expressive like a bird's. His love for her had grown deeper over the war years, like the roots of a tree that had fought the storms of winter.

It was indeed only through luck that Jun and Sayo had survived the latest raid. In one night, close to 100,000 Tokyo residents had died, 400,000 were wounded and a million left homeless from the attack of 330 B-29s.

As Jun and Sayo were not on duty that night, they had stayed in their shelter for the first hour or so. When they emerged, worried about their patients, bombs and fire blocked their way. It took them two hours of running through burnt-out areas to arrive at the hospital, and then they had worked all night and all day, trying to save lives, and to ease pain.

Thinking of that raid now, Jun turned to face Sayo. "If there's another raid like the last one, we'll die, you and I. Don't you think that at least you should go to Gumma or to the village where Yumi-san went?"

Sayo shrugged, and when she spoke, her voice was matter-of-fact. "Who'll take care of people at the hospital, then? We don't have enough doctors or nurses."

"But at least one of us must live for Shun, when he comes back."

"Jun-san, I want to be wherever you are. If I'm of any use to you and to the patients, I'm happy. I've already asked Yumi-san to take care of Shun in case both of us die," she said in a determined voice.

He gripped her hand tightly in his. "I'd like to be wherever you are, too, but don't think like a martyr. You have to think about your life, Sayo," he said.

"Think about yours. You're the one with the martyr mentality," replied Sayo.

In another half an hour, the train pulled in at a station with an unfamiliar name, but Jun knew it was the place to get off, since the platform looked like a deck of a military ship—crowded with dozens of young men, all dressed in navy blue, staring into space with deadly intent eyes. Shun had written in a letter that everyone at the camp had eyes haunted by death.

The air smelled of the sea. Except for a cluster of old wooden houses right next to the station, the area was enclosed by barbed wire. Beyond the camp was the ocean, where several military ships were lined up. The space inside the wire appeared strangely deserted, with only a few soldiers coming in and out of the rows of barracks: the others must already have gone off to the war.

At the front entrance to the base, a young sentry was standing, looking like a stone guardian dog by the gate of a shrine—ready to bite. Sayo bowed to him and asked if they could see Shun Imura. The sentry's eyes twitched. With a malicious glance at Sayo, he resumed his sulky guardian-dog face again, one tooth sticking obliquely out of his pursed lips. Jun repeated the same question politely, adding, "We came all the way from Tokyo. I understand that you allow family to see the new recruits."

The sentry moved his heavy lips. "Yes, but he's not here."

"Where is he, then?" Jun and Sayo both asked.

"In the hospital," the sentry said, looking away.

"The hospital? What happened to him?" they asked.

"You can go there and find out. It's up there, in that building," the dog said, sticking his chin and pug nose up to point out the direction.

They walked to the building, Sayo boiling with rage. "What right does that pug nose have to be so nasty, when Shun might be sick? Is that how the military teaches a young man to behave?"

The hospital was a prefabricated shabby structure, which looked ready to fall over with one gust of wind: the blast of a B-29 would not be needed here. The inside of the building smelled sick and stale. "This hospital cultures bacteria instead of killing them," whispered Sayo to Jun.

When they found Shun among the rows of beds jammed against each other, he resembled nothing so much as a dying fish among dead ones on a fish store's crowded slab. His eyes were bloodshot, his cheeks swollen, his lips purple and bleeding. A thick collar hung around his neck. He looked gaunt and almost ten years older, but when he saw his parents at the door, the eyes between the puffed lids lit up.

"Father and Mother! How did you find me? I didn't write to you that I'm here, so you wouldn't worry."

"So, who beat you up? It must be a man like that nasty sentry at the gate who did it to you. This camp must be a slaughterhouse," Sayo said, her face flushed with anger.

"The guy who looks like a dog?" Looking right and left, Shun whispered so as not to be heard by anybody. "He's one of them. He's called Bulldog. I was beaten by him every other day." With a grimace, Shun slowly sat up, saying, "I'd like to talk with you in a quiet place." With the help of a frame, he limped with his parents over to a corner of the cafeteria, empty because there was no food to serve.

"It's a tradition for officers and senior trainees to haze newcomers," Shun said, looking more relaxed in the room where no one else was around. "They beat me for speaking with insufficient respect for them, for coming one minute late to a meeting, and for dozing for a few minutes when I was night sentry. The other day I criticized a human torpedo and didn't volunteer for it. That's why I'm here."

"What is a human torpedo?" Sayo asked. "Is it another crazy, suicidal thing like a *kamikaze* plane? Will you be on a torpedo and kill yourself as well as the ship?"

Shun nodded.

"I'm glad you didn't volunteer for it," said Jun with a sigh.

"But they almost killed me because I didn't," said Shun.

"No wonder this country is losing the war. New soldiers go to war with broken bones. And they commit suicide with their own torpedoes," Sayo sighed.

"What happened to your neck, Shun?" asked Jun. "It couldn't be just a beating."

"I was kicked with boots, pounded by the metal head of a bayonet and left outside all night. I have a bad case of whiplash. Also a hip bone was cracked," said Shun, biting his swollen lip. Then he continued, smiling wryly, "In a way it's good that this happened. I'm allowed to stay away from them for a few days and they might have to postpone sending me off to war."

Opening Jun's medicine bag, Sayo began treating the wounds and cuts on her son's face and body. The big slash across his stomach, which was infected, particularly worried his parents. Jun examined his neck and hip and asked, "Did they take x-rays?"

"They would never use such fancy apparatus for a rebellious recruit. They wouldn't care if I died," Shun said.

After listening to his son's chest with a stethoscope, Jun said, "You're young, Shun. If you rest well and don't overdo it, these wounds will eventually heal."

"It's not up to me to decide if I can rest or not," Shun said, sounding resigned.

Hiding her tears, Sayo looked down and rummaged through the bag she had carried from home. On the table she placed a loaf of home-made bread and said, "I know you love bread, but this came out like a dumpling because I made it out of the mysterious ground powder given for rations. But I made this jam from the peels of the clementines in our backyard."

Shun thanked his mother and bit into the bread with a childlike smile. "I'm sorry I can't even serve you tea here, but why don't you eat some, too, Father and Mother? Both of you have lost a lot of weight," he said, scanning the faces of his emaciated parents.

Prodded by his father, Shun told them about the human torpedo episode.

"Last week, the officers assembled the new recruits and said, 'A great weapon called *kaiten* torpedo has been created. If any of you are burning with patriotism, and volunteer to die for your motherland, please raise your hand. With *kamikaze* planes in the sky and *kaiten* torpedoes under the sea we'll reverse the tide of war.' Out of fifty recruits, only a few, including myself, did not raise their hands.

"I happen to know that this is a ridiculous machine nobody should be allowed to use, because I've been sent to work on it as a trainee engineer," Shun said. "Some of the *kamikaze* planes at least destroy their targets, but the success rate of the human torpedo hitting enemy ships so far has been almost zero. It's a complete waste of life."

Shun sighed and continued, "I knew I wasn't allowed to talk back to the officers, I'm a sheep in a wolves' land, but on this occasion I felt I had no choice. I spoke up timidly, 'I understand that not too many successes have been reported with these machines. As a trainee engineer I know there is still a lot of room for improvement. Is it possible to give us a little time before . . . ?'

"Before I could finish my words, my cheeks felt violent slaps, fire sparked in my eyes and I fell on the ground, passing out. When I came to, I was in the officers' room. All the officers took turns yelling at me. 'You should be kicked out of the navy, but you're too dangerous to be let out. We'll give you the most deadly assignments.' Then they let Bulldog and the other senior trainees take over the physical side of the abuse.

"My speaking out made little impact on the volunteers. My bunkmate said, 'I can't take this interminable waiting for death anymore. If I have to die anyway, I'd rather choose a quick death.' Luckily, I don't think any of the volunteers has been sent out to die yet because not too many torpedoes are available now.

"It's no fun being labeled a coward and a traitor. Maybe I should've joined the crowd without protesting. I'm likely to die anyway," Shun said, staring into space with the same intent gaze of those young soldiers on the train station.

"You're no coward; it was brave of you to speak up. I'm proud of you, Shun," Jun said, his eyes gleaming with affection.

"Do you know how this torpedo looks, Father and Mother? It's painted all black—the picture of death," Shun said. "It's placed on the deck of a submarine and it'll be let off when an enemy is near. Its pilot decides the angle of attack with a periscope and aims at the target. But because he's underwater, he can't see much and easily misses the target. The terrible thing is that when he fails in his mission, he can't even save his life. He could open the hatch and climb out, but how would he survive at the bottom of the ocean? Nobody who has been launched has ever returned. They must have died from lack of oxygen," Shun said and closed his eyes in despair.

"Those officers who urge young men to die like that should be hanged," said Sayo, her face haggard from shock. "They're the ones who should go in the machine."

Nobody knew what to say anymore and they sat in silence. It was already pitch dark outside and the dim lamp did not light up the room much, nor their dark mood. Realizing it was time for curfew, Shun roused himself, faltering, and said in a determinedly cheerful voice, "I feel much better since you came to see me, Father and Mother. Aren't we lucky our family is intact? Let's all stay well until the next time we see each other."

Once again they were all quiet, wondering when that next time would be, or if indeed there would be one. Even now, Shun was not all that well. But Sayo managed to force out a smile. "No matter when that will be, let's pray we will all be well."

Both Jun and Sayo were reluctant to leave. "How long will you be staying in this hospital?" Sayo asked Shun.

"I hope at least a few more days," he told her.

Sayo's eyes twinkled as a bright idea hit her. "Can I stay with you as long as you are here, Shun?" she asked, and turned to her husband, saying, "Jun-san, is it all right with you if I stay here for a while? I'll make Shun all better."

"It's a good idea," Jun said happily, watching Shun's eyes glow. Jun had secretly been concerned about the extent of his son's wounds and the seriousness of the crack in his hip. Sayo would work miracles on them.

Returning home to Tokyo, Jun was relieved to find the house still standing, neither bombed nor burned. He had a meager dinner, but did not notice what he was eating, preoccupied as he was with his son. When they had hugged each other good-bye, Shun was so fragile his bones creaked. He clasped Jun and did not let go for a long time, probably thinking, just as Jun did, that this could be the last time they would ever hold each other. One large tear dropped into Jun's bowl.

He was washing the dishes when he heard a voice at the front door. "Good evening." It sounded like Yumi, except that her voice was usually at least three notes higher and far more lively; besides, she should already have left for the village. But when Jun opened the door, he found that it was indeed Yumi. Pale and crestfallen as a faded lily, Yumi was carrying a plain wooden box wrapped in a white cloth. Before Jun could say anything, she burst into tears.

"This was brought to me yesterday," she said through her sobs. "The official confirmation of Masao's death. This is supposed to contain his bones and ashes. I opened it and found a sprinkle of white sand. The man from the army office who brought it said, 'Congratulations. Your son died a glorious death in New Guinea.'

"'What kind of a glorious death was it?' I asked.

"'We don't know exactly. But the army believes that it was. New Guinea was a difficult place to be. Here's a letter reporting to you that your son was promoted to corporal, for his valuable contributions to the country,' the man said. He bowed five times, and left."

Jun asked Yumi to come in. He took the box from her, and was shocked to find how light it was. The lightness brought home to him that Masao was gone forever. That big, sturdy young man, reduced to a few sprinkles of false ashes in an empty box. They had swindled Yumi of her son with cheap words of praise, a meaningless military rank and a scatter of sand.

Yumi sat down on the couch, bent her face on her lap and wept. "I keep seeing him lying in a muddy jungle, asking for water and gasping for air," she said, trembling. Jun sat next to her and gently stroked her back. In front of his eyes was his bright-eyed young nephew, full of adventure and mischief, who had frightened Sayo with a birthday present of a crawfish and a beetle, had chased dragonflies with Shun until he fell in the *koi* pond, and had walked and run on tall bamboo stilts like an acrobat. He had turned into a good-looking man, the mirror image of his father.

Soon Yumi stopped sobbing and asked, "Where's Sayo-san?" Hearing his explanation, she sighed and said, "I hope Shun-san will be all right. There's so much craziness in this world."

Jun made tea for Yumi and himself. He placed a third cup of tea in front of the wooden box on the table and then sat down on the couch.

"Welcome home, Masao," said Jun to the box, patting it. "It was a long way to come home. But you're finally back with your mother. Let's drink tea together. You, your mother and I. It was a hard war for you. We are proud of you—you were always so brave. I'm sure you were courageous till the last minute. Now you can join your father in heaven: he's waiting for you there." Then Jun joined his palms together and bowed to the box, tears trickling through his closed eyes.

"I knew the chance that you'd live was close to nothing,

Masao, but as a mother, I never gave up hope for you, until this box came," Yumi said, touching the teacup to the box so that her son could drink.

Then she turned to Jun. "I just feel sorry for him having died for nothing. What did he live for and what did he die for? In order to be stung by a viper, or swallowed by a flood in the name of a holy nation?" Her body shuddered with anger.

Jun told her to drink her tea. She sipped it slowly, and gradually seemed to relax a little, the color coming back into her cheeks.

"Yesterday when I received this box, I almost felt like dying," Yumi said, moving closer to Jun. "Then I thought of you and Sayo-san. I shouldn't kill myself when death is so cheap. Nothing is gained if I kill myself. You and Sayo-san don't need another death when you're witnessing them by the hundreds in the hospital. I was supposed to go down to the village, but I couldn't do so without seeing you."

She leaned against Jun, who put an arm around her shoulder. They sat together quietly. It was lucky that there were no air raids that night. The luck might not last long, but Jun appreciated every minute of peace and silence given to share with Yumi. It was a sad occasion to mourn for Masao, but it was also a precious brief moment, possibly the last one, someone in heaven must have granted to the two who had always loved each other, but had been forbidden to express it.

Yumi was no longer the young girl Jun once knew; she would soon be fifty. Her hair no longer hung like an opened fan over her shoulder, nor in a split peach or oval chignon, but was tied casually in the back. Yet her face, with its delicate features lit by candlelight, was still as beautiful as it had been when she was a girl. She still tilted her neck, unintentionally coquettish.

Jun loved Sayo. He would never betray her, but was there anything wrong in admiring two women for different reasons? He now understood why his father had loved both Emi and

Hana. The fact that he had never been allowed to love Yumi made her more precious in his mind, like a flower in a forbidden garden.

Yumi was restless, knowing it was time for her to leave, but not willing to do so. She had the same sense of finality about this meeting as did Jun, not because she would go to the village soon, but because the world might end tomorrow. Life might end either for her or for him.

"Jun-san," she said, her eyes brighter, as she came up with an idea to prolong their last moments. "Can you put some music on for Masao? Very quietly, so as not to arouse the authorities."

"What kind of music? Mozart's *Requiem*?"

"No, something more cheerful and romantic. How about Beethoven's *Spring*? After all, it's spring now and Masao always liked the season."

As the music flowed, Yumi who had been casting her head down, looked up, her cheeks rosy. She saw Jun's eyes light up as he listened to the Beethoven he had not heard for a long time and said, "Masao must be happy, listening this music in heaven. I should be crying for his death, but this is so joyful it makes me feel like living again. Jun-san, why are we fighting this idiotic war, when there's such beautiful music in the world?"

"We are idiotic, aren't we, Yumi-san?" Jun said. "I used to think that people learn from past mistakes, and that history always makes progress. When I was young, I thought our life would be better when we grew up. But look at us. Wasn't the life we spent together at our father's house so much more enlightened than our lives now? Who imagined that this country that seemed so civilized with its beautiful houses, temples, tram cars and *kabuki* theaters and, above all, its nice people like you and sweet Tami-san, would ever start such an uncivilized war and destroy everything our father and his ancestors worked so hard to create?"

"Father and Mother fought a lot, but their fights were little comedies compared with the tragedies we have now," said

Yumi. Then, sitting up straight, her eyes sparkling, she said, "But, Jun-san, let's try to survive. As Isamu-san said in his shelter to me and Mother who was dying, some day soon peace will come. Everything is temporary and the sun will rise after the most terrible storm. And unless the Americans kill us all, you can start medical research again in a laboratory, which you always wanted to do, Jun-san. And maybe I'll write a story about this terrible war."

"How wonderful it would be to have the days again when we can do research, write stories, or listen to any music we like," Jun said, looking dreamy.

"In my story, I'll also write about your mother, Emi-san," Yumi continued, lost in reverie about the story she might write. "Did you know, Jun-san, that before our father died, he gave me an old wicker trunk that he told me not to open while my mother was alive, because dozens of letters my father and Emi-san wrote to each other were in it. So I opened it after Mother had died, but at the time I was so preoccupied with Hisao's death and Masao's whereabouts that I didn't read it all. The wicker trunk is now in the shelter Isamu-san built so it won't be burnt in a fire. I'll read the letters when the war is over, and write their stories, too."

Tired of talking, Yumi listened to music again, sitting close to Jun. Soon her eyes were closed and her head began to droop on his shoulder. Jun let her sleep for a while, watching her breathe peacefully. Her head rested on his shoulder and he could see her cheek right under his eyes. It was as soft as he had always remembered, but under her closed eyes were three wrinkles—tokens of hard times and sadness. They made her face look so melancholy that Jun had to fight the desire to kiss and comfort her. But he just watched her a moment longer and placed a hand on her shoulder gently, saying, "It's getting late, Yumi-san. I'll walk you home."

She stood up slowly. Dreamy-eyed and still reluctant to go, she put her arms around Jun. "Thank you very much for comforting me." She rested her face against his chest, and listened to his heart through his sweater. "Your heartbeat is so steady," she whispered after a while. Then, her eyes wide open as if frightened by something, she said, "Oh, Jun-san, don't die. Please survive the war."

Carrying Masao's box, Jun walked her home. A half moon, in the shape of a lemon, hung in the hazy sky. A searchlight was scrutinizing the sky, but no enemy planes were in sight tonight. The night air revived Yumi. "Jun-san," she said eagerly, "is there any way you can find someone else to take care of the hospital? Can't you ask the doctors in Gumma to take turns with you? Please do something so that you'll be in a safer place."

"It may not be easy, but I'll try," he replied. "I'll definitely send Sayo to Gumma as soon as she comes back. But, Yumi-san, if Shun survives the war and if both Sayo and I die in a raid, please look after him."

Yumi looked at Jun, her eyes wide open. "Of course I would. I feel as if he's my own son anyway. Sayo-san asked me the same thing. But don't talk like that. It's more important to do something positive to survive, Jun-san."

"I'll try," he said again, but the tone of his voice gave away his pessimism.

"Don't be so fatalistic," she told him, shaking her head. "You have to fight for your life. Please live for me, as well as for Sayo-san and Shun."

When they arrived at the front of Yumi's house, Jun felt as if he had come to the end of the world.

Yumi whispered, "Can I kiss you on your cheek just once, Jun-san?" Before he could answer, her lips were on his cheek, where they lingered. He kissed her, too. Then he quickly said *sayonara* and began to walk home. He looked back once and saw her standing alone in the silvery moonlight, watching him. He wanted to run back and clasp her in his arms one more time, but he made himself keep walking. He promised himself that he would remember the sweet taste of her cheek, soft as a magnolia petal, even after he died.

Sayo came back in three days. She reported to Jun, stamping her feet in anger, that the officers had already taken Shun out of the hospital. Because of her care, the infection on his belly was getting better, and the x-rays she insisted they take for his neck and hip did not look too bad. But those minor signs of recovery were enough to prompt the officers to take him back to the camp. The doctors told the officers that it was imperative for Shun to take it easy; otherwise he would be no good at all, and only be a nuisance on the battlefield. But how could she trust those cold-blooded officers to listen to anybody's advice?

When Jun told Sayo about Masao, she was saddened. Bowing her head, she said she should be more grateful that Shun was alive.

Yumi buried Masao next to his father's grave before she left for the village. Sayo visited Yumi and accompanied her to the cemetery. It was a sunny spring day, and along the way the cherry blossoms were in full bloom over the charred ruins.

"Let's pick flowers for Masao-san," said Sayo. They picked wild flowers from the burnt-out gardens until their arms were overflowing. Bees and butterflies followed them all the way to the cemetery.

It was one of the few places in Tokyo to escape the bombs. "It's incredibly peaceful here. Americans don't seem to be interested in the dead," Sayo said, taking in a deep breath with a rare sense of safety and peace. They decorated the new grave for Masao with the flowers. Yumi put half of her flowers on her husband's tomb.

"I asked around for a Christian minister to hold a service, but I couldn't find one. Masao wasn't a Christian anyway. So I'll just pray for him, and I'd appreciate it if you could, too, Sayo-san, since he loved you so much," Yumi said.

Together they bent their heads in the balmy sunlight, but

Yumi did not close her eyes. "I have trouble praying," she said. "When Hisao-san died, I thought I was being punished because I didn't love him enough. So I tried to be a better person. Since Masao went to war, I have prayed every day asking God to protect him, but my prayers haven't reached Him. Why do I have to be punished so much, Sayo-san? Perhaps after all, He may be a Western God. He may not like me."

"I don't know anything about Christianity, but maybe God doesn't like the way we are fighting the war," Sayo said.

"But why does God allow the Americans to drop bombs and murder so many thousands of civilians? Just before Isamu-san died, he made one of his cynical remarks about how the bombers, Christians though they may be, probably feel no guilt killing people, since they never see the faces of their victims."

"This war has made everybody crazy. God must be terribly angry," Sayo said.

"You should go to Gumma. Jun-san, too," urged Yumi. "Both of you have such a sense of duty about saving people's lives. It's admirable, but I want you two to be alive. Have you been reading the papers about the war? They predict more raids. Try to talk Jun-san into getting out of Tokyo, please, Sayo-san."

When Sayo returned home, she relayed Yumi's words to Jun. To her happy surprise, he had not only already made the arrangements for Sayo to be transferred to the hospital in Gumma, but he also had asked the administration to arrange for doctors to take turns working in Tokyo. They had promised Jun that they would accommodate his request.

Part of the reason for his request was that Jun had surmised from news reports and the reports of wounded soldiers, that the enemy's attacks on the mainland would become even fiercer. Starting from Saipan the previous year, the Americans had hopped the islands one by one, coming closer and closer to Japan—Guam, the Philippines, Iwo Jima and, currently, Okinawa, and they had won every battle. If they could launch planes from nearby islands, attacking the mainland would be far easier.

Yet it was the Beethoven violin sonata that he listened to with Yumi that moved him most strongly to do something to save his life. That music had been so full of love and joy of life that it lifted his dark spirit and gave him a renewed desire to live. With Western music forbidden, and the roar of bombs constantly reverberating in his mind, music had stopped sounding in his ears. Then came this piece, suddenly shining in his world like the most glorious day after winter. If someone could create such beautiful music, he thought, we all have hope. People could not all be as bad as they seemed to be now.

All that was godly about human creation—Beethoven and Mozart's music, Michelangelo and Van Gogh's art, the medical discoveries of Pasteur, Koch and Jun's Japanese mentors—could not be destroyed by the demons of war. The beauty of the mountains, the seas, the stars and the moon would not perish. If there were eight million gods in Japan, some of them would surely make it through the war.

If he survived the war and if peace came, then he would really begin again the research he had enjoyed so much, but which had been terminated by the earthquake, even though being a full-time doctor and dreaming of being a researcher was like being happily married to a lovely wife, Sayo, and longing for Yumi. Unrealistic dreams for now, perhaps, but if he were to live, the days might be back when he could listen to Shun play the piano and watch Sayo pantomime sumo wrestlers and laugh. They would invite Yumi for dinner, sing songs and talk about books. Although no one knew what defeat in the war would bring—he had already seen hell—how much worse could anything else be?

Jun's change of attitude pleased Sayo. She was excited about the move, and liked to talk with him about how they would find a small house in Gumma, in a spot nestled in green mountains, where sirens never blew and the drone of the bombers never threatened. Jun would commute from time to time to Tokyo. It would not be totally safe, but far better. Sayo packed her trunks, and was ready and waiting to go.

* * *

In the small *tatami* room of the village farmhouse Ken had rented for his family, Yumi lay on a futon. It was her third night here. For her own peace of mind, she kept by her pillow her air-raid hood and the thick silk floss-lined jacket Sayo had sewed for her, and a flashlight, even though Ayako had laughed at her, saying, "We've never had a single air raid here. No enemies are interested in a remote village like this. So relax and sleep well, Yumi-san." She imagined Jun and Sayo, dressed in white gowns and working in the hospital. Before she left Tokyo, Sayo had told her of their decision to move to Gumma. She hoped they would do so quickly.

Masao's death, though she had expected it for so long, had saddened her so much that she had not been sleeping well. But here she fell asleep soon, probably because of the fresh air of the country and her residual fatigue from the move. At midnight, though, a rumble from the sky woke her. Immediately she put her hood and jacket on and walked out of the house in the dark, but then realized that there was no shelter here. Ayako had told her there was no need for such a thing.

She saw a light flashing, and looked up. It was neither a searchlight nor an enemy plane, but lightning shooting down from the sky to a mountain. The rumble that woke her had been that of spring thunder, not a B-29.

A sudden gust of wind almost knocked her down. With it came drops of rain and a few more bolts of lightning, followed by faraway rolls of thunder. As in an air raid, the storm's onset was deceptively gentle, but then the whole sky was abruptly slashed by fat golden axes and zigzag saws. Thunder roared, shaking the sky and earth; the wind howled and the rain hit with a vengeance.

Oblivious to the drops wetting her face, Yumi stood frozen, mesmerized by the thunderbolts slicing the universe into pieces. She remembered Sayo's words: "This war has made everybody crazy. God must be angry." Yumi was sure that these bolts were

God's anger, that the wind and the rain were His shaking and His tears. She walked home slowly, her hood and jacket keeping all but her face dry and warm.

The next morning Ayako hailed Yumi cheerfully. "Didn't you sleep well? The nights here are so quiet, aren't they?" When Yumi mentioned the thunderstorm, she looked surprised. "I never heard it. We kept all the shutters closed."

Two nights before the day set for Sayo's move, she and Jun were working the night shift at the hospital. Because only emergency patients were admitted, there were only twenty-eight patients in the ward, a much lower number than they normally housed. Lately the nights had been calm, with no raid in Tokyo for over a month since March 10. The B-29s were busy killing people in other cities, Osaka, Kobe, and Nagoya.

About ten at night, the siren wailed, and the lights went out. Jun ordered all patients evacuated into the shelter beneath the hospital garden. Only six members of the staff were working that night—Jun, Dr. Yanase, and four nurses including Sayo. With two manning each stretcher, only three patients could be taken out at a time. Some of the patients were ambulatory, but the staff still had to go back and forth in pitch darkness several times.

Another siren went off, indicating imminent danger; Jun told the nurses to enter the shelter right away. "Doctor Yanase and I'll manage the rest."

As he and Dr. Yanase rushed out to get the remaining patients, Sayo ran after them, saying, "I'll come, too. Dr. Yanase, you are a big man. You can carry a patient in your arms, can't you?" They moved around the ward with a weak flashlight, looking for the few remaining patients. Some were so ill that it required the utmost care to lift them on to the stretcher and they had to be carried slowly without shaking.

The rumble of the planes grew louder. The western sky flushed several times, dyed red from fires caused by the incendiary bombs.

"It's time for us to go into a shelter," Dr. Yanase said and ran down the stairs, a lady patient in his arms.

"How many are left in the building?" shouted Jun from outside, bending down at the mouth of the shelter.

"Just one more," a nurse shouted back. "Yoneda-san. She's in room number three, upstairs."

Jun ran back out, saying, "I can take care of her myself. Sayo, Dr. Yanase, please stay here." From the entrance to the shelter, Dr. Yanase called, "Come back, Doctor Imura. It's too dangerous now."

Grabbing a stretcher, Sayo ran out, following Jun. When he turned back and saw her, he waved her away, shouting, "Sayo, you shouldn't be here. I can carry Yoneda-san by myself. Run back. If I don't make it, please live for Shun. I love you, Sayo."

The droning was shaking the earth and the sky. Jun saw bombs falling like a torrent of shooting stars. The faces of Shun and of Yumi flickered in his eyes, and tears splattered his face as he ran. His heart thudded loudly. "Do I have to die? Do all my dreams have to die?" The strains of Beethoven's *Spring* ran through his mind and he ran faster, saying to himself, Sayo, Shun, Yumi-san, I love you.

"No, Jun-san. I won't let you go alone." Sayo had caught up with him. She carried a stretcher in one hand; she used the other to grab his fingers.

Jun tried to talk her into going back once more. He said, tears rolling down his cheeks, "R-run back, Sayo. I love you. Thank you for being so sweet to me, but you must live. Live for Shun." Dropping her hand, he ran ahead of her and went inside the hospital. For a split second Sayo hesitated, but then she followed her husband through the entrance of the building.

A minute later there was an earth-shattering boom from the back of the hospital. In a second, the building burst into flames.

The next morning Dr. Yanase and the neighbors dug through the smouldering debris. They found the bodies of Jun and Sayo under a half-burnt wall. They were lying next to each other on their stomachs, his arm slung over her shoulder. Their faces were not badly burned. Their eyebrows were knitted and their lips twisted, revealing the extent of their pain, but their faces were turned toward each other. Yoneda-san's body was charred black. Three of the patients also died in the shelter during the night.

The next day Ken brought back to the village a newspaper that contained a report about a doctor and nurse couple who had died in the raid, trying to save the last patient left in the hospital.

Yumi read it, and then bent her face down on her lap without uttering a word. In her eyes titanic bolts, just like the ones two nights ago, cut the universe into pieces. The night she was awakened by the storm was the night they had died. God had been telling her what was happening to them. The wind and rain were the wailing voices and tears of Jun and Sayo. God must have been crying in rage and sorrow for the death of two such gentle people.

But, oh, why did you die, Jun-san and Sayo-san, leaving Shun and me? You were such martyrs after all. How painful it must have been, to be smothered, suffocated and burned to death.

Jun-san, I still see your eyes, brimming with tears while listening to Beethoven. Those radiant eyes told me that you really wanted to live and were now determined to. I remember the warmth of your chest when I embraced you. It was only eight days ago. The steady and rhythmic beat of your heart is still pounding in my ears. Is it really possible that there is no more beat and no more warmth in your chest? Will your lyrical voice, which always gave away the passion hidden in a shy man, never sing again? Will your dark indigo eyes gleaming like stars in love never open again?

And, Sayo-san, I had so many happy afternoons with you, drinking tea and watching our sons play. You were so worried about my being left alone that you dashed to my shelter at the time of the raid and told Jun-san to hold my hand, knowing how much I loved him. How grateful I was for your silent kindness. How I admire your courage for having followed your husband to save a patient. You did not let him die alone. Jun-san, you were a lucky man to have had such a loving wife.

You both saved countless lives in the bombings and fires, but nobody was able to save yours. Not even God.

The next morning, Yumi took the first train to Tokyo. Ken, who was greatly saddened by the death of his half-brother and Sayo, said that he would follow her soon, and would like to have a proper funeral for them.

"I'll come as soon as we fix all the power lines—the recent air raids over Nagoya and all the lightning and storms over this region have wreaked so much havoc. I feel as if I'm in almost as vulnerable a position as Jun-san and Sayo-san were. If you're responsible for a job and for people at your work, you can't abandon them and run away. I'll try to be as brave as they were, if the circumstances require it," Ken said to Yumi, his voice unusually grave.

When Yumi visited the site of the fire-ravaged hospital, she found it deserted. No doctors, nurses or patients. Not even the traces of the dead. A neighbor pointed out to her the wall under which the bodies of the doctor and the nurse had been found.

Climbing over the fallen roofs and windows, Yumi managed to reach the spot and sat down on the rubble. When she bent to lay down the bouquet of flowers that she had brought, she saw a gap between the wall and the ground, and jammed within it the scorched remnants of a stretcher. Under it was a dark-colored sea of coagulated blood. The blood brought home to Yumi the cold reality of their death. It was not just a bad dream, but an irreversible fact. She crouched down in despair.

Yumi sat and patted the ground. She kept patting, searching for the warmth of their bodies that might be left somewhere.

"Jun-san and Sayo-san, what a terrible way to die. But at least you were together, comforting each other and you went up to heaven together," she whispered, feeling the ground that was now wet with her tears, imagining Jun's head here, and Sayo's arms there. She cut her finger on a piece of glass, but she could only shrug. They were crushed under a wall among electric wires, broken medicine bottles, chairs and beds, and cut, burned, smothered, and electrocuted. How could a small cut on a finger matter?

After praying for a while, Yumi was about to leave when something red under the wall caught her eye. Using a metal stick, she managed to pull it out through the jumble of pipes and wires. It was a torn piece of a scorched scarf. It must be the scarf Sayo had been wearing around her neck. Yumi kissed it and said, "Hello, Sayo-san," trying to smile at it. Then she began to look for a keepsake from Jun. In the rubble, a patch of greenish marble glittered at her, as if asking for her attention. It was the fountain pen he had always kept inside his jacket pocket. Although only a charred black stick with a few specks of marble pattern left, the pen still seemed to Yumi a part of Jun. She held it tightly to her chest, as if it were his warm body.

She headed for their house. She was to wait there for Ken, who was supposed to come from Nagoya later in the day, to meet her in either Jun or Yumi's house, whichever was still standing. If both had been burned, they would meet at Taku's: its extensive gardens meant that out of the three Imura houses, it was the one most likely to be intact, for why should the bombers waste their time destroying greenery?

Unlike its owners, Jun and Sayo's house had been left untouched by the bombs. When she opened the door, she pretended they were there and called out, "Good evening, Jun-san and Sayo-san." For a moment she held her breath, hoping against hope, waiting for their voices, the bustle and the cheer that would welcome her into the house. "Oh, Yumi-san, we were hoping you'd come. Come in. Come in."

She noticed Shun's handwriting on a postcard in the overflowing letterbox. She pulled it out, and read a brief note written in a hurried scribble: *Dear Father and Mother, I'm on my way to Okinawa. I'm healing well thanks to Mum's loving care. Hope both of you are all right. Let's not forget our promise to see each other alive. Love, S.* Poor Shun. How would he take it when he learned that the promise had not been kept?

The sun was setting and, except for one wall that reflected the orange glow of the evening, the house was growing dark. Yumi sat on the couch, on the exact spot she had occupied nine days before. That evening Jun had sat next to her and consoled her for Masao's death. And now it was Jun who was gone, and Sayo, too. No one could console Yumi for their deaths. Not even God.

Yumi stood up and walked around the house. In a corner stood two big trunks—no doubt what Sayo had packed for moving. They looked forlorn, waiting to be picked up. Yumi wished she could send them to heaven to be with their owners.

On the wall hung two sweaters, a brown pullover and a pink cardigan. Yumi knew both of them. Jun was wearing the brown one the last evening she had seen him. It was worn out, with the arms curved round on the elbows and the shoulders sticking upwards; it looked like Jun himself. The pink cardigan was Sayo's favorite: she wore it at home like a uniform. The yarn had stretched and thinned out. It had the shape of Sayo, much thinner and elongated recently. "Oh, Jun-san and Sayo-san, you're here." Yumi smiled at the sweaters and cuddled them together in her arms. They were warm and smelled like them. She buried her face in them.

Yumi left for her own house, thinking that Ken might be waiting there. With everybody evacuated to the countryside, the neighborhood was as deserted as a ghost town, and it was eerie to walk alone in the evening. Strangely the area had been forgotten by the raiders, and she saw that her house was still standing.

She heard someone chasing her and felt frightened, but, as

she looked back timidly, she saw Ken catching up to her with quick steps, carrying two wooden boxes wrapped in white cloth.

As he came into her house, Ken said, “The director of the hospital met me at the station and gave these boxes to me. He said that the entire hospital board and all the staff had been saddened by the heroic deaths of the great doctor and nurse. They wondered if they could hold a funeral at the site of the hospital. I said, ‘I must talk to my sister, but this is wartime. It’s dangerous for so many people to gather in Tokyo. It would be nice if you could give a memorial service for them in Gumma, but let us give a private funeral in our family cemetery.’ What do you think, Yumi?”

“I think you gave him the right answer. Jun-san and Sayo-san would be dumbfounded if so many people showed up after they were dead, when nobody came to Tokyo when they needed them. If the hospital people cared so much about Jun-san and Sayo-san, why didn’t they do something before it was too late?”

“That’s how people are. It’s the same at our company,” Ken said, and shrugged.

Yumi made a comfortable bed for Ken in Masao’s room, which had been kept as it was when he left. She took the two boxes to her room. Unlike Masao’s, they were heavy, and inscribed on them were Sayo and Jun’s names in beautiful calligraphy. Yumi placed both boxes by her bed, kissed them, hugged them and slept.

The next day she and Ken held a quiet funeral. They buried Jun and Sayo beside Emi, Taku, Hana and Tami at the Shomanji temple. It was a warm April day. Thousands of petals of cherry blossoms fell gently like a snowfall and made a garland over their graves. Later, Ken returned to work, and Yumi to the village.

The village was in a small basin surrounded by green mountains. In the backyard of their rented house, Ayako worked on a vegetable garden every day. Busy at his various power stations and at the office in Nagoya, Ken was hardly ever there. They were fortunate enough to have had daughters instead of sons, but even the girls had been mobilized to work for the war effort. The eldest daughter worked in a factory, making parts for *kamikaze* planes; the second made bombs, while the third worked at a bamboo factory making spears. All of them stayed in the dormitories, and seldom came home.

Yumi spent her days moping like a wet towel, burying herself in a book or looking at the mountains. After watching her for almost a week, Ayako approached her. "Yumi-san, I don't know how to console you. My family hasn't been affected too badly by the war, so I can't imagine what I'd be like if I had to go through what you have. But don't you think the dead would be happier to see you come out of your mourning and be strong again? Why don't you take a walk, or help me in the garden?"

"I'm a city woman who's never worked in a garden except to dig holes for tulip bulbs, Ayako-san. I'd better go for a walk," Yumi told her.

"Then can you go to the Kiso Rapids, beyond that forest over there, and buy a few *ayu* fish from the bald-headed old man who's always there, fishing? We can have them for supper," Ayako said, pointing to the big forest near the mountains.

So Yumi went to the rapids, carrying a pail Ayako had given her. She walked along the rice paddy and through the forest. After following a long shady path, she suddenly felt the sun shine on her head. In front of her was fast-running water, jumping and dancing on thousands of small rocks, and making white splashes. The water was so clear that she could see a school of fish swimming and multicolored stones at the bottom reflecting the sunshine.

Yumi took her *geta* clogs and *tabi* socks off and dipped her bare feet in the water. It was so cold she cried out. The flow of the stream immediately tripped her, and she felt as if her feet had been stolen. But standing there, resisting the current, she felt happy to be alive for the first time since all of the recent deaths.

The warm sun dried her tears. The cold water teased her feet and made her smile.

She hummed to herself snatches from Schubert's *Trout*, a piece that Jun had often made her listen to. It must have been by a stream like this that Schubert had composed the quintet, listening to the constant sound of water hitting rocks and watching fish swim, flipping their tails and fins. Perhaps the sun had penetrated all the way down to the bottom of his stream, too.

Yumi looked up at the sky, stretching her arms and shaking them. "Hello, everybody up there," she said aloud, smiling. "Jun-san, Sayo-san, Masao, Hisao-san and Isamu-san. Do you see me? I'm fine. I hope you are, too." The sky was bluer than any she had ever seen.

She walked along the stream until she saw a bald old man. He stood with a bamboo rod in a quiet pool of water overlooked by the restless stream. He seemed to Yumi like one of those sleepy trees that had stood for a hundred years along the shore. On the bank nearby was a bucket, in which several glittering white fish were swimming.

Yumi said hello. The old man turned his head as slowly as if waking from a long sleep. Sounding bored, he asked, "How many you want?"

"Three, please."

With a hand that looked like a fossilized crocodile's paw, he grabbed the fish, which resisted, splashed, but slid into the pail Yumi had carried from home. She felt guilty for having disturbed the old man, and left quickly.

When she returned, Yumi talked to Ayako about him. Ayako said, "He lost his wife due to illness and his two sons in Guam and the Philippines recently. He lives alone now and spends all his time fishing." If that man could keep living in spite of the loss of his whole family, she should also be able to, Yumi thought.

Ayako insisted Yumi had to garden. "Working outside cheers you up. I was a city woman, too. But look at me. I'm as strong as a peasant's wife now," she said, showing her muscular arms and face as red as a yam. Yumi admired Ayako for her willing transformation to the life of a farmer from a life in the lap of luxury. Ayako's father was a baron and she had attended the peeress's school.

Hoeing and tilling under the sun was not easy and did not cheer Yumi up as easily as Ayako had suggested. Although she tried to shake off the images of the dead, they flickered in front of her, even in the second between lifting up a hoe and putting it down on the soil, and tears fogged her eyes.

Ayako said, "O-oh, watch out. You swung the hoe too far. Concentrate, Yumi-san." But the physical work was good for her after all. It was so exhausting that she had no more energy to cry, and slept like a potato at night.

One early morning Ayako cried out, "Yumi-san, come out. Little chicks are hatched." Yumi came out yawning, but burst out laughing at the sight of the lemon-colored fluff balls, their eyes like black beads and their legs like thin twigs. "What lovely creatures they are," Yumi said, watching them wobble in the garden. As the morning breeze combed the chicks' wispy feathers, Yumi felt the joy of rebirth after a long winter of sadness. The old wounds would eventually heal and life would continue.

In May, Germany surrendered unconditionally. With Italy long defeated, Japan was the only one of the Axis powers still left. Reading the news, Yumi asked Ken, "Why does Japan keep fighting when it's obvious we won't win?"

"If we surrender, the military would not only lose face, but also their heads on the guillotine. They don't want that," Ken said, looking weary. He had at first been an enthusiastic patriot, believing in the war slogan of establishing a greater East-Asia co-prosperity. But halfway through the war, he had realized that this was a losing battle and, being a realist, he did not see the point of continuing, although he kept up the façade of a faithful citizen.

In June, Okinawa fell after the death of 200,000 people. Most of them were civilians, among them boys and girls mobilized to the student corps. Even Ayako, who usually refused to read about losing battles, read the news three times and said with a frightened face, "I wonder what happened to Shun-san."

Yumi and Ken wondered the same thing. But they kept their fears inside and did not talk about Shun. The odds were too great against him. Every day and night, Yumi prayed fervently for him. Both Jun and Sayo had asked her to look after Shun in case of their death. She hoped she would be given the chance.

Summer came and all the vegetables were ripe in the garden. Watching Yumi pick tomatoes, Ayako said, smiling, "Yumi-san, your face is as red as a tomato. Nothing makes me happier than to see you like that, because you looked like a sick fruit when you came here." Ayako's own face had turned as brown as the earth.

While the city people were starving, they had more than enough to eat. *Ayu* fish was often on the table, too, because Yumi loved going to the rapids to wade in the water and visit the bald-headed man. She had told him that she had lost her husband in an air raid and her son in New Guinea, and now he smiled at her every time she came by to buy fish. He did not talk much, keeping his gaze fixed on the bottom of the water, but Yumi knew he was bearing his sadness in silence. She knew that a parent's grief over lost children never died.

On the afternoon of August 6, 1945, when Yumi and Ayako were queuing up for their ration of rice in the village square, a very old man with a long goatee walked in with a bamboo stick like the one Taku had once carried. Everybody wondered who he was, for none of the villagers had ever seen him before.

He stood in the center of the square and talked with big gestures, waving his arms around in the manner of an oracle, but his face grimacing in agony and sadness. "Doomsday has come. A terrible thing happened in Hiroshima this morning. Satan ignited his magic lamp and lit up the whole sky. Then a monstrous mushroom sprouted—the most virulent mushroom that has ever grown on earth. As it spattered its poison, the whole city turned into an inferno, burning hundreds of thousands of people, blackening and peeling their skin as if they were potatoes, blowing eyes out of sockets, and wrenching off heads, limbs and hearts. The wounded rolled and stumbled like roasted pigs. The wailing voices of agony—calling the names of children, mother and father, crying for help and for water—reached heaven and hell. In seconds, all the buildings had been flattened and the city had turned into a grave of burnt bodies, and the river was flooded with the dead, permanently dyed red."

The old man looked pale and asked for water. When a woman handed him a glass, he thanked her, gulped it down, and asked for another. His color had returned, but his face was still pinched with agony. Without saying another word, he walked slowly away in the direction from which he had come, leaning heavily upon his stick.

Yumi had detected a Hiroshima accent like her father's in his speech. Had this man traveled all the way from Hiroshima this afternoon? Or was he a messenger of God? An incarnation of Taku himself? And was it a true story? If it was, was this the ultimate punishment from the angry God? Or was this another of the mass killings by those faceless, guiltless murderers?

Later Yumi heard the same story on the radio. Three days later, another venomous mushroom sprouted in Nagasaki.

On August 8, Russia declared war on Japan.

At noon on August 15, 1945, Yumi and Ayako sat in front of the radio, trying hard to listen to an unprecedented broadcast by the Emperor. Static interrupted his metallic voice, unusually high for a man, and the fact that he spoke in the royal language set aside for the living god alone did not make it easy for normal people like Yumi and Ayako to comprehend. He called himself "Chin." To Yumi it sounded like the name of a dog.

But they did manage to hear the holy voice pronounce the words "an unconditional surrender." Ayako bent her head on the floor, bursting into tears. Yumi bit her lip and sat straight, but soon tears welled up and finally gushed out in torrents. She cried with relief that the war was finally over and with anger that it had not been ended earlier, before the deaths of Masao, Isamu, Jun and Sayo. Why had it begun at all? Without the war, Hisao and Hana would not have died either. And three million Japanese, including half a million civilians, untold millions in China and the rest of Asia, and countless people on the Allied side would not have died.

The rumors had been that American occupying forces with faces of monsters with horns would cut off people's noses and ears, chop off their fingers, rape women and then run over them with their bulldozers. The rumors were unfounded.

One day, several villagers came back to the square, smiling with excitement. "We saw three Jeeps, those olive-colored machines, race down the outside road, trailing clouds of dust. We crouched behind the rice paddy, but they saw us. Do you know what? They're as tall as giraffes, but have no horns. They smiled and threw these to us." The villagers proudly showed off boxes of tobacco, and gave to the hungry children the chocolates and crackers they had received.

Once she had recovered from the initial shock of defeat, Ayako had begun to laugh out loud, overcome with happiness and gratitude that peace had finally come and that her family was alive and well. But she did not laugh with Yumi. Once, Ayako, who was having a good time with the villagers, joking and laughing, cupped her mouth with her hands, when she saw Yumi coming. The villagers bent their faces down. Yumi was a constant reminder of the misery of war to the happy survivors who were already trying to forget it.

Ken and Ayako were anxious to return to Nagoya where their house was standing intact, and to be reunited once again with their daughters. They told Yumi that she was welcome to live with them, but Yumi did not want to be a permanent parasite.

At the end of the summer when Ken and Ayako went home to Nagoya, Yumi took a train to Tokyo, after thanking them for having been so kind to her.

After a long train ride, during which she was jammed like a potato in a sack, she took a city tram to the stop nearest her house. Then she dragged her feet toward home, overloaded with bags on her back and in her hands. She used to enjoy the walk to her house through a market and a quiet residential area, but now she often closed her eyes as she walked, because every corner she turned was a wasteland of burnt-out ruins.

Only with her eyes shut did the colorful image of what had been return to her: a toy shop with her favorite Japanese doll in the window, a teahouse where she had sat and drunk bitter green tea with red-bean cakes, a pickle shop smelling of vinegar, and the old houses with stone gates and evergreen shrubbery.

Everywhere in the ruins, men were working tirelessly like ants who build another anthill no matter how often the old one is destroyed. But they were only building barracks with plywood and tin, as if they did not believe anymore in making anything long-lasting after the earthquake and the destruction of war.

Yumi trembled when she found her whole neighborhood, which had been intact on her last visit, flattened. As she turned the last corner to her street, Yumi told herself to be prepared to find her house in ashes, but when she really saw it was no longer there, her head reeled and she sank down in front of the fallen door.

It was the last straw. The war had deprived Yumi of a husband and a son, her best friends Jun and Sayo, and now it had plundered her of her home. What did she have left to live for? She felt as if she had been stripped naked, abandoned by the whole world and by God. She howled like the stray dog she almost was, forgetting all the stoicism and dignity she had maintained with Ayako and Ken. There was nobody around to care. All around her there were only charred ruins.

Where were the piano, the books, the sheet music and the

records Jun had given her? Where were the beautiful kimonos and *obis* Hana had bought for her? Were there no more pictures of Masao making funny faces at his father, or of him riding on his bicycle, his hands waving in the air, smiling proudly? Fate had not allowed Masao to live long, but was his mother not even allowed to keep his image? And where was the happy photo of the handsome Hisao and his young bride? The sweet one of young Tami and herself looking like dolls with ribbons on their heads? And the picture of shy Jun-san in his student's uniform at the *kabuki* theater standing next to Yumi in her yellow kimono—the one she used to hide in her desk drawer to look at in secret? Where was the faded brown photo of beautiful Hana standing like a proud peacock and pock-faced Taku with his meek eyes only half open? The past would never return, the dead would never come back, and even the pictures were lost.

Yumi did not think she could ever get up again. She was tempted to sleep right there. The evening had turned into sultry night; she could sleep under the stars, the stars of Hisao, Masao, Jun and Sayo. They would protect her; they would cry for her and console her. She would sleep one last night on the ground where her home used to be, pretending everything was as it had been, with everyone in her family still alive.

She lay down on the flattened door and watched the millions of stars that the war victims had turned into. At least they did not have to hide themselves any longer for fear of being shot down, although they were still shedding tears of chagrin. Yumi wondered which star was who, and decided that the two silvery ones sitting near Mars were Hisao and Masao, and a pair of the brightest stars shining like two blue jewels were Jun and Sayo. As she gazed at them, she could hear them speak. "Yumi-san. Don't be so discouraged. We'll always protect you from here," Jun said, his starry eyes, which used to gleam with love, having turned into a real star and shining like the most beautiful one in the entire sky. "It's not a good idea to sleep outside," Sayo said, shedding warm beams. "Why don't you go to our house?"

"You are right, Sayo-san. I shouldn't sleep here," Yumi said, slowly rising to her feet, although she did not think she could walk any farther. She staggered down the street, dragging her luggage behind her.

From a block away she saw that Jun's house was still standing, and that strangely, it was not dark, but lighted. Yumi was so startled that she rubbed her eyes to check that she was not dreaming. Could it be Shun? Or Jun and Sayo? The possibility that Shun would be there was as slim as the return of his parents. The news from Okinawa had convinced Yumi of his death. She still prayed daily for his return, but with little hope, for she had prayed fervently for Masao for two years, and look what had happened to him.

Probably it was another homeless person like herself, who had found a convenient empty house to sleep in. But then again, it might be a burglar, or perhaps even the American soldiers who had just landed. Yumi felt as panicked as the times when she had to creep into her dark underground shelter by herself.

With careful, stealthy steps, she neared the house. A shadow was moving in the kitchen window—that of a young man resembling Shun. Mistrusting her eyes, she studied the silhouette once again. This young man had thick unkempt hair, but the profile, with its slim nose and thin cheeks, reminded her of Jun.

"Shun! Shun!" Yumi screamed, and began running so fast she tripped over the bags she had been dragging. Hearing the loud voice calling his name, Shun opened the door, came out on to the street, and helped her get up off the ground.

Shun was on crutches. One trouser leg was dangling from the knee.

Yumi did not know what to say. "Shun, you lived," she said, choking on the words. "You lived!" He hugged her so tightly she could not breathe. They cried on each other's shoulder until Yumi felt faint. She somehow made it to the house, Shun clumsily carrying all her luggage for her. He made her sit on the couch, and sat next to her as Jun had done. She felt as if Jun was sitting beside her once more. Shun had always looked like his father, and now he resembled him even more strongly, perhaps because of the emaciation of his face.

Shun said that he had been back for five days. He had gone to the ward office and found out about his parents, and had been devastated and crying ever since.

"On the last day Mother was with me at the hospital, she said, 'When the war is over, let's climb Mount Fuji, all of us.' On the ship returning back here, I was so happy about finally coming home to see Mother and Father that I said to myself that even with one leg, I would climb Fuji-san with them. I remember Father had said, 'When you come back, let's set up a telescope in the garden and watch the stars. Please don't die, Shun.' So I tried hard to survive for their sake, even when I wanted to die. I thought they would do the same for me. Oh, why did they die? Why?" Shun crouched over his thighs, his hands covering his face.

Yumi stroked him on the shoulder. On his bent back, just under the collar of his shirt, she could see a patch of violet-colored, thick scars from burns. His right hand, which he kept clenched in a fist, looked as if it had been dyed with pink paint.

"You had bad burns, didn't you, Shun?"

He pulled up his shirt to show her his back and she almost cried out in horror. A third of his back was like a map painted with dark blood. He opened his right hand. Four of the fingers were stuck together, pink skin joining one to the other.

"You can't play the piano any longer," Yumi said, stunned. In her ears was the Mozart sonata he had played on the day he left for the war.

"I can't. It's too bad. But I'm back alive from a place where almost everybody else died. My body is deformed with one leg gone, the scars of bad burns, and fingers that are all stuck together. But the fact I'm alive is truly a miracle. So I'm grateful. I wish Father and Mother could have seen me like this before they died. They would have been proud of me for managing to survive."

"They are proud of you, up in heaven," Yumi said, cupping his deformed hand with hers.

At first he was reluctant to talk about the war, but after a while he said, "Do you know, Aunt Yumi? I met the most beautiful girl in a cave where they had the hospital I was taken to for my infected leg. Her name was Mina. She was only sixteen, one of the hundreds of the Lily Student Corps. She worked so hard, bringing water, handing out medicine and changing dressings for the hundreds of wounded.

"A surgeon told Mina to hold my limbs so I wouldn't move. This military butcher liked to chop off anything that came his way. While carrying food and medicine from my ship to the island, I had been hit by a bullet. By the time I was brought in to the cave hospital, the leg was badly infected. I protested about it being chopped off. The butcher didn't like my rebelling. He yelled at me, 'Do you want to die of gangrene or septicemia?'

"My leg was chopped off with a saw, without anesthesia. Mina was holding down my limbs, trembling and weeping, and she helped him clean the cut and wrap it with bandages. When it was all done, she whispered to me, 'I hope it'll heal well,' and smiled at me in tears. It was the most beautiful smile I'd ever seen."

"Maybe she was your mother who came from heaven to be with you," Yumi said.

"Two days later Mina was killed. The commander saw no more hope in winning the battle and let the students go home to their parents. As soon as she and two dozen other students went out of the cave, excited to go home, they were all shot to death right there. I didn't die because I stayed in the cave, immobile." Shun closed his eyes, the image of the girl in his mind.

"When I was finally able to walk on crutches, I left the cave because someone said the battle was over. There weren't any more sounds of guns. But in two minutes I was hit by a burning flame-thrower. I don't know who did it. I let myself fall on the ground and rolled around. The flames on me eventually went out, but I was in unbearable pain. I staggered to my feet and looked for water. The only water I could think of was the sea, which was down the hill. I thought that if I had to die, I wanted to die in the sea. I started, but I fell down on the road and couldn't get up. In my eyes were Father and Mother. 'I wish I could see you once more,' I said, and cried. Then I must have passed out. After a while, I heard some voices and opened my eyes. I almost fainted again, because in front of me were two tall American soldiers with machine guns and bayonets. 'If you surrender, we'll rescue you,' the shorter one of them said. I understood their words, thanks to your English lessons, Aunt Yumi. I nodded. I knew I might die even if I was rescued, or they might kill me. But I thought any way of dying would be better than roasting to death, my body covered with scorching burns, on that sweltering hill.

"The taller one hopped down the hill like a child on a picnic, carrying me all the way. 'We won the battle,' he was shouting. I realized the battle of Okinawa had really ended. The shorter one said, 'Take it easy. His burns hurt.'

"They took me to one of the several huge hospital boats floating offshore. People were so kind to me. Everybody. It's strange the people we called enemies were nicer than some of the Japanese officers I had worked for, or the butcher who had cut off my leg. They treated my leg, which had become infected again, as well as the burns. My doctor, Dr. Young, said that it was a big shame my leg had been cut off.

"Anyway, it was because of them I survived. Without their care and good food, I would definitely have been dead. Dr. Young said surgery could be done on my fingers and back. He knew all about the latest medical advances. He inspired me to study medicine. That way I could continue my father's legacy—and my mother's."

He turned to Yumi, then, and smiled. "You must be exhausted. I'll make your bed." Hopping on one foot, he took a futon from a closet and made a new bed in Jun and Sayo's room. "I've learned to do everything on crutches," he said.

Before leaving the room, he gazed at Yumi, his dark eyes the exact copy of his father's. He said, "I heard about Masao. You must be very sad about him. So, Aunt Yumi, we'll make a good match. You'll be my mother and I'll be your son." He hugged Yumi again.

"Do you mind if I live here, Shun? My house has burned down, as you've probably seen. I could live in my parents' house, if it's still there."

"You are my mother now. Please live here, although I know Grandpa's house is intact. I went to look for you there first. Do you know that Aunt Kana is living in the teahouse with her lover? She said she'll marry him soon. There was an American officer looking into the western wing. When I asked if I could do anything for him, he said that he would like to confiscate the house for the Occupying Forces' use. 'There aren't too many livable houses around,' he said. So you won't be able to live there anyway."

After Shun left, Yumi looked around the room. On a dusty bookshelf stood a faded wedding picture of Jun and Sayo. It made her smile because they looked so young and happy, beaming at each other. Yumi lay herself down on the soft futon. She turned off the light, but their beaming faces were still in her mind. They must be smiling like that in heaven, now that their son was back home. He had brought back spring after the long hard winter, reviving hope of life. Yumi had not been allowed to love Jun, but she now had his son to look after.

"Aren't you proud of Shun, Jun-san and Sayo-san?" she whispered to them. "He is so very sad about losing you and he'll carry the wounds of war for a lifetime, but he has a positive outlook on life. He'll work hard and live a long, good life. He'll continue both your legacies in medicine. Maybe Ken-san can help him have surgery so he can play the piano again. I'll help him as much as I can, Jun-san and Sayo-san. So rest in peace."

Sleep came easily to her at such a long day's end. Peace, finally, after the long ordeal of the war.

Yumi roamed a garden full of beautiful flowers. She wondered where it could be. It must be a dream since the flowers were more exotic, their aroma more intoxicating, than any she had ever known. She looked around and saw the triangular roof of the teahouse poking out over a bush, and the square top of the western wing behind the pine trees. Isamu was poking his head out of an azalea bush in his camouflage helmet and shooting Kana with his measuring stick. So this must be Hana's garden after all. As Shun had told her, the whole place was intact; Hana had dreamed of making an eternal garden, and it had managed to outlive both people and the war.

From the direction of the western wing, Yumi heard a cat growl and a dog whimper. It must be Hana and Taku. A bird-chirping laugh startled Yumi and she looked back: it was her long-gone sister Tami skipping cheerfully in the flower garden, her round face shining like a full moon.

"Let's play hide and seek," Tami said. After counting to ten, Tami began to run around the garden, where she found everybody who had long been missing: Hisao, Masao, Isamu, Jun and Sayo. They had been hiding under the bush, in the maze, and inside the shelter under the mound. They all came out smiling, looking young and healthy. From somewhere far away, the music of a *koto* was heard and Jun ran to look for his mother. Soon he came back, blithely talking with Emi, a peach-colored cat following them wagging his stubby tail. Behind them was Lee who had been found trimming a hedge. After a while, Shun came hopping on crutches from Okinawa; Ken and Ayako arrived from Nagoya.

Taku and Hana invited all of them to tea. They talked and laughed merrily, but suddenly the sky grew dark, and a storm with thunder and lightning scattered people back into their hiding places. In a few minutes, the sun was back and it was all quiet again, but Yumi could not find anybody in the garden except Ken, Ayako, Kana and crippled Shun.

The trees had grown and thrived while the people were fighting; the flowers had returned every year to bloom. Unmoved and unimpressed by the war, the rocks in the rock garden had continued their slumber of a thousand years. In the pond, fat *koi* were swimming away in eternal solitude, indifferent to the short lives of the people around them, all the people who had so recently filled this place.

GLOSSARY

Diet	Japanese Parliament.
furoshiki	A square sheet of cloth for wrapping and carrying things.
geta	Footwear made of wood.
go	A strategic board game played with black and white stones.
kabuki	Japanese classical drama played with male actors and female-impersonators.
kamikaze	Divine wind. When Kublai Khan tried to invade Japan in the thirteenth century, storms sank his ships. At the end of World War II, the Japanese hoped the divine wind would blow again to sink enemy ships and planes.
konnichiwa	Hello. Good day.
kotatsu	A heater placed under a table covered with a futon to keep one's feet warm.
koi	Carp that can live longer than humans.
koto	Thirteen silk-stringed Japanese harp.
miai	A meeting with a view to marriage.
mochi	Rice cake made by pounding cooked sticky rice.

ninja	A secret agent in feudal times with magical powers of stealth and concealment.
obi	A long and wide sash used to tie a kimono.
oden	Soup made with fish cake, fried tofu, *konnyaku* (devil's tongue starch), seaweed, squid, Chinese cabbage, and white radish.
okasan	Mother.
omikuji	Fortune-teller. A prophecy written on a piece of small folded paper that is found in shrines.
saké	Japanese rice wine.
-san, -sama, -chan	Used after a name to show affection and respect: *-sama* is for addressing one's superiors; *-chan* is an endearment used in speaking to children and among close friends.
sayonara	Good-bye.
sensei	A professor, teacher, and doctor. Used after a name to show respect.
shogi	Japanese chess.
sumi	Chinese or Indian ink. One can write or paint with a brush dipped in *sumi*.
tabi	White socks that are worn with *geta*.
tatami	Rush mat, a standard floor covering for a Japanese living room or a bedroom.
tsuno-kakushi (horn-hide)	A traditional box-shaped white cloth a bride wears on her head. There are several explanations for its purpose: for hiding a horn that a woman grows when jealous, as a symbol of purity, or a device to keep the head warm and free from dust.
zabuton	A cushion used to sit on a *tatami* floor.
zaibatsu	Financial conglomerates.